THE MADONNA MURDERS

THE MADONNA MURDERS

PAMELA CRANSTON

SHP
ST. HUBERTS PRESS

OAKLAND, CALIFORNIA

Chapter epigraphs are by Archbishop and Metropolitan Anthony Bloom from: *Meditations: A Spiritual Journey Through the Parables*, published by Dimension Books, Denville, N.J., © 1971, and *Living Prayer*, published by Darton, Longman & Todd, Ltd., London, © 1966.

Metropolitan Anthony Bloom was Metropolitan of the Diocese of Sourozh under the Patriarchate of Moscow until his death, August 4, 2003.

This book is a work of fiction. Every effort, however, has been made to represent historical events as accurately as possible. The characters and incidents portrayed and the names used herein are fictitious and any resemblance to the names, character, or history of any person is coincidental and unintentional.

Library of Congress Catalog Card Number: 2002096505
ISBN: 0-9724163-0-7

Published in the United States of America
Printed in Canada

∾

With love and gratitude for my brother
DAVID CURRIE LEE, D.Ed.
(1953-1995)
Educator and Russian Scholar

CHAPTER 1

"We must start on a real pilgrimage, a long pilgrimage."
Metropolitan Anthony Bloom
Meditations: A Spiritual Journey

Monday, October 22, 1990

It's not often that a classroom of diverse, savvy Episcopal seminarians in Berkeley, California, is ever collectively astonished by anything. But when Andrea West flashed the slide of the Icon of Kazan onto the screen, everyone sat up and gawked. "Wow!" somebody whispered from the back.

Andrea warmed with a surge of inner satisfaction. She almost felt as if she had painted it herself, as if the icon belonged to her, like the portrait of a distant family relative. She never grew tired of gazing at it.

"It's quite something, isn't it?" she said. She paused to let every one bask in the radiance of this momentary vision.

Andrea stood behind the humming projector and studied the slide. The Russian icon of the Madonna and Child, painted on wood, depicted two figures. One was a woman with wide almond eyes, an oval face brown with age, and a long, slender Russian nose. The other was an infant, whose small face was nut-shaped and wizened, with eyes as inscrutable as an old man's.

Apart from the two faces, the rest of the icon was overlaid with an ornate covering made of pure gold, which outlined the figures of the mother and child in relief. The gold plate was embossed and studded with hundreds of rare gemstones: huge green emeralds cut in ovals and squares, blue sapphires, tiny diamonds and large round pearls. An arch of red rubies adorned the crown over Mary's head, while white glowing pearls, encircled by diamonds, decorated the icon's bottom rim.

"This is the Icon of Kazan. Today is her feast day," Andrea said, breaking the hush to continue her lecture. "It's one of the most venerated Russian icons in the world. In fact, it will be here in the Bay Area touring the Orthodox churches soon. The gold and gemstone cover is called a 'riza' and that alone is worth over four million dollars. Money is nothing compared to its real value—it's considered miraculous. Legend has it that, during the War of 1812, General Kutusov prayed with this icon to bless the Russian army as Napoleon's troops stormed towards Moscow. Many people still believe that it has healing powers and can cure blindness."

"Do you think that's true?" Christie Matthews asked abruptly from her seat in the front. Andrea felt her stomach tighten as she heard a faint edge of belligerence in her student's flat suburban voice.

Andrea breathed deeply to center herself. "Frankly, Christie, I don't know. It's hard to say. There is such a fine line between myth and reality when you're dealing with the spiritual realm. Remember, in this course we're talking about the symbolism of good and evil. Last week we talked about how the Crystal Skull, possibly of Aztec origin, symbolizes death and possibly is the embodiment of all evil. Today we see here an image from Russia that represents the essence of life and all good—but I don't think we should be too literal about it. Sometimes, when dealing with inner truths and ancient myths, we go beyond the reach of facts."

"So you think this all is just a myth?" Christie grumbled, glancing around the room for support.

"I didn't say that," Andrea moderated her voice on purpose. "Remember what I said before: ever since I first heard of the Crystal Skull, I've been amazed at the way people project their own unwanted evil onto this inanimate object. I have some personal theories about it, but they're not important right now. What do you think?" Andrea reached into her bag of teaching tricks to dodge Christie's latest attack.

"I think you're side-stepping the fact that you have blatantly presented us with occult images under the pretense of spiritual theology."

Andrea could not see Christie's cheeks in the dimly lit room, but she sensed that, like hers, they were reddening. A few students adjusted themselves uneasily in their chairs. One or two sighed with exasperation.

Andrea smiled to herself and parried, "If an icon of the Virgin and Child is an object of the occult, then I think at least half of Christendom is in a great deal of trouble." A handful of students chuckled.

"I wasn't talking about that—I meant the Crystal Skull. It's satanic! How dare you show it in a seminary classroom?" Christie's voice raised another note on the decibel scale.

"Ahhh," Andrea said in a low soft voice. "So tell me, Christie, what is more evil: talking about evil or censuring talk about evil?"

"You weren't just talking about evil," Christie argued. "You've sanctioned the Crystal Skull by refusing to believe in its satanic power. The Bible says Jesus acknowledged the existence of Satan. Why can't you? You're just playing into the hands of the demonic."

Andrea felt herself growing defensive and feared the focus of the class might be knocked off track, but she remained composed. "I sanctioned nothing, but I think you prove my point exactly. These objects have a way of raising up our most powerful projections: the things we most deeply fear and the things we most deeply yearn for. Your reaction to my slide of the Crystal Skull clearly shows how these spiritual archetypes hook us."

Christie slammed her book shut and said, "Come on! This is a bunch of Jungian psychobabble. I can't take this anymore." With that she grabbed her books and bag, and strode out of the classroom, failing to avoid the cliché of slamming the door behind her.

"Christie!" Andrea called after her, but the troubled student had gone. The volcano, which had threatened to erupt all semester, had finally blown and there was nothing Andrea could do about it.

Everyone sat motionless in their seats, stunned with mute embarrassment. An awkward silence hung like smoke in the darkened classroom. The only noise in the room was the rumbling slide projector throwing its shaft of hot white light onto the screen. Andrea felt frustration and anger rising up inside her, but she stifled these feelings for the sake of the task at hand. Everything, she believed, was a teaching moment, even conflict—or rather, *especially* conflict. All eyes in the classroom were upon her.

"John," she asked calmly, "could you please get the lights?"

John ambled over to the wall and flicked on the lights. With a click, Andrea switched off the projector. The picture of the Icon of Kazan disappeared like a mirage. Brushing back the crown of her lush, wavy black hair, she walked easily to the front of the classroom. Leaning against the edge of the table, she folded her arms and surveyed her students. Her dark brown eyes sparkled brightly behind her tortoise shell glasses, "Thoughts, anyone?"

2

After class, Andrea hurried down the corridor to her office when the faculty secretary stopped her. Sally slyly handed her a pink message slip, "Here's a voice from your past." Tall, gawky and fifty-something, Sally had the knack of making a new dress look like a rumpled bed sheet thirty minutes after she had put it on.

Andrea awkwardly juggled her load of books and took the message. "Thanks." Her eyebrows lifted slightly in surprise. The scribbled note read, "Call Michael Beech. Urgent."

An intuitive flash of foreboding raised a red flag. She recognized the number from the De Young Museum and glanced at her watch. No time to call. She always felt thwarted where Michael was concerned. What on earth could he want? He never called with an emergency.

"So." Sally placed a hand on her hip. "Don't keep me in suspense. Are you going to call him back or not?"

"Maybe," Andrea grinned. "The way things have gone between us, I'd rather get a call from my dentist. Anyway, I can't call him now, I'm looking for Christie Matthews."

"She's in the Dean's office. By the way, the Dean wants to see you, too. What's going on?"

Andrea's lush black eyebrows furrowed. "It's too complicated," she said. "I'll explain later."

"He doesn't look very happy," Sally warned her. "You know what happens when he gets mad. His neck turns red and that vein in his forehead pops out. I think he's working up to a big one."

Andrea took a deep breath and gathered up her courage. "Wish me luck."

"How about a novena instead? It sounds like you'll need it." Sally gave her the thumbs-up sign as Andrea walked stoically past her to Dean Ferguson's office. Andrea felt the muscles tighten in her back as she walked down the seminary corridor. Instinctively, she wanted to run in the opposite direction, but she kept going. She paused near the Dean's office, wiping her clammy hands on her skirt, then firmly knocked on the heavy oak door.

She could hear voices inside, and then Dean Ferguson opened the door. Andrea watched as he clasped Christie's hand and said, "Thank you for your input, Ms. Matthews. I'll be in touch with you soon." He gave Christie a salesman's smile, and then looked at Andrea sternly.

As Andrea passed Christie in the doorway, she saw that Christie's face had a set, self-righteous look about it. So it's war, Andrea thought, and fought to keep her heart from sinking to her shoes.

"Christie," Andrea paused, stopping to touch the younger woman's shoulder, "couldn't we have talked this out first?"

"It's beyond that, Ms. West. Excuse me, please, I have to go," Christie brushed past her.

Andrea sighed and stepped into the Dean's office. "What did she say?"

Dean Ferguson stood facing the window with his back to her. His hands were folded behind his back like a schoolmaster. Dressed in crisp black clericals, the Dean was a short, slight man whose closely cropped hair had lamentably begun to thin. He prided himself on descending from pure Scottish stock, and mentioned it often. Like many Scotsmen, he was an exacting man with a sense of humor the size of a thimble. Somehow, his inordinate sense of responsibility had a way of making even ordinarily reliable adults feel negligent.

Andrea was always puzzled about why he remained committed to the Episcopal Church, known as it sometimes was for its flabby thinking. And to think he held a position as a seminary dean in liberal Berkeley, of all places.

The Dean's rigorous perfectionism was a frequent topic in the staff lounge. Andrea once quipped to Sally, "I think the Dean's going to have to spend a lot of time in Purgatory for his 'virtues.'" And she meant it. Still, he was a good administrator, and that's what the Trustees had wanted.

Dean Ferguson stared out the window across the grassy yard, then turned and looked at her sharply. "Please, take a seat," he gestured stiffly.

Andrea's body tensed. "No, thanks. I prefer to stand for executions." She hoped humor would help. "Besides, we have chapel in a few minutes."

"Yes, of course," he said dryly. "But I think you may want to sit." There was no arguing with his tone of voice. Andrea sat down on the sofa. The Dean began to pace. "I know this is a bad time to bring this up, Andrea, what with your final dissertation presentation tomorrow. But I think you ought to know that Christie has dropped out of seminary." He paused for dramatic effect. "She says it's because of you."

Andrea's mouth opened a little. She shut it again and pondered the appropriate response. "I'm sorry to hear that."

The Dean moved away from the window and sat down a little too primly in the brown leather chair behind his massive oak desk. "Are you? She says it's because of your class on the Crystal Skull. She says you've gone New Age and have introduced occult ideas into your lectures. Evidently, she was going to talk with you directly, but after praying about it, she felt the Lord was telling her to leave." He leaned in his chair towards Andrea. "What's more, Christie says she's going to tell her husband to cancel his $50,000 pledge to the new building fund! Andrea, just what the hell have you been doing?"

"Nothing—nothing beyond teaching a regular class of Anglican theology!" Andrea felt her own neck growing warm. "There isn't anything New Age or occult about it."

"Then what's all this talk about mystical healing, Jungian archetypes, psychic phenomena and Crystal Skulls? That sounds pretty New Age to me."

Andrea sighed. "She misunderstood what I was doing."

Andrea thought to herself that one of the unfortunate things about working for a seminary, which survived chiefly on student tuitions, was that it sometimes accepted second-rate minds with first-rate pocketbooks. Not that the students here were slow, by any means. In fact, five students in the first year class already had Ph.D.s from other professions and she admired them for having the guts to begin another career in middle age, which would slice their salaries in half.

The job of a seminary, as she saw it, was not to produce Thomas Aquinases, but to educate able pastors who could work with their hearts as well as their heads. Nevertheless, every year the administration always managed to select a few with religious glaucoma: rigid fundamentalists who refused either to think or grow.

"Obviously somebody miscommunicated," Dean Ferguson glared at her. "Tell me, what is the Crystal Skull?"

"It's a jewel, made of clear quartz crystal, about five by seven inches high, shaped in the form of a human skull. It's supposed to have evil powers. Just superstition, really. Mere projection." Andrea gestured. "Look, all I was doing was showing slides of different types of religious art: icons of the Virgin Mary to symbolize good, for example, pictures of things symbolizing evil, like hex signs, the Crystal Skull and medieval paintings of Satan, to prove how these ideas effect us beyond an intellectual level. Christie's reaction just proves my point."

"She seems to think you were promoting something akin to Satanism, especially with all that talk of paranormal experiences."

Andrea stood up. "Oh, really! You should know me better than that. I simply used material from our mystical tradition—nothing terribly unusual. Besides, all this about Satan is pure nonsense!" Andrea found herself getting angrier than she wanted.

"Christie Matthews doesn't seem to think so. She takes it all quite literally and she thinks you're desecrating the educational process. Next thing I hear, you'll be introducing the Goddess into the Creed!"

"That's next semester..."

"This is serious, Ms. West."

"I am serious. Whatever happened to the good old Anglican value of healthy doubt? Of living with ambiguity? Of being able to question and debate? Not to mention academic freedom! What do you want me to do, go after her on my knees? Change my course content?"

"You may wish to consider some modification."

"I can't believe this is happening. In an Episcopal seminary at the end of the 20th century!" Andrea glared.

The Dean tapped his pencil impatiently on his blotter and glowered at her. "I don't think I need to remind you that you're in no position to argue." She could see the vein on his blushing forehead beginning to bulge.

Andrea froze in fear at his somber tone. "What do you intend to do?"

He snapped his pencil in half, "It's not what I'm going to do—it's what you're going to do. You just lost us $50,000. Go think about it and then tell me how we are going to clean this mess up!"

Andrea knew she was cornered. She felt trapped and bewildered. "How can I fix it?"

"You're the doctoral candidate. You go figure it out. Now get out of here before I throw you off the faculty altogether." The Dean put on his reading glasses, looked down and began thumbing through a stack of files. The vein in his forehead throbbed noticeably.

She backed towards the door. "I'll see what I can do," she said rather icily, aware that she had just caved in to his pressure. She knew this was a job for him to solve, not her. She decided to wait a week or two to re-negotiate things with him, after their tempers had cooled. But now, fuming with fury, she exited his office as fast as she could.

Andrea leaned into Sally's office. "Battered, but not beaten," she announced with relief.

The older woman gave her a sympathetic, motherly glance. "It looks like you need a good hot cup of tea. Want to join me in my office?"

Andrea paused. Chapel was definitely out of the question now. She felt shell-shocked and angry, but she somehow collected herself. "Thanks, but what I'd really like is a good stiff drink. Too bad I hate hard liquor. No, I think I'll just go home and relax."

"Don't forget Michael's call," Sally reminded her.

"Oh, damn!" Andrea glanced at her watch. "I might as well get it over with. What else could go wrong today?"

"We could have a big quake on the Hayward fault."

"Very funny," Andrea smiled ruefully. "Thanks, Sally. I don't know what I'd do without you."

"I'm sure you'll think of something. You usually do," Sally gave her a canny look and turned towards her typewriter. "Now go home and take a nice nap for me."

Andrea walked down the hall and closed her office door. As she grabbed a wad of Kleenex from the box on her desk, she realized she was trembling. Conflict always left her drained. She kicked herself for not resigning. Quitting, however, was a step she couldn't afford to take.

Damn the Dean and damn the almighty dollar! She shook her head. How could Christie have done this? It galled her that people thought religion was so simple. Black and white thinking short-changed both them and God.

To her, this kind of literal thinking was like the fishermen who went trawling over an ancient oyster bed. They were content to catch the fish swimming near the surface of the water, but had no idea that a deeper and more luminous treasure lay embedded in the muddy bottom below. Ignorance and fear (which they disguised as principles)—and, perhaps, the inability to swim—kept them from diving to the murky depths. Only those willing to brave the mysteries of the unknown and the darker currents of doubting reason had a chance of retrieving the Pearl of Great Price. No pain, no gain. Life was not about being financially secure nor about having the correct answer, but about finding one's soul. Andrea wondered if the Dean still had one.

3

Unfolding the pink message slip, Andrea thought that maybe seeing Michael would help. At least he made her laugh. She picked up the phone and dialed the assistant curator's office at the De Young Museum. Hopefully Michael was calling about her book deal. "Here goes," she murmured, and gripped the receiver nervously. She felt her pulse rate quicken as she listened to the phone ring.

Michael Beech had been an old lover of hers at Stanford. Then, after her divorce from Gareth, she and Michael had re-met two years ago and begun seeing each other again. Their relationship had run hot and cold until last year, when it ended abruptly on the night she learned that Michael was suddenly moving to West Hollywood to live with a man.

Michael's plummy voice came onto the line. "Andrea, how lovely! I was hoping it was you. How's the God business these days?" His voice lilted with a faint hint of a Yale accent, although she knew he was raised in Georgia. Michael's glib banter was one of the things she had both loved and hated about him, like having too much tinsel on a Christmas tree.

"Terrible, but no doubt better than the way the vicious world of art and museum politics is treating you." Andrea observed the icy tone in her own voice. Wishing she could pour out all her fears and anger about Dean Ferguson to Michael, like the old days, Andrea was determined to sound nonchalant. She picked off some withered violet leaves from the plant on her desk.

"Yes, isn't it awful how the supervisors always get their grubby little hands in the cultural pie?" Michael said with his usual urbanity. "This work on the new art wing is nearly driving me bonkers." Andrea sat back in her chair as her former lover treated her to a detailed account of the complications he had to suffer while building an art museum out of a rundown library. "It's like trying to turn Superior Court into a dance studio," he complained.

At thirty-seven, Michael Beech was the rising star of the San Francisco art world and, despite his silk smoking jackets and his gold rings, Andrea knew he took art and his career quite seriously. High Beauty was Michael's credo in life. He was also damned good at his work.

"But I didn't call you to burden you with my political bickerings," his tone unexpectedly changed. "I know this is last minute, but I need to see you." Andrea's heart skipped a beat. She sat up, not quite believing what she heard. She could tell he was dead serious. "I want your opinion about some work I'm doing."

"What work?"

"An icon."

"Oh." Her voice fell. "By the way," she said hoping to lighten the mood. "How is Hans?"

"The truth is, Andrea," Michael hesitated, "Hans left me. Dropped me like a stone. Then he got killed in a motorcycle accident last May."

This stopped Andrea cold. "Oh, Michael, I had no idea. Why didn't you tell me?"

"It all happened too fast. I suppose I couldn't face any of it at the time—not until it was all over. It was too humiliating and painful."

"I'm so sorry." She couldn't think of anything else to say.

"Thanks." She could hear his voice contort with grief.

Knowing that distraction would help him feel better, Andrea asked, "So, tell me more about the icon."

"I'm sorry, Andrea, but I can't say more right now. I'll explain when I see you."

"And by the way, where is your letter of recommendation for my book? My agent is getting antsy."

"We can talk about that over lunch. How does twelve-thirty sound?"

"You mean today?"

"Of course. Have you ever eaten at Greens Restaurant? They have great food and I know how you're always fretting about your girlish figure. My treat."

"You're worse than a snake charmer," Andrea couldn't keep herself from laughing. "If they serve pasta, I'll be right there. Twelve-thirty at the latest. I suppose I could make it back in time—assuming traffic isn't held up on the Bridge."

"Of course you can," Michael said. "I promise we'll be through by one. We wouldn't want any of your budding saints to feel neglected."

Andrea smiled, quite used to his teasing, "Thanks. I'll make sure they put your name on the prayer list: under St. Jude, for lost causes."

"Blessings on you, my child," he intoned. "I can use all the help I can get, just as long as they keep the Supervisors off the list." Then he said warmly, "Andrea, it will be good to see you again. I really need you on this one," and hung up.

Whatever it is, Andrea thought, he must really want it bad.

4

Glad to leave the suddenly stifling confines of the seminary campus, Andrea stuffed her papers in her brown leather briefcase and bolted from her office. Outside, the sharp autumn air felt as bracing on her face as a cold compress. She loved this time of year. She ran down the staircase, past a brick wall covered with crumbling sycamore leaves, towards her car in the parking lot below.

Over on the Cal-Berkeley campus, noontime bells rang a Bach fugue from Sather Tower. Already in full momentum, the carillon rang out its metallic melody loud and clear. Andrea loved fugues and all sorts of complicated things. Strands of contrapuntal music floated in the mild blue air like a tangled mass of invisible ivy, weaving and lacing together their braids of inextricable silver sound.

Normally, the bells gave her cause for rejoicing—a musical reminder that she had climbed the academic ladder so well and so fast. It had taken her only five years to reach her present position: a Ph.D. degree looming and a guarantee of being professor of Anglican theology and spirituality at the Episcopal Church Divinity School in Berkeley.

Today, however, she wondered gloomily if the bells were tolling the death knell of her job. She didn't stop to listen, but hurried into her car and drove out of the parking lot towards San Francisco.

As she sped towards the Bay Bridge toll plaza, Andrea caught a glimpse of the bizarre wooden sea sculptures that locals had built in the marshy mud flats of the Bay. They were like wooden pterodactyls, antiquated and pre-historic. And here she was, one day before her dissertation defense, wondering if she was doing the right thing. Was this what she really wanted? To be a respectable seminary professor in sensible shoes and dull tweeds, with Dean Ferguson running her life?

She knew she could never fit properly into any other profession, but the image of being old and alone loomed before her like one of those twisted specters standing out in the stinking mud flats of Emeryville. It was all so very nice, so wonderfully Anglican—but it was so damn safe.

5

Twenty minutes later, Andrea drove into the huge parking lot at Fort Mason in San Francisco and parked. She surveyed the immense warehouses before her, took a deep breath to expel her nervousness and strode into Greens Restaurant. Owned and operated by an American community of Zen monks and nuns, Greens was considered one of the finest vegetarian restaurants of nouvelle cuisine in the city. The view overlooking the shimmering blue-green waters of the Bay was a big draw, too.

Through the large pane-glass windows, Andrea glimpsed the Golden Gate Bridge in the distance, dropped on the landscape like a movie set. Close by, gulls paraded the decks of sun-drenched sailboats, which bobbed and swayed in their berths in the Marina below.

Andrea slipped into the restaurant bathroom to straighten herself before proceeding further. She peered at her long oval face in the mirror, and applied some fresh lipstick to her full mouth. Michael once teased her, "You know, your lips are too sensuous for a seminary professor. Almost a bit film noir," and he touched her bottom lip. But she hadn't believed him.

Yet, as she surveyed herself in the mirror, she had to admit that there was something faintly exotic about her. It frightened her a little. "You have the most alluring eyes," her mother always said. "Of course, you get that from me. You know the saying: 'Scratch a Russian and find a Tartar.'"

Andrea brushed her thick black hair and surveyed her tall figure. She was dressed stylishly and carefully in low brown heels, a flowing tan skirt, brown tweed jacket, and a white blouse with an amber brooch at her neck. She looked every inch the Berkeley seminary professor she was preparing to become. Only today she wasn't sure if she were happy about it, or even if it would happen.

Out in the restaurant, Andrea peered past the gigantic redwood burl sculpture and searched the pine tables, looking for Michael. She spied him at the far end of the restaurant, seated by the corner window out of the sun. He was casually reading a book and when he saw her, he waved solemnly at her.

"Sorry I'm late." She glanced at a large abstract canvass of green and oranges that hung above his table and wondered if he was going to frown at her for her tardiness. But instead he stood up, came over and kissed her on the cheek.

"Not to worry, dear. I've been a real jerk recently. Are we friends again?"

"That depends on what you mean by friends." Andrea hung her purse strap on the back of her chair and sat down.

"What's the price of forgiveness?" Michael peered at her over his glasses.

Andrea crossed her arms defensively. "Is that a personal question or a theological one?"

"Both, but don't answer. At least not right now. I'm starving." He handed her a menu and scrutinized his own menu closely. "After so many people simply raved about this place, I decided I had to come here. They said it was the only restaurant in town that doesn't make tofu taste like soggy newspapers. Not that I'll order it, of course. What will you have?"

"I don't know. A salad, I think." She saw Michael looking up at her, his eyes dancing merrily. "Don't you dare say a word!"

His grin revealed a dimple. "You look great, Andrea—not a day over thirty-five."

"You always had a way with compliments..." she tossed back as he turned to his menu. She studied him discreetly. He hadn't changed much in the past year: thirty-seven, tall and lean, with a fine nose, straight blonde hair flecked with gray, he was flawlessly dressed in a gray wool pin striped suit with a fresh blue cornflower in his buttonhole. He wore a Cubist tie, a black watch, a thick gold bracelet and a gold Stanford ring on his little finger. She thought his face looked tired. Pouches and shadows brooded under his eyes.

At that moment, a well scrubbed, rosy-cheeked waiter with a shaved Zen monk head approached their table. He bowed slightly, then kindly and efficiently took their orders.

Andrea sipped lemon water from her glass. "So what's this big mystery you urgently needed to see me about?"

Michael dipped warm sourdough bread into a yogurt and cucumber sauce. "Why do these people always have to wear their health on their sleeves?" He turned and looked out the window at the boats bobbing on the blue water. "Do you think the sea lions will come back to roost on our piers again this year?"

She looked at him with amusement. "Come on, Michael. You're avoiding the subject. What is it?"

He took out a small gold snuffbox from his inside breast pocket and, with his usual mock gesture, offered some to her. She smiled and shook her head. He tapped a small pile of tobacco powder on the top of his knuckles, sniffed hard, then blew his nose with a white handkerchief.

"Ah, much better," he sniffed. "Well, dear, there is a rare and valuable icon I want you to look at."

Andrea raised her eyebrows. "You've already said that."

"Forbes over at the De Young Museum got a call a few weeks ago from a man in Spain who runs some arch-conservative society dedicated to the Virgin Mary. They want to have one of their special icons re-appraised. It's so valuable they even built a basilica for it. They plan to send this icon on a grand tour of the U.S. before they officially give it to the Pope, and they want us, or rather me, to take a look at it for their insurance company."

The waiter set their plates before them. Andrea's plate was awash with fresh spinach, goat cheese and pine nuts. Michael raised his wineglass to her and said, "To us. And to the icon."

"Not so fast. I don't come in package deals." Andrea did not raise her glass. "I don't understand. Aren't there other people at the museum who can give you a better second opinion? After all, you're the one who's the icon expert, not me."

"But they don't have your spiritual instincts," Michael buttered his bread. "I don't need you to look at the technicalities of dating the icon. I've checked it out with a Russian colleague of mine who says it's authentic, all right, but I have my own theories about that. What I want is for you to get a feel for it. You know, what sort of spiritual baggage it's carrying, etc."

"Sounds mysterious. Tell me more."

"It's the Icon of Kazan."

"Not the Icon of Kazan?"

Andrea felt her blood trilling inside her.

"The very same, miracles and all. Even the gold riza has been restored with all the original diamonds and emeralds, and a few new sizable gems added, as well."

Andrea could hardly control her pleasure. "What do you want me to do?"

"Just come with me to the Holy Virgin Cathedral to see it."

"When?"

"Tonight. For Evensong, at six thirty."

"That soon? Oh Michael, you know I'd love to, but I can't! I have a class at two, then I have to get ready for my dissertation defense before the doctoral committee tomorrow. Can't it wait?"

"Nope."

"Why not? What makes this so important?"

"I can't say right now. You'll have to trust me."

"That doesn't give me much to go on. What if I said no?"

"Then you don't get my letter of recommendation."

"You're joking!" Andrea sat back stunned.

"Only a little." His eyes shone; but Andrea had seen that look before. "No letter, no contract; no contract, no book. I don't imagine your Review Board at the seminary will like that much. It's as simple as that."

"You blackmailer."

"Don't be so dramatic."

"Dramatic!" The sound of Andrea's voice made the couple at the next table stop and stare at her. After this morning's encounter with Christie Matthews and the Dean, her temper threatened to unravel like a frayed rope. She shot up out of her seat. "You run off with that garden lighting expert from West Hollywood and then you expect me to drop everything just for lunch and a kiss?" She collected her purse and stood up to leave. By now all eyes in the restaurant were upon her.

"Andrea, sit down. Don't make a scene." Michael squirmed in his seat, his cheeks reddened.

"I'll make such a scene you'll think this was Lincoln Center!" She hurriedly grabbed her coat and purse, nearly knocking over a water glass in her haste. By now her Russian temper had gotten the better of her.

Unnerved by this unusual outburst, Michael coaxed her to sit down again. "Please, let me explain."

Andrea glared at him. "This better be good." She sat down on the edge of her chair.

Michael examined his fingernails with a pained expression. "I shouldn't have said that. I'm sorry. It was inexcusable of me, I know. I screwed up with Hans, too. But my sexuality has never been a mystery to you. After all, we did have an arrangement."

"Some arrangement."

"Andrea, I never meant to hurt you." He took her hand into his and looked straight into her eyes. "We have been through too much together and I love you too much for that. You're my spiritual sister. Ever since Hans died, I've had to keep working or else go crazy. I'm desperate. I need you. I need your gift. Something weird is going on. I can feel it." A hint of fear flickered in his eyes.

She paused, sensing real urgency behind his plea. "Let me think about it."

He raised his hands in surrender. "Of course, think about it. But I promise you, it will be something you'll never forget." He mopped up his sauce with some French bread. She could smell the garlic from where she was sitting. "You should try this fettuccini sometime, the dried tomatoes are perfect. So, let me tell you about the new Matisses that have just come in..."

Michael's words washed over Andrea, an inaudible rush of babbling sounds. She suddenly had the overwhelming sensation that the two of them were falling towards the bottom of a deep well. She tried to crawl to a distant light, but couldn't reach it. Fear encircled her like a whirling tornado. Something was terribly wrong, but what? She knew she needed to get away to sort herself out.

She stood up, collecting her purse. "I'm sorry Michael, I can't stay. I'm too upset to eat right now." Then she hurried out of Greens, fighting back tears.

6

Andrea wiped the tears from her cheeks as she drove her car away from the restaurant. Strange that Michael should call when she was feeling the most vulnerable. He'd never taken the initiative in their relationship before. Was this icon business the only thing he wanted? But the more she thought about it, the more she realized how impossible it would be to ever get Michael to settle down. Unfortunately for her, no one else was even in the running.

Since her divorce from Gareth and beginning a Ph.D., time for relationships had flown completely out the window. Seminary, of course, killed all chances she had of dating anyone. First, there was no time to meet available men. Second, although there were plenty of mature straight men on campus, most of them were married. Any involvement with her colleagues or students was strictly out of the question. As her seminary ethics professor once so aptly put it, "Don't fuck the flock."

When she wasn't teaching or working on her dissertation, she was left alone at night with her cat, stuffing her face with low-cal popcorn and watching another episode of Masterpiece Theater. Her love life had become as exciting as the history of concrete. Michael had simply served as a habitual stay against loneliness.

Andrea turned a corner onto Bay Street and headed towards the Bay Bridge. She'd first met Michael at Stanford University in the early '70s, where they'd studied together in the Art History department. She'd attended a few classes and read a handful of books to keep a "gentlewoman's" C average. Michael, on the other hand, was as cavalier about school as he was about everything else, he never studied at all yet somehow managed to get the best grades.

She remembered visiting him in his dorm. Unlike the other students who had The Who or The Doors blaring from their rooms, Michael had built his own pine harpsichord (from a mail order kit) and played it for hours. In winter, he carried around a large black umbrella, which sported a brass duck handle. And in the spring, when most students were walking around barefoot in Levi's, Michael would stroll into the cafeteria wearing a white three-piece suit—emulating Tom Wolfe.

Oddest of all, he attended church—an Episcopal Church—and volunteered on the side to wash dishes at a local soup kitchen. There had been rumors that he had even gone to his local parish priest to talk with him about ordination, but nothing ever came of it. A walking anachronism, Michael was a hopeless 19th century Romantic beached on the shores of the 20th century.

In short, to most of his peers, Michael Beech was an enigma. But Andrea was fascinated by him.

They became friends, then lovers, during the winter of their junior year abroad when they traveled to Florence, Italy, to study Classical and Renaissance art. He was the wit and life of the tour.

The Mediterranean sun, the art, the hearty food deliciously swamped in garlic, the heady red wine, and the gusto of the Italian soul had intoxicated both of them. His vulnerability and feminine sensibility had touched Andrea deeply, like the first night he tentatively kissed her fingertips.

She smiled now, at the thought of them in that upstairs room in the old Palazzo, lying naked between crisp white sheets smelling of lavender after he'd made his first fumbling efforts at lovemaking.

Since she was a virgin too, she'd hardly known how bad he was at it then, but simply was grateful for his embraces.

Their love affair continued all semester, although they had sex only a handful of times—much to Andrea's frustration. Michael always seemed to be in love with love but not with her; yet she was the one he always came back to.

It was during this time that she learned more of the truth about Michael Beech: that he was born and raised in Thomaston, Georgia, sprung from an old line of southern Dixiecrats that went as far back as DNA. His family never forgot nor forgave General Sherman for crushing their plantation in the Civil War, and still assumed they were part of the landed gentry, although they had no land.

One of Michael's favorite stories was a family anecdote that had taken place back in 1910. His grandfather and great-grandfather were riding in a carriage by the new Plaza Hotel in New York City, which was fronted by a statue of General Sherman on horseback being led by an angel. His great-grandfather looked at the statue, knowing full well who it was, and inquired, "Who the hell is that?" "Don't you know, father?" Michael's grandfather had asked. "Why, that's General Sherman." The old man eyed the statue suspiciously and snorted, "Just like the damn bastard to ride a horse and make a lady walk."

Michael's father, now dead, had been a lawyer, aloof and passive, hence not a very successful one. His mother, still very much alive, was small as a wren but like many southern women, dominating. Michael once told Andrea, "You should have met my parents: my mother was like a small tidal wave—my father was like the Dead Sea." Since Michael was the youngest and the only male child, his mother and his three sisters treated him like salt-water taffy—something to push, pull or prod for their own devices. To survive, he developed the knack of out-manipulating them all.

His father had also been a devout Southern Baptist. As a boy, Michael was sometimes made to attend a small wooden Baptist church in the woods, whitewashed by the congregation every spring because the tropical sun made the paint blister. Michael told Andrea, "It used to embarrass me to go there, but mother always said it would help me remember what not to become. It worked."

By the time he was seventeen, Michael served as crucifer and later as part-time organist at his mother's local Episcopal church. In college he went through a devout phase, often slipping away to pray kneeling on the hard stone chapel floors for hours. As he grew older, this, too, would change. By the end of their trip to Italy, Michael had become a budding first-class art expert, specializing in Byzantine and medieval art; a passion that would eventually replace his zeal for religion.

It was Michael who, with his passion for Bach, T.S. Eliot and C.S. Lewis, first opened Andrea to the bizarre idea that God—and the church—might have anything meaningful to say to her or her soul. A year later, she had, on her own, surrendered to the Mystery and reclaimed the religion her father had raised her in. She became an Episcopalian. She would always be grateful to Michael for that, for she finally had found a place to belong.

But at that very moment, recalling their luncheon conversation, Andrea wasn't feeling very grateful to Michael at all. She didn't know whether to be angry with him or sorry for him, or both. She could always get someone else to recommend her book. But who? There was not another icon specialist around who knew her theoretical work as well as Michael did. Assuming she had done her work well, a letter from him virtually guaranteed publication.

Did he really mean he'd withdraw his letter of support for her book or was he just saying that to manipulate her? Had she over-reacted? Staying home might give her a few more hours to study but, on the other hand, if she didn't know the material by now, it was too late. She was terrified that if she refused to join Michael at the Cathedral, he might really carry out his threat.

Not going might jeopardize the fruit of five years of mind-bending work. The topic she had chosen for her dissertation was on "Theological and Spiritual Parallels in the Orthodox and Anglican Traditions." Michael's letters, she had hoped, might help to turn this paper into a book. And Harper's would never accept her book without his endorsement, of this she was sure. He had been a feather in her cap, and if she decided not to play his game, she might lose it, and perhaps him, forever.

CHAPTER 2

"To pray in the absence of God, to know that God is there but I am blind; that God is there but I am insensitive is an act of His infinite mercy not to be present to me while I am not yet capable of sustaining His coming."

Metropolitan Anthony Bloom
Meditations: A Spiritual Journey

At the same time as Andrea drove away from Greens Restaurant on the San Francisco waterfront, across the Bay in Piedmont, Alex Menshikov climbed out of his car in front of a large mansion that loomed before him.

He stood for a moment in the gravel driveway and surveyed the solid three-story stone building. It appeared cramped and out of place, as if some architectural magician had dropped a honey-colored English manor house from Sussex into this old, moneyed section of Oakland. If the house had been a person, it would have been a square-shouldered English banker. The roof pitched softly, reflecting the white sunlight off the shiny gray slates; two brick chimneys perched, poised like tightrope walkers, on its peak.

Alex remembered the classical yellow buildings from his youth in Russia, decorated with white trimming like a wedding cake. Nothing like the old palaces of St. Petersburg, he thought.

Inhaling his cigarette down to the nub, he winced, then flicked the butt into the bank of green ivy and strode swiftly towards the front door. After adjusting his brown corduroy coat over his broad shoulders, he pounded the door with his fist.

A tall thin woman with short black hair and black glasses, wearing a white blouse and long nightwatch plaid skirt, opened the door. Alex instinctively recoiled from her sharp, small-breasted body. He felt like a colossus by comparison.

"Mr. Menshikov." She did not smile at him. Exhaustion had drawn dark circles under her eyes like two brown coins placed on tissue paper. "We weren't expecting you so soon. Cecil said you were coming later." There was a note of disapproval in her Oxbridge voice.

"Something's come up, Miss Thorpe," he said. "It's urgent." He ran his knobby fingers through his shaggy white hair.

She raised an eyebrow in silent inquiry, "Well, we mustn't let you keep us in the dark. Please follow me." She led him towards the living room; Alex followed, looking around the room with curiosity. "Since we last talked three weeks ago," Priscilla Thorpe said, "I'm afraid Mrs. Saxon-Briggs' condition has deteriorated. She eats little. Refuses to touch anything but tea and Melba toast. The doctor says her cancer is advancing. You know, they've been treating her with chemotherapy, which is part of the problem. It upsets her stomach. We're very worried, especially Cecil and Edith, who always take these kinds of things so personally."

"Sorry to hear that," Alex said vaguely, busy inspecting the large framed oil paintings marching up the grand white marble staircase which dominated the spacious reception area. Alex speculated about their worth. He turned to Priscilla. "And you, do you take this personally or are you hired to be a detached nurse?" He looked at her with a curious mixture of playfulness, boredom and disdain.

Priscilla Thorpe drew herself up to her full stature, "Mr. Menshikov, I have been with this family for thirty-five years. It's not simply a question of a job. It's the right thing to do."

"Right."

Priscilla opened the door into an anteroom. At his right, two white cabinets, scalloped like huge shells, were built into the wall, each faced with slender Doric columns. He expected the shelves to be filled with rare English porcelain figurines, but instead found an exotic and varied collection of colored quartz crystals.

Some of these stones were in their natural roughhewn state, jagged as glass teeth. Others were neatly cut, shaped and polished: amethyst, rose, smoky topaz and citrine quartz. In the middle of this collection, mounted on an ebony stand and glowing under a faint purple light, stood a human-shaped skull made of flawless quartz. It was five inches high by seven inches wide, about the size of a Bocce ball.

Alex stopped and studied it closely. It looked eerily too human. As he examined the jaw, clenched in a deathly grimace, he felt as if the hollow eye sockets were staring menacingly at him. "What's this?" He pointed at the macabre sculpture.

Priscilla, who had already passed it, turned back. "That's the Crystal Skull. Mrs. Saxon-Briggs was on the expedition when it was found in the Belize jungle in 1927. It belonged to her father. She inherited it from him. It was used in ancient Mayan rituals."

"You mean when they sacrificed virgins?" Alex leered.

"Perhaps." Priscilla was not amused.

Alex thought that probably nothing amused her. "You don't really believe that."

"Mr. Menshikov, you don't have to take my word for it. Ask Cecil, he's an expert archeologist in Mayan antiquities."

"Who cares?" Alex shrugged his shoulders.

Their conversation stopped as they overheard a man's voice, with a Canadian lilt, booming from the living room. "This mosaic's case has turned the whole antiquities world upside down," he said. "This means that any government could claim that any art piece stolen in war was rightfully theirs, no matter who had legally bought it later."

"What about all those antiquities in the British museum? And the Elgin Marbles?" A woman with a mousy voice answered.

"My point precisely. They should leave well enough alone."

"Yes, dear, but what if it was really theirs in the first place?" the woman meekly countered.

"I say all's fair in love and war. They lost it fair and square; the new owners should keep it fair and square."

"But Cecil, dear, isn't it a question of who really owns the art?"

"Exactly. As it is now, antiquities dealers will have to start buying liability insurance, just like doctors, to protect us from malpractice. Then watch the price of art shoot through the bloody roof!"

"Oh dear, we could never afford that."

"And you wonder why it's so hard to earn a living selling antiquities these days!" Cecil groaned.

As Priscilla and Alex stepped to the threshold of the expansive rectangular living room, Alex quickly took in his surroundings. The room had twelve-foot high, light blue ceilings and large windows. A white frieze circled the pale yellow walls. There were three people in the room: a man and two women.

Alex already knew Cecil Durant. He was a short, stocky man with sandy hair and ruddy cheeks, red as Rome apples, which propped up a pair of round wire glasses. He draped his elbow on the mantelpiece.

His wife, Edith, sat demurely on the couch. She was about to say something when Cecil spotted Priscilla and Alex and bounded over to them. He gave Alex's shoulder a hearty slap, "Good to see you again, old man!" and took charge, as usual. "You know my wife, of course." Edith smiled wanly at Alex as he nodded to her. "And this is Mrs. Hannah Saxon-Briggs. Hannah," he raised his voice audibly so she could hear, "Mr. Menshikov is here. The man we've hired."

"You mean, I've hired." Mrs. Saxon-Briggs snapped. She had been scratching out a letter at a mahogany triangular desk facing the window overlooking an English formal garden, and now turned painfully in her chair to examine him.

Alex saw that she was dressed like the Grand Dame he had imagined her to be. She wore a long, emerald-green silk bathrobe with Chinese brocade embroidered down the front, and a long strand of pearls dangled over her ample bosom. Two rings, her gold wedding band and a huge emerald engagement ring, rattled on her bone-like finger.

Mrs. Saxon-Briggs' metal walker stood handily beside the desk. Her snow-white hair was set in a fancy French twist, which had two hairpins falling out. Despite her frailty, Alex saw that she had once been a matriarchal powerhouse—tall, big-boned and domineering. I know how to handle these kinds of people, he thought. Just cut through the bullshit, jolly them up and don't be intimidated. Alex made a courtly bow to her.

"We've heard a lot about you from Cecil," she said to Alex. "I hope you can live up to all our expectations."

"That depends," Alex frowned. "Things have started to unravel. Michael Beech is onto us. We'll have to act fast. We're going in tonight."

Cecil stopped and stared at Alex. "The bloody bastard! But you're crazy. We can't go in tonight. We'll never be able to pull it off."

"We will if you follow my instructions for once," Alex shot back.

"Impossible!" Cecil pulled a pipe out of his breast pocket, which he had just placed there a moment before, and mashed the tobacco angrily with his thumb.

Edith Durant gave Alex a thin enigmatic smile, as if half to apologize and half-defend her husband. "Are you sure you have it right, Alex?" She sat with her hands folded in her lap, rather doe-like, with large luminous eyes.

Alex thought to himself that there was at once something both wise and childlike about her. "Positive," he said. "Beech told me himself he was going to the Cathedral tonight to do the carbon dating. If he gets those samples, we're finished."

2

They had been deliberating for some time, when an older woman holding a tumbler of scotch on the rocks suddenly fluttered into the room. "Oh, I didn't disturb you, did I?" The Countess, at seventy plus, was petite, no more than five foot three, but her stateliness, combined with silver hair pulled fashionably back, made her appear taller.

Alex, seeing that the Countess clearly meant to interrupt them, glared at her angrily. He said to Priscilla, "You didn't tell me she was going to be here. How much does she know?"

The Countess twisted the string of white pearls, which dangled down her red designer jacket and pouted. "Really, Alex, you don't need to be rude." She spoke with a part Continental, part American twang, as if time had faded her Russian inflection like fabric kept too long in the sun. She sank affectedly into her chair, clanking her ice cubes as she sat.

She'd always reminded Alex of one of those sophisticated dowagers before the Revolution who used to collect the brightest intelligentsia for their salons, like dragons hoarding treasure in their lairs. Her age showed. A little too much white powder covered her wrinkles; red rouge caked heavily onto her protruding cheekbones.

"How is your little art import business doing, darling?" She eyed him coyly, blowing parallel streams of smoke through her nostrils.

"Fine, how's your extortion business doing?" Alex growled at her.

Pretending shock, she said, "Give us a kiss and let bygones be bygones." She put down her old fashioned gold and ivory cigarette holder and held her hand out, beckoning him to take it, but he merely looked at her disdainfully.

Alex said, "If she's in, I'm out of this."

"Alex, she knows everything," Priscilla said. "She has been part of the Inner Circle for years. The Durants said they wouldn't do anything without her. We didn't tell you because we thought you might not join us if you knew."

"If you drop out," Cecil said, "we want the $100,000 back."

"I can't do that."

"Well then, my dear," the Countess gloated like a cat, "you have no choice."

"It looks that way, doesn't it?" He glared at her again.

Mrs. Saxon-Briggs broke the silence. "Can you get everything organized in time? I don't want there to be any mistakes." Her voice sounded dry and raspy. She coughed twice, trying to clear her throat.

"There won't be any, not if I can help it. I assume everyone knows what to do. It should be simple, provided we all stick to our plan." He surveyed the room. Everyone nodded. Alex asked Priscilla, "What about the Countess? Where does she fit in?"

"We thought it best she stay here and take care of Hannah."

"Rubbish! I don't need any taking care of," Mrs. Saxon-Briggs protested. "I'm not a child that needs baby-sitting!" Then she lapsed into an intense coughing fit.

Priscilla went to fetch a glass of water and soon returned. She lovingly helped the older woman drink it until at last she regained her voice. "This must go smoothly. I want the Icon of Kazan back before I die," Mrs. Saxon-Briggs rasped. "I must have it. It's my only hope." Leaning forward over the walker, she struggled to rise to her feet. "Hannah, you must never attempt to stand up alone," Priscilla gently scolded her. "You know how shaky your balance is."

"Stop mollycoddling me!"

"I'm not mollycoddling you," Priscilla retorted. "I'm just trying to prevent a fall like last time..."

Hannah Saxon-Briggs said, "I want this done quickly and smoothly. Nothing can go wrong. I must have that icon." She leaned forward, placed her hands on the walker, and struggled to move her feet. Priscilla Thorpe scowled and helped her to her feet and together they began slowly moving towards the door.

Alex watched as Edith left the room to retrieve her knitting bag from the cupboard by the Crystal Skull. She whispered to Alex on the way back, "You know, the Icon of Kazan is a miraculous icon. It's known for its powers of healing. It is especially important that we get it for Hannah." She sat down again on the sofa with her knitting on her lap and began to click her needles rhythmically.

"You're not serious," Alex laughed.

"I am," Edith stated. "This is no ordinary icon. When Hannah owned the icon before, we would often gather to meditate around it."

"We have a great love for her," Edith said dreamily.

"Mrs. Saxon-Briggs?" Alex asked.

"No, the icon," the Countess chipped in. "She has a personality of her own, you know. So does the Crystal Skull. They used to be like two cats together, they couldn't stand to be separated for too long." She smiled serenely at Edith, who returned her look.

"I see," Alex said, sounding doubtful. He noticed that Cecil remained pointedly silent.

"I don't think you do," Priscilla said. She shot an icy glance at Edith who failed to catch it. "But that doesn't matter. All we want is the icon."

"Don't worry. You'll have it in your hands by nine tonight," Alex said.

"Good." Mrs. Saxon-Briggs turned to her secretary. "Priscilla, make sure you wire the rest of the money to his Swiss account and arrange for a ticket to London. Now, if you don't mind, I think I'll retire to my room. This has tired me out. Come along, Priscilla."

The Countess rose and joined the two women as they left the room. "It's much too chilly in here for me," she said and gave Alex a spiteful look.

Alex waited until they had gone, and then said to Cecil and Edith Durant, "Let's go over the details again."

3

Michael sat behind his massive ebony desk at the De Young museum and jotted a note to Andrea. He signed his name at the bottom of the museum stationery with a flourish and dropped a small brass key into the envelope. After sealing and stamping it, he slipped it into his inside coat pocket, reminding himself to mail it on his way to the Cathedral.

That done, Michael sat back in his plush desk chair, locked his hands behind his head and recalled his meeting the week before with John Hart. Hart was the Director of the Holy Virgin Society, who had hired him to appraise the Icon of Kazan. Michael wished he could forget the memory of Hart's fat, sweaty handshake and the look of his rumpled brown suit with its side pockets sagging like saddlebags on a beat-up horse.

Hart had suggested they meet in one of the more expensive restaurants adjacent to Golden Gate Park. "For reasons of security," he half-whispered and wheezed over the phone. Michael had wondered what all the fuss was about. Why should a Catholic religious society have to worry about security?

Michael had finished his coffee, wiped the corners of his mouth with his cloth napkin and laid it neatly folded on the table. "What's so important that you couldn't tell me in my office?" he'd said to Hart.

John Hart had looked over his shoulder, then handed Michael a tiny flat brass key. "The Major thought you should have this, just in case. It's a safe deposit key."

Michael looked at the key quizzically. "Who's the Major? And in case of what?"

"I can't tell you his full name. He prefers to remain anonymous. The Major was the one who tipped us off about the icon being a fraud, says he has important family papers to prove it."

Michael sat up with interest. "Really, and how do you know he's telling the truth?"

Hart spoke in a hushed tone. "We don't. Not until we see those papers. He says they'll prove the age and identity of the icon. There's a strange group of people hooked up with it. He said he had the names and addresses of all the members of this art ring. I think he called it the Inner Circle. He would know."

"Who are they?"

"We don't know. The Major won't tell. I think he's trying to protect his sister, who's somehow involved with them, but I don't know for sure."

"Who's she?"

"I don't know that either. Believe me, I asked."

"So why didn't he just give you the papers?"

"He wants you to examine the icon before he gives them to us. Says it has to do with family honor. He wanted you to have a key in case anything happened to him. He has the other key."

"What does he expect to happen?"

"Anything could happen. The Major said he's being watched. He used to work for US intelligence, so I'm sure he knows what he's talking about. He's retired now, over seventy. Fortunately, he's fit as a bull. An old army man. Russian stock. Runs five miles a day. Also, he thinks his phones have been tapped."

"How can he tell that?"

"He knows. Your phones are probably tapped too. If I were you, I'd have them checked."

"What makes you think all this isn't just a bunch of paranoid nonsense dreamed up by a retired spook?"

"Mr. Beech, the Major's not crazy. I'm just passing on to you what he said to me. I advise you to take some precautions, just in case." Hart crumpled up his napkin and tossed it on his plate. "For our insurance company, of course."

"Ah yes, the insurance company." Michael had drained the last bit of wine from his glass. "How could I forget? They're running the whole country!"

Returning to the present in his office, Michael felt his gorge rise. "Hart's an ass!" he said aloud. Nevertheless, the possibility that what Hart had said might be true nagged at him. This would be one of the greatest art scandals of the century and it would certainly make his career.

Michael picked up the phone to dial another call, when he heard a strange faint mechanical noise rasping on the other end of the line. His face blanched with sudden realization. "Shit!" He slammed down the receiver hastily, took out the letter from his pocket, ripped it up and began writing another letter.

4

Andrea glanced at the wall clock and noted that the time was almost up. Quickly summarizing the details of her last point, she read to her students from her notes, "'With these words, Richard Hooker routed, with one stroke of genius, the Catholics' ambition for power and the Calvinists' penchant for doctrinal purity.'" She ended and scanned her class. "For next week, please read chapters four through eight of Wolf's book *Anglicanism* and MacQuarrie's chapters on the Sacraments. Any questions?" There were none. "Then I guess that's it for the day."

Suddenly the room erupted with a gabble of voices and the sound of metal chairs scraping across the linoleum floor as twenty seminary students filed out of the classroom. Some stopped to ask Andrea questions, others to schedule appointments, and still others simply to chat. She liked most of her students and loved teaching them—all except the occasional antagonistic one, like Christie.

Alone now, Andrea removed her glasses, placing them on her notes by the podium, and picked up an eraser. After each class, she erased the green chalkboard as a kind of ritual to help her unwind. She smiled to herself as she remembered one of her colleagues, a brilliant theology professor, who would write on the blackboard then absentmindedly clutch his suspenders while he taught, leaving conspicuous white chalk marks on his black clergy shirt. She dusted off the chalk from her own jacket, grabbed her briefcase and hurried to the parking lot below.

As she sat in her car, she thought about her conversation with Michael. She regretted losing her temper with Michael and truly felt bad for him. Maybe she should go to the cathedral and apologize. But why was she so hesitant about seeing the icon? She had wanted to see it up close for years. Was it her pre-exam jitters or something else? What was she really afraid of?

What had Michael said? He wanted her to come and get a "feel" for the icon. Ever since their trip to Ravenna, he knew she had this hidden gift. He called it being psychic. But it wasn't quite like that. She could never read people's minds and her flashes of ESP were few and far between.

Her first experience of this gift happened when she was nearly seven years old. Following her parent's messy divorce, she moved with her mother and brother from the wealthy suburban town of Scarsdale, New York, to her mother's home in San Francisco.

Her mother, Marina Roevich, came from a prestigious family of Russian painters who fled Russia in 1922, after the Revolution, and eventually settled in California. Maria was at heart a passionate woman, but also a temperamental artist and a devout Russian Orthodox believer. Andrea's father, Sam West, an upwardly mobile American of the 1950s, was a born conservative; so conventional that he thought cornflakes were interesting. His religion was convention-al too, what she later called a "Christmas and Easter" Episcopalian.

Though he rarely went to church himself, he refused to let Marina and the children attend the Russian Orthodox Church. Early on, he put his foot down and said, "What? Attend a Russian Church? Then Joe McCarthy's boys would really be after us." But Andrea later realized he just disapproved of her mother's church; he thought it was primitive and odd. This and a series of roaring fights contributed finally to her parents' divorce in 1961.

She remembered her first Easter Vigil in California in 1962. Her brother Nicky had just turned eleven, old enough to stay up at night an hour longer than she normally could. On Easter Eve, her mother took her, after some coaxing, to her first Orthodox Midnight Easter Vigil at a small, whitewashed Orthodox Church on Green Street. It had a tiny blue cupola on the roof and on one side a large glass encased icon, of the Face of Christ, badly in need of restoration. All she could remember was shivering in the damp windy fog, along with a crowd of two-hundred worshipers, trying to shield the flame of her slim white candle while the deacon intoned the opening sentences with such a deep bass voice that the walls almost shuddered.

Then came the big push inside into the crowded wooden church. It was all too overwhelming: the low ceilings and wooden floors, the red Persian rugs, the big iconostasis with three doors, an assortment of icons and the smell of beeswax votive candles on the wall; elderly women stooping to kiss the icons and one old man weeping and repeatedly kissing the floor. The thick smell of lilies and rosewater, mixed with white clouds of musky frankincense, lingered pleasantly in the air. The choir and the fat bearded deacon, jangling the bells on the thurible, droned on and on, while Andrea, with no place to sit, stood until her legs ached. She felt faint with hunger and exhaustion.

As she watched this living communion of saints, these older churchgoers in front of her, something trembled and shook loose inside her. Then a bolt of energy coming out of nowhere shot through her like a warm laser. It was as if she had been pushed through an invisible scrim into another world: a world of her deepest roots, but a world incomprehensible and filled with awe and terror, joy and fear. It was her first real experience of God: God—not as some approachable Person but as Mystery in the raw, deeper than outer space itself.

Her confusion and fear nearly swallowed her alive. Suddenly she felt like she was suffocating. She gasped for air. Panicking, she shoved her way through the crowd, out the narrow door and down the front steps onto the sidewalk, panting rapidly. Her mother rushed out to her quickly. "Are you all right, sweetheart? What is it?"

Andrea shook her head and cried, "I can't breathe."

"Put your head down between your knees." Andrea did as her mother ordered. "That's it. You'll be fine after some fresh air, then we can go back into the church." Marina rubbed her daughter's back to soothe her.

"No. I don't want to go back," young Andrea said stoutly. She began to cry and bite her thumb. Her mother collected Nicky, who was equally happy to go, then took them by the hand and left.

This memory abruptly faded as the screeching wheels of a braking truck roared past. Andrea's thoughts returned to the present, "And I never entered another church again," she said aloud to herself. Until Ravenna. Michael opened her eyes to new wonders. The great 6th century mosaics in the Basilica of San Vitale gave Andrea her first inkling that there might be a God who believed in her, even though she didn't believe in Him. The possibility of this scared her half to death.

Ravenna changed everything. It seemed so simple and natural at the time. The pictures spoke to her and the gift, like a shaft of gentle interior sunlight, had come. Again, the memory of it still made her feel safe and mellow.

She inexplicably discovered that she could sometimes see into people as if their souls were made of glass. She could smell holiness—or evil—like the smell of sun-drenched sheets or conversely, rotten eggs. She simply had an inner capacity, something like a spiritual Geiger counter, to know how people were feeling, spiritually and physically. On other rare occasions, this psychic awareness would come with the capacity to heal or even more rarely, to see into the future. But these were never anything that she could control, as much as she would have wanted to.

Michael's request was so simple. What harm was there in that? They could view the Icon after Evensong, then she could leave, drive home to Berkeley and still have time to prepare for her meeting the next morning.

The problem was, of course, that this inner spiritual gift had gradually dimmed, then died six months ago, after she finished her dissertation. She had often wept and raged at God about it, but both her inner and outer sky seemed empty. It was as if the prayers she shot up to heaven hit the ceiling and came crashing down to her on earth. In short, while she still believed in God intellectually, she feared that she had lost her faith. She felt empty as a tomb. Dead inside. Everything else was play-acting.

Then it became clear to her: she didn't want Michael to know. It was one of the few things she could do better than him. A few years ago, his brief dabbling in religion had changed from a flicker of enthusiasm to a devout aestheticism. Maybe she could tell Michael there was nothing to feel. No explanation needed. He'd never know the difference.

CHAPTER 3

"Each of us is an image of the living God, but an image which, like an old painting that has been tampered with, overlaid or clumsily restored to the point of being unrecognizable, yet in which some features of the original survive; a specialist can scrutinize it and, starting with what is genuine, clean the whole painting of its successive additions."

Metropolitan Anthony Bloom
Meditations: A Spiritual Journey

Alex Menshikov stamped his feet and shivered in the cold twilight outside the corner grocery store at 26th Avenue and Geary Boulevard by the Russian Orthodox Cathedral. It had begun to drizzle heavily. He adjusted the canvas pack slung carelessly over his left shoulder, and pulled up his collar.

He scanned the street, looking for the Durants' Dodge sedan. No sign of them. He checked his watch again. Six o'clock. "Come on, come on!" he muttered to himself. "Christ, where are they? Why try to work with these amateurs? Maybe I'm getting too old for this kind of thing?" Alex stopped to examine himself in the store window and straightened his posture, trying to look younger.

As big as Alex was, he felt minuscule compared to the golden onion dome of the Holy Virgin Orthodox Cathedral across the street. A few elderly Russian worshipers struggled up the front steps into the cathedral. Men over eighty, with faces like creased leather, climbed the steps slowly, bending double over their canes. Years of suffering were etched into every line. The blue-haired women dressed in black coats and red and black floral scarves coaxed them up the stairs, chatting in Russian.

He recognized these old parishioners; their faces reminded him of their old servant Gregory. These faces could still be seen in every church between Odessa and Omsk. Some spoke a little English, but most preferred to speak in Russian. They were the last remnants of the White Russians from his parents' generation who had emigrated during the '20s. These were the lucky ones.

Since the Orthodox Church had acted as the mouthpiece for the Tsar, Alex understood why, after 1917, the Cheka so viciously tried to annihilate the church and all its trappings of faith and power. He knew that over twenty million people were arrested or murdered for religious and political dissent during Stalin's purges. Between 1917 and 1938, the number of clergy alone shrank from 300,000 in Russia to a mere few thousand. They even killed his hometown parish priest.

Alex had heard many tales from his uncle: how Komosol leaders, for instance, had placed stolen icons in the vestibules of their bath houses then, dressed only in towels, used them as target practice before stepping into their baths.

Russian refugees, however, had begun flooding into the U.S. long before the Revolution. Boatloads steamed in at both Ellis and Angel Islands during the Russo-Japanese War of 1904 and continued long after 1917. Alex knew this because he was part of that later incoming tide.

These White Russians, like his own family, had suffered much to flee Russia immediately after the Revolution, but at least they were still alive. Leaving all property and wealth behind, they escaped with nothing but the clothes on their backs and their small icons in their vests. They fled west through Poland and Paris, or East by way of Harbin or Shanghai through Manila or Yokohama, ultimately landing in San Francisco.

Alex looked at these elders with a strange mixture of contempt and nostalgia. Contempt because he knew that these White Russians persisted in clinging to the last shreds of Tsarist Russia when all hope of a counter-revolution had disappeared decades ago. Contempt because they were cowards. They didn't stay to fight. They were not present to see the disaster of the Civil War, his country lying in ruins and the cream of Russian nobility and the intelligentsia wiped out like flies. They had been spared these brutal realities and so could afford to cling to their illusions a little longer. Much longer.

But he felt a wave of nostalgia for them, too. Nostalgia because, like it or not, aristocracy was in his blood. During the Civil War after the October Revolution, his parents and grandfather fled from St. Petersburg to their estates in the Ural Mountains not far from Omsk. Here in their summer cottage, they carved out for themselves a wholesome but harsh lifestyle. He was born there in 1927, the grandson of a prince. But what did that mean anymore?

He revived distant memories of his grandfather's summer dacha, the purple mountains, the old peasant servant Gregori, and of the time at age four when he snuck after them to watch his grandfather and father, dressed in tweed knickers, shoot grouse in the fields, not for sport but for food. He especially loved the early mornings, when the mist still hovered in the zebra-white birch groves and shrouded the green clattering leaves into silence. At his feet, bright red poppies and golden wheat spread like a vast Persian carpet across the open rolling hills.

During those first warm summers, his family even managed to retrieve a bit of their old elegance with their abundant food and wildflowers. But this was soon devastated by the long cruel Siberian winters and the years of forced collectivization. His mother, Anna, used to paint vivid pictures of what they once had: a huge palace on the Neva River, jewels, servants, titles and a history that went back to Tsar Peter the Great. Now they survived on sunflower seeds, horses' oats, milk, eggs, berries and very rarely a chicken. The army had choked off the roads, the lifeline to the markets, so that whole villages starved. When the winter passed, the army would come in, clear out the corpses, leaving villages perfectly intact to allow new people to settle there.

Somehow, through various false papers and identities, Alex's father, Andrei, had managed to stay alive during the early waves of Stalin's purges. He was arrested six times, usually held only a month or two, and then released. His seventh arrest was much harder. After weeks of beatings and political brainwashing, he was finally released to go home—but only after he agreed to collaborate with the secret police called the NKVD, the precursor to the KGB.

In 1934, Andrei joined the Communist party and was ordered

to help exterminate the local Kulaks, the prosperous peasants who resisted Stalin's efforts of collectivization. As a neighbor, he had worked closely with many of them on their farms. Andrei's delicate and spoiled sensibilities broke under the strain of it. His moods swung between violent rage and despair. "When the forests are cut, chips will fly," his father once said.

As a boy, if the wind was right, Alex could hear the distant sound of gunshots in the black piney woods. One night, his father came home late, sullen and reeking with vodka. His red, watery eyes looked vacant one minute and desperate the next.

He could still see the terrified look on his mother's face as she crouched sobbing by the fireplace. "No, Andrei, don't shoot us! Please don't shoot us!" And his father staggering there, wild-eyed, the revolver trembling in his hand. Ten-year-old Alex tackled his father by the waist and shouted, "No, Papa! Please, Papa!" When he dropped the gun, the bullet ricocheted off the stone hearth, just missing his mother.

Finally one night, in 1937, the inevitable knock came at their front door. Alex was the first to spot the green hatbands of the secret police. The KGB took his father away. By then, Andrei was so beaten down, that he went without a whimper. His mother fled with Alex in case the police came back for them too. Later Alex heard conflicting rumors: that his father languished in Lubyanka Prison, until he was shot, or that he was forcibly drafted into the Soviet army, where he was sent to the front lines of the Finnish War and was never heard from again. He never learned the truth.

Bloody bastard deserved it, he thought bitterly. His father had been weak and spineless. His father, son of a prince, had become, through cowardice, a mass murderer—a tool of the State. From that moment on, Alex had determined that nobody would ever pin anything on him. The best way to survive was to be independent and strong. And to trust no one.

He took one last drag on his Pall Mall, flicked it to the ground, and then mashed it with his foot. Alex looked at his watch. It was now 6:10 p.m.

A beige sedan pulled up and parked down the street into a partially hidden service driveway of the cathedral. Cecil and Edith Durant nodded to Alex from their car.

2

Everything had been carefully planned. Months ago, Cecil had cleverly maneuvered himself into a part-time position as a security guard with the very agency the church had hired to protect the Icon of Kazan. After weeks of stealth and manipulation, he arranged to be scheduled on the evening shift at the cathedral, which he was about to begin.

Alex was relieved to see Cecil charging towards him, dressed in a navy blue uniform. Edith straggled along behind, clutching her purse, looking every inch like the church-lady, but there was no sign of Priscilla Thorpe.

Alex hissed to Cecil as he made to pass, "Where is she?"

"Hannah fell," he grunted. "Priscilla said she couldn't come."

"Damn! You'll have to be the look-out."

"We'll manage." Careful not to blow his cover, Cecil strode on to the cathedral to play his role.

A few minutes later, appearing eerily calm about the whole thing, Edith likewise came to the cathedral door, placed a scarf over her head and went inside. Pretending to be a worshiper, she distracted one of the elderly Russian ushers by asking him questions about the cathedral and drew him away from the vestry door towards the counter of holy cards, candles and black cord Russian rosaries.

The diversion allowed Alex to slip through the double brass doors, carrying his pack with his tools and black cassock inside. He turned right and went through the side door under the hanging pendulum clock to the maze of halls and rooms below.

3

Andrea checked her watch as she rounded the corner towards the Holy Virgin Cathedral. It was 6:20 p.m. exactly. On time. Michael Beech was climbing the cathedral steps alone when she hurried up behind him and tapped his elbow. "I changed my mind."

He turned, genuinely surprised, and gave her a quick hug. "Glad you could make it."

"I can hardly wait to see it," Andrea said, peering over Michael's shoulder at the crowd clustered around the Icon.

"You'll have to wait your turn, but it'll be worth it." He opened the heavy glass double-door of the cathedral for her and stopped. Surveying the crowd of assembled worshippers, he said, "This service will be larger than usual. You can tell because Orthodox clergy are here from all over the West Coast. See."

The place seemed to be swarming with clergy. Andrea looked around and saw a number of bearded men dressed in black cassocks gliding quietly among the parishioners. Some stopped to talk with them, others made their private devotions at separate icons, while still others went behind the iconostasis to make last minute preparations.

As she studied the church, comparing it with her previous memories, she noticed a priest dressed in a black cassock with a long peppery beard, looking at her with piercing eyes from under his thick eyebrows. When she returned his gaze with a puzzled look, he turned quickly away and moved to speak to some parishioners. Then he was lost in the crowd.

Andrea wondered what that was all about. She knew that Orthodox priests were allowed to marry but maybe this one had been celibate too long. She thought no more of it.

"Evensong will begin soon," Michael said. "Excuse me while I talk with Sergei." He left her while he made arrangements with the aged sexton by the front counter. Andrea was quite happy to peer through the great glass wall that divided the vestibule from the nave into the cavernous cathedral.

Inside, the cathedral walls were covered with ornate icons and designs. On the walls around the room, someone had painted twenty-foot icons of saints and archangels in bright red and golden tunics. Not one inch of the walls was left untouched.

There were no pews. Most people stood in place to say their prayers, while the older members sat in wooden chairs in the back

set up specifically for the frail elderly or pregnant mothers. Still others, older men and women, clergy in tattered cassocks, made their
rounds throughout the church, kissing their favorite icons of Jesus,
Mary, St. Nicholas, and St. Herman, as if to say hello.

One woman, with dyed red hair and bad teeth, hovered over
the counter where holy cards and piles of thin beeswax candles were
being sold. Andrea bought two candles, one for herself (as interces-
sion for her dissertation defense tomorrow) and one for the soul of
Hans. The woman glumly took Andrea's bill and gave her change,
then with a gesture she invited her to sign the guest book. Andrea
was pleased they made an effort to reach out to newcomers and
signed her name and address. After a moment's thought, she penned
in Michael's name as well.

When Michael returned to her side, Andrea said, "I signed in
for you. They don't keep attendance, do they?"

He shook his head. "They could never be so organized. Maybe
I'll get the gift shop catalogue now."

Together, Michael and Andrea left the narthex and stepped onto
the polished pine floors under the three-story dome. Andrea looked
up and overhead saw painted on the ceiling of the dome a huge
mural of the icon of Christ in Judgment, the Pantocrator. "It's almost
as wonderful as Ravenna," she whispered.

Above the altar, on the wall behind the iconostasis, (also covered
with icons and gold filigree), was a beautiful large icon, a blue pregnant Byzantine Mary, the Virgin of the Sign, looking down upon
them with outstretched arms. The unborn Christ child blessed the
people from her womb with an upraised hand. Andrea didn't know
why, but she felt deeply moved by this icon.

Pointing at a painting of the Archangel Raphael, she said,
"Michael, I haven't seen work like this outside of Russia!"

"You're not likely to," he said. "Father Mench once told me he
helped Father Kiprion, who painted all these murals and the dome.
He was the last of the great Russian iconographers who learned his
skills in the old country, under the old masters. He was a real genius,
don't you think?"

"Absolutely," Andrea said vaguely, too dazzled to take in much of what he said. It was as if she had stepped inside a shimmering jewel. This effect was heightened by three glittering gold and crystal chandeliers suspended overhead.

She saw that special icons were placed on stands strategically around the room, a dozen on each side. They looked as homey as family photographs. Each had next to it a large round brass candle stand on wheels, which could hold banks of thirty slim white candles. One particular nativity icon, a scene of Mary, Joseph, and Jesus in a stable, caught Andrea's eye, "Michael, look at those lines of the stable roof, why are they all crooked? Didn't the iconographer know about perspective?"

Michael studied the Christmas scene. "Not at first. None of the early medieval painters did, until Leonardo. Later iconographers were forced to follow a rigid style in order to render theological dogma through their art. They never believed in 'freedom of expression' or the search for 'realism in art.' That wasn't the point. To the iconographer, icons were a theological tool, just like the Bible. That's why the perspective is all askew, it's because the painter wanted to convey another sense of reality."

"So what we are looking at is a picture of an altered state of consciousness?"

"Sort of. To the Orthodox, icons are supposed to be windows to heaven. The fifth dimension, if you will. And the primary action which every figure in an icon is doing is prayer."

"And, none of them cast any shadows. Like St. Anthony in the desert."

"Right. The old iconographers believed that the starting point of all perspective in an icon was the viewer. They called this inverse perspective. Iconographers deliberately distorted normal perspective, such as slanting a stable roof the opposite way, to show how God breaks into our everyday lives and turns everything upside down. Icons are also supposed to depict scenes of heaven on earth. These scenes look weird, not because heaven is warped, but because we are. It is a visual attempt to show how skewed our perspective is compared to the reality of Grace."

"Hmmm," Andrea mused. "That's how C.S. Lewis described our

capacity to sin; he called it being 'bent.' Do you believe that?"

"I tend to side with the Epicureans—man is no more good than the soup he eats. Morality is primarily a matter of digestion."

"I think you've sided with the cynics instead." Andrea smiled, suspecting he was pulling her leg on purpose for the sake of argument. "But what about Genesis and the idea of God creating us originally good?"

"Always the optimist, I see. I'd love to continue our little theological discussion, but we don't have time to talk now." Michael watched the acolytes move into the sanctuary. "The service is beginning."

A parade of two Bishops, four priests, two deacons and four altar boys, all dressed in badly soiled white and gold silk vestments processed into the sanctuary. One three hundred pound deacon, a man with a long gray beard and a deep bass baritone voice, boomed out the introit. Above in the balcony, the choir of men and women responded antiphonally, "*Gospodin...*"

As the service progressed, Andrea watched with fascination an old Russian woman, dressed in a raincoat and wool beret, who came to an icon near them. She had a bulbous nose and a face creased with webbed lines. She exchanged a warm glance with Andrea, who felt immediately akin to her. A holy sister. She watched as the woman tucked a quarter into the tin box, lit a white candle and kissed the side of the Icon three or four times before placing her candle in the stand. The woman knelt with both knees on the ground, kissed the red carpet before it, and then kissed the icon again. Andrea was stunned by her devotion and utter lack of self-consciousness. Secretly, she felt jealous of her and sad on her own account, because she felt so spiritually empty.

Andrea closed her eyes and inhaled the honeyed air mingled with the scent of beeswax candles and frankincense. The rhythmical, rich chanting between the deacon and the choir lapped through and over her like the recurring waves of a deep ocean. She could have stood there forever.

4

Michael touched her elbow. "It's over now," he whispered. Members of the congregation slowly straggled out towards the narthex, chatting amicably with each other in Russian.

Andrea blinked, "That was quick."

"Not quick enough," Michael mumbled. "These people think that if it's good enough to do once, it's good to do it nine times. Now," he said eagerly, "let's see what we've really come for."

Michael stepped up to the Icon of Kazan, opened his case and took out a packet of brushes and a large magnifying glass. "Now it's up close and personal," he said. "Let me show you the pièce de resistance." His eyes danced brightly.

Michael bowed deeply to the icon, crossed himself, and kissed the corners of the icon three times before lighting a candle and placing it in one of the brass candle stands. He said a silent prayer. Andrea then did the same.

The Icon of Kazan was laid on an ornate wooden stand about four feet high. The sacristans had draped it with a large garland of a hundred budding white roses, each one as perfect as if it had been made of porcelain. The icon stood on the red carpet between the gospel podium and the steps leading up to double doors of the iconostasis, revealing the altar decked with white linen and large red sanctuary lamp behind.

The riza, or icon cover, was made of pure gold and overlaid the entire icon except for the face and neck of Mary and the infant Jesus, who stood to the right. Artisans had hammered out the gold riza copying the shape of the child's torso and the Madonna's head and shoulders. Sixteen large rectangular emeralds, surrounded by diamonds, rubies and even larger diamonds circled the diamond and pearl-studded crown on Mary's head. One oddly shaped emerald surrounded by diamonds was placed in the middle of Jesus' chest; his raised hand was outlined by rubies. A large blue sapphire was placed over Mary's heart. Andrea wondered if the placement and colors of the jewels meant anything. She knew that green was the traditional color of healing.

"At last we meet," she whispered as she kissed the icon with a qualm of awe and trepidation. Immediately she smelled the strong perfume of rose water on the icon itself. At closer inspection, the icon and the riza appeared even more refined and delicate than she thought possible.

She stepped back and was unable to tear her eyes away from the Madonna. "She's so beautiful!"

Michael nodded, "People would give anything for this beauty."

"Have you noticed that curious look on her face?" Andrea said. "This sounds like a cliché, but there's something enigmatic about her, like the Mona Lisa."

Michael nodded his head and remained silent. Andrea continued to stare at the icon. The smooth, gentle moon-face dispelled her feelings of emptiness. Her sense of lostness fell off her like an old cloak. Her body became quiet. Her shoulders lowered and the tightness in the center of her chest and stomach flowed out. She sighed audibly. As she stared at the eyes of the Virgin Mary, she began to notice a quiet, delicious inner burning sensation in the middle of her chest.

With this, the eyes of the icon seemed to sparkle with a playful but deep luster. Even the skin of the face of the Virgin seemed to shine with a quiet ecstatic joy. To Andrea, the eyes felt almost hypnotic, with a compelling, tender quality. The more Andrea looked, the more she realized that she was being looked at as well, by eyes that poured over every inch of her soul, but with compassion. A compassion, filled with mirth. It was as if the icon was pouring liquid sunlight into her. All sense of time disappeared. Seconds seemed like hours. Because of the joy she felt, she almost began to weep, but she controlled herself. This was too special to talk about.

She once heard Bishop Timothy Kallistos Ware say that the only way a worshiper could properly view an icon was with one's eyes shut. She closed her eyes again. The warmth was still there and inside her.

"Well?" Michael asked.

"It's very special," Andrea said. "But I can't describe it now." She didn't want to profane the experience by talking about it. She followed the old Zen adage: 'Those who don't talk, know; those who talk, don't know.' "I'm tired, Michael. I've had a pretty long day. Let me think about it some more."

Michael crossed his arms, a gesture he used whenever he was about to pontificate about something. "Of course, this is an old enough piece, but I think it was painted no earlier than 1750, give or take a few years. Some art appraisers say this icon was painted in the early 13th century. The problem is that soon after it was 'miraculously found,' two other copies of the original were quickly painted. I think this piece is one of those two copies."

"You mean it's not the 13th century original, as some claim?"

"Right. The Holy Virgin Society bought it for half a million dollars, assuming it was the original, and up to now were saying it was worth nearly five million."

"Was that fraud or a mistake?"

"I'm not sure yet. But somebody knew what he was doing. I've come here to check out some last minute details before blowing the whistle. Everything is ready to go."

"This is pretty wild stuff," Andrea said. "Are you sure you know what you're getting into?"

"Quite sure."

Andrea suddenly looked at her watch, "I have to go! Can we see it again?"

"So soon?" Michael said with dismay.

"You're lucky you got me at all. Remember, my dissertation defense is tomorrow."

"Sorry, I forgot. Thanks for coming." Michael said gratefully. "Really." He kissed her cheek. "I'll call you tomorrow to see how it all went."

"Say a prayer to the Holy Virgin for me!" Andrea called out over her shoulder.

5

The sky was dark when Andrea hurried down the front steps of the cathedral. The rain had stopped, but dank fog from the ocean billowed and swirled like smoke around the pinkish-yellow glow of the street lamps. Everything was cold, wet and bleak.

Andrea thought to herself, "How odd. I feel like Dorothy who's just stepped from the Land of Oz and into Kansas again. I've gone from living color to black and white. I guess that's what the Orthodox liturgy is supposed to do, heighten our senses to the sublime."

As she walked, she rummaged through her purse looking for her keys. She always liked to have her keys ready before she got into her car—it made her feel safer. Not looking, she turned at the corner and bumped shoulders with a woman wearing a navy-blue overcoat and a paisley scarf, who walked quickly past her. As she did so, Andrea recognized the faint vanilla scent of Shalimar perfume, one of her old favorites.

"Oh, I'm sorry," she said feeling foolish. The woman quickly turned her face away, muttered something curt, and moved ahead. Andrea instantly felt as if she had passed an icebox. She shivered and all the hairs stood up at the nape of her neck. As she unlocked the front door of her car, she turned to look back at the cathedral. The woman had disappeared. Except for the cars on Geary Street splashing through puddles, Andrea was alone.

6

Michael stood in the now nearly empty cathedral and watched Andrea leave with a pang of fondness. He knew he had betrayed her love and realized deep down how self-centered and shallow he had become. Or maybe he had always been. He was the kind of man who rarely looked inside himself. Like many narcissistic people, he feared that if he did, he'd find nobody home.

Tonight, however, seeing the Icon of Kazan through Andrea's eyes had somehow changed him. Her spiritual depth was so obvious it cut him to the quick and it convicted him. He ached for the faith, which he had long since discarded and he ached, as much as he could, for her.

Being superstitious, he made it a practice before beginning any work on an icon to say a short prayer. This time he said one in earnest to the icon, or rather to the Virgin Mary, for Andrea and for himself. Perhaps for their future together.

"Ardent Intercessor, Mother of the Lord on high! Pray to Thy Son, Christ our God for all and save those who have recourse to Thy Powerful Protection..." he muttered, praying with all his heart.

Then eagerly he set to work examining the back of the icon. By a long-standing arrangement with the church sexton, Sergei, Michael was allowed to stay for an hour after the worship service to examine the icon. Sergei, who was slightly deaf, was a small mole-like Russian. He looked too frail to push a broom, but he nodded when he saw Michael and then went back to the cathedral undercroft to finish sweeping.

Michael heard the footsteps of the security guard outside in the narthex. I can't believe they don't have tougher security here, he thought. Only one security guard for this icon? I guess it costs too much money.

Michael's plan was to take some wood samples from the icon for carbon dating later. Working fastidiously, he took a sharp X-acto knife and cut a sliver of wood from back of the icon, then unscrewed the riza from the icon itself. He chipped away a fragment of the gesso where the icon had already been badly damaged in the past.

Spotlights twenty feet above the chandeliers cast three eerie shafts of light onto the wooden floor of the cathedral. A crowd of dim faces seemed to be peering down from the wall at him. Michael had the creepy feeling that he was being watched. He looked around into the shadows of the cathedral. Everything was dark. Behind the iconostasis, the dim candlelight of the red sanctuary lamp glowed in the dark over the altar. Hot wax sputtered in the glass. It was difficult for him to see as clearly as he would have liked.

From time to time, he heard Sergei's footsteps, the sound of closing doors and the rhythmic brushing of the big push broom knocking the floor. Sometimes there were voices. Michael assumed the sexton and security guard were having a chat.

He was so absorbed in his project that he barely noticed the sound of another door opening silently from behind the iconostasis.

Out of the corner of his eye he saw the large figure of a bearded
Orthodox priest in a long black cassock genuflect in front of the
altar. Michael ignored him and went back to his measuring and chis-
eling tiny fragments of paint and wood.

A gruff Russian voice erupted from behind him. He started
with fright, half-turned, barely catching a glimpse of a black cassock
and gray beard towering over him before he felt something hard and
metal crack into his skull. He collapsed unconscious onto the floor.

Poor bastard, Alex Menshikov thought. He carefully unscrewed
the back of the Icon of Kazan from its stand, wrapped it in a large
clean white felt cloth, and set it on the floor. Then he took another
icon from his shoulder bag, exactly the same size and shape as the
Icon of Kazan, complete with a fake gold riza and green glass emeralds, and placed it on the stand where the original one had been. It
fit perfectly. He screwed the glass case into place over it.

He took a cloth and wiped his fingerprints off the gold case.
Then he clasped Michael's hands and dragged his body across the
waxed floor, up the steps of the iconostasis, through the royal doors
where he laid him out behind the altar.

Returning to the spot where Michael had fallen, Alex hastily
rubbed the waxed wooden floor with a towel. He tucked the real
Icon of Kazan into his bulky shoulder bag and carefully hoisted it
over his shoulder. A noise rustled in the back dark corner.

"Cecil?" Alex hissed, but there was no reply. Alex nervously
grabbed his tools and hurried silently out of the sanctuary.

CHAPTER 4

❧

"The real battle takes place in the hearts of men and women, between love and hatred, light and darkness, God and him who is the murderer from the beginning."

Metropolitan Anthony Bloom
Meditations: A Spiritual Journey

Tuesday, October 23, 1990

Early next morning, Sergei arrived at the Holy Virgin Cathedral to begin his usual routine. Shuffling into the sacristy where the communion vessels were kept, he pulled a can of cat food from his coat pocket, peeled open the top and spooned some ground fish into a small dish. He put the dish down on some newspaper in a corner, and then opened the door, which led from the sacristy into the basement. At once, a gray cat bounded out and trotted to her food. Sergei laboriously bent over and gently stroked the cat's plump body. The cat vibrated under his gnarled hand as she purred and ate hungrily.

"You little fatso. You eat better than we did in Stalingrad." Then he set about his regular chores.

First on Sergei's list was to set up the prayer books for the morning's service. He took out his wad of keys, humming a Russian kontakion under his breath, unlocked the back door to the sanctuary and slowly walked in. He glanced at the altar in passing, and then froze.

There, stuck in the center of the altar, was a long pearl-handled silver dagger. A pool of red blood saturated the white fair linen. Sergei swore under his breath, quickly crossing himself.

He stepped back in fear. Only then did he see Michael Beech's body lying in the shadows behind the altar with his throat gashed open. He screeched.

Michael's body and arms were stiff and waxy yellow. A sticky river of blood trickled down the sanctuary steps onto the floor of the main church itself.

Sergei crossed himself twice and hurried out of the church to the nearest phone as fast as he could totter. He never noticed the candle in the sanctuary lamp hanging over the altar. The whole lamp had been turned upside-down on its chain and hot wax, like Michael's blood, had poured out and hardened on the polished floor.

2

By 8:30 a.m., the whole front of the Holy Virgin Cathedral along the sidewalk was sealed off with yellow police tape. Four black squad cars, a mobile homicide crime lab, an ambulance and two mobile television vans topped with radar were parked out front. A burly Irish traffic cop stood in the middle of Geary and 26th Avenue and waved traffic through, attempting to prevent morning commuters from rubber necking past the crime scene.

The garbled noise of static burst randomly from the squad cars, disrupting the quiet of the fog-shrouded streets. Already a crowd of curious spectators had gathered, craning their necks to see what had happened. Most of them were joggers, kids on their way to school, a few housewives dressed in bathrobes and slippers, plus some commuters, erect with brief cases, waiting for the express bus heading downtown.

Police and detective crews filed in and out of the building. Technicians from the photo lab worked inside, taking videos and stills of the body. Then the crime lab assistants dusted the place with graphite for prints, took blood samples and searched around the altar area for shreds of clothing, hairs and any possible miscellaneous pieces of evidence. The Coroner came, inspected Michael's body, ate a jelly donut and pronounced him officially dead.

After Detective Lt. Tony Catelano finished arguing with Adams from Forensics on the front steps of the cathedral, he called Officer

Jergeson over. "Where's Yazwinski?"

"He got transferred," the rookie answered. "I'm here to take his place."

"You think you can take his place?" Catelano snapped.

"No, but does two years working South of Market and the Haight count?"

"It'll help, given the stuff going down today. Let me show you something." Catelano nodded towards the sanctuary.

The two men went inside and approached the double doors of the iconostasis. The fetid sweet smell of the corpse clung to the air like a Walgreen's perfume.

Tony shivered. "I hate it in here. Reminds me of my days as an altar boy." They swung open the gilded doors and came face to face with the altar. The large bloody knife stood erect where it had been stuck the night before. Michael's body lay where it had been dragged.

"Jesus!" Jergeson said.

"You might want to watch your language around here. Weird, huh?"

Jergeson moved to take the knife from its wound in the altar.

Tony held his arm. "Don't touch that! Get Forensics in here. Adams, where the hell are you?" he shouted.

"So, what do you think?" Jergeson asked.

"Hell if I know. Anything can happen in this city."

"Maybe it's some kind of ritual abuse or something."

"Hell, that slit is more than some abuse. Maybe it's a set up to make it look like it was. Has anybody else seen this?"

"I don't think so."

"Good. I don't want the reporters getting wind of this, or we'll never get them off our backs. I'll take care of them. Get Adams over here immediately and have him tell the team I want this case cleared up within forty-eight hours. You, go talk to the clergy and find out, if you can, who was here last night." He shuddered slightly as Officer Jergeson walked away. "Christ, this stuff gives me the creeps."

The TV camera crews, reporters and photographers stampeded Catelano as he stepped outside the cathedral. They all shouted at once. "Can you tell us who the victim was?" "Who found him?" "When?" "Was he shot?" "Any suspects?"

He held up his hands and bellowed, "Take it easy. You'll get to see the police report like everyone else when it's passed out at the station. Until then, I have no comment." He nodded to *Examiner* reporter Keith Carlton. "See you tomorrow, buddy." Then he walked through the double doors of the cathedral, which were guarded by a patrolman who folded his arms across his chest like an ancient keeper of the Gate.

A red-headed reporter, resembling a shoe salesman hyped on speed, shouted after him with pen poised in hand, "Lieutenant, do you think the Chief's going to use this as an excuse to get the Mayor to beef up the police budget he wants?"

Tony swung back to him. "Look, Preston, we've had bodies dropping in this town like fleas off a dead dog all year, and you ask me if the Chief is going to play politics with the Mayor over this case? Of course he is. He's going to fight like hell to get the budget we deserve, just as he always does. So why don't you think up something really important to ask me?"

Preston stood there scribbling too fast to notice the other reporters smirking at him. Keith Carlton, relaxed as ever, grinned over at him. "You know, Preston," Keith said, "That was a really dumb question. Why don't you go back to work for the *San Francisco Progress* or something?"

Preston looked up puzzled. "That paper died years ago."

"That's what I mean."

Just then, the paramedics wheeled Michael's body down the steps, wrapped from head to foot in a black plastic body bag and strapped tightly to the gurney. The reporters watched soberly and silently as it was hoisted into the ambulance for its trip to the morgue.

"I hear he was only thirty-seven," Keith finished his notes and stuck a pen behind his ear through a mass of shaggy brown hair. "I hope he's into recycling," he said ruefully, thinking of the next process that awaited Michael's body.

Preston wondered out loud, "You know, I hear some men get

erections just before they die. Do you think that's so?"

"God, Preston, get a life!" Keith walked away. Corpses always made him feel slightly nauseous, but he never let on.

Although he was a new beat reporter for the *Examiner*, Keith Carlton was by no means green. Despite his experience on smaller urban newspapers, both on and off the police beat, he still hadn't completely steeled himself to the sight of blood. This year, he had seen one too many murder victims to suit himself. Unlike some of his colleagues at the Hall of Justice who were more leg men than writers, Keith didn't thrive on the macho, grisly aspects of the police beat; he couldn't wait to get off it to do some real writing. Political writing.

But this case looked intriguing, he thought. Mysteries always fascinated him. He could see the headlines now: MURDER IN THE CATHEDRAL. Maybe he could get into the city room with this one. But where was the political angle?

3

It was cold and foggy when Andrea awoke. Feeling drowsy, she lay cozily under her warm blankets and listened to the soothing sound of rain battering the roof over her bedroom window. She loved the patter of rain. She fumbled for her glasses, put them on and groped for her alarm clock.

It was nearly 7a.m. She rolled over in bed, accidentally kicking the calico cat that lay on her feet. It meowed and jumped off the bed indignantly. "Sorry, Gwyneth," she muttered. She put on her red and white silk Chinese robe, brushed back her long black hair and padded barefoot to the kitchen, where she put the kettle on for coffee.

Andrea lived in what was originally a summer bungalow in the Berkeley hills, among the cypress trees and usually above the morning fog. Normally, her living room picture window displayed a wonderful panorama of the flat lands of Berkeley and the Marina leading to the slate blue bay and a view of El Cerrito and the Richmond Bridge, but this morning everything was socked in by dense clouds.

She never listened to television during the daytime; instead she played her favorite morning tape, the *Symphonic Dances* by Rachmaninoff. Serene but passionate underneath, with a hint of a blue note—like her.

She went outside and picked up the paper wrapped in plastic, but tossed it unopened on the dining room table. She was too nervous to read. She wished she could see Father Peter right then but knew she'd have to wait for their lunch appointment at noon. He had been her spiritual director, colleague and moral support for three years, and he knew all about her and Michael. He was always so sensible and compassionate. If anyone could give her a pep talk, he could.

She leaned against her kitchen counter and fantasized about her mentor. Though he was nearly fifty, Father Peter's hair and bushy beard were still jet black, laced only with a few flecks of silvery gray. Like many ordained professors from England, he wore a tweedy jacket and black clericals. He wore a wide "dog collar" that went around his neck Anglican style, instead of the bits of white squares which many Anglo-Catholic and Roman Catholic clergy wore.

But what especially amused Andrea about him was that, now he was in America, he usually wore fitted blue jeans with his tweeds and clericals. A Durham Dean wearing denim. Perhaps it's his funny way of breaking out, she thought. How English. How very typical. It's as if the bottom half of him wanted to be sexy but the upper half thought better of it. This, of course, only made him dearer to her. In every other way he was the model of pastoral restraint, respectability and even style. She hoped he would someday have the guts to wear his blue jeans in Durham.

Andrea finished her coffee and looked at her watch, "Oh, shit!" She ran to the bedroom, showered and then dressed in a stylish suit, looking very tweedy and academic.

She slipped into her pale blue trench coat, slung her purse over her shoulder, and collected her pile of books and papers. Reciting dates of Church history aloud to herself, she made sure the cat was out, locked the door securely and dashed to her car.

4

"Well, I think those are all the questions we have for now, Miss

West," Dr. Thomas said. "We shall see you after lunch, at 2:00." He was a Presbyterian minister who, she thought, with his bow tie and big ears, looked like former Senator Paul Simon from Illinois. He looked over his bifocals at his two colleagues, and they agreed they were finished with their questions.

Dr. Thomas was one of three examining faculty members supervising her final dissertation presentation at the Graduate Theological Union, commonly called the GTU. Students called it "Holy Hill." It served as the umbrella organization for a dozen different seminaries—Catholic, Protestant, Orthodox, Buddhist and Jewish—including the Episcopal seminary where Andrea taught.

The other two faculty members were Dr. Marcia Wilber from the Protestant seminary, who was rather dumpy and decidedly more evangelical than Andrea was, and who had a special interest in healing ministries; and Father Juan Serrano, a handsome, brilliant Jesuit from Spain, something of a mystic, an avant-garde liturgist and a major liberation theologian. Of the three, Andrea found him the most intimidating and fascinating.

Andrea stood up and smiled with relief. They shook hands all around. "Thank you, those were challenging questions you asked," she said. "Especially yours, Father Serrano, about the social critique that liberation theology has of Jung's perspective about myths, icons and archetypes."

He nodded. "Yes, I sometimes wonder whether we worry too much about the inner meaning of things when there are lots of hungry people in the world who can't eat meaning but need bread."

"Yes, but why then are you a liturgist?" Andrea countered.

"Ah," he gave her one of his charming smiles. She knew he had set her up for the question. "Because somewhere along the line in the Central American jungle I learned that one does not live by bread alone but by every Word that comes from the mouth of God. But that Word has to be based in radical action. The first radical act of the Word is to celebrate the Mass. It's that simple."

"Of course," Andrea smiled in return. "I quite agree." Too bad he's unavailable, she silently mourned.

Dr. Thomas coughed. Poking his glasses into his left ear to satisfy an itch, he said to Father Serrano, "Isn't there some paperwork we need to attend to in the administrative offices?" Father Serrano nodded and bowed out of the room.

As Andrea left, Dr. Marcia Wilber nudged her elbow and whispered, "Father Serrano is always tough on the good ones. Don't worry, you'll do fine." Andrea thanked her and left the brick building, quite pleased with herself. She felt exhausted.

"Thank God that's over!" she said to herself, and walked briskly towards the cafe, pleased about seeing Father Peter.

5

Andrea bought the afternoon *Examiner* newspaper at the corner and then found a small table at the back of the coffee shop to read in quiet. A blonde student waitress came and took her order. "Decaf coffee for now, thanks," Andrea said.

She opened the paper and saw the story below the fold on the front page of the *Examiner*. "No!" The anguished tone in Andrea's voice made a couple at the next table turn their heads and stare at her with curiosity.

The headline read: MURDER IN THE CATHEDRAL, and it continued: "A 37 year old man was found beaten, with his throat cut inside the Russian Orthodox Cathedral on Geary and 26th Avenue this morning. Police say the man died from multiple injuries, but a further autopsy from the Coroner's office is pending. He was discovered this morning about 7:30 a.m. by the cathedral janitor."

She skipped to the last paragraph and read the last line: "Cathedral and museum officials said the immediate motive for the murder was unknown. In recent days, the cathedral has been exhibiting a valuable holy relic, the Icon of Kazan, but that appeared to be untouched. Nevertheless, police said they were investigating robbery as the possible motive for the murder. The identity of the victim has been withheld pending notification to his family." Andrea noted the by-line: Keith Carlton.

"Oh, my God! Michael!" She sat in stunned silence, pale and shivering. Feeling suddenly nauseous, she raced to the bathroom.

6

Rolling over in bed, Alex Menshikov awoke himself with his snoring. He groaned and put his hand up to his forehead; it ached as if someone had slapped him with a tire iron. God, he thought, I have to stop drinking Boris' martinis. He rubbed his eyes, and then pressed his head between his hands to relieve the pain. Yesterday's clothes still clung to his sweaty body, and his tie was wrapped around his neck. He dimly realized that he stank like a pair of dead Adidas.

Looking at his watch, he tried to focus his eyes. It read 12:30 p.m. "Christ!" He sat up in bed. "I missed the fucking plane."

Alex pulled himself out of bed, stripped down, put on a fresh tee shirt and underwear, and then went to hunt for a cigarette. A package sat near the envelope filled with fifty-dollar bills. Travel money. He felt a quiet sense of triumph. He had done it! He had pulled off the icon heist of the century. It was the culmination of a career that had begun long before he joined the army, though he didn't realize it at the time.

It had started when he was ten, after the time of his father's final arrest in 1937. Alex and his mother escaped by train in a coal car to Harbin, Manchuria, then to Vladivostok. It was a thrilling train ride for a young boy, despite the coal dust, the crowded cars smelling of stale body odor, raw onions, and the fear of the railroad police. In Vladivostok, his mother supported the two of them by teaching English and translating for the military.

Alex quickly became street-wise, first learning the tricks of the pick-pocketing trade from Hang Jin, a Chinese orphan with nimble fingers and fast legs. Within a year, he could expertly snatch gold watches and bracelets from Russian matrons and sell them on the black market for good money. He always told his mother he earned it chopping wood, but he did that just to build up his biceps.

1937 was the watershed of his life—the year of supreme sorrow, high adventure and the drab mediocrity of Uncle Nathan. Nathan Pratt was an American soldier stationed in Manila who came to Vladivostok for a month's leave. He was a somber man from Kansas who joined the service to get off the farm. At 30, he had high ambi-

tions and a mean streak, which showed whenever he was contradict-
ed, which Alex did often.

Nathan had met his mother in Vladivostok, courted her with a
flurry and finally convinced her to come to America with Alex.
Nathan was kind to his mother, but backhanded to Alex. One day,
Nathan spotted him working a crowd on the street. He grabbed Alex
roughly by the collar, and lifted him until his face was two inches
from his, "You little punk thief," he hissed. "If I catch you stealing
again, I'll beat the living be-Jesus out of you."

"Let go of me, you bastard!" Ashamed and red-faced with anger,
Alex flailed at him but missed.

"You're nothing but a spoilt little prig," Nathan laughed at him
and threw him to the ground. "You think the world owes you everything."

"I'll show you!" Alex seethed silently. And from then on Alex
always operated away from the areas where Nathan might catch him,
wary of another violent encounter.

Trapped in this explosive triangle, the three of them headed for
Manila and on to California. He had dreamed about California for
years—the place where it never snows, where oranges grow all year
around and where there is always enough food. Alex was eleven
when the three of them landed at the Immigration Offices on Angel
Island in 1939. They had come, like the 15,000 Russian immigrants
before them, crazy with hope and desperate dreams.

So many of his people had settled in the Western Addition by
1928 that it was called Little Russia, while Fillmore Street was nick-
named the Nevsky Prospect of the West. Since it was where most of
the middle and upper class Russians lived, his mother made sure they
settled there. The poorer Russians settled on Potrero Hill.

Many of them were Molokans, members of an Orthodox sect,
divided into two groups: the Postojannye or "the Steadfast" (the
majority of whom lived on Potrero Hill), and the Pryguny or "Holy
Jumpers," the Orthodox equivalent of Holy Rollers. Like the Amish
in Pennsylvania, the Molokans practiced communal living and clung
to their ethnic dress, but two hundred years of persecution by the
Orthodox Church had forced many of them to flee Russia. Because

of this, many Molokans supported the Bolshevik coup in 1917. In fact, one of Alex's best friends in school had been a Pryguny—only because he knew his mother disapproved of them.

Angel Island was Alex's first experience of the narrowness of the prevailing American attitudes towards immigrants. Spurred on by the myth of the "Great American Melting Pot," the induction process virtually wiped out all foreign languages and culture, and treated him and his people like cattle.

The Russians were the ones most susceptible to this cultural erosion. By the mid-1940s, Little Russia had all but disappeared. Most of the new Russians in San Francisco quickly achieved a new affluence and blended more and more with the general population, losing much of their Russian identity. Only their food and religious observances, whether Orthodox or Jewish, distinguished them.

The Pratts later moved out to the fog-enshrouded Richmond District near the ocean, and even later, down the Peninsula to San Mateo. Except for the elders who clung to the old ways and the old Slavonic religion, most Russians had become completely American-ized. And Alex was one of them. Almost.

When the World War II came, Alex was eager to fight. In 1943, he was big for sixteen, so he lied about his age and enlisted. Instead of sending him to the Pacific, the army was quick to use his language skills in Russian, French, and German, and soon promoted him to the espionage division on the Eastern Front where the Russians were rapidly gaining ground. While in U.S. intelligence, he was forced to collaborate with the Soviets and the Americans against the Germans. But he also tried on his own, with nightmares of purges teeming in his brain, to destabilize the Soviets as much as possible. Here he began his private war against the Communists. It became his religion.

This was also when he got his first taste of the Soviet black market and the real horrors of war. Law had long since ceased to have any meaning for him after he saw what the Soviet police had done. "The law's a wagon, it goes where you turn it," Alex often bragged. Soon he became a master driver.

He saw the siege of Leningrad firsthand. The famine was so severe that old women would sell him their precious icons for a can of Spam and a crust of bread. It was so cold, his nostrils froze together. People would drop dead in the street and no one would stop. Wagons went around three times daily to pick up the corpses. Cannibalism was rife. There were tales of dead babies being boiled for soup. Alex became disgusted with people and politics. For himself, survival was the only thing. The only way you got ahead was by beating the system. He became expert at this.

After the war, it was easy for him to set up connections between Paris and New York, so he started a lucrative black market trade in stolen Russian art. For him, it began as a mission of sorts— to save valuable pieces of his Russian heritage from the destruction of the Germans and the Communists. So why shouldn't he earn his living from it? And he did, handsomely.

But last night was the capstone of his career. He remembered how greedily Cecil had pored over the Kazan Icon when he handed it over to them. He inspected it carefully, scrutinizing the front and back while they had all watched patiently.

"Well?" Mrs. Saxon-Briggs snapped.

"It's the same one, all right," Cecil said. "You can see the faint triangle mark I branded on the back left corner of the icon in 1964." He took a clean white cloth and wiped the riza before setting it back on its stand.

"How did it go?" Priscilla eyed Alex.

"Cecil almost got us caught."

"What?! You took so long I had to distract the custodian so he wouldn't see you," Cecil glowered at Alex.

"I thought you said he couldn't see his broom."

Mrs. Saxon-Briggs stamped her cane on the floor. "Enough, you two! You should show more respect." She nodded to the icon.

Cecil shut his mouth and fumed. Alex smirked and folded his arms.

Priscilla took an envelope from the side desk and handed it to Alex. "Here's your ticket to London for tomorrow and the receipt from your Swiss account where we wired your money. The rest is in cash, as you requested. You will see it's all in clean new notes."

Alex took the envelope in his thick hands and thumbed the

bills, making sure the money was all there. "You're efficient as usual, Miss Thorpe. We missed you at the cathedral."

Priscilla shot him a cold glance. "Mrs. Saxon-Briggs demanded all my attention."

"And I'm sure you gave it your all," Alex said. "By the way, Cecil, who was that woman with Michael Beech?"

"What woman?"

"The one wearing the light blue raincoat. She left right after the service was over."

"You saw a woman with Beech wearing a blue raincoat?" Priscilla asked.

"Yes," Edith said vaguely, "she had thick, wavy black hair. She and Beech talked for the longest time in front of the icon after everyone had gone."

Priscilla frowned. "Do you think she knows anything? What if Michael Beech talked with her? What are you going to do about her, Alex?"

"Nothing," he said. "My job's done. That's your problem. Thanks for the cash. If you ever need anything, don't call me." He gave them a sarcastic salute. "Enjoy the picture. Don't worry about me, I can see my own way out."

As he strode out of the room, he heard Mrs. Saxon-Briggs comment, "Horrible man. A trouncing bore."

"Hear, hear," Cecil said.

"You can always get rid of that kind with money," the Countess said with contempt.

7

The Countess' remark had pissed Alex off so much that he'd stopped off at his favorite bar on Haight Street, the Assyrian Zam Zam Club, for a few drinks. The bar itself was a time warp, a throwback to the 1940s, with a juke box that played "As Time Goes By" and other lounge music from World War II.

Boris, easily the shrewdest man in San Francisco, had run the Assyrian Zam Zam Club for forty-five years. He was tall and thin,

always immaculately dressed in a vest and tie, with an oily black hair-
cut slicked straight back. If asked what nationality he was, he'd say
with his deep baritone voice, "I am an ancient Assyrian!"

You had to pass muster to stay in Boris' place. That meant you
had to like his martinis, which fortunately were the best in town. If a
couple came in and asked for Irish coffee, Boris would lean over the
bar and sneer at them, "This is a bar. We don't serve coffee. If you
want to drink Irish coffee go down to the fern bar on the corner."
The thing that Alex liked about Boris was that he never pretended to
be good.

It was a city institution for those in the know. To Alex, it was his
second home, where he often spent long nights, like last night. Next
thing he realized, it was morning and he was back in his own bed
nursing a hangover.

"That screws that," he said aloud. He stood up, picked up a blue
bathrobe hanging limply over the arm of a Queen Anne chair, and
stumbled into the bathroom.

Alex Menshikov lived in a large three-floor classic San
Francisco Victorian house with a crow's nest built opposite Alamo
Square. It had high ceilings and elaborate gold leaf molding around
the edges of the green Morris wallpaper, crystal chandeliers, potted
palms and huge stone fireplaces.

Clothes were scattered all over the house: shirts were draped
over burgundy velvet Victorian sofas, shoes were tossed on the hardwood floors. His heavy claw-foot oaken dresser belched open drawers as if it had five tongues. Books and papers bulged out of bookcases haphazardly. Ashtrays sat with mountains of cigarette butts in
them and some had spilled on the rugs. The room smelled smoky
and stale as an English pub.

Icons with silver and cloisonné rizas, Victorian oil paintings,
original Soviet Revolutionary posters, plus signed pieces by a host of
other lesser Russian artists, hung crookedly on the walls. Many were
works, which he had smuggled out of the Soviet Union.

Now that the Soviet Union had dissolved, allowing freer trade
and travel across the borders, Alex had busily re-organized his smuggling and black market connections, while maintaining a proper

position in the business community as a "respectable" arts dealer. Given the poverty he had experienced as a boy, Alex insisted that he live in style and luxury. His flourishing "business" in antique art and icons insured that he lived accordingly.

He went down to his front door, where the afternoon paper had been thrown, picked it up and read the headlines slowly as he walked inside. He stood still for a moment as he read, MURDER IN THE CATHEDRAL and anxiously scanned the details describing Michael's death. Back in the kitchen, he slammed the newspaper down on the oak table, poured piping hot water into his coffee maker and sat down. "God Damn! A fucking murder?"

Thoughts raced through his brain as he desperately tried to retrace last night's steps. He remembered going to the cathedral, putting on the false gray beard, the long black cassock and playing his ludicrous role as priest, then hiding in the back until the church was all clear—except for him and Beech. He remembered knocking him out and dragging his body behind the altar. I'm sure he wasn't dead, he thought. His body was still warm when I dragged him behind the altar.

But a nagging doubt ate away at his self-justifications. You fool, you know it takes a while for dead bodies to cool down. It doesn't mean he wasn't dead.

He sat down and ran his trembling fingers through his white hair. Maybe I did kill him. Who else saw me? Think, Menshikov, think!

He remembered seeing Michael Beech talking with that young woman in the pale blue raincoat. He remembered seeing her clearly because of her face: the full lips and the dark thick eyebrows. Its beauty arrested him, it was erotic and soulful like a good Russian's. No, it was something else. Something about her face haunted him. It reminded him of someone; it reminded him of his old lover.

That woman in the raincoat was the last one seen with Michael Beech. He was no fool. Once Michael had carbon dated the icon, it wouldn't take him long to discover it was a fraud. Perhaps the girl knew as well. He only knew one thing, he had to find her. Quickly, he went upstairs, dressed and left his house.

CHAPTER 5

∾

"To find oneself face to face with the living God is something of grave, fateful consequence. To meet God is always a 'crisis' and in Greek the word 'crisis' means Judgment."

Metropolitan Anthony Bloom
Meditations: A Spiritual Journey

Recovering from her trip to the bathroom, Andrea found her seat in the cafe and sat down. She felt as if she had just been kicked in the stomach. Father Peter was due to arrive any minute. She would, of course, tell him the heartbreaking news.

She grabbed a napkin from the canister on the table and wiped her tears away. "Not Michael!" She put her head in her hands. Inside herself, she felt the turmoil of terror and confusion twisting like a corkscrew. Immobilized. Should she go to the police? Should she tell them everything? Including Michael's half-hearted attempt at blackmail? She was one of the last people to see him alive. What would they think of that?

Father Peter approached her table as she was still mopping her face. "Thank God you're here," she hugged him impulsively, clinging to his damp tweed jacket, which always smelled of wool and tobacco; it was the comforting smell of safety.

"What's this?" he asked, holding her away in his arms to look at her pale face. He mocked her playfully, "Did your orals go *that* bad?"

"It's not that," she set her jaw grimly. "I wish it was! It's much worse! Michael Beech is dead. He's been murdered." She slowly lowered herself back into her chair.

"What? When? Are you sure?"

Andrea struggled to control her tears. "He was killed last night. The sexton at the Orthodox Cathedral found him dead this morning." She shuddered. "Here, read this."

He scanned the article quickly. "It doesn't say his name, are you sure it was him?"

Andrea avoided his dark sympathetic eyes for fear of breaking down completely. "I'm sure. I was with him last night at the cathedral. I had to leave early to get ready for today."

Father Peter's face contorted at seeing Andrea in pain. "I'm so sorry." His wide, black eyes almost duplicated those of Rouault's Christ.

"Now I feel as if it was all my fault. If I had stayed, maybe Michael wouldn't have been killed."

"Or maybe you would have been killed too," a quiver of emotion flashed through his face. Father Peter paused to let the reality of this statement sink in for both of them. "Here, have some water." He handed her a glass from the table. "Don't work yourself up into a guilt you don't deserve. God knows, we all carry around too much of it as it is..."

Andrea's eyes brimmed up with tears. "I can't believe he's dead. I just left him hours ago."

"It's a nightmare," he sighed. Father Peter took her hand in his and said softly. "Tell me what happened. Don't spare me anything."

"Michael was in trouble and he knew it. He called me here the other day. He said he had to tell me something important, but that he couldn't talk about it over the phone, so I met him at Greens Restaurant yesterday. The upshot of it was that he took me to see the legendary Icon of Kazan with him last night—you know, the one I've been teaching about. He threatened not to review my manuscript if I didn't, though I knew he was only half-joking."

"Half-joking?" Father Peter scowled. "Sounds dicey to me."

"Michael could really be a bastard sometimes..." Andrea admitted, smiling weakly. "He usually got what he wanted."

"No doubt," Father Peter mused, and took out his brown pipe.

"So, anyway, what choice did I have? I went. Besides, I've wanted to see this icon for years. We went to the Holy Virgin Cathedral and, after evening prayer, he showed me the icon. It was gorgeous. He suspected there was some art fraud going on and he was about to do the last bit of research that night to prove it."

"Did he say who was behind this?" Peter asked. Unable to smoke in cafes in Berkeley, he was content to clean the bowl of his pipe with his pocketknife.

"No, but I suspect he knew," she said. "And I think he was scared. He wasn't normally so secretive about things. His style was much more flamboyant. I think he was really trying to play this straight."

He tapped the bowl into a paper cup. "Does anyone else know about this?"

"I don't think so. I'm not sure."

"And you say you were one of the last to see him alive?"

"Yes, except the sexton in the church." Andrea stared mournfully. "I wish I hadn't left him so early last night. I feel terrible. I'd like to murder the bastard who did it," she said with a sudden blaze of fury.

"I can see why you'd feel guilty, but it's not your fault. This is damned awful." They sat silently for a moment.

"Peter, what should I do? I'm in no shape to take the rest of my exam today! It all seems so meaningless."

Father Peter laid his pipe down on the table and gazed at her with soft eyes. "Just because one life has been lost doesn't mean you have to destroy yours. My suggestion is that you keep on as planned. Get your dissertation done. You know your stuff. You've been prepared for weeks. Years. I know your shock and grief must seem unbearable right now, but you'll just have to put it aside. Don't ruin everything you've been working for."

"No, I guess that would be dumb," she admitted. "Maybe I should just get it over with."

"That's the spirit! Then you'll have plenty of time to get to the bottom of this. But I think your exams are the least of your worries."

"What do you mean?"

"Two things really. You said that Michael blackmailed you, in jest you say, and that you were the last one to see him?"

She nodded tearfully.

"That's not going to look very good on a police report. I think you'll have some questions to answer at the police station. But worse, I suspect that whoever killed Michael might have been around long enough to see you with him. Maybe the killer thinks you know something too."

Confused, Andrea asked, "What? I don't know anything!"

"Andrea, I think your life may be in danger."

She blanched. "So what do you suggest? That I should march myself down to the nearest police station after my exams?"

"It couldn't hurt," he answered, tucking his tobacco pouch back into his side pocket. "At the very least, you might find out some more details about Michael's murder."

Andrea looked at her watch, "Oh, my God, it's almost two o'clock! My exams start in ten minutes. Got to run. I'll do that later." Scrambling for her purse and coat, she accidentally bumped the table as she rose, splashing the coffee across the table. She smiled clumsily but Father Peter waved her mishap aside and adroitly stopped the spill with a paper napkin. Uncoiling himself from his chair, he stood up and gave her a warm hug, "Don't worry. You'll do fine."

"Thanks, Peter, for listening and helping me to sort things out." Her eyes grew moist.

"Anytime. Call me and let me know what happened."

"Of course!" She strode quickly out of the coffee shop towards the seminary.

2

After his daily morning workout and swim at the Presidio Officer's Health Club, the Major showered, dressed and went to order a sparkling water at the Health Club bar.

At seventy, Major George Vashkovsky was a small, muscular man with a brown weather beaten, gnomish face. His big ears, black eyes small as pebbles, and crooked nose gave his Russian heritage away immediately.

"Jimmy, give me a Calistoga," he said, wiping his crew cut with a towel. He fished for some bills out of his wallet.

Jimmy dug a glass into the ice and popped off the bottle top.

"Major, did you see the headlines? There's been a murder up at the Russian Cathedral."

"What are you talking about?"

Jimmy handed him a copy of the mid-day paper with the head-lines about Michael Beech's murder. The Major stared at it silently, poker-faced. "Perverts!" he said and tossed the paper back. "See you later, Jimmy." He pushed some change towards him over the counter and strode out of the bar with his glass.

He went immediately to the newsstand, bought his own paper, and then sat in the lounge by the window to read the article careful-ly before lunch. The Major scanned the front-page closely. Damn! They've really bungled it this time. Amateurs!

He knew the Saxon-Briggses had gone off the deep end thirty years go when their passion for collecting expensive religious art had turned into an obsession with the occult. Cecil Durant was behind that, feeding them all this nonsense about psychic emanations and other spirit worlds. Cecil had formed a psychic club around himself, calling it the "Inner Circle," and told them all they were gifted seers. It was bad enough that Priscilla Thorpe got roped into it, but when his sister joined, that was the last straw. But now they had gone too far.

He thought about the options open to him. He could either do nothing and wait to become number two on their hit list (which was not an option), or he could steal the icon papers back. Either way, he'd have to work fast. But first...

Skipping lunch, he tucked the newspaper under his arm and briskly strode out of the Officer's Club.

3

The copper gutters that rimmed the Piedmont mansion reflect-ed the bright noonday sun and sent a shaft of white light spilling onto the living room floor. Priscilla, who had been reading, looked at her watch impatiently. She stood up abruptly and announced to the group in the living room, "The mail should have come by now, I'll go see."

She walked down the gravel driveway to the locked gates and checked the outdoor mailbox. It contained some letters, a few bills and the mid-day paper. She looked at the headline, hastily tucked the paper under her arm and trotted upstairs to her room.

Meanwhile, in the living room, Mrs. Hannah Saxon-Briggs sat holding a knobby cane in one hand and a magnifying glass in the other, inspecting the Kazan Icon on the wooden stand in front of her. She made discreet hums of approval from time to time.

"Magnificent! Magnificent!" she said in a hushed voice. "The icon hasn't lost any of its power, has it?" she asked the others.

"None, I'm sure," Cecil Durant said. "In fact, if anything, it has gained power. Can't you feel it?"

"It makes the whole room glow," Edith agreed.

"Father used to say he even slept better when the Kazan Icon and the Crystal Skull sat next to his bed," Mrs. Saxon-Briggs said. Turning to Cecil she asked, "Could you build an alarm system in my bedroom so I could keep them there safely?"

"Of course," he said. "No trouble at all."

"You can feel the emanations coming from it right now," Edith Durant said in a ghostly voice, having already turned her gaze inward. "How clear the invisible light is!"

"Yes," Mrs. Saxon-Briggs sighed. "There is a real peace in this icon. Just look at Her eyes! The last time we meditated with Her, I felt better for a week."

"We can get you feeling better again. There's no time like the present!" Cecil said. He stood up and arranged four chairs around the icon.

"Where is Priscilla?" the old matron asked as she fussed with her handkerchief.

"Getting the mail, I expect," Edith said.

"It's scandalous how bad the mails are here! In England we used to get them twice a day. Priscilla!" Hannah called loudly.

After a moment, Priscilla came in carrying a bundle of letters. "Betty said lunch will be twenty minutes late today. Here are some letters for you."

"Oh, bother the mail, Priscilla! We're going to sit with the

Icon," Mrs. Saxon-Briggs said. "Would you like to join us?"

"Of course," Priscilla said, sitting down by Mrs. Saxon-Briggs while Cecil and Edith sat opposite. Their knees almost touched. The Icon of Kazan sat on the stand in the middle of the four of them. They all held their hands and closed their eyes.

Presently Edith began to chant the word DEUS. It resonated almost like a growling noise deep in the pit of her stomach. The sound vibrated through the bodies of the two women sitting next to her, making them feel its faint buzz as tissue paper on a fine toothed comb. Then they joined her in the chant. DEUS, DEUS, DEUS they chanted.

The sound ebbed and flowed above them and around the room, quite disconnected to them, circling around the rim of the ceiling as if they were sitting in a crystal glass and a wet invisible finger was making tones along the rim. They continued their chant, pulsating slower and softer, until after twenty minutes they barely hummed in an audible whisper. Cecil, Edith and Priscilla focused their inner wills toward the Madonna.

Then in the silence, a great cracking sound came from the icon and shafts of white light reflected off the mirror above the fireplace. Cecil looked and noticed that Edith was oblivious to this but that Priscilla, who sat with her eyes closed, suddenly appeared transparent. He could see through her, as if she were a ghost, so that the back of the chair she was sitting in appeared quite visible. She sat with her back ramrod still.

Startled by this unexpected emanation, Cecil anxiously shifted in his chair and cleared his throat loudly. The hum and the vibrations came to a quick stop. The other three resumed regular consciousness with a jolt. Edith, looking vague, as if waking from a deep sleep, returned from her trance. Mrs. Saxon-Briggs, who had fallen asleep, raised her head from her chest and looked about, blinking and confused. Priscilla stared at him with fierce owl-like eyes.

"Well, I think that's quite enough for one morning, don't you, Mrs. Saxon-Briggs?" Cecil said nervously.

"What? Did anything happen?" Mrs. Saxon-Briggs looked about the room.

"Nothing much, just a few emanations of energy from the icon," he lied.

Priscilla looked at him pointedly, aware that a lot more had occurred than he had said.

"Do you think it will cure me?" Mrs. Saxon-Briggs asked hopefully.

"Better than radiation therapy," he said. "We have the Source of Life here!"

"Good. We shall do this again tomorrow. Now leave me, I am feeling a bit tired and peckish. What time is it?"

"Almost lunch time." Edith glanced at her watch.

"I hope cook has made some shrimp briquettes and salad for lunch. Oh, and bring a bottle of white wine, I do believe my stomach is feeling a little stronger!"

Priscilla, who had remained silent throughout, stood up brusquely and said, "I'll get it," and turned on her heel to leave.

4

Priscilla Thorpe waited to speak to the Durants until after Mrs. Saxon Briggs had retired upstairs for her after-lunch nap. She stood by the living room fireplace and waited for Cecil and Edith to come into the room. "Cecil, please close the door behind you." She nodded to the sofa, "Sit down. I have some bad news."

He closed the door and remained standing, "If you don't mind, I think I'll stand. I feel as nervous as a cat in a cold bath." Edith, however, sank demurely onto the sofa.

"Read this," Priscilla scowled, thrusting the mid-day paper with the murder headlines into Cecil's hands.

He read it quickly and then almost threw it into his wife's lap. "I knew we couldn't trust him," he fumed and began to pace back and forth agitatedly. "It's all your fault."

"What did I do?" Edith sputtered.

"Cecil, stop that stupid pacing. Get a hold of yourself," Priscilla said. "You agreed Mr. Menshikov came with the very best of references. How did we know he'd bungle the job? How could you let this happen?"

Edith sniffled and looked at the fire burning in the fireplace, "The poor, poor man. He was so young."

"Stop your sentimental rubbish," Cecil barked at his wife. "He was about to ruin everything. It's probably just as well he's dead."

Priscilla picked up the newspapers and reread the article slowly, "It says here that the Icon wasn't stolen. They don't know yet that the other one is a fake. At least that gives us a little time."

"But not for long. What if they catch Menshikov and he turns us in?"

"Don't be silly Cecil, Mr. Menshikov is in London, remember? We already planned for all possible contingencies," Edith said.

"But we didn't plan for this!" Cecil thundered.

"No, we didn't," Priscilla said curtly. "It was a horrible accident. But there's no use crying about it now. We have to get on with it and protect ourselves as best as we can."

"Then you better invest in a couple of bodyguards while I'm still around." Alex Menshikov stepped out from behind a side door, pointing a gun at them. "I hate to be crude, ladies and gentleman, but if I go, we all go."

"You idiot, you're supposed to be in London!" Cecil's face grew apoplectic.

"Let's just say I didn't like the guy who was driving the plane."

"Cecil, keep your voice down," Priscilla whispered. "And put that stupid gun away." She glared at Alex.

He glowered back at her. "How do I know you aren't going to blame the whole thing on me?"

"Well, you killed him, didn't you?" Cecil accused.

"How do I know you didn't do it?"

"That's ridiculous!"

"Who's to say Mr. Menshikov didn't hit him harder than he expected?" interrupted Priscilla. "But we'll get nowhere if we keep fighting among ourselves because, as you say, 'If you go, we all go.' And we wouldn't want that, now would we? So, Alex, one more time, please put your gun down. Don't go off half-cocked like a crazy Russian. We aren't going to turn you in."

Alex latched the safety catch again and stuffed the revolver into his pocket. "O.K., but I'm going to keep my eye on you."

"I think you better keep an eye on that young woman with Michael Beech last night," Cecil said.

Priscilla pressed further, "And you forget, we still don't have the papers."

"What?! Jesus, I thought you had them already."

"The Countess tried, but failed. The Major hid them somewhere. We have to find them, or there will be no more chances."

"I bet the girl knows," Cecil said gloomily.

"We don't even know who she is," Alex protested.

"Yes, we do," Edith spoke up out of her long silence. "She and Michael Beech signed the church guest book last night. I made a point of looking at it before the service began when I went over to sign it. Her name is Andrea West, and she lives in Berkeley."

"Andrea West?"

"Well," Priscilla said calmly, "since Mr. Menshikov got us into this mess, I'm sure he'll be able to get us out of it." She smiled slyly over at him.

"We'll see," he said. "But I warn you, I'm going to keep my eye on all of you." And with that, he left the room.

5

After a grueling afternoon of questions and answers, Dr. Thomas stood up and shook hands with Andrea, "Congratulations, Ms. West. We've all agreed you've passed with flying colors. Well done."

Dr. Marcia Wilber beamed broadly at her from the other end of the table and Father Juan Serrano said, "Let me know when you want to turn your dissertation into a book. I'd be glad to help." Andrea wondered how to interpret his brief lingering look.

Both surprised and touched by his offer, Andrea bowed modestly, "Thank you. I thought you were always cool about interdisciplinary fields."

"In your hands, both theology and spirituality become clearer, more integrated, instead of being made murky, as so many theologians do. I applaud you." He smiled shyly then pointed his gaze to the floor.

Andrea blushed. "Thanks, maybe I'll take you up on your offer." She couldn't tell if he averted his eyes because of religious obedience or because of some other more complex feelings.

Dr. Thomas stretched his back, "It's been a long but productive day. I say we all go home. Please send my secretary your dissertation and your final paperwork, so the Trustees can vote on it at their spring meeting. I think it will go very well."

"I'll send them to her as soon as I can," Andrea assured the panel. "Oh, and thank you for knowing my work so well. Your questions were right on target. I appreciate all the attention you put into this."

"It's one of the advantages of being such a small school," Dr. Thomas said. "Now go home and celebrate."

Something inside Andrea twinged, knowing this was the last thing she wanted to do. However, she put on her best professional face, thanked them all again and left the building. When she reached the sidewalk, she looked up to heaven. "Thanks, Michael."

As the autumn sun set earlier these days, it was quite dark when Andrea reached her front door at six o'clock. She knew she should have gone to the police station, but she was too exhausted to drive across the Bay. I'll call from home, she rationalized to herself.

Because of the impending exams, she had let her refrigerator go bare, so she stopped at the market on her way home. At her front door, she struggled with a bag of groceries in one arm while she rummaged in her purse looking for her house key. Gwyneth meowed loudly for dinner on the other side of the door.

As she opened her front door, she felt something obstructing it. When she pushed harder, she heard wood scraping on the floor but got the door open. She flicked on the front hall light and gasped.

Her whole house had been trashed. One of her dining room chairs lay on the floor in front of her. Cupboards and drawers were left opened, clothes, papers and books were strewn all over the floor, plants toppled over, cushions scattered. Her library and bedroom were equally trashed. The sliding glass door onto the deck was left wide open.

She heard a noise in the back yard. Her first instinct was to run out after it, but her better sense stopped her. My God, what if they are still out there?

She bolted out the front door, jumped into her car and drove down the hill to the nearest corner store to phone the police.

Two squad cars were at her house within twenty minutes. She gave them the house key and watched from the street above as they opened the door and went in shoulder first, guns out and held high. They quickly inspected the rooms in silence. Not a sound anywhere. One of the officers went outside into her back yard. Andrea sucked in a deep fearful breath.

After a long five minutes, the officer in charge shouted up the stairs, "There's no one here." Andrea walked down her brick steps and went inside, much relieved. The officers asked her a lot of questions and wrote up a police report about the break-in. Oddly enough, nothing seemed to be missing.

"Looks like a routine burglary to me," Officer Morse said. "You probably scared them off before they could get anything. Do you have any idea what they might have been after?"

"I don't know. Perhaps some jewelry and some silver. I can't tell," she answered honestly. "But I did know the man who was murdered at the cathedral this morning. Do you think that had something to do with it?"

The officer taking notes looked up with surprise. "What was his name?"

"Michael Beech. He worked for the De Young Museum. He was working on an appraisal at the Russian Orthodox Cathedral."

The officer closed his note pad. "I think you ought to come down for questioning first thing in the morning. I'm sure your input will be very helpful. Just call the Homicide Office in San Francisco, they'll direct you where to go. You can get the number from the phone book."

Andrea assured him she'd be there. She ushered the policemen out and with trembling hands double locked the door behind them.

Paranoid about another break in, she went throughout the house inspecting all the doors and windows, making sure they were tightly locked.

She stopped and surveyed her belongings now scattered all over the house. Her normally secure world had been violated beyond all comprehension. This time she knew she'd have to tell the police everything.

She sank down onto her sofa, emotionally exhausted. Gwyneth brushed up against her leg and nagged greedily for dinner. Andrea picked her up and hugged her, "I don't suppose you do windows, do you?"

CHAPTER 6

"We are encompassed on all sides by worries, concerns, fears and desires and are so inwardly perturbed that we hardly ever live within ourselves— we live beside ourselves."

Metropolitan Anthony Bloom
Meditations: A Spiritual Journey

Wednesday, October 24, 1990

The waitress with limp hair, already looking haggard from her morning's work at the Line Up Cafe, stepped up to the table. "Ready to order, guys?"

Keith Carlton tossed his menu towards her. "I'll have the usual: hash browns, two eggs over easy and coffee."

The waitress looked at Detective Lt. Catelano sitting opposite him. "I'll just have a steak and eggs with hot sauce on the side, a small orange juice and coffee. Thanks." He pushed the other menu towards her. She scribbled down their orders, took the menus and left.

"Going easy this week?" Keith kidded.

He patted his ample stomach, "My wife says I should go on a diet. If I did, my mother wouldn't know what to do with herself."

"Would that be before or after she fed you a mountain of spaghetti and meat balls? Or is death by pasta her modus operandi?"

"Hey, at least my mother can cook, which is more than I can say for yours."

"Can I help it if I didn't know TV dinners weren't haute cuisine until college? My mother had to work for a living, remember?" He settled back into his seat. "So, how's this cathedral case going?"

"Not as fast as I'd like. I had hoped to have this thing solved by now. We should get the coroner's report in by Monday, although it will probably state the obvious. Beech's head was bashed in pretty bad. And, off the record, his throat was cut and a knife was found stuck in the altar. The lab is still analyzing other clues."

"Amazing how this city goes in for weirdness. You think it was a ritual killing?"

"Could be. The shrinks are looking into it."

"Any other leads?" Keith sipped his coffee slowly.

"Maybe. I'll know later this morning. I'll tell you what I know only if you agree to sit on it for a while."

"You don't make it easy for a guy to do his job."

"Hey, I'm just trying to do mine. If you wait, you'll have so many scoops you'll think you're an ice cream parlor."

"I'm all ears."

"We got a report from some beat cops in the East Bay about a routine burglary. It turns out this woman was with Beech Thursday night. It appears from the cathedral guest book they were there together. We called her and she's coming down this morning."

"You wouldn't want to say who this suspect is, would you, old pal?"

"No, not yet."

"How did she sound?"

"Nervous," he grinned. "Jergeson said she had a sexy voice on the phone."

"Do you think they were lovers?"

"Haven't got a clue."

"Well, I demand to get a interview. My legions of inquiring readers must be kept informed."

"We'll see, Carlton. One thing I can say, you've kept your nose fairly clean. Not like the guy you replaced."

"It doesn't pay to dig up dirt where it doesn't exist," Keith said, remembering his predecessor, who reported a scandal in the Police Department, which was based on rumor and innuendo.

"Especially on my beat," Tony said. "Good reporters get the facts when the time is right...We're pretty sure we know the motive," Tony paused and sipped some coffee.

"So come on," Keith demanded. "What is it?"

"Robbery. Someone took a valuable religious painting. What do they call it? An Icon."

"I thought you said that nothing had been stolen?" Keith looked puzzled.

"That's what we thought at first. But some big shots in the church hierarchy called a jeweler to examine the jeweled cover, just in case. This morning they called back with the results. It turns out the icon was switched with a fake. They discovered the emeralds were made of glass."

"Thanks for my next story. You know, my mother's Uncle Isaac had something to do with an icon once," Keith mused. "Not much, of course, because he was Jewish. He married old Aunt Ethel, which you can be sure caused quite a stink in her Presbyterian family. He was twenty-five in 1905 and was still living in the Urals. Uncle Isaac was raised an Orthodox Jew, but he was good friends with the local village priest. When the Tsar started the pogroms against the Jews, he ordered thousands of them to be killed. So when the soldiers came and were about to kill all the people in his village, Uncle Isaac gathered everyone in the town square. Then he ran to the church, brought out an icon and held it over everyone's heads The soldiers saw it and left town."

"Sounds pretty far-fetched to me," Tony said.

"Doesn't it. Everybody in the village said it was a miracle and tried to persuade him to become Christian, but he refused. He said God made as many miracles happen through Moses as He did through Jesus, so why should he change? When he came to this country, he tried to fit in by marrying Ethel but secretly hoped to make his sons and grandsons as Orthodox as he was, but they ignored him. Poor guy, he never got over it; he died from a broken heart."

"Yeah, it's tough dealing with folks from the old country..." Tony said empathetically. "You should see my grandparents!" He groaned.

"I have!" Keith smiled at him.

"That's not all the news," Tony continued. "I thought you'd like to know some church group in Spain has put out a big reward for this icon."

"How much?"

"$500,000."

Keith whistled, "That could keep a guy in caviar for a long time."

"Just thought I'd mention it."

"Are you hoping to get the reward money or do you want me to do your work for you again?"

Tony ignored his playful jab. "I want to take a look at Beech's house up on Pacific Avenue later this afternoon. Want to join me?"

"It depends upon whether I can gather up any crumbs from your witness after you question her this morning. I've also got a couple of other deadlines due by mid-afternoon or Bernstein's going to kill me."

"Suit yourself," Tony shrugged. "You know my number."

The waitress laid two plates in front of them. "Careful, they're hot. More coffee?" They held out their mugs for a refill.

Keith eyed the strips of steak on Tony's plate, "You know, it's amazing what they can do with tofu these days."

Tony gave him a long, steady look and chuckled softly.

2

Andrea stepped through the dirty glass doors of the San Francisco Hall of Justice and walked through the metal detector after a moment's wait in line. At 10:00 a.m., the Hall of Justice echoed with the sound of muffled talk, the tramp of feet, elevator bells ringing and doors slamming. Up on the fourth floor, as she walked down the long sterile corridor, her heart pounded rapidly.

The words Homicide Division were inscribed in large black letters on the frosted glass of an old office door. She knocked, and then stepped inside the small reception area to find herself face to face with a redheaded receptionist. The woman glanced at Andrea with a slightly bored look.

"What do you want?"

"Inspector Catelano, please. My name is Andrea West. I was told to meet him here regarding the Beech case."

"Wait a minute, I'll call him." She pressed the intercom button. "Inspector, there's a woman here to see you." She looked at Andrea wearily. "What's your name again?"

"West, Andrea West," she said.

The receptionist announced Andrea's name over the intercom. "Should I send her in?" After a brief pause, she turned to Andrea. "He'll be out in a minute. Have a seat."

Andrea sat down nervously. Three men laughed on the other side of the half-glass partition. Then a paunchy middle-aged Italian, dressed in a wrinkled suit, punched through the door, hollering to one of his colleagues down the hall, "Tell Miller to pay up on the ball game or he doesn't get the spread on the Niner's," Catelano yelled. Seeing Andrea, Catelano quickly put on his game face and immediately greeted her with what passed, for him, courteousness and professionalism.

She stood up as he approached her, noting his rumpled tie.

He smiled amiably at her and sized her up in a glance. "I'm Detective Tony Catelano. Thanks for coming in, Ms. West. Please, step inside."

She held out her hand, which Tony shook awkwardly. "I hope I can help," she said anxiously. They stepped into his small, drab office: all desks, computers, papers, phones and partitions.

"Whew," she said, feeling a blast of intense heat, "it's hot in here."

Tony had loosened his tie. "Yeah," he said, his face looked a little flushed. "This is the Office from Hell. Maintenance keeps the heat on all year round." His shirt stretched tautly around his torso, moist with sweat, even though it was October.

Officer Jergeson was already sitting in a chair in the corner, stone-faced. He didn't say a word. The tall, sandy-haired rookie had become a regular fixture in Catelano's work life. His navy suit was impeccable. He had a small tape recorder, a note pad and a stack of papers. Tony Catelano offered her a wooden chair and closed the door.

"You've already talked with Officer Jergeson by phone." Jergeson nodded to Andrea. Tony sat against his desk and folded his arms across his belly. "So, tell us what you know about Michael Beech." His rich baritone voice soothed Andrea's nerves.

"How long have you got?" she said half-joking, looking at her watch.

"As long as it takes," he smiled. "Provided you keep to the point."

"I've known Michael since 1973, but I hadn't seen him for many months until Thursday," Andrea said. She briefly explained their recent relationship and how he asked her to meet with him at the Russian Cathedral. Tony shot a glance to Officer Jergeson.

"So, you were with Michael Beech the night he died?"

"Yes. He called me on Thursday to have lunch with him and asked if I could attend a church service with him to see the Icon of Kazan. He said he was doing some research on it for some people who wanted it re-appraised."

"You had lunch with him?"

"Yes, at noon on Thursday, at Greens' Restaurant, the one at Fort Mason." Andrea watched as Officer Jergeson took notes steadily.

Tony leaned forward, "Who wanted the icon re-appraised?"

"I don't know. But he told me he thought it might be a fraud. He was afraid someone was after him. He said he thought his phones were being tapped."

"When did he tell you this? At lunch?"

"No, Thursday night, after the service."

"Do you have any idea who or why anybody would want to kill him?"

"No. Well, the icon is very valuable."

"No other reason?" Tony eyed her shrewdly.

"None that I can think of." She thought it wise not to mention its miraculous powers yet.

"So Michael Beech had no enemies? Perhaps an associate of Michael's from the museum?"

Andrea laughed out loud. "Sure, he had lots of enemies, but none of them would ever have the guts to do this. He could be a real bastard to small-minded people."

"When did you last see him?"

"I left him just after the church service ended because I had to prepare for an exam the next morning. That was Thursday night, about 9:00 o'clock."

"What time exactly?"

"I guess more like 8:50. It was dark out then. I remember hearing the time announced on KCBS news."

"Did anyone see you leave?"

"A few. There was only a handful of people present when I left, members of the Altar Guild, the sexton and the old Russian cashier at the front counter, who'd sold me a candle."

"Busy people. And they didn't know who you were?"

"No, although Michael might have told someone there about me beforehand. I don't know. I signed the guest book."

"What were you wearing that night?"

"A light blue raincoat, a tan skirt, a white blouse and a brown tweed jacket."

"Not the most conspicuous clothing, I'd say," Tony commented. He shifted in his chair and changed direction. "How did you first meet?"

"We went to Stanford together and traveled in Europe for a while in the mid '70s."

"Were you close? You said you and Michael Beech used to be lovers," he pared his thumbnail with an end of a paper clip. "Who broke that off? You or him?"

Andrea stiffened slightly in her chair, "I don't see what business that is of yours."

Tony sighed, "We need to examine all the connections and possible motives involved, Ms. West. Just doing our job."

"Our love affair ended by mutual agreement about two years ago." She felt a twinge of pain at the thought of this.

"Because?"

"It just wasn't working."

"Because he was involved with a man in LA, wasn't he?" Tony eyed her closely.

"How did you know that?"

"As I said, Ms. West, we're just doing our job."

"All right, yes, but the man died. Michael was completely shattered by it."

Tony looked at his watch, "We're running out of time. Is there anything else you think we ought to know?"

"No, not that I can think of. Except one thing. Not related to Michael, but to me. You know already that someone broke into my house last night."

Tony looked at Officer Jergeson and then nodded to Andrea, "Yeah, but we'd like to hear your version of the story."

"When I came home, I had trouble getting into my house and when I got inside I saw that someone had completely trashed it. The patio door was left open. I thought I heard someone in the garden, but I was too afraid to check. I called the police and they came right up. They searched around but found no one."

"Anything taken?"

"I don't think so. Nothing big like a TV, jewels or stereo."

"Have we got your numbers and address?"

"I gave them to Officer Jergeson last night when he called."

"We'll need more information. If you don't mind, stop by our receptionist and fill out our questionnaire. It keeps the bureaucrats busy."

"If you find out anything, please let me know," Andrea said. "And feel free to call me if you need any more information."

"Don't worry, we will." Tony's eyes bored into her. "In fact, you can count on it." The two men rose as she stood up to leave.

Andrea paused in the doorway, "I hate to sound pushy, but this break-in really rattled me. Could you arrange for some squad cars to cruise my neighborhood for a while, just in case they return?"

"Sorry, that's out of our jurisdiction, but we could put in a word to the Berkeley police for you."

Andrea paused to consider this proposal "Thanks, I'd appreciate it. You're sure it's not a bother?"

"No bother. Just part of our job," Tony flashed the first hint of a charming smile at her.

She stepped out of the office, breathing nervously. Somehow, from the looks they gave her, she didn't feel reassured about the interview. The detective's cool but courteous manner had left her with such a sinking feeling in her gut that she wondered if he considered her a suspect.

3

Andrea was still filling out the forms for the secretary in front, when Keith Carlton, wearing a shirt and tie, blue jeans and a corduroy jacket, breezed through the office door past her. Andrea couldn't help but notice when he came up behind the desk and gave the secretary a friendly squeeze. "Maggie, I hate to tell you this, but you've got bags under your eyes. Not staying up too late at rowdy parties are you?"

"You know I'd never do a thing like that," she said with her permanent scowl, not showing how he really got to her.

"Todd in?"

Maggie jerked her head toward the back offices, "In back."

Keith went to the open door and shouted, "Hey, Todd, how am I going to win the Pulitzer if you guys don't put out your night reports on time!"

The officer, dressed with his shirtsleeves rolled up, came to the door. "Carlton, you'll get them just like everyone else," he growled. "The boss has 'em. Keep your shirt on, they'll be out in a minute." Then Todd went back inside. Keith stubbed out a brown Sherman's cigarette in the sand ashtray, glanced at Andrea, as he did all women, and then surveyed the police log tacked onto the bulletin board.

Andrea spied him out of the corner of her eye. Looking about age forty, he was handsome despite being slightly over-weight, not too tall and he had wavy brown hair, which needed a slight trimming. His round glasses and a high-ridged nose betrayed a hint of education and breeding. He oozed charm but with just enough toughness to make him sexy but not really dangerous.

A line-up of FBI Most Wanted pictures, print outs from the preceding week and various other lists were also posted. He flicked through a sheaf of the papers, then stood and read some of his own notes.

Andrea gave the clipboard back to Maggie, "I think that's just about everything."

"O.K., Ms. West. We'll call you if we need anything else."

"Thank you. And if you could, please let me know if they get any leads on the Beech case. It's really important to me." She strapped her purse over her shoulder and pushed open the door.

Intrigued, Keith stuffed his notes into his pocket and trotted after her as she left the office. "Excuse me, did you just see Inspector Catelano?"

As he moved towards her, she felt unexpectedly flustered inside. Nevertheless, she eyed him warily, immediately sensing that if she said anything at all, her privacy would crumble to bits. "Who are you?"

She felt him give her the subtle once over as he spoke. "I was wondering if I could ask you a few questions."

"What about?" She was tired of answering questions.

"Keith Carlton," he offered his hand. "I'm working on this case for the *Examiner*."

She ignored the offer of a handshake. "Oh, so you're the one who wrote that horrible tabloid story about Michael's murder."

"It wasn't that horrible," he sounded offended.

"It wasn't that sensitive. It was more like Geraldo than Bill Moyers."

He shrugged, "My editor liked it, that's what counts."

She looked at him coolly. "I have nothing to say to you."

He followed after her. "Is it true you and Michael Beech were lovers?"

"Where did you get that?" Andrea stopped at the elevator and glared at him. She hated pushy people, particularly pushy men. "I told you, no comment."

"Just a guess." He grinned playfully at her. "You had no wedding ring. I just put two and two together."

Andrea looked at him indignantly. "I don't have to talk with you."

Keith saw the red rise up her neck. "Have you ever noticed

how radiant you look when you're angry?"

"You better work on your people skills or your newspaper career's in the toilet."

"I guess you don't want to discuss the case over a cup of coffee then?"

"I don't think my business concerns you." She hit the elevator button again.

"For someone who's supposedly innocent, you're a bundle of nerves. I think you know more than you're telling."

"My best friend has just been murdered! And now you've just spent the last five minutes being incredibly rude and arrogant and you expect me to talk? You don't even know me."

"Nevertheless, I'm correct," he said. "Reporters have to learn how to read people very well. Sixth sense."

"Don't you have to go interview somebody about a UFO?" Finally, the elevator door opened and she walked in. Keith stood still in the middle of the corridor, staring after her as the door closed.

Officer Jergeson, who had observed this tiny interaction, came up behind Keith and smirked, "Carlton, I got to hand it to you, you always had a way with women...."

"Thanks, Ted. You know, I've seen the daily tracking polls showing our favorite Police Chief pulling ahead of the Mayor. If they split the absentees, you can just pay me then, so we won't have to stay up too late."

"Those are O'Shaughnessy's polls," Ted quipped. "What do you expect from them, reality?"

4

Andrea's place was still a shambles when she returned home, but she decided to leave it for the afternoon. She felt too upset to eat lunch, so she switched on her answering machine and listened to four messages. Two were from friends of hers who knew Michael and were calling to share their grief. One was a consoling message from her mother, Marina, and the last was from Michael's priest.

Father Hunter was Rector of the Episcopal Church of the

Advent in San Francisco, one of the last bastions of old style Anglo-Catholicism on the West Coast. Andrea listened intently. She knew he hated leaving messages on phone machines.

He spoke with a calm voice, "Andrea, this is Father Hunter. I heard about Michael in the afternoon paper. It's tragic, just tragic. Anyway, I'm calling to let you know I'm here if you want to talk and also to ask your help in arranging the funeral. Since you knew so many of his friends, maybe you could contact some of them? We plan to have the funeral here at church on Sunday afternoon at 4 o'clock. Call me tonight if you can."

Andrea wrote the messages down and reset the machine. She felt exhausted but knew she needed to call him to arrange the details of the funeral. When she dialed, he answered immediately. "Advent Rectory," he said. Andrea explained she needed to keep the conversation brief, which he understood. They worked out the logistics of the funeral, which would be an Easter requiem.

Nothing dreary about it, not for Michael, Andrea thought. He would, as in all things, go out with a splash. Lots of flowers, classy music, but no wreaths. Michael hated funeral wreaths. He thought they belonged in horse derbies. And champagne and fancy hors d'oeuvres afterwards.

She deliberately said nothing to Father Hunter about being with Michael the night he died and hung up. Then she phoned the friends who had called her to relay the funeral plans. Hearing their voices made her briefly break down in tears. They cried too and said they'd take care of everything except the service. "No, I prefer organizing it myself," Andrea sniffled. "Michael would roll over in his urn if I didn't."

The crying spell made her feel so much better she decided to tackle her library to take her mind off things. She put a Mozart CD on loud and set about to reorder her strewn books back on their shelves.

While she was putting her family pictures in their places around the room, she noticed that an old picture of her and her mother was missing. It was her favorite picture, taken when she was a chubby five-year-old clutching a sand bucket on the beach, while her mother sat next to her smiling in one of those old 1950s striped bathing suits. Her mother must have been around twenty-eight then. She still was something of an exotic beauty, with a Russian oval face, almond eyes and glossy black hair. People often said Andrea took after her mother, but she never believed them. She couldn't see it.

"I know this picture has to be somewhere here." She searched for it frantically. She stopped and tried to think where she last saw it. But the last place had been on this very bookcase. "Damn!"

Then she got the creeps. What if the intruder took it with him last night? Maybe he was some sort of sex pervert who liked to snoop around the homes of single women and collect pictures of little girls?

She shivered and wondered if she should tell Catelano. Her instincts told her not to, it was safer not to get involved. Andrea suddenly felt as if all this chaos was more than she could take. Instinctively she did what any Russian woman would do. She phoned her mother.

5

"Nothing was taken, except I can't find the old photograph of you and me," Andrea said.

"What do you mean?" Her mother's voice was shaking.

"You know the one Dad took of us on the beach on Shelter Island when I was six? I kept it on a shelf in the library. This morning, I noticed it was gone."

"Why would a burglar steal a thing like that? You must have misplaced it."

"Mama, I haven't touched it in months!"

"You're telling me that someone broke into your house last night for no reason at all, messed it up and left taking only a photograph? Not even some silver or jewelry?"

"Right. Why would anyone do that?"

"I don't know," Marina said.

"It's creepy. I'm getting paranoid."

"Darling, do you want to spend a few nights with me here in

the City?"

"Thanks, Mama, I think I'll be O.K. The police said they'd cruise by. A lot has happened in the past couple of days and I just want to spend some time alone for a while. You understand don't you?"

Marina sighed. "You were always like that. Even as a child, self-reliant to a fault. I don't want you to get hurt, that's all. Promise you'll call me later."

"I promise," Andrea reassured her mother. After changing the subject to her brother Nicky, Andrea said good-bye. As soon as she had hung up she looked around her trashed living room and suddenly wished she could have felt as confident as she sounded on the phone. I can't believe this is happening, Andrea gestured to the sky.

6

Simultaneously, across the Bay, Alex sat at an antique desk in a small back room in his house. On the table was a sophisticated receiver, connected to a wire that stretched to a pair of earphones he had on over his ears. He listened carefully to both Andrea's conversations with Father Hunter and her mother, Marina.

He carefully noted the time and place of the funeral. When they finished, he tuned the receiver to stand-by, then went downstairs and poured himself a stiff glass of vodka and drank it with one gulp.

7

At Andrea's house, the mail was usually delivered at mid-day. She stood in her hallway sorting through the pile of letters and bills, when she saw one with familiar handwriting. It took her breath away. It was from Michael. It was written with an ebony fountain pen in his usual flamboyant handwriting. Andrea ripped open the envelope and eagerly read the letter. Inside were a brass key and a note dated October 22nd. The note read:

"My dearest Andrea, I want you to have this key to my apartment in case something happens to me but I don't expect anything will... You'll think I'm crazy, but I think my phones have been tapped. I'm not sure. I want you to have this just in case. I have taken appropriate precautions. There are papers about the Icon of Kazan in my safe deposit box at the Bank of America on Montgomery Street. The box number is #36. I left the key to the security box in the Russian black lacquer box on the mantel. Be careful. All my love, Michael."

Andrea's eyes welled up with tears. Then she shivered as if a cold, dark shadow had crept behind her and she now knew she was in danger.

8

Andrea saw Michael standing there, just as she had seen him on Thursday night at the cathedral, but now in a billowing cloud of white mist. He was dressed neatly in his gray pin-stripped suit with a blue cornflower in his buttonhole, with perfect creases down his pant legs. He stood in the middle of the polished pine floor of the Russian Orthodox Cathedral, illuminated in a pool of white light that shone from some unseen spotlight above. The cathedral was full of icons, but they were all the same—large icons of Our Lady of Kazan circled him like mirrors.

She halted, stopped as if by some invisible force. She wanted to rush up to him and say, "Michael, you're not dead! The papers were wrong. I know they're wrong." She couldn't get the words out of her mouth. She was paralyzed.

Michael stood in the beam of light with his arms folded, a picture of righteous anger demanding justice. His eyes blazed furiously. He demanded, "Find her!"

"Find who?" Andrea at last found her voice. "The icon?"

"Find her." Michael spoke firmly and quietly. He gazed at her in silence for a minute, then slowly stepped out of the spotlight and disappeared into the white mist. Andrea rushed towards the light, looked around and saw no one in the cathedral but herself surrounded by a dozen images of the Icon of Kazan. "Michael," she cried, "come back! Tell me more!"

"Michael!" Andrea called out in her sleep, and awoke with a jolt. She lay in bed, her heart pounding rapidly. She broke out into a slight sweat; all her delayed dread and fear came flooding back to her. Glancing at her digital clock on her bedside table: she saw it was 3:22 a.m.

She lay still and tried to sort out her dream. Since she didn't have these kinds of vivid psychic dreams often, they always came as a surprise to her. She knew they were authentic by the strange feelings of terror and joy she felt. This dream was too powerful for her to ignore; the weight of it pressed relentlessly and indelibly upon her soul.

"I have to find the Icon of Kazan. Michael wants me to find the Icon of Kazan." She lay in bed thinking about what to do next, until her eyelids became too heavy for her to keep open.

CHAPTER 7

∽

"St. John Chrysostom tells us: 'Find the key to your heart; you will see that this key will also open the door of the Kingdom.' This is the direction our search should take."

Metropolitan Anthony Bloom
Meditations: A Spiritual Journey

Sunday, October 28, 1990

It was fifteen minutes before Michael's funeral. Already, the church was crowded with a wild mix of Michael's friends from the art world and the SoMa bar scene. Andrea was amused to see the polished museum staff and docents, wearing designer suits, sitting next to punk-looking Generation Xers with purple hair and rings piercing their eyebrows, noses, lips and God-knows-what-other-less-obvious places, besides members from the Gay Men's Chorus and the AIDS Quilt Project. The miracle was that they all mingled sociably together.

Andrea sat next to her mother at the end of the front pew, which also contained Michael's mother, Leonora, and his three sisters, Melissa, Melinda, and Melody. The four women in Michael's family were all bottle blondes from Georgia, who periodically dabbed their mascara and blew their dainty noses on lace handkerchiefs. They dared not look around.

Michael's mother, Leonora, whose fashion sense was frozen in 1954, was a petite, brittle woman in her late 60s. She wore a prim navy blue suit, a netted hat and white-gloved hands in which she properly clutched her small gilded black leather edition of the 1928 *Book of Common Prayer*. She stared straight ahead, clench-jawed, afraid that if she turned to see her fellow mourners she might be transformed into a pillar of salt like Lot's wife.

Andrea had always felt uncomfortable and put-off by Michael's mother and her stiff, overbearing ways, but today she felt sorry for her because, with Michael, the family dynasty had died. At least that's how she knew his mother felt about it.

She was glad Marina could briefly attend the funeral before racing off to see an important client. Michael had never been a favorite of her mother's, so Andrea saw it was a great concession that Marina decided to attend.

"Do you think someone from the Museum murdered Michael?" Marina whispered to Andrea as she turned to scan the crowd.

"Mama! Turn around. What a thing to ask, and at this time!"

"Just wondering." Marina marked her hymnal with her program. "Everybody else is talking about it."

At that point, as she sat in her pew, Andrea could have cared less about gossip. She was wondering whether she would survive reading aloud the Old Testament lesson from Job without weeping. Michael's ashes had been packed tightly in a rectangular cedar wood box covered with a small white pall and were placed on a stand in front of the altar. She could hardly bear the sight of it. Her heart ached as she was forced to accept Michael in this new form; she barely contained her tears.

The four-foot Paschal candle stood erect in its stand beside the ashes. Michael's mother had bought a huge basket of white roses and placed it in front of them. Michael's family, at his request, had asked their guests not to send flowers but to donate the money instead to the AIDS Foundation and Coming Home Hospice. Andrea liked that. Michael could be difficult sometimes but deep down he had compassion.

The service began promptly at four. Father Hunter processed in slowly behind a tall, somber male crucifer and two teenage acolytes with punk haircuts, dressed in white albs and pink Adida running shoes. He wore a white chasuble, which symbolized the Resurrection and the joy of Easter, and shiny black leather shoes.

Everyone rose as Father Hunter solemnly recited the opening words from the burial office. "I am Resurrection and I am Life, says the Lord. Whoever has faith in me shall have life, even though he die..." he intoned as he processed down the aisle.

Since Father Hunter thought the prerogative of the pulpit belonged to clergy alone, there were no spontaneous eulogies from family and friends, however some were allowed to read prepared statements. At Andrea's insistence, he let her read Michael's favorite poem by Gerard Manley Hopkins: "As kingfishers catch fire, dragon-flies draw flame;/As tumbled over rim in roundy wells"... which she did, without letting her emotions show. Since he knew Michael Beech well, he did the rest of the preaching himself. Mercifully brief, Andrea thought.

An able choir of men chanted in the balcony behind them. Two soloists from the San Francisco Opera Company; one, a fine soprano, who had been persuaded at the last minute to sing excerpts from Fauré's Requiem, joined them. Together they sang it well.

Throughout the funeral, Andrea felt nothing but a numb ache as she struggled to suppress a flood of feelings. She was pleased at how well she controlled herself until the congregation sang "Amazing Grace," during which she finally broke down and wept.

As she was returning red-eyed to her pew from the communion rail, she was dismayed to see the reporter, Keith Carlton, standing in the back of the church. He nodded to her solemnly. She flickered a faint smile and sat down. By now her head was throbbing; she felt in no mood to deal with reporters.

When the service had ended, Marina politely stayed long enough to offer her condolences to Leonora and Michael's sister. Then she warmly kissed Andrea good-bye and whispered in her ear, "Tell me how the reception went later."

After the funeral, the mourners packed into the parish hall, where Michael's friends and family had hosted a lavishly catered reception. People lined up two deep by the banquet table, hungry as baby birds, then for two hours, they laughed, hugged and swapped anecdotes about Michael while swigging champagne and munching on shrimp cocktails, brie, pâté and cucumber sandwiches.

Halfway through the reception, Keith Carlton trapped Andrea between the punch bowl and a stack of chairs in the corner.

"Nice reading, Andrea."

"Are you following me?" She tried to move away. She still had a headache.

"Not quite," Keith grinned. "I had to come here anyway. But now that you mention it, that's not such a bad idea."

"Don't you ever quit?" she hissed at him.

"Not when I can smell a good story."

"What don't you understand about 'Go away?'"

Keith looked a little pained as he realized he had overstepped her bounds. He backed off apologetically. "I get the message. Perhaps I should apologize for being so pushy yesterday," and offered to shake her hand.

Andrea took his hand cautiously. "Why don't you apologize for being pushy just now? If you're trying to impress me, it's not working."

"It looks like we've started off on the wrong foot again," Keith sighed. "I realize you must be terribly upset. This is probably the last place you want a reporter nosing around your private life. But I have a job to do. Keith Carlton; I'm with the *Examiner*."

"How could I forget? Will you please excuse me, I better go and deal with Michael's mother."

"Wait, Andrea," he said softly. "Please, if you really do know something, I think your life may be in danger. Maybe I can help."

She stopped for a moment, caught off-guard by the genuine concern in his voice. "How do you know? What's in it for you?" She speared a pink shrimp on her plate.

Keith blinked. "I have my sources. I don't want to see another person killed, story or no story," he answered honestly. He took out a box of Sherman's from his shirt pocket. "Mind if we go outside?" They stepped into the church garden where Keith pulled out a long brown cigarettelo, lit it with a plastic lighter and inhaled. "If I see another homicide, I think I'll go crazy," he confessed.

Andrea said softly, "I imagine seeing all that violence changes your faith in human nature."

"It does," he frowned a little. "I would rather help change the conditions which breed such violence in the first place."

"Now you're talking," Andrea said, pleased to see he had a heart after all and wondered if his jaunty edge belied a deeper gentleness. "How would you do that?"

He shrugged. "I'm a political writer. I see covering politics as my patriotic duty. First Amendment and all that. If the people aren't informed, they can't vote."

"Admirable sentiments." She eyed him with new respect.

"If I may ask, how did you get mixed up in all this anyway?" Keith asked. "It's an odd thing for a seminary professor to do."

"Almost a professor. I've been a graduate student so long," she laughed, "I don't know what a professor would do."

"And is seminary where you learned how to fend off nosy reporters?"

"Where do you think I was born, in a test tube?" Andrea snapped. "Why does everyone think people in seminaries are plaster of Paris saints? Michael and I were old friends. We went to school together."

"That's why you're here. But why were you there? At the cathedral with him the night he died?"

She balked. "What are you talking about?"

Keith always had a weak spot for strong women, but this one couldn't lie her way out of a paper bag. One thing he knew for sure, she didn't kill Michael Beech. "Well, it's a relief to see that the seminary is one of the few American institutions left that doesn't teach you how to lie."

She gave in, amazed he had called her bluff. "How did you know?"

"I heard at the police station that they were going to question a woman who was with Michael Beech at the cathedral. Two and two equals four. If that's true, you may end up as fish food in the Bay."

"If we talk, are you going to print what I tell you in the newspaper?"

"It's up to you."

"Has anybody ever told you you're a bastard?" She smiled wryly at him.

"Often." His eyes danced mischievously. "Want a watercress sandwich?"

2

Keith glanced around the garden to see if he was being watched and edged a little closer to her. "Are you allowed to have dinner with a bastard," he asked seductively, "or do your seminary rules prohibit it?"

"What do you want, a date or an interview?" Andrea quipped, but her pulse sprinted as she could feel his gaze meeting hers. She reminded herself to stay cool.

"How about a little of both?" He looked intently at her, but relaxed, letting her make her own decision. She noticed that he smiled, but his eyes looked soulfully serious. Maybe there was more to him than she knew? She decided to see if he had any grace under pressure besides his usual steamroller approach.

"Does this Mel Gibson approach always work with women you meet?"

He grinned. "No, but I thought I'd give it a shot. Besides, I'm getting hungry and I don't like to eat alone."

"Is there anything you like to do alone?" Andrea tested him again. To her, a person's religion was always what they did with their solitude.

"Besides vote? Can't think of anything, unless you count writing, computer chess, and counting stars."

She looked at him, surprised. "You star gaze?"

"Only at night." He adjusted his glasses. "I don't have the right equipment for daytime."

"How unusual, for somebody who seems so," she paused to find the right word, "elemental."

He let her little jab pass by. "Let's just call it my connection with nature and the need to keep things in balance. That and pool. Someday I want to write a book, *The Art of Zen and Pocket Pool*."

Intrigued, Andrea asked, "Zen and pool. Tell me more."

"How about if I explain at dinner? Anyway, I've got a few hunches about Michael's case I want explore with you."

She hadn't had an honest date in months, and she longed for any distraction from this intolerable loneliness and grief. For all his glibness, she could sense that Keith had a good heart and that they were temperamentally compatible.

She decided to take the risk, "OK, you win. But on one condition, if we talk, you must promise not to print the story in the paper until we both agree it's the right time."

"Fine, but only if you agree to talk with my editor when my deadlines are due. How does Kimball's sound? It's not far."

"Let me say goodbye to Michael's family and I'll be right with you," she flashed a brief smile and went to find Leonora.

Neither one of them saw Alex Menshikov standing among the crowd, watching them intently.

3

The smooth sounds of a jazz trio—piano, bass and drums—echoed through Kimball's jazz club, re-built from an old brick warehouse. Keith and Andrea sat eating in an elegant dining area tucked upstairs among well-dressed clientele on their way to the Symphony.

Keith rolled his fork in his clam linguini. "Did anybody ever tell you you'd make a dream date for Narcissus? You never say anything about yourself."

"I thought this was a date with Narcissus."

"Ouch! Below the belt. Do you always fight this tough with your friends?"

"With Michael I did," she said bitterly. "It was the only way I could survive."

"Why bother? Why not let yourself thrive with someone else?"

"I don't think this is the right time to ask that question."

"Sorry. My former wife was like that. Can't live with them, can't live without them."

"So you were married?"

"Once, but it's over now and too painful to talk about. I have a daughter, named Katie. I send money regularly but I don't see her much. My ex-wife and I parted on good terms but I wish I could see Katie more." He looked sad. "Kids grow up too fast these days."

"Why did you split up?"

"She always used to accuse me of having itchy feet. At first we traveled a lot together, but later, after she had Katie, she didn't want to go anywhere, which I understood, but I had a writing career to get off the ground. Since our divorce, I've been to Central America, Russia, Nepal, Borneo and Japan," he cocked his head to see her reaction. "In between small newspapers jobs around the country. Then I landed this job at the *Examiner*."

"Russia, huh? What made you start globe-trotting?"

"I was born and raised on the north side of Chicago. From a good working class family. They were decent, but it suffocated me. My father was an engineer who worked for Kodak, and my mother was a homemaker. They're both dead now."

"I'm sorry," Andrea said sympathetically, briefly thinking how awful it would be for her to lose her own parents.

"That's life," Keith shrugged philosophically. "I had the usual siblings: one older brother and sister. My folks were the only Protestants in a Catholic neighborhood, which sometimes made life challenging, especially when I had some relatives in Skokie who were Jewish. It was tough growing up because the boys from the Catholic school would try to beat me up when I walked home from public school. It got so bad, I'd play hooky and run off to the pool hall."

"And became a pool shark?"

"No, but it's how I learned to fight." Keith broke off a heel of bread and buttered it. "And to cope."

"And your parents?"

"If my father was alive and saw what I was doing now, he'd kill me. He thought real men only worked with their hands. Though I guess he relented after I earned more money from shooting pool during college than processing pictures part time for Kodak. But an old photographer named Jack Weinstein got me interested in photography and eventually I earned a scholarship to the University of Chicago to study journalism. In the summer, you could tell me apart from the rest of the kids in my class by my pasty pale face."

As he talked, Andrea realized she could listen to him for hours. He talked with his hands, he talked with color, and he was a natural born storyteller. "When was that?" she interrupted. "Did you get drafted to Vietnam?"

"No, I got a student deferment, but my brother was. He was killed in the last days of the war. About to go on leave, too. It really ripped us up. That's when I started to question everything. That and Watergate pretty much turned me on to political journalism, which is what I would like to do until my ship comes in."

She sipped from her glass of wine, then asked, "Is there anything else you really care passionately about?"

"Lots of things. Besides photography and politics, I care about traveling, pool, baseball, outer space and working with words. These seem to make the most sense to me. And I guess you could also call me a news junky. I picked journalism in college, because it was the only course that would give me credit for reading newspapers all day long. Somewhere along the line I got hooked for better reasons."

"You and George Orwell," Andrea observed, noticing he hadn't fully answered her question. "Didn't he write the essay, *Politics and the English Language*? I remember he once said something like: 'The great enemy of clear language is insincerity'? You don't strike me as being overly sincere," she said, testing him.

Keith said softly, "Only the insincere man knows how hard true sincerity is to achieve." He looked humbly at her from behind his glasses. His gaze took her breath away. As she looked into his eyes, she glimpsed spiritual depths in him, which he himself didn't completely know.

"Well, at least you're honest. That's a good start," she laughed approvingly. "So what is this hot news you're dying to tell me?"

"The Holy Virgin Society has put up a $500,000 reward for the missing icon." He explained to her that the original was replaced with a forged copy. "If I find the Icon of Kazan, I can stop chasing all those stupid ambulances and homicide vans and work City Hall. After that, I'd like to be rich enough to do some exotic travel writing, human interest stories of people and places with a slant on the mysterious."

"So, you really do like people, after all," Andrea teased.

"They fascinate me endlessly. Especially you. Your turn. Tell me about you and Michael. I want to get the story right about him."

Keith finished his last bit of pasta.

"You never give up, do you?"

"It's an occupational hazard with us hack reporters." His grin did not betray his resolve.

To Andrea's surprise, she could almost hear the current humming between them. She felt totally at home with him, able to say anything. Keith cocked his head attentively as she told him about the past two days.

She told him all about Michael, about her lunch with him at Greens, about their visit to the icon at the cathedral, about the break-in at her house and the curious fact of her missing photograph. Taking a risk, she even told him about her dream.

It was a relief to speak about all this—especially to someone outside her seminary circle where gossip was rife. She hadn't realized how lonely she had been and how much she needed to talk. Luckily, he was someone who could listen well.

"So," Keith asked, "you think Michael knew something that got him killed?"

"Yes, he told me he thought the Icon of Kazan was a fraud."

"That's what I heard down at the police station. Do you know if the Holy Virgin Society had any hint of this beforehand?"

"I don't know. If so, why would they put up a $500,000 reward for it in the first place?"

"Good question. Which causes me to suspect either they didn't know or they're paying a lot for a cover-up. But it seems obvious to me that if the thief, or thieves, could make a duplicate of the Icon of Kazan good enough to fool the authorities, then they were no ordinary burglars. There's got to be people who know about making icons and people who know those people."

"Michael told me about a man named Father Mench, who used to work with Father Kiprion—he painted the icons in the Cathedral."

"Do you think you could contact Father Mench for me?"

"I don't know him, but I know others who could." Andrea toyed with her spoon. "I think there's something else you ought to know."

"Sound away." Keith leaned back in his chair.

"Michael sent me a key to his apartment the day he died. I got it in the mail yesterday."

Keith sat upright. "Why did he do that?"

"He wanted me to get a safe deposit key before the police arrived."

"What's in the safe deposit box?"

"He said I'd find some papers about the icon."

"Maybe that's why someone broke into your house the other night. They were looking for the key."

"Yes, but why would someone take my photo?"

"That seems quite understandable," he said and grinned at her.

"You certainly know how to lay it on, don't you?" Andrea said, but secretly was pleased. "Do you think they took the picture because they liked the looks of my mother or me at six? It doesn't make any sense."

"I think we should go get that key," Keith said. "Before someone else does."

Andrea looked up abruptly from her plate. "What do you mean we?"

"I'm not going to do this all alone," Keith answered. "And you certainly aren't going without me. What if somebody follows you?"

"What if somebody follows us?"

"I think the two of us could handle him."

"You think so?" Andrea looked dubiously at him. "Isn't Michael's house already sealed off by the police?"

"So what? The police have already come and gone. Besides, you can prove Michael gave you his key and left instructions for you to go in if anything happened to him. We'd be in and out of there in a flash."

"True, but I feel so underhanded about it—like it would be trespassing or something. Why can't the police solve this?"

"Didn't you just tell me they think you're a suspect?"

"They said everybody's a suspect."

"Except you're number one. Who's going to take care of you, if you don't? What about your dream of Michael? If that doesn't sound like divine intervention I don't know what is."

"I thought you didn't believe in God."

"I don't, but you do. Let's just call it the Forces in the Universe. Maybe part of your spiritual work involves solving this mystery."

"Now you're sounding like my spiritual director," Andrea said ruefully, recognizing that he had hit a deeper cord than he knew.

"Good. But what if I'm right? Don't you think Michael would want you to get involved, to ask some hard questions?"

"You're suggesting I do a lot more than ask a few questions."

"Andrea, you won't be safe until we get those papers—and for that, we need the deposit box key."

"All right, I'm convinced." She rose abruptly. "Let's go."

"Right now?" He looked up at her with surprise.

"The more we know, the safer I'll feel. I can't face any more chaos." She dropped her folded napkin on the table, slipped on her coat and walked out with a determined step.

Keith hastily dumped three twenties on the table to cover the bill, gulped down his last bit of wine and hurried after Andrea.

4

The cold and blustery fog blew through the cedar trees, making them creak and clack in the dark. Andrea felt the damp night air seep through her bones. "Hurry up, we can't stay out here forever! Somebody will see us." She shivered and rubbed her arms to stay warm.

"Hold on, I've almost got it," Keith said, fumbling at the key-hole ahead of them in the dark.

They were standing outside in the back garden of Michael Beech's house trying to get in the basement door, which the police had not sealed off with yellow tape. Andrea heard the squeak of metal as Keith jimmied the knob and pushed at the door. Keith said, "It seems to be stuck."

"I remember Michael always complained about this door being hard to open. Something about the wood swelling. You have to push down hard with your shoulder."

Keith leaned with the full force of his body weight and rammed the door with his right shoulder. It exploded open with a bang and sent Keith hurtling forward and down two steps onto his chest with a thud. "Christ!"

"Are you all right?" Andrea stepped down and peered through the threshold into the black hole of the basement.

"Yeah," he groaned struggling to his feet. "Jesus, why didn't you tell me there were steps there?"

"I forgot," she said, feeling lame.

There were the scrape of a chair leg on the cement floor, and the dull sound of cardboard boxes and glass shattering. "Are you OK?" she asked again.

"I'm fine. Just hope the damn thing wasn't a Ming vase."

"It probably was, knowing Michael. He used to store his mother's old china down here."

"Great! Does your short-term memory work well enough so you can tell me where the stairs to the house are?"

"I think they're at the other end. To the right."

Keith flicked his lighter and held it overhead to try to get his bearings. She slipped in quickly and stood behind him. He put the light out again.

"We don't want to be seen, do we?"

She felt strangely exhilarated standing here in the dark with this stranger. She could feel his nearness and smell his body, which was pleasantly sweet. Her blood pulsed and the ache inside her hammered home the fact that she hadn't slept with a man for a very long time. Much too long. "You lead the way," she said.

He groped for her hand and together they weaved through the obstacle course in Michael's basement, bumping inadvertently into a rake, which clanged to the floor.

"You'd make a lousy burglar," Keith whispered.

"Thanks for your support," she muttered. Just then, overhead, Andrea thought she heard something above on the floorboards. "Shhhh! Did you hear that?"

"No, what was it?"

"I thought I heard footsteps."

"I think your imagination is working overtime. Where do those stairs go?" He pointed to a flight of stairs by the wall.

"To the kitchen. Look, are you sure we should do this?" she asked nervously as they climbed to the top. The kitchen door was locked. "What do we do now?"

"What kind of lock is on this door?"

"I think it's just a latch."

"Stand aside," Keith whispered. Andrea stepped down and pinned herself against the wall as Keith took a step back and rammed the door with his left shoulder.

It refused to open. "Damn!" Keith rubbed his shoulder. "This is getting to be a bad habit."

Andrea suppressed a laugh.

"Do you want to try it?" He looked at her indignantly.

"Sure," she said, examining the door closely. She took out a long thin nail file from her purse, slipped it through the crack by the doorjamb and slid it up towards the latch. The latch flipped up with a faint clatter. "Brains always work better than brawn, my mother used to say," Andrea said sweetly as she stepped over the threshold.

"Very funny," Keith answered sourly.

So, he hates to look stupid, Andrea thought. Like me.

Her eyes, now accustomed to the pitch dark, easily adjusted to the interior of the house, which was dimly lit by the amber street-light outside. They stepped quietly through the dining room and the den to the front living room. Andrea jumped as lights shown on the wall from a passing headlight.

"Get down," Keith motioned with his hand.

She crouched on one knee and pointed towards the fireplace. "The Russian lacquer box is up on the mantel."

Keith scurried over to the other end of the room and picked the small lacquer box off the mantelpiece. Andrea could hear something rattling inside it. "I think I've got it!" He flicked on his lighter again to inspect the box, and then snuffed it out again.

Just then, out of nowhere, an indistinct dark figure burst from behind the floor-length curtains by the bay window.

"Look out!" Andrea yelled.

Keith turned in confusion and raised his arm, but it was too late. Something hard came crashing down on him. Andrea saw two bodies fall to the ground, the one on top wrestling with Keith in the darkness. The intruder slammed him hard in the gut and fled into the hallway, opened the front door, and then ran out down the street. Andrea stood frozen with terror.

5

Anxiously, Andrea bent over Keith's body and felt for a pulse. Thank God, it beat strongly, but he was unconscious.

She quickly grabbed a glass of water from the kitchen and splashed it in Keith's face. He came to with a start, "Oww!" he groaned and held his shoulder in agony. "I can see you're a real Florence Nightingale!" He writhed in pain. "Ahhh, shit! I think something's broken."

Andrea said sternly, "I'm taking you to the hospital."

"Oh, great! And I thought we were going to have a nice romantic evening together."

"Good try. Did he get the box?"

"Of course. What do you think he came for?"

"Did you see his face?"

"He hit me from behind. For a short bastard, he really had a lot of muscle." Keith shivered.

"You're going into shock." Andrea looked concerned. She quickly tore off her jacket and wrapped it around Keith's shoulder's.

"Careful!" he winced. His teeth chattered.

"Here, let me help you up." She bent over him. "Put your left arm around my neck. How does that feel?"

"Magnificent," he groaned, "never felt better."

With some difficulty, she straightened her back and hoisted him up, and then she steadied him as they shuffled out the front door to her car parked around the corner.

As they left, they didn't notice that someone sat in the dark green Mercedes across the street, watching their every move. Andrea pulled her car out with a screech and left. The Mercedes headlights lit up like yellow lanterns, illuminating the misting nighttime fog in the dark. The car followed them at a safe distance.

6

At the hospital, the doctor asked the usual questions and filled out the usual forms. X-rays were taken. Pain medication was given. In the end, Keith had a fractured collarbone.

"Give him plenty of medication," Andrea told the nurse in front of Keith. "He's the worst patient I ever saw."

"Never be stoic when you can get lots of legal drugs," Keith grinned. Andrea waited while the medical team took him away to have his collarbone set. Then he was sent to bed for the night. Soon, he fell asleep in his hospital bed, exhausted.

Andrea decided to stay until she was sure he was asleep. He tossed fitfully on the bed, groaning anytime he moved. She examined his face, freed from the pain by sleep, and liked what she saw. There was something almost boyish about him. She smiled. Really quite tender, she thought. Then, feeling drained, Andrea closed the door and left quietly.

7

At midnight, the Major sat in his overstuffed chair by the fireplace and silently watched the fire lick the thick oak logs perched on the grate. He turned the black Russian lacquer box slowly in his hands. It was not a one-of-a-kind piece, but the design was rare enough. The gold picture on the cover, painted with fine-hair brushes, was of a fiery archangel, more like the Firebird, coming to Mary at the Annunciation.

Small brass keys to security box #36 lay on the table by his side. Now they can't pin anything on me, he thought with satisfaction. He pulled the screen across the hearth and rose stiffly from his chair.

He stopped in the downstairs bathroom and inspected his face in the bathroom mirror. He touched his left eye with his short stubby fingers. It was swollen and bruised and already turning violent shades of black, red and purple.

Still think you're a punk fighter, do you? Running the tap, he soaked a washcloth in cold water and pressed the cloth gingerly against his throbbing eye. He hissed from the sharp sting. You can't fight like you used to, you old fart. Nevertheless, he still felt a certain pride—after all, he'd brought down a man half his age. He took off his shirt and flexed his arm muscle—still, he had to admit he had the element of surprise and superior military training on his side. Otherwise, it would have been impossible. Nope, he threw the washrag down, I can't do this any more. I'm finished.

With that, he hauled himself painfully up the stairs to his bedroom, pulled down a suitcase from the upper shelf of his closet, and began to pack methodically and quickly.

8

Alex sat in his library nursing a glass of vodka and pondered his dilemma. He was in deep shit this time. Michael Beech was dead. If Alex had killed him, he hadn't meant to, but there it was. What a huge puzzle. He knew he had hit him hard, but when he pulled Michael under the altar behind the iconostasis he distinctly remembered feeling Michael breathe. It couldn't be.

Just his luck. The loopy members of that damn Inner Circle had their icon, and he certainly had his money, but he was also stuck with a defunct airplane ticket to London, and a possible murder rap on his head.

He rose from his chair and went over to the wet bar, where he poured himself another shot from a square crystal decanter and began to pace back and forth across the Chinese carpet.

Right from the beginning, things at the cathedral hadn't gone according to plan. Maybe it had been a set up all along? Where had Cecil really gone? He was nowhere in sight as Alex left the cathedral that night. Priscilla Thorpe and that aristocratic old biddy were too evasive the other night. They certainly wanted him to leave town fast enough. They never trusted him, he was sure of that.

What bothered him most was Andrea. How did she get mixed

up in this? He took another gulp of vodka. Obviously, she knew Michael Beech well enough to join him that night at the cathedral. What exactly did she know? And how much?

He went over to the polished oak desk and picked up the photograph of six-year old Andrea and her mother. After looking at it for a long while, he put it down again. He wanted to pound his chest and bellow to the sky like their servant Gregori did the night he learned his father Andrei was taken away.

Fine, so he had screwed up, but they weren't going to get him this time. Not like his father. He would die first. Alex turned suddenly and violently, with an oath, shattered his shot glass in the empty fireplace.

CHAPTER 8

❧

Monday, October 29, 1990

Andrea attended Monday morning chapel at the seminary as usual. One hundred faculty and students said Morning Prayer from the *Book of Common Prayer*, complete with rich organ music and antiphonal psalms, chanted from side to side, which reminded Andrea of how the monks used to chant the psalms in choir.

Andrea felt a wild hodgepodge of feelings. She was torn between fear and elation, grief, anger and foreboding. One the one hand, her common sense filled her with a feeling of dread that she was getting in over her head. On the other, her heart filled her with exhilaration from the night before, despite her real grief about Michael. So as she stepped out of the ivy-covered brick chapel, she caught herself absent-mindedly humming and thinking, not of God, but of Keith Carlton.

Father Peter Ashton appeared suddenly at her elbow. "You're chipper this morning."

"Am I?" She felt suddenly exposed.

"You said you'd tell me how everything went." As her spiritual director, Father Peter knew her well enough to pry openly. He offered, "Time for a cup of coffee?"

Andrea felt torn and guilty for two reasons. Number one, normally she was meticulous about grading student papers but, on this autumn day, she had an attack of spring fever. In fact, she was so eager to see Keith that she was tempted to hand the papers back late; but her responsible side would never let her do that.

Number two, she always enjoyed seeing Peter, but she didn't want to tell him about her adventures over the weekend. Certainly not about last night.

"Sure," she waffled, "but a quick one. I've got tons of work." They walked together down the hill, past the Stalinist gray dorms on the north side of the Cal campus—the windows were opened wide and rap music pounded out from above.

They found a small table in the back of a quiet cafe down on Euclid Street. A Mozart string quartet played discreetly over the sound system overhead.

Father Peter sat back comfortably, "So how did your dissertation defense go?"

"Very well. Father Serrano asked the best and hardest questions, of course. That part was tricky. Dr. Wilber was a dear and Dr. Thomas really didn't have a clue as to what I was talking about. But it worked out in the end. It certainly makes one reassess higher education."

Father Peter laughed, "I think you'll find that every vocation has institutional hoops which must be hazarded—seminary graduate programs are no exception. I heard from Father Serrano that you did more than very well: you did brilliantly. I expect you should be getting a letter in the mail from them confirming your Ph.D. any day now. I'm proud of you, Andrea. Well done. I knew you could do it."

She blushed, both embarrassed and pleased that her mentor praised her so highly. "Thank you. I hope you're right! I could never have done it without you."

Fr. Peter nodded his thanks. "What about the Icon of Kazan? Did you go to the police?"

"Wednesday morning."

"And?"

Andrea suddenly felt mildly irritated by his older brother proprietary stance and avoided his eyes.

"They took my report."

"I'm sure that was painful." His voice radiated sympathy.

"It could have been worse. You were right. The Detective said everyone is a suspect. At least at first. Even me. But I'm glad I went," she peered nervously into her coffee cup.

"You, a suspect? I don't believe it. Unless they had some reason to believe you were hiding something from them. But you have nothing to hide."

"Of course not." Andrea looked up at him and smiled. The jumble of divided emotions tore at her like dogs struggling over a bone. She wanted to pour everything out to him like in the old days, but felt ashamed, as if she had been somehow disloyal. She wasn't quite sure to whom.

There was Keith, or rather the possibility of Keith. But then, there was Peter. Peter, with his intense mystical eyes, who had depth and soul and who knew her so well. Usually he could see right through her. Finally she decided to say something more. It was the truth, but not the whole truth.

"I think you ought to know my apartment was ransacked the other night," she added.

Father Peter's face froze. "You weren't there, were you?"

"No, I was out grocery shopping. By the time I came home, everything was a mess."

"You must have been terrified!"

"I was."

"Do you need company tonight?"

Andrea blinked at him, and her heart went to her throat.

"I could ask Sheila. I'm sure she'd be glad to come over. You know how she cares for you." Andrea heard a horn blast outside the coffee shop and inside, the clang of coffee cups being washed up behind the counter.

"No, thanks." She peered down at her coffee. "That would leave you alone with the kids and you already have your hands full. I'll be fine. I called the Berkeley police and a squad car goes by periodically."

"What were they after? Did they steal anything?"

"I don't know," Andrea lied, remembering the missing photograph.

"I hope you're not getting in over your head," Peter said, giving her a stern look.

"Don't worry, I won't," she said, a little too breezily. But she knew she had already passed the point of no return.

2

Andrea's energy for teaching her morning class had dropped like a deflated balloon, but she soldiered on. She summarized her lecture: "Lancelot Andrews, along with two other famous Caroline Divines, George Herbert and John Donne, set an indelible mark on the Church of England in the 17th century. That's because they dared to breathe the mystical spirit into their life, their work and their art. Their lives, their prayers and their poetry continue to inspire us to see the sublime in ordinary things.

"Their solution was to embody what we call the 'Via Media,' the 'middle way,' between the Catholic and Protestant positions which had so polarized Europe during the Reformation, and breathed new depth and tolerance into the Church of England. Along with Cranmer's new Prayer Book, these Caroline Divines raised the language of religion to new heights. Thus they established Anglicanism once and for all as a legitimate spiritual and theological alternative to the religious landscape of their day—and ours." She closed her notebook.

"Next week read chapters 12 and 13 on 'The Wesleys and Pietism in the 18th Century' and the rise of the Evangelical move-ment. Your papers are due in two weeks. This time," she surveyed her students over her glasses, "No late papers."

The classroom echoed with the gabble of voices. Good, Andrea thought, at last I have the afternoon off. Struggling with feelings of eagerness and guilt, she found she had been obsessing about Keith lying in the hospital all morning, which was unusual for her.

It was all her fault, she told herself. Without her, he wouldn't have gotten hurt. But it was he who first suggested it. No doubt the same man who burgled her house was already at Michael's when they snuck in. The least she could do was to visit Keith and apologize, she rationalized.

An hour later, in the hospital in San Francisco, Andrea told her-self she was on a mission of mercy. But when her stomach began to flutter as she approached the door to Keith's room, she began to real-ize what was really happening. The other half of her didn't give a damn and went straight ahead anyway. She knocked on the open door gently.

Keith's sleepy voice called, "Go away! No more pills!"

Andrea hated the antiseptic smell of hospitals—the dead recy-cled air in drab waiting rooms and the stench of Pine-Sol disinfec-tant on the habitually washed floors. She cautiously tapped the door. "I thought you might be wanting a visitor." She carried a card and a potted plant of rust colored chrysanthemums. Keith rolled towards her, looking bleary-eyed and bruised from the black eye he suffered.

He sat up in bed, "You're a sight for sore eye, so to speak." He beamed at her, despite his shiner.

"Stay still," she chuckled. "You never stop, do you?" She held the pot of flowers in her arms. She caught herself fantasizing how he looked under his blue and white hospital gown. His collarbone was taped and his right arm was bent in a canvass sling to prevent excess movement.

"Not if I can help it. This place is like a morgue." Noticing the flowers, he waved his left arm towards the windowsill. "You can put them over there. The nurse will water them until either I die or they do."

She laughed. "You look like a tractor ran over you."

"Yeah, a monster four-wheeler. That guy was small, but he was built like a brick wall. He probably eats baby robins for breakfast," he snorted. "Big help you were—all you did was scream."

"Yeah, but it made him leave, didn't it?"

"Sure, right over me." He moaned as he tried to shift his weight to make himself more comfortable.

"Did you notice anything about him?" Andrea asked.

"Not really, although I don't think he was very young."

"Do you remember what the lacquer box looked like?"

"It was black with some scene of a Russian peasant girl and

large orange figure on it. I couldn't tell if it was a big bird or an angel."

"I remember that box!" Andrea said. "It's the Annunciation of the Virgin Mary and the fiery bird was the Archangel Gabriel. It was Michael's favorite."

"If you say so."

She sat down on the end of his bed. "So what are we going to do now?"

"We?" he looked at her. "Darlin', if you haven't noticed, I'm out of commission for a while. You're on your own. Don't forget, you're the only one who knows the bank and the vault number. No matter what the police do, you're going to have to stay two jumps ahead of this bozo."

"Maybe the murderer forced the information out of Michael before he killed him." Andrea's eyes watered at the thought of this.

"I don't think he would have trashed your place if that was the case. The murderer knows you know where the safe deposit box is and wants to get you first."

"Don't remind me..."

"If he waits too long, he knows you could set up a trap for him; you tell the police, he goes to the bank, and wham—they nab him."

"Maybe he's already gone to the bank. Maybe he went today."

"Maybe he has, but you won't find out unless you go after him. You've got to beat him at his own game."

"But I don't even know who he is."

"I bet you could find out. Next to Michael, you know more about the Icon of Kazan than anybody else. You have to start hunting." Keith threw off the blanket exposing his handsome legs. "Geez, it's warm in here. Anyway, somebody in the church is bound to know the history behind the icon."

"Probably. I'll ask around. I vaguely recall the icon was shown at the 1963 New York World's Fair. In some sort of fancy pavilion. I remember seeing pictures of it as a kid in *Life* magazine. It caused a big splash back then. The public library ought to have copies of the old magazine on file. I could start there."

"Just let me know what you discover so I can write about it

later," Keith grinned.

"Sure, if you give me the byline." She poked his good shoulder. "What about you?"

"I'll be all right," he said. "As long as they let me keep popping these pills. They'll probably discharge me later today or tomorrow. You know how HMOs shuffle people in and out these days: a broken collar bone—one day, open heart surgery—three days, brain transplant—four days..."

"I'm sorry I got you into this mess." Andrea said and rose to leave.

He smiled at her. "I wouldn't want to be in this mess with anyone but you. Hey, you know what you could do for me?" He leaned seductively towards her. Andrea's heart pounded.

"Could you get me those Sherman's out of my jacket?" He pointed. "I'll just have one outside before bedtime."

Andrea fished his cigarettes out of his pocket and waved them before him. "This could be the perfect time to stop smoking," she said with mock sternness. "You know the hospital rules."

"I'll stop tomorrow," he growled through a smile.

Andrea stuffed the pack in her pocket. "I'll just go see what I can dig up." She smiled mischievously and strutted out of the room.

"Bring those back!" Keith whacked his bed with his left arm in frustration. "Damn!"

3

Andrea sat at a large oak table in the periodical room of the decaying San Francisco public library. Across from City Hall, the exterior of the library blended well with the beaux-arts Civic Center, but the interior was crumbling and threadbare from over use by the city's homeless population as a daytime lounge.

On her left, a large volume of bound *Life* magazines for 1963 and 1964 lay by her elbow. She had just spent the past hour leafing through each one for the article she'd told Keith about.

The dated photographs brought back old memories that still pinched like scar tissue. She remembered how just after her parents split up she, her mother and Nicky moved to California. She used to cry herself to sleep every night, wishing her Daddy would come home, but he never did. She used to be jealous of all the other little girls who had fathers, but now the pain of the old wound had burrowed so deep it was forgotten. Almost. She sighed and flipped through the *Life* indexes.

She found a small and disappointing article about the Icon of Kazan in one of the October 1963 editions. A photo of Jane Mansfield dressed in a swim suit dominated the cover. The photos had smudged because of the bad printing job; the colors were a dull brown and pea green. It showed the icon at Orthodox Pavilion at the World's Fair, but it had few details.

She tapped her pencil on the table with frustration. "Damn!" she mumbled. "Another dead end."

A few minutes later, after finding the correct microfiche film for the same month and year for the *New Year Times*, she took her turn at the overhead viewer. Half an hour later, she found what she was looking for at last: the November 16, 1963 New York Times article, with an illustration.

It read: "The Russian Orthodox Greek Catholic Church of America announced yesterday that it would buy a famed icon, the "Virgin of Kazan" from an English woman for $500,000. The ten by thirteen-inch wood panel was painted in Kazan, Russia about 1400.

"A silver gilt riza, covering all but the faces of the Virgin Mary and Jesus was added about 1600. The riza is studded with more than a thousand diamonds, emeralds, rubies, sapphires and pearls, some reputedly donated by Catherine the Great.

"The Kazan icon, credited with many miracles, was in the Moscow Cathedral until the 1917 revolution, after which the Bolsheviks sold it. It is now privately owned. Mr. Cecil Durant, an archeologist and antiquities dealer from Victoria, Canada, is currently holding the icon in trust for the owner and acts as private consultant. The painting has been on display in the US and Canada for the last few months and is now at the Holy Virgin Protection Cathedral, 59 East 2nd Street, New York City. The icon will be shown at the Protestant-Orthodox pavilion at the World's Fair."

"That's it!" Andrea pounded the table, which caused a short female librarian wearing bifocals to look up from her computer with curiosity. Andrea smiled contritely back at her, then returned to scribble down the details into her notebook. She glanced at her watch. It was 4:40 p.m., almost closing time. Better hurry to the nearest phone to tell Keith the news.

4

Keith was propped up in bed watching the 'Niner's game on Monday Night Football when he heard a soft knock at his hospital room door. "It's open," he called.

"That was obvious," Tony Catelano said, standing in the doorway. Keith noticed he didn't look happy.

"Have a seat. It's almost half-time and the defense looks like they finally came to play." Keith was glad to see a familiar face, but wasn't so sure he wanted it to be Tony's.

"I forgot to bring the flowers and candy."

"Forget the flowers and candy. Give me a smoke? I'm out."

Tony patted his pockets, "Sorry. Remember, I quit. What happened? You look like a piñata after a birthday party."

"Yeah, look at this," Keith pulled his hospital gown away at the shoulder, revealing a flaming purple bruise.

"How color coordinated. What the fuck happened?"

"I fell off my ladder painting the house."

"You don't own a house, but I'd pay big money to watch you try to paint one."

Keith laughed, "I got mugged."

"Following the icon story, right, with Miss Seminary?"

"You're a regular Sam Spade, aren't you?"

"Someday Keith, your testicles are going to get you into big trouble."

"How much trouble can she get me in?"

"You're here, aren't you? Maybe she's some psycho, who knows? They're the ones who look the most innocent."

"You really think she did it?" Keith asked incredulously.

"Look, why don't you just leave the detective work to me. You can report on it later, OK? There might be fewer dead people in this town."

"I wasn't killed."

"But you might have been!" Tony countered. "Keep your nose where it belongs. I don't want to see you messing around with this case anymore."

"Aye, aye, Captain Sir." Keith saluted him.

"If you don't, I'll make it so hard for you to work around the station, you'll wish you had an assignment in Kuwait."

"Cute. Besides, you'd never stand up to the publicity war I'd wage on you if you did."

"Maybe. You're not important enough for the paper to risk one. Maybe I should just let you hang yourself on your own rope."

"I'll let you know if I do."

"It's your neck," Tony shrugged.

"Thank you for pointing that out to me." Keith turned his face away.

"OK, let's drop it. So, when are they letting you out of this hell hole?" Tony asked.

"Tomorrow morning. Not soon enough."

"Good. Need a ride?"

"Miss Seminary, as you call her, is picking me up."

"You're making a big mistake, Carlton," Tony shook his head.

"I know what I'm doing."

"Let's hope so." Tony changed the subject. "When your shoulder heals, maybe we could get in some straight pool?"

"Yeah, sure. And I'll kick your ass again, even with my shoulder tied up!"

"Right, Minnesota Fats! See you later. Remember what I said."

Keith waved him off as Tony stepped out of the room. "Sure. Thanks for coming."

5

Tuesday, October 30, 1990

It was almost noon when Andrea parked her car in front of Keith's two-story Victorian walkup. He lived opposite Dolores Park in an apartment next to a Hindu health food restaurant. Keith opened his door and gingerly maneuvered himself out of the car. "I feel like an ice cube that's been tossed around too long in a martini shaker."

"Here, let me help," Andrea said, and came over to his side to give him a hand out of her red Honda.

"I think I can make it on my own from here. Want to come in?" Keith looked up at her as the wind blew wisps of black hair away from her face. His eyes looked tenderly at her for a moment, and she thought he was going to say something but thought better of it.

"Sure, but only for a while. I have to get back to work." She followed him upstairs as he slowly climbed. Once on top of the landing, Andrea smelled stale cigarette smoke and air full of everything except oxygen. Inside, the living room decor looked at best erratic: Aladdin meets Alan Ginsberg, she thought. Bright modern 1950s furniture clashed with the Victorian architecture. The place was a mess. But to her, the room felt both warm and alive. Andrea liked the feel of Keith's energy here.

Several red Persian rugs were scattered over the hardwood floors like a Mid-Eastern bazaar. A huge clay pot with a potted palm stood in one corner of the room. Small Grecian urns, African ebony statutes, Mexican pottery, Tibetan singing bowls and ashtrays lined the shelves.

A floor-to-ceiling bookshelf covered one whole wall of the living room. It was overstuffed with books, papers and quartz bookends. Enlarged color photographs hung on the white walls, portraits of native women, children and old men from Central America, Borneo and Nepal. Andrea admired them immediately.

"What fabulous photographs. Who took these?"

"I did. I took the one you're looking at in El Salvador the day the Jesuits were murdered two years ago," Keith said matter-of-factly as he walked into the kitchen. "Want anything to drink?"

The photograph of women wailing in the church square momentarily pained and distracted her. "No, thanks," she said, composing herself. She noticed a pile of camera equipment by the sofa. "What were you doing there?"

"When I was young and stupid, I did a free-lance job covering the FMLA rebels in El Salvador. Nearly got myself killed by the junta."

"That must have been scary."

"Deeply scary. I'll tell you about it sometime."

Andrea looked around the apartment. Despite the mess, and perhaps because of the eastern artifacts, she felt unusually at home. The place was truly a disaster: empty Anchor steam beer bottles stood on the tables; socks, shirts and underwear were tossed in a pile; the ash trays were full; piles of newspapers and books were stacked everywhere. He used one pile of books as a doorstop to the bedroom. One brightly colored Gauguin poster of a naked Tahitian woman bearing papayas hung crookedly on the wall; a baseball glove lay on the floor in the corner by the potted palm.

"It looks like someone trashed your place, too!" Andrea said.

"It always looks like this," Keith came back into the room with a bottle of Calistoga water.

She cringed, "Can't you keep a window open or something?"

"No, because of burglars. Drugs in the Park."

"Why don't you move?"

"I would if I could. Can't afford it yet. I have a state of the art computer all set up with a modem and a laser CD/DVD system. Not to mention my cameras and telescope." He sheepishly picked up his clothes with one arm and tossed the pile into a side closet.

"Hungry?" she asked him. "How would you like some soup?"

"Sure! There are a few cans in the cupboard. Excuse me while I get out of these stinking clothes." He clutched a change of clothes to his chest and padded barefoot into the bathroom.

After moving some darkroom equipment away from the kitchen counter, Andrea found some bread and cheese, a can of clam chowder, and a saucepan. She put the soup in the pan and switched on the stove.

While he was dressing, she snooped around his apartment and scanned his bookcases. Keith had an exquisite antique chess set made of jade and onyx set up on his coffee table, with the pieces still in play. He probably plays both sides by himself, she mused.

Over his computer and printer, he had two dozen writing and reference books. There was a large collection of rare leather-bound books, many dating from the 17th and 18th centuries. There were plenty of modern novels and mysteries, good ones, plus computer books, travel books and maps, and reference books in Russian, French, and Spanish. He had many history, journalism and political science books, but more surprisingly, also some psychology and philosophy books: Joseph Campbell, Jung, Suzuki, Sartre, Camus, Marx (both Karl and Groucho), Hegel and Thoreau. Lots of Thoreau, all fourteen volumes of his journals. At least he's well read. A smart man.

"I didn't know you liked Thoreau," she called from the living room, thumbing through one of the journals. He said something inaudible from the bedroom. She had a passion for Thoreau. His work evoked such a sense of place that it made her nostalgic for New England and her childhood. Now she appreciated him as much for being a brilliant writer as well as a mystic.

When the soup had heated, she deftly made grilled cheese sandwiches, and then set them on the dining room table. "Lunch," she announced. Keith stepped out, looking more comfortable, wearing a green corduroy shirt and a worn pair of blue jeans.

"This isn't much," she said, "but it's all I could find."

"Smells great." He sat down gingerly at the table. "I'm starving." He took a bite out of his cheese sandwich and said, "So where do you want to begin?"

Flustered, Andrea answered, "You mean with the case?"

Keith winked at her. "Of course."

"It will take me a while to find this Durant guy. I have a few contacts with the Orthodox Churches. I'll begin with them."

"Wish I could join you. It's too bad you have to deal with Russians in the process."

"What do you mean?" Andrea asked defensively. "Are you a conservative or something?"

"No, I am a Chicagoan. I grew up with Russians in my neighborhood. Russians are brute barbarians," he grinned. "And that's their good side."

Andrea chuckled. "Yes, we can be that way." She regretted agreeing with him, deeply aware of the shadow side of Russians. "Most of the time, I feel more American than Russian, but I can't help being fascinated by them. Real Russians live life with such passion! Such color. You've only got to listen to their music to feel it. Americans are like Melba Toast by comparison."

"So, you're Russian?" He looked at her cannily and not without intense interest. "Silent waters run deep."

He leaned over to kiss her but she evaded the maneuver and said, "You have to get to know us." She tweaked his nose and rose from the table. "I better be going," she said quietly and collected her purse.

"Call me and let me know what happens," He stood up and ushered her to the door. They stopped at the threshold. "Sorry for being so pushy the last few days. I couldn't help myself. You've been really sweet."

"I take that as a compliment." She smiled and kissed him on the cheek. "Take care of yourself."

He rubbed his cheek softly, "So there's some hope?"

She grinned. "Don't hold your breath. I gotta go." She opened his door to leave.

"Thanks for the lift," he said. "Let me know what else you find out. I'll call you."

"I'm sure you will," she said. "The press never sleeps."

"In case you haven't heard, neither do hospital patients. The first thing I'm going to do is take a long nap," With that, he shut the door after her.

As she stepped buoyantly down to her car, Andrea was surprised to catch herself humming again. She didn't know she was being watched.

6

Andrea's mind was racing as she put her car into gear and pulled away from the curb. She ached for sex. It had been too long. But in these days of AIDS, one could never be too cautious. Besides, all this was happening too fast. Much too fast. It wasn't like her college days, when she could jump into the sack with anyone she wanted any-time—not that she ever did much of that. My love life has always been hopeless! She moaned. I always pick the wrong men. Yet, she remained hopeful and stayed on the pill.

She was too bookish to date in high school. At Stanford, Michael Beech had been her first experience of sex, such as it was. Later when she was twenty-six, starting graduate school at Christ Church, Oxford, studying theology, she met Gareth Williams, while they were both on retreat at a Franciscan monastery. The young bearded Welshman, who once was an Anglican monk, had swept her off her feet.

There was something about his passionate Celtic nature and his love of creation, which spoke to her. She fell in love with Gareth the moment she saw him in the monastery barnyard holding a newborn lamb in his arms and feeding it with a baby bottle. She introduced herself. They talked and kept talking intensely for the next three days straight, even missing Compline each night.

Within eight months they were married, living in a cold-water flat in Oxford barely surviving on fellowship grants and income from various non-profit social service jobs. Their marriage was doomed from the start: the Welsh vs. Russian/American cultural differences and the financial strain eroded their alliance. When they argued, they were like two steam engines colliding at full speed.

At last, his old vocation kept nagging at him, until Gareth left her eight years ago to return to the monastery. She understood, but felt more devastated than if he had slept with another woman. Who can compete with God? It was humiliating.

She stepped on the gas and headed for Van Ness Avenue and the offices of the Orthodox Church in America, at Trinity Cathedral on Green Street. She had called earlier and made an appointment to meet with Father Dmitri Stokovich, the resident priest, to talk with him about the Icon of Kazan.

Andrea had decided to begin her hunt here, rather than at the Holy Virgin Cathedral because she knew that the OCA clergy would speak good English and because they knew her mother.

She also knew a thinly-veiled rivalry existed between the different Russian Orthodox Churches in the city and that it would be difficult to find any consensus of opinion regarding the recent history of the Icon of Kazan—or anything else, for that matter. To non-church people, the differences between the sects often seemed minuscule and irrelevant. But Andrea, who had a passion for Russian history, knew these differences were born in blood.

One of the things, which had always fascinated Andrea, was the Russian Underground Church because her Aunt Nadya had been a member. As Nadya retold the history, she soon learned just how devout and divisive church politics could be. They loved hard and they hated hard.

Most astonishingly, she found, the roots of that underground history started right here in San Francisco. At first, there was only one Orthodox Church, which was the congregation of the Orthodox Church in America (often called the OCA), on Green Street, which she intended to visit today. They regarded themselves as the true heirs of the Russian Orthodox Church in the West.

Seeking to evangelize the New World, Tsar Alexander II sent missionaries east to establish Russian Orthodox Churches, which flourished in Alaska, Canada and Northern California until the Russian Revolution in 1917. Things changed when the Orthodox Bishop of San Francisco, Bishop Basil Bellavin Tikhon, a small man with a pointed beard, was elected Metropolitan of Moscow in 1907 and sailed back to Russia.

In 1918, he was elected Patriarch—the Orthodox equivalent to the Pope—of the whole Church in Russia. During this time, a group of priests, who called themselves the "Living Church," aided by Soviet police, illegally seized the Patriarchate headquarters. Patriarch Tikhon was placed under house arrest and in 1923, after two humiliating trials, Bishops from the new "Living Church," defrocked him in a public trial, reducing him to the status of a layman. Andrea remembered Nadya saying bitterly, "In 1925, the GPU starved Tikhon to death at the Botkin Hospital in Moscow. They exterminated him like a common rat."

Then came the Great Terror: Stalin's brutal persecution of the church in Russia. By 1938, only 4 of the 138 Orthodox Bishops had survived, but thousands of priests, monks, nuns, and untold millions of lay believers, perished in the Gulags. Afterwards, throughout all of Russia, only 4,225 out of 30,000 churches remained standing. Members of the Church like Nadya, who somehow managed to survive the purges, were henceforth disenfranchised as "enemies of the people," and so the Underground Church was born.

Ever since, the Underground Russian Church has regarded Patriarch Tikhon as its patron saint. Just think, Andrea mused with pride, he started right here in San Francisco.

Two of the Orthodox Churches in San Francisco were spin-offs from these events. The first, the Holy Virgin Cathedral, where Michael was murdered, was built by the Russian Orthodox Church in Exile. The second, St. Nicholas Church on 15th Street, was formed as a mission of the Orthodox remnant that stayed in power after the 1917 Revolution. Her mother, Marina, dismissed them as Soviet collaborators. Neither of these churches recognized the apostolic validity of the other and rarely spoke with each other.

Trying to get them to come to any agreement about the icon must have been impossible, Andrea thought. She knew it would be equally impossible for the police to get any information from them now, especially since Michael had been killed in the Cathedral. Whenever the state stepped in, old Russians shut up like clams, but she was half-Russian and had nothing to do with the state. Perhaps she had a chance of discovering something about Michael's death. The prospect of this possibility sent a bolt of electricity through her body.

She found a place to park two blocks away from Green Street and walked to the corner where the small, white, bright blue-domed OCA Cathedral stood. She remembered, once again, her first visit there as a child, the time she almost fainted. She stopped for a moment outside and gazed at the huge icon of the Face of Christ posted on the front of the church. His eyes gazed back at her from a sea of green serenity. She went to the side door and rang the bell.

Expecting to see Father Dmitri, Andrea was startled when Luba, the old, short, red-faced parish secretary—an old friend of her mother's—answered the door.

Luba's body almost filled the open doorway. She stretched out her sweaty round arms and shouted, "Andreochka!"

She grabbed Andrea in a great bear hug and kissed her twice on the cheeks enthusiastically, then stepped back and wagged her finger at her. "You have been away too long and you've come back to make your confession to the priest, no?"

"Yes, I've come to see Father Dmitri, but not about that. Is he in?"

"He's not here now," Luba said escorting her down a long, narrow, musty corridor. "He's gone to the hospital to be with Marie Chelnokoff. She is really dying, finally."

Andrea giggled to herself when she remembered seeing Luba for the first time at age six. "Mama," she had asked, "Why does that lady over there have such a big mustache?" "Hush," Marina had scolded her and smiled at Luba when she turned towards them in the crowd. Andrea spent years praying Luba had never heard her because Luba's temper was notorious.

Luba led her now into the cramped parish offices where she worked. She offered Andrea a wooden chair and then sat heavily behind her own faded wooden desk. A large wooden Orthodox cross dominated one wall, while in the upper eastern corner of the room an icon of Mary was set below some peeling pea-green plaster. On the desk, an old Remington typewriter sailed like a barge in an ocean of papers and used stencils.

In short, the room hadn't changed in thirty years and was as chaotic as ever. Andrea knew it was Luba's way of maintaining control of the parish and of Father Dmitri, who couldn't administrate himself out of an egg carton.

"I'm sorry I missed Father Dmitri," Andrea said, noticing the stacks of holy cards, black-knotted prayer cords and devotional manuals scattered on the shelves. "I thought he could help me with some important questions about the murder in the cathedral last week." She was sure the whole Russian community had heard about it by now.

Luba shook her head, raising her eyes towards the blistered ceiling and crossed herself. "Such blasphemy!"

"Maybe you can help?" Andrea suggested. "I need to know who killed my friend Michael. He believed that fraud was involved when the Icon of Kazan was originally sold. Now it's gone."

Luba eyebrows shot up. "He was your friend?" She sighed wearily. "It's tragic, tragic," she said, waving her puffy hand. "The Holy Mother will not be pleased."

Andrea wasn't sure if Luba was more upset about the stolen icon or Michael's death. She sat on the edge of her chair and related her findings excitedly. "Luba, I think I've got some clues! I've discovered that the Orthodox Churches here wanted to buy the Icon of Kazan in 1963. Do you know anything about that? Or who the original owners were?"

"My memory is bad, very bad. I heard this from old Archbishop John. He said icon was moved to the great Kazan Cathedral in St. Petersburg in 1721 and stayed there until June 29, 1904, when it, along with all the treasures of the cathedral, were stolen. They caught two thieves, but where the icon went, no one knows. It was big scandal in Russia. Big scandal. They say this icon was smuggled out of Russia after Patriarch Tikhon was arrested. You know about Tikhon?"

Andrea nodded.

"Yet another Kazan icon was also at the Kazan Cathedral in Moscow," Luba continued.

Andrea interrupted her, "You mean another copy?"

"To be sure," Luba nodded. "Metropolitan Theodosius was Tikhon's Chancellor during the Revolution. He knew all about the church money and the treasures."

"What happened to him?"

"He was young priest in San Francisco, but left his family to go serve in Russian army as chaplain during World War I. He was caught in Moscow after Revolution but they let him go. He secretly helped the Patriarch until Tikhon was arrested. In 1922, he escaped Russia and came back here to his family. Some think he knew what happened to Kazan Icon. But he was eaten up by ambition. I think he disowned his family so he could become Bishop."

At this, Andrea shook her head with disapproval, for she knew that only unmarried clergy could become Bishops in the Orthodox Church. "Would his family know about the icon?"

Luba shook her head, "Nyet. His children turned against him. But who could blame them? Such a tragedy! He had two children before the Revolution and two after—twins, a boy and a girl. Then he was elected Metropolitan of all Russian Orthodox Churches in North America in 1934. Him, they didn't have much to do with."

"Do you know who they are? Where are they?"

"His wife died in maybe 1920. Heartbreak, I'm sure. The first two children have already died. I don't know where the other two are. One twin went into the army. The girl had big ideas; she married a Russian from the old royal family. More than that I do not know. Check with army, if they let you."

"Why wouldn't they?"

"He did top secret work during the Second War. A U.S. spy."

"It sounds like he might know something about the icon." Andrea jotted down a few quick notes.

"Maybe," Luba said. "We never heard where the icon went until after the war, when suddenly it shows up in London at Christie's in 1945. Do you know that when Elsa Tripp's uncle saw it there, she said it cured his arthritis? That's when some rich English lady bought it for lots of money. I don't know how it came to Christie's."

Luba stopped and blew her nose loudly. "Please excuse. I have a cold."

"So sorry," Andrea commiserated, praying she wouldn't catch it. "Do you happen to know who she was?"

The old woman coughed and stuffed the worn handkerchief up the sleeve of her navy blue dress, then continued, "The English lady? No, she worked through middlemen. We never learned her name. Then in 1963, she wanted to sell it for over $500,000. Why? I don't know. Our Archbishop wanted to start a fund drive with the other

Russian churches to buy it and then build a special shrine for it here in San Francisco, but he could not raise the money."

Andrea knew the old in-fighting had a lot to do with it. "Who do you think stole the icon?"

"I don't know. He is no good person, whoever he is. No common thief would dare steal it. Everybody knows the Kazan Icon! It would be crazy to steal it for the money and then hide it. No, these thieves are thinking of something else. It is bad, very bad. I feel it in my bones."

"Who was her appraiser?" Andrea asked, testing her to see if she knew about Cecil Durant.

"Names I can not remember. You should check with Anna who has the files in Santa Barbara. She might know. I'm afraid I have no more answers. Maybe you should talk with Father Mench?"

Andrea stood up and kissed Luba on the cheek. "Of course! I intend to. You've been a great help! I'll come back to see you and Father Dmitri again."

Luba took one of the Holy cards from the stack by the windowsill. "Perhaps you should have picture of the Holy Virgin?" She handed Andrea a small six-inch copy of the Icon of Kazan: the gold, jewel-studded riza with the faces of the Virgin Mary and the infant Jesus peering through strings of pearls. Andrea looked at it and noted the prayer for protection on the back. She accepted it gratefully, "Thank you. I will treasure this."

"Good luck. Our prayers go with you." Luba waved good-bye to Andrea as she left the church. "Tell Marina we need help with the bazaar at Christmas."

"I will. God bless." She blew a kiss to her and then left the building.

7

Andrea called Keith as soon as she returned home. "How's the shoulder?" she teased. "Ready for a quick game of racket ball?"

"Very funny. Any news? I was just thinking about you."

Andrea flushed but quickly refocused. "Nothing except that the woman who used to own the icon bought it through Christie's of London." She recounted all the details Luba had told her. "I think this Durant is the key. Know how to find him?"

"I don't know, maybe through some art association. What about Father Mench?"

"I hope to see Father Mench as soon as I can," Andrea said, walking with her cordless phone to a comfortable corner of her sofa. "I'll phone him tomorrow. Since you're lying around like a couch potato, why don't you make yourself useful? Can you find out if Durant ever had any dealings with Christie's in London?" Gwyneth sprang onto Andrea's lap and began to knead her thigh with her claws. Andrea frowned, gently moved her paws and stroked her soft fur.

"How am I going to do that?"

"You're the professional sleuth around here. Don't they teach you how to do research in journalism school? Maybe Michael knew him. Why don't you look on his old Rolodex? I could phone his secretary for you."

"I bet the police have the Rolodex," Keith said gloomily. "Besides, we don't even know if Durant's name is in it."

"Please, just find him. I'll call you tomorrow."

8

Alex Menshikov switched off the listening device, and jotted down the name. He rose, turned out the light in the study and then left.

CHAPTER 9

❧

"It is not in vain that Sartre has said, 'Hell is other people.' But while we exclude the other we imprison ourselves also in irremediable loneliness so that in the end the same French writer could say, 'Hell is ourselves.'"

Metropolitan Anthony Bloom
Meditations: A Spiritual Journey

Wednesday, October 31, 1990

Mrs. Saxon-Briggs hadn't meant to eavesdrop on their conversation. She had been feeling queasy all morning and thought it better to have lunch in her bedroom, listening to her favorite news show on the radio. She was on her way to the kitchen to tell the cook to make up a light lunch of tea and eggs, thrusting the steel walker in front of her until she caught up with it, when she passed by the living room and overheard them.

She had that odd ability, as many partially deaf people do, to hear selectively. She was not nearly as deaf as many supposed, meaning that she was often unable to take in voices which sounded in particular ranges, but whenever the subject of a conversation was about herself or things she was vitally interested in, it was remarkable how much her hearing improved.

Cecil's voice was the loudest of all. "What do you mean she called her lawyer?" This stopped Hannah up short in her tracks.

Priscilla's voice was calm and coldly rational. "Hush, Cecil. Just what I said. She put a call in to Chase this morning."

"Whatever for?" the Countess hissed. "Doesn't that old witch have enough to do around here?"

"If I knew why, I'd tell you," Priscilla said indignantly. "I wish she'd have gone through me first," she sighed. "She always gets things hopelessly muddled."

"You don't think she's changing her will?" Cecil's voice betrayed a note of fear. "Not after all we've done for her. We had an agreement."

"Yes, Cecil dear," the Countess answered, "but maybe she's going a bit gaga. Some people do at her age, you know."

"No, she had her reasons, I'm sure of it," Priscilla said.

The Countess asked, "What are we going to do?"

"Call Chase, of course," Priscilla said briskly. "We need the facts first, then we decide."

Hannah Saxon-Briggs bristled at this and had a mind to storm into the room to give them a tongue-lashing, but her curiosity got the better of her. She thought conversations overheard about oneself was the next best thing to reading someone's mail, and she wanted to hear more, no matter how painful it might be.

A kaleidoscope of emotions whirled within her as she listened. Mostly she felt a wave of indignation. "Old witch?" The Countess was the one born gaga. "Muddled." Indeed! She had more common sense than all of them put together. How could Priscilla, of all people, say that? She'd show them who was muddled... Yes, indeed, she had phoned her lawyer, but not for the reasons they supposed— which made her think about calling him again.

How different things were before her husband Edward died. She ran this house like a ship then. Edward Stanton, banker, wealthy financier, all-around social gadfly, addicted golfer and collector, had been her husband for thirty-two years, on paper at least. It was a marriage of convenience, arranged by her adopted father, Robert Saxon-Briggs, more for his convenience than hers, she'd later realized. Nevertheless, she forgave her father this bit of patronal domination and still adored him.

Oh, what magnificent travels she and her father had exploring the Yucatan and the Amazon together! But things changed after the Crystal Skull was found in 1927 on her father's first expedition in the Yucatan jungle. He had gone searching for the great lost Mayan temple city called Lubaantun, "the City of Fallen Stones," and found it.

By then, he had begun to dabble in the occult. After her initial skepticism was overcome by a few remarkable coincidences, which led them to Lubaantun, the lure of his enthusiasm for the supernatural seduced her, too.

Somewhere along the line, he had stumbled upon Cecil Durant, then a young archeologist, and discovered similar interests. The Countess, who seemed to have some strange connection to Cecil, was referred to the Saxon-Briggses through a fellow disciple of the Georgian mystic, George Gurdjieff.

Edward, of course, never had anything to do with either the supernatural or running the house. He was much too busy at the bank or at the golf course to worry about the day-to-day details of domestic maintenance: whether the cook had ordered the best tenderloin or the maid polished the silver without stealing it. He handled the business side of things—trusts, futures and mutual funds—helped by Priscilla, who started with them fresh out of secretarial school. By the time she discovered that Priscilla and Edward once had an affair (although he was forty years her senior) he was already dead and Priscilla had become so indispensable to her that she didn't care anymore. When Hannah's husband died, she took back her maiden name: Saxon-Briggs.

Yet, as she listened to their conversation, she also felt a vague sense of uneasiness, which someone who was more self-aware than she, might have characterized as a touch of fear. This was caused more by the tone of their voices than anything they said in particular. Except for a decidedly superstitious quirk, she was a practical, nononsense woman bred to dismiss such unpleasant intuitions out of her consciousness, which she did immediately.

She hobbled into the kitchen and ordered her lunch, then took her in-house elevator up to her bedroom to rest a while. She had nodded off listening to the noonday recap of the BBC on National Public Radio when she was awakened by her two Pekinese dogs barking as the Countess breezed into the room carrying a tray.

"Hannah, here's your lunch," she said. "Feeling poorly?"

"It's nothing." Hannah sat up with difficulty as the Countess placed the tray on her lap. "Please have Priscilla bring up the afternoon paper when it comes."

Not used to being ordered about, the Countess stiffened. "I'll tell her," she said and quickly left.

Hannah sipped her tea and made sure the Countess was long gone before she picked up the phone by her bedside and dialed her lawyer's office. She dimly heard the secretary say: "Leach, Straphe, Levy and Chase" when she felt suddenly faint. The four corners of her room spun upside down and she collapsed back onto her chaise-lounge as the phone receiver bounced off the table and dangled in the air.

2

It was noon. Chow time, Keith thought. He had just spent the morning searching for Durant's name at the De Young Museum and the San Francisco Library, but with no luck. Keith's pager hummed at his hip. He looked at the number and saw it was from his city editor, Jeff Bernstein, and went to find the nearest phone. When he dialed the *Examiner* office, Bernstein's line was busy, so he spoke with Tom, the crusty veteran copy editor, instead.

"Carlton? It's been ages. I heard you were going on Worker's Comp," he roared. He spoke with a deep voice that resonated up from the bottom of his lean six-foot-four frame.

"Don't you wish," Keith bantered. "Tell Bernstein I'm following up on some leads about the murder in the Russian Cathedral. I got nothing better to do. I'll call in my copy later this afternoon."

"You better get it in fast. Herr Himmler was ready to give the story to Manning because he hadn't heard from you."

"He can't do that!"

"He almost did."

"Tell him this is my story!"

"Since when did they make you City Editor?"

"Please, just tell him. I'll try to get a hold of him later." Keith slammed down the receiver, "Dirty bastard."

Keith grabbed lunch at a crowded diner on Hyde Street, the best greasy spoon in the city. It was only a block from the main Library and many city workers, politicos, labor hacks and newsmen ate there regularly and were all equally abused by the Greeks who ran the place. It was a good insider's place to hang out.

While waiting in line for a seat, he decided to use the restaurant's phone. He pulled out the list of Russian names he had gotten at the De Young museum. Andrea had called ahead for him and arranged a meeting with Michael's secretary with the promise that the *Examiner* wouldn't put the museum in a bad light. He had just spent the morning in Michael's office searching his database and Rolodex for Durant's name, but came up empty-handed. He did find, however, a few promising Russian names and decided to follow up on these.

He tried Alexander Savodnik's number first, but there was no answer. The second name on the list was a Vera Markevitch from the Richmond District; she ran an antique store and specialized in the sale of Russian heirlooms. He dialed the number. The phone clicked on the other end and an older woman's voice with a thick Slavic accent answered, "Yez."

"Hello, I'm in the market for some icons and I wonder if you have any for sale?"

"No, I don't have any," she sounded bored.

"Do you know any icon dealers in the Bay Area? I mean ones that deal with expensive icons?"

"Sure, there are some down Peninsula."

"How about appraisers?"

"They are there, too. Why you want to know?" she asked suspiciously.

"I'm doing some research for a friend of yours, Michael Beech," he said. There was silence on the other end of the line. "Dawn, his secretary, gave me your name." The line clicked off suddenly in his ear.

Keith looked at the receiver in his hand, "Boy, these people are paranoid." He thought he'd check the San Mateo Yellow Pages.

He deposited another quarter in the pay phone and dialed his boss. "This is Carlton. I hear you're trying to reassign the Beech story to Manning. With all due respect, you can't do that."

"The hell I can't. Where have you been anyway?" Bernstein demanded.

"Hanging out with Nurse Ratchett. Look, I've got some hot leads on this case. Manning will only bungle it."

"Well, at least he'd send us some copy."

"I'll have some copy for you this afternoon. This Beech murder case might be hotter than we thought. I need to keep at it for a while."

"OK. Just don't forget you got other stories out there. And we print this newspaper every day, if you get my drift. No excuses this time, or Manning's got it for sure. "

"I'll call you."

"It better be good. I'll give you a few more days," Bernstein said, then he hung up.

As Keith slid into a vacant seat at the counter, he wondered how he was going to get Andrea to type and e-mail his copy, when he remembered his promise to hold off printing the story.

He realized he had just painted himself into a corner and didn't know which way to turn. But there was nothing he could do about it now. He ate a cheeseburger and quickly scanned the sports section, before gulping his coffee on his way out of the Coffee Shop. He never noticed the large white-haired man in a brown leather jacket standing by the corner. Keith walked past Hastings School of Law and hopped onto the Hyde Street bus going downtown. A few moments later, Alex hailed a cab and followed him.

3

Andrea parked her car outside the Eastern Rite Our Lady of Kazan Catholic Church in the San Francisco Richmond District and glanced at her watch. "Damn, I'm late!" Never liking to keep people waiting, she rushed out of her car and walked briskly up to what she thought would be the church. Instead, she was confronted with a three-story brick house. The front porch of this brick and stucco house had been converted into a small narthex, complete with a small blue cupola over the entrance.

A weathered sign on the side of the building said in English and Russian: Our Lady of Kazan Eastern Rite Catholic Church, Father Karl Mench, Priest. Divine Liturgy: 10 a.m. Sundays, 6 p.m. Wednesdays and Fridays. Confessions by appointment only.

She rang the front doorbell and, after what seemed a long time, heard the sound of approaching feet. A gaunt, medium-sized priest in his late 60s, with salt and pepper hair, wearing black clericals and a Roman collar, greeted her at the door.

Andrea was immediately impressed by how skinny Father Mench was. His cheekbones protruded profoundly and his face was pale, with a faintly yellowish pallor. He blue eyes could have cut cloth. She wondered if he was ill or if he had been fasting.

The priest offered his hand, "Good afternoon, I am Father Mench, but you can call me Father Karl, if you like. How shall I call you, Miss West?" His eyes danced kindly. She noticed he spoke with a curious Slavic accent, which she knew wasn't Russian.

When Andrea shook his hand, she noticed it felt quite cool and clammy. She had begun to think that perhaps he was unwell. "Please, call me Andrea. Sorry I called on such short notice. Perhaps I should come another time."

He dismissed her statement of concern with a wave of the hand as if it was a bothersome fly. "It's nothing. Please come in," he said, leading her through the front hall. He stopped just before his study. "Would you like to see the chapel?" he asked, almost as a kind of test.

"Yes, please," Andrea said. This seemed to satisfy him. He led her down the long hall, past the parlor, into a living room, which had been transformed into a chapel.

The dark room seemed dingy in the late October afternoon light. There were no pews, but a large red Persian rug lay in the middle of the worship space. The only light was from the flickering amber votive lights standing sentinel to the icons hanging on the walls.

She could dimly see at the far end of the room a portable iconostasis screen, a hanging red votive lamp above the altar, icons and statues of the Virgin Mary in three places. A wooden baptismal font was placed to the side in one corner. The place looked shabby compared to the majestic grandeur of the Orthodox Cathedral on Geary Boulevard.

They paused in silence for a moment at the back of the chapel, then he entered, genuflected and crossed himself, as she did the same. "You see, this chapel is dedicated to Our Lady of Kazan," he said proudly. Then he was silent again, with an unusual stillness. She wondered if he was praying. She prayed a silent prayer to Mary that this interview would lead to something. A clue, anything.

After a few minutes, he led her into his small, cluttered study. He gestured to the best seat in the room and invited her to sit down as he bent slowly into the wooden chair opposite her.

"So, how can I help you?" He sat back and rested his ascetic hands in his lap.

His kind face immediately put Andrea at ease, so that she spoke with more candor than she expected to. "I was a friend of Michael Beech," she began seriously. "He was murdered last week at the Russian Cathedral."

He shook his head sadly, "Ya, I remember him. It was sad, very sad."

Andrea leaned forward. "He often spoke of you. I know that he was doing some work on the Icon of Kazan when he was murdered. I wonder if you might know something about the icon." She paused, unsure of how open he would be with her.

"You know the story about the icon, how it was originally found?" Father Mench looked her straight in the eye.

"A little. Tell me more," she said.

"It was during the reign of Ivan the Terrible in 1579. Kazan is on the east bank of the Volga River and it was several times sacked by the Tartars and burned down. It was always restored, but again burned down. There was a soldier whose house burned down. He was planning to build a new house near his burned one when his eight-year-old blind daughter, named Matrona, heard the Blessed Virgin tell her to go dig and she would find an icon. The girl went and dug, then found an icon, wrapped in scarlet rags. Instantly, she regained her sight. Soon, there were more miracles: blind people got their sight, the lame walked. Then the Archbishop of Kazan had it enshrined."

Father Mench pulled on his ear, interrupting his own monologue, "That Archbishop was some smart man," he grinned, then continued. "In 1612, the Polish army invaded. Then they called the icon to Moscow. Through Her, the Russian troops—only one battalion—threw the Poles out of the country. In 1812, during the time of

Napoleon, General Kutusov, he got the icon and took it under his coat and said to the army, 'This is the Liberatrix and Defendrix of all Russia'".

"Wasn't Napoleon driven out of Russia because it snowed early that year?" Andrea asked.

"Ya, ya!" he said excitedly. "They prayed to Our Lady and she drove the French out."

"It's interesting that God used non-violent methods..." Andrea mused aloud. "Do you know who owned the Kazan Icon before the Holy Virgin Society?"

He leaned back and closed his eyes. "It was owned by a rich lady with a funny English name. In a minute, I will think of it. I never met her. She worked through a middleman, a Mr. Cecil Durant. You know him?"

Andrea shook her head, "No, but I've heard of him. Wasn't he an antiquities dealer or something?"

"Ya, that is it," he smiled. "First he was a Canadian archeologist, who later got into the art business. He said he was old friends with this rich English lady. Everything was done through him."

"When you said 'everything was done,' what do you mean, 'everything'?" she asked.

"Well, I was the one who got the Holy Virgin Society to buy this holy icon." He stood up and pointed at a frame hanging on his study wall. It was an 11 by 17 inch document, written in bold and rather crude calligraphy commemorating and witnessing the sale of the Icon of Kazan to the Holy Virgin Society.

It read: Be it known that on Sunday, May 24, 1970 at the Catholic Russian Center of Our Lady of Kazan in San Francisco, the miraculous icon of Our Lady of Kazan was returned to religious devotion under the custody of the Holy Virgin Institute after 52 years of private ownership." It was signed by Mrs. Bryce Parker, (Holy Virgin Society Representative); Fr. Karl Mench (Chaplain, Holy Virgin Society/Catholic Russian Center); Cecil and Edith Durant, Ms. Priscilla Thorpe, administrative assistant, plus 40 signatures of people acting as witnesses. At the bottom, a red wax seal and ribbon were attached to it.

Andrea hurriedly copied the information down in her notebook. "This is impressive," she said.

"Ya, it is," he said. He painfully sank back onto his wooden chair. Andrea showed her concern but he brushed it aside.

"You don't mind if I take notes, do you?" she asked.

"No, please. If it will help to find the Holy icon."

"How did you come in contact with Mr. Durant?"

"He contacted me. See, he had the right idea from the first. He wanted the icon to be sold to a church not, not," he stammered, "not to be in a private home."

"Where was the icon then?"

"He had it."

"He had it?" Andrea's eyebrows rose.

"Yes, in custody for the rich lady. As I said, she didn't want to deal with business."

"When did he first contact you? Do you remember? Was this before the New York World's Fair?"

"No, after. This was, I would guess 1967 or '68. He tried to go to the other Orthodox Churches before but it was no good."

"When was this? What happened?"

"Around 1964 and the World's Fair. The natural thing was for the Orthodox Churches here to buy it. At first, Archbishop John had the idea for the World's Fair to build a replica of the Fortress Cathedral from Moscow right here in San Francisco and to keep the Holy Icon there as a shrine. But raising the funds was necessary," he paused and wiped his nose with a cloth handkerchief and continued.

"He opened a bank account for the icon only, but sad to mention, while it was there not one cent was paid into the account. Not even one cent of dollars!"

"I was in New York," he continued. "Several times I went to the Orthodox Pavilion where the icon was. They made a copy of the wooden Orthodox chapel still in Fort Ross, California, built when the Tsar was claiming part of the West Coast for Russia. The Icon of Kazan was the main attraction. The last time I was there, I saw one wall of the chapel stuffed with boxes to the ceiling." Father Mench spread his arms to show how high. "Archbishop John explained to me, 'they are all candles'. He had launched an appeal to the people that he would burn candles in front of the icon if they wished to pay for them. He told me, 'These are all paid for. Day and night I have to burn candles!' But not one dollar came into the thing."

"Anyway, he concluded the World's Fair with a deficit. I heard they wanted to collect $500,000 to build the shrine to house the icon. So. All what he had gotten, in the end, was only $64,000. And then he had to return some of that money. In the end, I heard the rich lady said, 'I don't want to have anything to do with that man!' She was very angry with him."

"So that's why the Russian Churches in San Francisco didn't buy it," Andrea said. "They tried and failed."

"Yes, and the lady wanted a lot of money for it."

"How much?"

"I don't know. Money I don't mix in. It was quite much. So. The years went by—1969, in January. Mr. Durant, he called me again and said, 'Father, do you remember me?' I said, 'You are the million dollar icon.'" Father Karl laughed spontaneously at this, exposing two rows of thin brown teeth. "He said, 'Yes, I want the icon to go back to the Catholic Church. Maybe you know somebody who would be interested?' I thought, 'Hummmm,' but didn't say a word. I looked at my small congregation, what you see here, it would be impossible. But I didn't want to let him down, so I said, 'I'll see what I can do.' 'Oh, thank you very much, thank you very much, thank you very much!' he said."

"So what did you do?" Andrea was enthralled.

"First, I knew the Roman Catholic Archbishop had finished a successful $15 million fund drive to build a school, an old people's home and St. Mary's Cathedral. I thought, 'Hummmm', maybe there is some money left over. So I called him. He told us to meet him at the Chancery Office on Church Street."

"So, Mr. Durant came, with a shopping bag." Father Karl cackled quietly, "No one would have guessed it contained this special icon. The big Archbishop said, 'So this is the great treasure of the Russian people.' Mr. Durant began to tell him that it dated from the 15th century."

"15th century?" Andrea's mouth dropped open.

"Ya, see, he told us he took the riza off and then he saw that the gesso on the wood was very thick and coarse. This proved the date."

"That's odd, I heard it was dated from the mid-18th century," Andrea used the information she got from Michael to test him.

Father Karl looked disturbed by this new fact. "I don't know. I would like to talk to him about it." He shifted uncomfortably in his chair. "So. The Archbishop said, 'Yes, I am quite willing to accept the great treasure of the Russian people if you bring me a benefactor who will put up the money.' There we were, square one." He sighed.

"Then what?" Andrea turned the page of her notebook and wrote rapidly, recording the convoluted journey of the icon from owner to owner down through history.

"Finally, on the Feast of the Immaculate Conception of the Virgin Mary—for me, a big, big feast day, she got me out of trouble once, maybe she can do it again, I thought—I wrote the Holy Virgin Society in Spain."

"To who?"

"The head of the Holy Virgin Society, Mr. John Hart. They have a magazine with two million subscribers. I thought, they could redeem the icon and honor it. He liked the idea and raised the money. In five years, they paid it off. Very fast."

"Sounds like he knows his business."

"They bought it only on two conditions, first, that when Russia is free, the Icon of Kazan should be restored to its proper owner: the Russian Orthodox Church in Russia. But only if they first rebuild the Cathedral of Kazan in the Kremlin where it was housed until the Revolution. And second, that all who gave money for the icon be commemorated in a golden book."

"Do you know where Cecil Durant is now?" Andrea asked, fervently hoping he would.

"No," he shook his head, "I don't know where he is."

Finding herself at a dead end, Andrea decided to change the subject. "Father Mench, you have seen the Icon often. I know there are old legends about the Icon of Kazan healing people, but do you believe the Icon of Kazan still has miraculous powers?"

"Ya, ya!" he said, his eyes shining with a soft, transparent joy. "I have seen one myself!"

4

From the start of this conversation, Andrea had decided to suspend all her disbelief and remain as open as possible. "What happened?" she asked.

"It happened when I went to visit the icon at their shrine in Spain in 1970. I had just con-celebrated a liturgy in the Byzantine chapel and was going downstairs to lunch when suddenly, a crowd came out, leading a man, holding him under the arms. He had had a heart attack. So they led him into a bedroom off the corridor there with a nurse and doctor. The doctor looks up and says, "'I am very pessimistic. I don't think he will live to see the morning.'" Father Mench shook his head gravely.

"Now it was 11 o'clock at night," Father Mench continued. "A priest there, Father Hobart, he told me, he thought, 'Maybe I can give a blessing with the icon.' So there was nobody else, just a nurse was there. The sick man was sleeping, and Father Hobart with the icon. He holds the icon," Father Mench held his arms out as if holding the icon horizontally over the body, "and gives a blessing over him. Then he takes the icon up and retires. The next day, the man went up and joined the pilgrimage."

"That's pretty amazing!" Andrea blurted, realizing this was not the time or place to poke holes in his story.

"So. You see this is modern kind of miracle, not just like in old centuries," he laughed loudly. Clearly Father Mench loved to tell stories and loved an attentive audience even more. He looked mischievously at her, "You know the story about Bishop Pike?"

"I live in the Episcopal Diocese of California, how could I not know the story!" Andrea remembered what she had heard about Bishop Pike, who was the controversial Bishop in San Francisco from 1958 until 1966. He was a brilliant liberal theologian who questioned the doctrine of the Trinity. As a result, he was the second Episcopal Bishop ever to be tried for heresy, but later was acquitted.

He was famous for his wit. Andrea remembered a story she once heard about Bishop Pike that happened the day Stalin died. During the regular Communion service, Bishop Pike prayed for Stalin's soul. Afterwards, a self-righteous church lady stormed up and scolded him, "How could you pray for a man like Stalin? Why, he didn't even believe in God!" Pike said without blinking, "He does now." And so does Bishop Pike—Andrea thought.

"You remember how Bishop Pike ended?" Father Mench cocked his head playfully to one side. His words brought Andrea back to the room.

"Yes. He became a little strange at the end. Didn't he hire psychics to contact his dead son after the young man had committed suicide? He always blamed himself for leaving his son in London. And then there were the heresy trials. I think he got very depressed. He and his second wife traveled to the Sinai desert, where he fell off a cliff and died."

"Ya. That was the stupidest thing they could do, to separate. They had a car with five wheels, right? If they had taken that spare wheel and put it on fire, a column of smoke would have gone up and Israeli planes would have seen it immediately. Do you know why that happened to him?"

"No why?" Andrea sat alert intrigued to hear gossip about her own community.

"Mr. Durant had the Icon of Kazan in a vault of the Bank of America downtown. There were times when he was there, when people could come and visit the Icon. About a year before the Bishop Pike died, he and some Russian friends came one day to see it. They went into the private viewing room, then the Bishop sat on a table and..." Father Mench stopped in mid-sentence, making a gesture of inhaling a cigarette, and blew imaginary smoke out of his mouth with a deep exhalation.

"He blew smoke at the Icon of Kazan?" Andrea looked astonished. Andrea remembered how her mother always forbade her father to smoke in any room where an icon was present.

"Ya. Even Mr. Durant was horrified when he saw this."

"No kidding?"

"Ya. He said one of the Russians leaned over to him and whispered, 'That Bishop will be a dead man in six months'. And it was true. It happened. Naturally, the Blessed Virgin doesn't like something like that."

"So you think the Icon can curse as well as bless?"

"Sure, why not?"

Andrea bit her tongue at this and changed the subject. "One Church publication I've seen says the icon appeared sometime in 1917 in London for sale. Do you know anything about that?"

"Well, then, that would point to the Communists after they secured power. They needed fast money to run the government. Everything was in ruins – the cities and farms destroyed—Civil War. How could they finance it? Ahhh, there was the Church. So, they began ransacking the churches for gold and vestments. Mr. Durant told me he knew a very big businessman in Los Angeles who went to Russia in the 1920s."

"Wasn't that Armand Hammer?" Andrea guessed, remembering the well-known travels of that wealthy businessman.

"Maybe," he said. "This man once took Mr. Durant into a room full of church vestments with gold threads, silver, silk and precious stones, everything. 'How did you get them?' he asked. The fellow said, 'I was in Moscow and Leningrad in 1918 and 1919 for some business. In the Kremlin, they had a big hall with long tables where they had heaps of these treasures: icons, chalices, and vestments gathered from all the churches. I asked, 'What are you going to do with them?' They said, 'We burn them down then the metal we gather,' 'How much money do you think you can get out of that?' They mentioned a sum. 'I'll give you double the sum if you give me those vestments.' 'Oh, take them, take them, we don't need all this stuff, we need the money.' So. He bought them."

"Do you think the Icon of Kazan could have been buried among those great treasures?"

"Certainly, it was underneath. In 1918, they sold only for gold and English pounds, nothing else."

"Who bought it?"

"I think maybe a rich South African with gold. Maybe it went from there to an English crown colony. It could have easily gone to England."

"How did this rich lady get the icon?"

"She inherited it. After the Second War another collector bought it from Christie's. He had an adopted daughter, and this was the rich English lady. Her name I can't remember."

Andrea noticed that Father Mench was looking very tired. "Before I go, may I be rude enough to ask you a personal question. Are you originally Russian, Father? Where do you come from?"

He chuckled, "I have been here in the Paradise of the Working Class now since 1974. I grew up in Czechoslovakia and went to seminary there before the War." His face became grave and creased with pain. "Then I was imprisoned in a Soviet concentration camp from 1944 until 1949. That is why my health is so bad."

Andrea rose and extended her hand. "I'm so sorry to take up so much of your time. You've been a great help. Thank you."

"It was my pleasure." He smiled broadly. "Come again." He rose and clasped both her hands in his warmly, then he ushered her to the front door.

He paused at the threshold and said, "There is an Abbot who knows the rich lady. His name is Father Seraphim. Her husband gave them much help. He is Abbot of a monastery in the mountains, north, near Willits. You call him. He will know how to contact her. I write the number for you." Andrea handed him a pen and her note pad to write on. He scrawled the name and number with a shaky hand.

Andrea thanked him again and left the house. Father Mench waved good-bye, "Tell him you met me. Father Seraphim, he is very special."

Andrea almost floated to her car she was so exhilarated. So are you, Father Mench, Andrea thought. So are you. Then she drove away, feeling more alive than she had in years. The chase was everything.

A green Mercedes parked half a block from the church waited a few minutes, then sped after her.

5

When Andrea reached home, she switched on her answering machine. There were two messages from students asking to see her tomorrow after class. The third was from Keith: "Hey, gorgeous, this is Keith. I have a few questions. Call me." She phoned him immediately. "So, what did you dig up?" Andrea lounged comfortably on the sofa in jeans and a warm sweater.

"My shoulder's fine, thanks... Nothing specific. I called one of Michael's connections, a Mrs. Markevitch but she hung up on me," he said.

"Scared," Andrea said flatly.

"How'd you guess?"

"Because I know her," she said. "She's Vera Markevitch, my godmother, but I haven't seen her in years. She runs an antique business in the Avenues. I forgot Michael knew her. He knew everybody. Lots of older Russians don't trust prying strangers."

"Think maybe you should follow up on old Vera, since she's so jumpy?"

"I think I could arrange something," Andrea twisted the phone cord around her index finger. "I had a good long talk with Father Mench, who told me about Cecil Durant and the woman who sold the icon to the Holy Virgin Society. He doesn't know where they are, but he gave me the name of a Father Seraphim who might. I also got lots of background about the icon and the war of 1812. Don't know how useful it will be in the end. It looks like people have been chasing after this icon for the past century."

"Now, why doesn't that surprise me?"

"What did you find out?" Andrea asked.

"You mentioned Christie's in London, so I looked up their references to icons and found some interesting stuff. The articles were written in 1935 and they came from *Art World* and *The Collector*. They're all about this South African millionaire named Solly Joel who loved to collect art. He apparently got the Kazan Icon in Poland in the 20's or early 30's, perhaps sooner, and kept it, I presume. Want to hear?"

"Sure, I love eccentric millionaires. I'm all ears."

"Back in the '30s, Solly Joel was popularly known as the 'King of Diamonds'. Get this, at the time of his death he was one of the two or three richest men in the British Empire, excluding the King. It seems he got his fortune from his uncle, Barnato Isaacs, who spent his early days dancing as a sidewalk clown for pennies in Soho. Old Uncle Barney, starting with only £300 and some boxes of bad cigars, hit upon the raw patch of diamond-stuffed clay, now called Kimberley, early on in the first great South African diamond rush."

"Sounds like winning the Lotto jackpot," Andrea laughed.

"There was more than luck involved," Keith said wryly. "Solly had a brother, Woolf, and a cousin named Jack Joel, who, with Solly, formed the Barnato Brothers Mining Company. Together they built up the business until they eventually re-bought the Kimberley Mines and joined with Cecil Rhodes to form the international Diamond Syndicate.

"But Solly Joel's real chance came after Cecil Rhodes died at age fifty-one."

"Probably from exhaustion," Andrea interrupted.

Keith chuckled, "Uncle Barney, who had become a Park Lane millionaire, fell or jumped from an ocean liner on his way to London in 1897." Keith added, "And if you believe that, I got a bridge to sell you."

"Solly sounds like a real ethical character."

"Wait, there's more." Keith went on, "Solly Joel inherited the lion's share of the business and when his brother Woolf was killed by a blackmailer, another large share went to him."

"Surprise, surprise," Andrea feigned.

"In the end, he controlled the Diamond Syndicate, as well as most of the gold and copper mines in South Africa. He owned huge blocks of real estate, shares of railroads, chain stores and investment trusts. When World War I broke out, he forced his shareholders and the British government to withhold diamonds from the market until prices shot up."

"Kind of like the J.P. Morgan of Britain," Andrea said.

"He was a splashy guy, too. Not puritanical and withered like J.P. Morgan," Keith said. "He had white hair and a beard and was tall, very dapper. When he first came to London, he always wore a bouquet of six full-blown roses. Later in life, his tastes changed and he always wore an orchid instead.

"He lived in huge mansions and gave money away like water. He was so rich that all through the Depression he kept a full stable of stud and racing horses, a big yacht, a town house mansion and a huge country estate at full strength."

"You know, you gotta like the guy," Andrea said. "These days, millionaires buy houses huddled together in real estate developments that look like K-Marts and think they own the world because they have a mansion and two Jaguars!"

Keith answered, "I guess his estate was held in probate for a long time because it wasn't until 1935 that his art collection, including the Icon of Kazan, was put up for auction."

"Do your articles say who bought it?"

"No, unfortunately.

"How did he get the icon?"

"I don't know."

"Well, it's all very fascinating, but where do we go from here?" Andrea asked.

"The main thing is to find Durant. I guess I could contact Christie's while you visit Vera. You stick to the Russians and the churches, since you talk their talk."

"That sounds like a good idea."

"OK, enough about work. When am I going to see you again?"

"Tomorrow's a really busy day for me, but I think I can squeeze you in."

"Mmmm, squeezing sounds good...."

Andrea laughed as she blushed from her neck to her ears, which she was glad Keith couldn't see, "You're hopeless! Don't you ever get serious?"

"Lots of times. I'll show you tomorrow. I'll pick you up at seven for dinner."

6

Alex switched off the listening device and fiddled with a paper clip distractedly as he pondered his four dilemmas.

First, there was something that bothered him about the job at the cathedral. It was too disjointed. It hadn't gone as planned. Then Beech wound up dead. He didn't like it. He didn't trust Cecil and Priscilla and who knew what that old bitch, the Countess, would do.

The second dilemma, of course, was Andrea. And now that this reporter Carlton was sticking his nose in, it made things worse.

Then there were the papers in that safe deposit box. He knew the Major had one key to the deposit box and that Michael Beech had the other, but the Major had refused to tell Michael what the papers said. What he didn't count on was how the Major got a jump on him, and on Keith, the way he did. And what if the police had frozen Beech's assets?

The question was: where was the Major? If only he knew what those papers said. One thing he knew, he had to get to that safe deposit box before the Major did. Feeling restless and hungry, he decided to go out to get something to eat and then head for Boris' Club to think everything over.

7

Tired from a long, intense day of classes, Andrea soaked in a long bubble bath after her conversation with Keith. The hot water in her tub ran so loudly, she didn't hear the phone ring. After twenty minutes, feeling warm and silky, she put on her nightgown and bathrobe and settled in for a nice quiet evening with Gwyneth of music, television, and a microwave dinner.

On her way past the telephone, she noticed the flashing red light and flicked on the switch. An unknown male with a strange deep Russian voice sounded ominously on the tape: "Keep out of this if you know what's good for you. Keep out!" She could hear him slurring some of his syllables. Then the tape clicked off.

She played back the tape again. The same baritone voice repeated the threat. She hastily switched off the machine and realized her body was shaking. She felt completely unnerved. She felt a whirlwind of emotions: sad, curious, adventurous, timid, and now most of all, terrified.

She dialed the phone. "Hi, Mama, it's me." Her voice trembled. She had just wanted to hear her mother's reassuring voice again, but what could she tell her? About this absurd message? About Keith? About their break-in together and his getting hurt? About her confusion? About Michael's connection with Vera?

"Darling, how are you? Are you OK? No more burglars, I hope."

"I just got a bad phone call, Mama. Some man warning me off the case. I'm safe, but emotionally I'm a wreck."

"You're not getting mixed up in this are you?"

"No, Mama. Really."

"I know you, Andrea, you get on one of those salvation kicks and then there's no stopping you. Think of all that time you wasted trying to save Michael."

"Mother!" Andrea protested, "I never tried to save Michael. If anything, he saved me—he kept me from going crazy in college." She fought back her tears. "I know you didn't approve of Michael or like him very much, but he was a dear old friend of mine. And for that alone you should mourn for him."

"Yes, I'm sorry, dear. This must be horrible for you. Have you called the police?"

"Not yet. Have you seen Aunt Vera lately? How is she?"

"I guess she's well. I haven't seen her latley. Why do you ask?"

"Just some dissertation research I'm doing." Andrea hated lying to her mother and she wondered if Marina could tell.

"Do you have a policeman you can talk to about all this?"

"Yes, a Detective Tony Catelano."

"Well, let me know if you hear of anything," Marina said. "When are you coming to dinner?"

"Soon," Andrea inquired after her brother, who rarely wrote anyone letters, before hanging up the phone.

Marina placed the receiver down and turned, "She's asking questions about Vera." She glared at the man sitting opposite her.

CHAPTER 10

∾

"To be blind to the invisible, to be aware only of the tangible world, is to be on the outside of the fullness of knowledge, outside the experience of total reality which is the world in God and God at the heart of the world."

Metropolitan Anthony Bloom
Meditations: A Spiritual Journey

Alex Menshikov watched Marina closely, almost covetously, throughout her phone conversation with Andrea. He sat like a burly bear in her large, overstuffed easy chair clutching a glass of vodka in his round fist and scanning Marina's lavish living room. It was filled with expensive Persian rugs, books, icons, bright expressionist art, golden Russian wooden bowls and purple sequined pillows. This was one of the few places, which reminded him of home. Her artistic eye had really paid off in her interior decorating business. He waited until she hung up the phone.

"Does she know about us?" His eyes narrowed. He sipped his drink slowly as he relished the sight of Marina again. She had put on weight, but he could still see the beauty he first knew in Paris, and later in Westchester County, in the 1950s—dark, musky and exotic as cardamom.

"No, I could never tell her. I tried many times. Sometimes I wish I had." Marina trembled, not from fear, but fury. "Right now I'm glad I didn't," she said. "You bastard! Why have you come? We agreed we wouldn't see each other."

"I'm sorry. But I heard Andrea was mixed up with this murder at the cathedral."

"What do you know about Andrea?"

"I can't say. Marina, this is dangerous stuff. If you know what's good for Andrea, you'll tell her to keep out of it."

"How dangerous?" Marina frowned at him. "How do you know?"

"I just know," he said curtly and shifted his gaze to the 19th century oil painting of a Russian Church. The tall, stark white building, capped with a blue star-clustered dome, stood against a dense green curtain of fir trees. He admired it for a moment, feeling suddenly nostalgic. Was it for his homeland or his youth, or both? He couldn't tell.

He remembered how, during heavy Russian blizzards, the churches, acting like lighthouses, would toll their bells unceasingly to help travelers find their way in the whiteout. He knew he had long since lost his way. He remembered being a boy, dancing and leaping in the new-fallen snow, with goose fat smeared on his face to protect against the cold, and smelling the crisp, woody scent of pine everywhere around him.

And he remembered his first passionate night with Marina, when Sam was away on a winter's business trip. They had tried hard to be good, but neither of them could dampen their desire any longer. He could still feel her hot voluptuous body under his. Better than any drug. And meanwhile, outside, the soft white falling snow muffled sounds all around. It was a memory he wished he hadn't had just then. I'm getting too old for this, he winced inwardly. "Your uncle's painting reminds me of Sverdlovsk before the War."

"Don't change the subject," Marina snapped. "I don't believe you. You always were a liar!"

"Never to you," he said softly.

"That's a lie."

He raised his voice. "Never to you. Who never showed up in New York? Who ran away to California? Who never answered my calls? Who?" He slammed his shot glass down on the table. "And you dare call me a liar?"

Marina raged at him, "Don't you see, you idiot? I had to go. I had two children to raise. If Sam knew about us, the courts would have given Sam custody." Her tears smudged her mascara, painting wet gray lines down her cheeks.

"That's your excuse."

Instantly, Marina shot back, "And what did you do?" Her black almond eyes glared at him. "Nicky and Andrea needed a father, not a black market vagabond who would disappear for months behind the Iron Curtain. God, how you made me sick with worry. Then you'd suddenly show up when you were hungry and your socks needed washing!"

"What else could I do?" He shrugged. He sighed bitterly, "I knew nothing else then." He looked at her red, teary face, "I suppose it's too late now."

"Too late for what?" She laughed bitterly. "Oh, no, you don't," she shook her head. Marina's eyes blazed at him warily. "You're not going to wrap me around your little finger anymore. You can't get away with it now."

Alex stiffened. "I'm getting out of here. It's no use. I thought I'd try one more time, but it's hopeless." He strode to the front door then stopped there. "I was only trying to do you both a favor. If Andrea keeps this up, she's going to get hurt. At least I won't be responsible." He turned to her, "And when that happens, don't blame me!"

"And what makes you think I won't tell the police about you?" She shoved her face close to his.

He grabbed her chin, "You won't. Because the shame would be too much for you." Then he opened the front door and left.

"Get out, get out!" Marina threw a black ashtray at him. It hit the half-opened door with a thud and shattered on the front landing.

2

Thursday, November 1, 1990

Young Dr. Hawthorne took Hannah Saxon-Briggs' pulse for the second time in two days, then gently laid her wrist back onto her bed by her side. He took out his cold stethoscope, slid it under her nightgown and deftly listened to her heart beating in her chest. Then he examined her eyes with a small flashlight, "No sign of numbness?" Hannah shook her head no. "Eating OK?"

"I have no taste for food," Hannah complained. "It's hard to swallow."

Priscilla hovered over the proceedings like a hawk, "We feed her very well, but she doesn't want to eat much."

"That's not too unusual. Older sedentary people don't eat as much as they used to. I can't see anything wrong, but I think you should go in for some tests." He scribbled out some orders on a piece of paper and gave it to Priscilla for safekeeping. "Go in as soon as you can, when you're feeling up to it." He spoke more loudly to Hannah and patted her arm. "Take care of yourself. I'll be checking on you at the end of the week."

He collected his medical bag and turned to Priscilla, "Don't worry, I can see myself out. Call me if there's a big change." Priscilla smiled at the doctor as he left and promised she would. Hannah's two Pekinese dogs scampered frantically after him, their claws clicking on the hardwood floor.

Priscilla stood at the foot of Hannah's bed, "We're lucky he makes house calls. Is there anything I can get you?"

"That's because we pay him to. A double scotch would be nice. I hate all these medical shenanigans—tests, hospitals, pills." Priscilla turned to fetch the drink but Hannah was still in the mood to talk. "Why do you think this is happening to me?"

"What do you mean?" Priscilla stopped and looked intently at her employer.

"I don't seem to be getting any better. I thought the icon was going to heal me."

"Perhaps you, we, have failed the icon in some way. I wonder if she is angry because you ordered us to steal her from the church."

"I was afraid that was the case." Hannah looked away towards the wall. "Then it's hopeless. Maybe I should give her back to the church."

"No!" Priscilla's voice was louder than Hannah wished. "You can't do that. The police would certainly link the robbery to you and we'd all get into trouble."

"I could tell them I got it through an intermediary."

"They wouldn't believe you and you'd have to provide proof of sale. Grand theft is no laughing matter. You wouldn't want to end your days in a federal prison?"

Hannah shuddered at the thought. "Impossible. Chase wouldn't let that happen."

"Lawyers can't do everything. Perhaps we could hold a séance and apologize to Our Lady. I'm sure she could diagnose your mysterious illness. I think she's feeling a little neglected. We need to build her a shrine here in your bedroom."

"Yes, Cecil would be good at that. He's so handy. Have him come up after lunch so we can discuss the details. I think I'll rest now. I've had an exhausting morning. The scotch can come later." Hannah leaned back in bed and wearily closed her eyes.

3

The mail at seminary usually arrived by late morning, after the ten o'clock classes. As Andrea ambled downstairs to pick up her mail, two of her colleagues—Father Tyler, a monumental man dressed in baggy black clericals with a radiant black face, and Father Little, a tall southern gentleman dressed in shorts and an old Princeton sweatshirt—stood like Tweedle-dum and Tweedle-dee by the reception office sorting through their letters.

Both professors loomed as large as their intellects—which were vast. Father Little had just returned from playing basketball and was all hot and sweaty. Red faced, he puffed loudly, trying to catch his breath.

"By the sound of your breathing, I see your game hasn't improved much." Father Tyler laughed loudly at his own joke.

"Hey, at least I get out there. Where were you this morning?" Father Little teased.

Andrea squeezed her way in between them. "You'd think they'd put the mail boxes some place more convenient," she grumbled, feeling cranky from too little sleep the night before. She pulled a pile of papers, some letters, a few newsletters and the latest edition of the *Anglican Theological Review* off the shelf and began to sort through them.

The two professors looked at each other. "What's eating you?"

Father Tyler asked jovially. "Feel like talking about it?"

Andrea looked up from her mail vaguely. "What did you say?"

"You seem kind of preoccupied."

"What do you mean?" she said flatly. "Everything's fine."

"That's a dead give-away," Father Little chimed in. "The ol' 'fine' answer. Sure nothing's bothering you?"

Usually, Andrea enjoyed kidding around with these guys but not today—she had too much to do and too much on her mind. "Seminary wouldn't be so bad if it weren't for all the helpful ministers," she remarked, only half-joking.

Father Tyler chuckled, "That's an occupational hazard around here."

"Half the job of seminary is to knock the do-goodism out of students and to teach them how to love," Father Little said. "Not always the same thing. You know, Chuck, the faculty basketball team would be much better if you were on it this season."

She ignored them and looked at a small white envelope in her pile of mail. Her name was typed in the center: Andrea West. No address, or return address or even a postmark. "This is odd," she said.

Father Tyler looked at her with curiosity, "From a student, perhaps?"

Andrea ripped open envelope and pulled out the note. Typed in capital letters were the words: I SAW YOU AT THE CATHEDRAL. STOP NOW OR YOU'RE DEAD. Andrea could not believe her eyes. Instantly, her stomach turned somersaults; she felt as if she was in some nightmare. Her home had been invaded, now so was her place of work.

Trembling, she stuffed the note back into the envelope so the others wouldn't see it.

She asked Gail, the student receptionist, "Did you see anyone strange around here this morning?"

"No, but you know how it is when classes get out. Anyone can come and go and I wouldn't notice."

"Not bad news, I hope," Fr. Little looked concerned.

Andrea suddenly couldn't speak. "Excuse me, I'm late." She pushed past them through the glass doors of the administration building and trotted towards the brick chapel. She stopped and sat on a wooden bench under the Japanese maple, which lazily dropped its flaming leaves, like red paper stars, on the brick sidewalk.

Oh God, why was she playing detective like this? Her rational side told her to stop now, to go straight to the police and tell them everything, but she knew the note might only incriminate her more. Andrea, you're a professor, not a murder detective. Who do you think you are? This is the stupidest thing you've ever done.

But the other side of her, the side she didn't show much, her headstrong, defiant Russian side, said to hell with them. There were two things she hated most in life: one, not being in control and two, not being able to solve a problem. The adventure of chasing this mystery had become almost an addiction. In fact, she had dedicated her whole life to chasing the biggest mystery in the universe— namely God—so why shouldn't she go after the smaller ones as well?

If she gave up now, part of her would die inside. She would cease to be authentic. On the other hand, if she didn't give up now, she might end up dead and cease to be altogether.

This dilemma was intolerable. Her head said one thing, but her heart told her another. All she knew was that, since this whole thing had started, she had never lived so intensely or so freely in her life.

Underneath her cool intellectual exterior blazed a romantic nature that yearned for passion and adventure as surely as the poet Ezra Pound once devoured a bunch of tulips, on stage, in the company of Yeats. Andrea's tulips would have been red.

Andrea slowly scrutinized the letter again, carefully noting the punctuation. She spoke out passionately. "They can't stop me. I'll show them."

"You'll show who?" A male English voice sounded behind her.

Andrea, startled, turned. Father Peter Ashton stood behind her, his face creased with worry. "I came looking for you because Chuck Tyler said you looked upset. Are you OK?"

"I'm fine," she said brusquely, slipping the letter unobtrusively into her purse.

He sat down and examined her face with searching eyes. "What is it?" He spoke softly.

Andrea felt her eyes beginning to brim with tears. She sighed and told him a half-truth, "I've been getting death threats warning me off the case." She studied the red maple leaves on the ground.

Peter's face paled. "Have you called the police?"

"It just happened. Obviously, somebody doesn't want me to find the icon or Michael's murderer."

Peter said stiffly, "I thought you said you weren't going to get involved in Michael's case."

"Well, I am. Or at least I've started to be," she hedged.

"What do you mean?"

Andrea hesitated. She tried to think of what she could say without implicating herself and Keith. "I've begun to do some more research on the Kazan Icon. You know I've always been interested in it."

"Andrea, you're hedging." He looked at her shrewdly.

"Look, Peter, I didn't tell you because I wanted to protect you."

"And I don't want to protect you?" He raised his voice with unusual anger. "Andrea, this is utterly stupid. This is a job for the police. Do you have any idea what you're getting into?"

"Of course I do, but I think it's worth the risk."

"Well, I don't. You're being irrational. As your friend, Andrea, I beg you to stop this craziness right now."

"And what if I don't?" He had gotten her Russian temper up.

"Then I shall have to advise the police so they can protect you from your own stupidity." He looked fiercely at her. "Andrea, stop. Think for a moment. This isn't like you." His eyes bore down upon her with all the compassion he was capable of. "You have too much to lose. Don't throw it all away because of your pride or your fear of failure."

"Look, I don't need anybody psychoanalyzing me. Nor do I need an older brother. I already have one, thank you. I appreciate your concern but I can handle this on my own." She turned away from him fiercely.

Peter shook his head, "You know I can't forbid you. I just hope you know what you're doing. I worry about you, that's all."

"I know you do. You'll be happy to hear I've been talking with the police and I plan to keep doing so." Andrea shook inside as her self-confidence began to crumble into self-doubt. It would have been easy to stand firm if he had been autocratic, but his compassion always did her in. She felt like spilling the whole story, but she mustered up her courage and contained it. "I can't help it, Peter. I have to go ahead with this. It's important."

"For whose sake? Yours or Michael's?" He scrutinized her carefully. She averted her eyes from his.

"Both, I suppose. And for God's sake."

"Aren't you manipulating God to suit your own ends?"

"No, but how else should I proceed?"

"With common sense, I should hope. Just be careful. Let me know what happens, OK?"

"Of course." She stood up and kissed his cheek, then turned her back on him and walked off, more abruptly than she would have wanted, leaving him standing there under the maple tree. As she walked down the steps past the chapel, inside she felt as if some part of her had just died. It was the first time she had lied to Peter. She felt like Judas Iscariot, who had betrayed Jesus with a kiss.

4

Andrea was thankful she had a full load of teaching all day to keep her mind off things. After her last class, she stepped into her office and checked her answering machine to see if she had any messages, particularly from Keith. There was one from him and one from her mother.

Marina's rich voice resonated on the tape, "Hi, Andreochka. I hoped you would be home by now. Call me. I'm very worried, Andrea. I don't want you to get mixed up in Michael's case. Let the police do it. It's too dangerous, " she warned. "Please call me."

Even Mama wants me to stop, Andrea sighed with exasperation. If I told her what happened this morning, she'd have a fit. Not feeling up to a scene from her mother, Andrea decided to call her later. She phoned Keith instead.

"Keith. We've got to talk." Andrea realized her hand was shaking. "Are you free?"

"What's the matter? Are you OK? When?"

"Are you always this perceptive? Actually, I'm not OK. I'll explain when I see you. Dinner, tonight?"

"Give me an hour and I'll be right there," Keith answered.

In the restaurant, an ageless young Asian waiter took their orders. Keith dipped a wedge of rice cake into some hot peanut sauce. "It's amazing how this Styrofoam tastes so good," he said. "So, tell me what's going on?"

"What hasn't been going on?" Andrea lamented. Over dinner, Keith listened attentively as Andrea told him about her meeting with Father Mench, the death threats and her talk with Father Peter.

"It seems everybody wants me to stop the search. And Detective Catelano really is going to love this," Andrea groaned as she showed Keith the note.

Keith inspected it and handed it back to her. "The note almost infers I did it," she said ruefully.

"On the other hand, if you can prove you didn't write it yourself, it may be the best evidence to drop you as a suspect in this case."

"What do you mean?"

"Well, now we know that the murderer saw you with Michael at the Cathedral. You have a witness, even though they might be framing you. You know you didn't kill Michael, and I know you didn't kill him. Our job is to convince the police you didn't and that the one who wrote this, did. You don't remember seeing anyone unusual that night?"

Andrea, who was never very good a details, racked her brain, "I don't remember. Everyone was unusual at that service. Michael most of all."

"I think you should call Tony and tell him now about these death threats, but in a general way. You don't have to be too specific. The least he can do is beef up protection for you."

"Yes, but won't that put a monkey wrench into our investigation?" Andrea absent-mindedly stroked the stem of her wine glass with her long, elegant fingers. This touch did not go unnoticed by Keith.

"They're just going to cruise around your home, not tail you.

They've got too much other work to do. And so do we. We don't know who this mystery icon lady is yet. I think that's the way to go."

"I was going to phone Father Seraphim tomorrow morning. Maybe I should call Detective Catelano after that," Andrea said, putting her fork down.

"Who's Father Seraphim?"

"You know, the Abbot in the monastery up near Willits. Father Mench said he might know how to contact this lady."

"What's his connection with her?"

"Father Mench said he knew her well."

"It sounds like he's the missing link." Keith enjoyed watching Andrea working through this puzzle.

"If I call Tony," she asked, "do you think this note will help?"

"It can't hurt. Besides, Tony wants us to stay out of this case anyway—let him do some footwork!" Keith scooped up a forkful of noodles.

"You know him better than I do. Do you really think he would arrest me?"

"When Tony is on a case, he hunts like a cat. He moves very slowly, letting things add up, then strikes when the time is right. I think the longer you wait for him to come to you, the more trouble you're in."

"That's reassuring," she said dubiously.

Sensing Andrea's anxiety, Keith changed the subject, "You don't really believe Father Mench's stories about the miraculous icon do you?" His eyes glinted merrily as he gazed at Andrea over his glasses.

Andrea shifted in her seat. "I don't know." she looked at her plate shyly, "I believe in God, but I'm no fundamentalist, if that's what you mean. I think biblical criticism is very important, but it has to be balanced with devotion and a healthy mysticism. You know, the heart, mind, body and soul working together. There is nothing worse than excessive rationalism; it petrifies the soul."

"What about all those miracles like Jesus walking on water and raising the dead? How do you know they aren't fantasy or medical ignorance? Wishful thinking or maybe just the power of suggestion?"

"I don't know. There's such a fine line between real miracles and

superstition, between the natural and the supernatural." Andrea
stalled, not wanting to share too much of her own experience of
these things. "And then there are the mystics. You can't just write off
people like Julian of Norwich, or St. John of the Cross or even Jesus
himself. There's too much to it."

"Why not? I think they were all just crazy—too much fasting
and too little sex, if you ask me." Keith speared a tomato with his
fork and held it up for inspection.

She wondered if he was trying to get her goat. "Maybe. But let
me ask you this. If God wanted to make a miracle happen, do you
think God could do it?"

"Assuming there is a God, I suppose God could."

"Right. It also depends on what you mean by 'miracle,'" she
smiled, sitting back in her chair.

"You sound like a Jesuit. Splitting hairs. Angels on a pin and all
that."

"Thanks; I take that as a compliment. The problem is that most
of us think about miracles too literally, supposing every word of the
Bible is written as fact. All it really is, is a metaphor attempting to
describe experiences of reality that can't be described any other way."

"That's what Joseph Campbell called myth."

Andrea raised her glass to him. "Correct. I'm impressed. Sorry,
but I'm going to have to give a little lecture now. The Gospels were
not written as Jesus' biography, but are theologies in story form
attempting to describe this phenomenon of Jesus. In the Middle
Ages, Aquinas had a problem with miracles too and tried to tackle
them by talking about natural law. He said God and nature were
divided in terms of the 'natural' and the 'super-natural', which led to
the old mind/body split of Descartes."

"I think, therefore I am," Keith quoted.

Andrea nodded. "Rationalists, ever since, have taken this tack
with a vengeance. But physicists and theologians today are questioning this and are turning more towards a holistic model. Maybe some
phenomena, which some of us call miracles, are really natural events
that we can't explain or haven't scientifically discovered yet. Look
how long it took us to discover electricity, or our ability to make and

fly jet planes. I bet the Islanders in Papua New Guinea think 747s are miraculous, too."

"But electricity and jet planes are provable."

"True, but even science has its limits—any physicist will tell you that. At first everything depends on theories. Which is another word for faith, I think." Andrea was enjoying this exchange.

"Hmmm. If you put it that way, light particles seem to be pretty miraculous, the way they can be a line and a particle at the same time. Then there's the question about the formation of life."

"Exactly. I like the way Theodore Roethke put it when he was asked to describe poetry. He said, 'Poetry doesn't happen so much by inspiration as by taking down the barriers.' I think the same applies to miracles. It involves taking down the barriers."

Keith was pondering this last sentence when the waiter brought their check. He palmed it. "This is my treat."

"Is this our first date?" Andrea smiled playfully at him and tossed her folded napkin on the table.

"You can call it that," he smiled and leaned forward. "Let's go back to my place, take down the barriers and see if a miracle happens..."

Andrea wavered but she resisted, "One thing about you, you're persistent. I may reconsider when you come up with a better line. Sorry, I need to go home."

"This is my last offer," he grinned at her, but she knew he was serious.

She hated to be pressured and responded glibly. "What are you, a close-out sale or something? Look, I don't make quick decisions buying clothes. I certainly don't make quick decisions about men." She caught the twinge of hurt in his eyes. "Sorry. That was too flip. I just need some time, OK?"

"I understand," he said. "I've been through the marital wars myself, remember?" They rose from the table. "May I escort you out to your vehicle?"

Andrea smiled. She liked his ability to be flexible.

"How's this for sincere chivalry?" He held out his good arm.

She took it and let him escort her out of the restaurant.

CHAPTER 11

∽

"I would like to stress that encounter with God is dangerous. It is not without reason that the eastern tradition of Zen calls the place where we find God, who we seek, the tiger's lair."

Metropolitan Anthony Bloom
Courage To Pray

Friday, November 2, 1990

Andrea sat with her head in her hands in the interrogation room at a steel table opposite Detective Catelano and Officer Jergeson, who took notes as usual. She couldn't believe what was happening to her.

The tape recorder hummed imperceptibly near by. Detective Tony Catelano had phoned her before she had a chance to phone him, and ordered her to come in immediately for questioning, which he was now doing methodically and calmly. He paced in front of her chair. "So you admit you had an argument with Michael Beech Thursday afternoon just before he was murdered?"

"Yes, but it wasn't a big one."

"Not according to some eye witnesses at Greens Restaurant. They said it got pretty loud. Ms. West, you don't seem the type who loses her cool very often. What happened?"

Andrea shifted uncomfortably in her seat. "Michael was never good at scheduling things. He invited me to lunch to persuade me to see the icon that evening. I told him I couldn't go because I had to prepare for my dissertation defense the next morning. My whole career was riding on this." She gazed steadily at the detective.

"Go on," he said, quietly.

"He said he wouldn't write a reference letter for me if I didn't go. He said it half-jokingly."

"Half-jokingly? Or was it blackmail?"

"That's a loaded word."

"And eyewitnesses said they heard you use it."

"I exaggerated. Michael had a way of manipulating people to get his own way. But usually he did it with humor. This wasn't one of those times." Andrea smiled ruefully.

"What did you do?"

"I blew up at him but I calmed down later. Afterwards, I left the restaurant and drove back to the seminary in Berkeley, which gave me time to think about it."

"What changed your mind?"

"Why should a little hurt pride get in the way of my career? I had been planning to study that evening, but I figured that if I didn't know the material by then, it was too late. Besides, I had always wanted to see the Icon of Kazan. I'm teaching a course on it."

"So I gather," Tony leaned forward in his chair. "In fact, you've been interested in the Icon of Kazan for a very long time, haven't you? You're obsessed with it."

"Well, yes. No." Andrea said, flustered. "Not in the way you think. How did you hear this?" The faces of Christie Matthews and Dean Ferguson flashed through her mind.

"I'm asking the questions right now, Ms. West."

She was startled by his brusque response to this simple question, but quickly regained her composure. "I've always been fascinated with the Icon of Kazan because of its holiness and its history. Some Russians call it a healing icon. By the way, I gather the icon was stolen after all. Do you know who took it?"

"We were hoping you'd know. No one noticed it was gone at first because whoever took it replaced it with a phony: the jewels on the second one are made of glass. Whoever copied it was very clever and had a lot of resources at their disposal. But we have no way of knowing if the icon had already been stolen by the time you saw it. Maybe the one you saw was a fake."

"I've seen photographs of the original. It looked like the real one to me. But Michael was the expert; he had been working on it for a long time. I think he would have noticed if someone had switched it."

"Was there anything else he mentioned that seemed unusual?"

"I've already told you he thought it was a fraud. Which surprised me."

"Is that so?" Detective Catelano slipped a sly look to Officer Jergeson.

Andrea nodded. She didn't like the flow of his questioning and frowned anxiously. "Are you going to arrest me?"

Tony studied her warily and said, "Not yet. But don't go anywhere for a while. As I told you, until we know all the facts, everybody's a suspect. Is there anything else you think we need to know?"

"I can't think of anything," she looked at Tony coolly. "But if I do, I won't hesitate to call you."

"Thank you. I think that's all for now. You can go."

Andrea collected her purse and coat with relief and left the building.

Tony tucked some files under his arm, poured himself a cup of cold water from the water cooler on his way from the interrogation room, and sank into his office chair with a grunt of frustration.

Officer Jergeson followed behind. "You think she did it?"

Tony rubbed his chin. "I don't know. I really don't know."

2

Andrea sat in the driver's seat of her car and shook for a solid three minutes. It had been a harrowing interrogation. The questions rattled her so much that she'd forgotten to mention the death threats, which Keith thought, would clear her name. But perhaps it was best she hadn't. The police already had a bad impression of her. They'd be angrier if they knew she was snooping around.

She felt as if she was in the middle of a Kafka novel: as if the hand of fate had thrown her before a menacing tribunal when she had done nothing wrong. The injustice of it burned in her like a cinder stuck in a fire grate.

She longed to talk with Keith, to pour out the whole awful

experience, and headed for the nearest phone. She found one in a swank cafe south of Market Street. She put a quarter in the slot and dialed Keith's home number. The phone rang five times before his answering machine clicked on. Andrea thought she had better not leave a message. Frustrated, she slammed the phone down on its hook and sat down at a table with a decaf latté to think things through. More than ever, she knew she had to solve Michael's murder—not just for his sake, but also for hers.

As Andrea sipped her coffee, her conversation with Father Mench kept rolling over in her mind. In 1968, "the rich English lady" wanted to sell the Icon of Kazan, which she inherited from her father, who was a wealthy art collector. Who was she? If she were still alive, she'd be ancient. Was she the woman Michael spoke about in her dream when he said, "Find her?" Why did she want to sell such a valuable piece of art? Did she need the money? Why did she want to remain anonymous?

And why did she only work through Cecil Durant? If he was such a good appraiser, why did he claim two different dates about the icon's age? Unless, of course, he falsified the dates on purpose. A 13th or 14th century icon would obviously fetch a healthier price in the art market than one from the 18th century.

Then again, why would a supposedly reputable businessman just vanish? There wasn't a business or home listing for Durant anywhere. She wondered if he was listed in one of the official art catalogues. And what about academic credentials? She thought of the names inscribed on the document on Father Mench's wall. Who was Priscilla Thorpe?

The questions nagged her like pestering black flies. But she knew obsessing about them wouldn't answer anything, so she let them simmer awhile. She made a list of things to do and phone calls to make that day: first, call Keith; grade papers and send them to the registrar; go shopping; and finally, call Aunt Vera and Father Seraphim. She underlined the last items. She looked at her watch. It was eleven o'clock.

In the cafe phone booth, juggling a heavy yellow pages book with one hand and holding a note pad in the other, Andrea found the section labeled "Art and Antique Dealers" and Vera Markovitch's listing. Good old Aunt Vera, her godmother. When she was very young, Aunt Vera sometimes baby-sat for her and Nicky when her mother had to go out for some evening events. This didn't happen too often.

What a strange, suspicious woman Vera was. She'd never acclimated to this country very well. Never spoke much English, or ever tried to. She was politically very conservative, and religiously superstitious. Although she was always friendly, Andrea never felt like she ever approved of her family. Not really. They were too modern, too American. Unlike Vera, they didn't constantly brood over the dark past.

The receiver was lifted after four rings. "Hello," the deep Slavic female voice on the other line said.

"Hello, Vera. This is Andrea West, remember me?"

"Andrea! Of course, such a stranger you've been. This is big surprise. Last time we speak, I saw you and your Mama for lunch at that miserable restaurant on 9th Ave. You were about to begin college again. How can I help you?"

"I can't talk about it over the phone. I need to talk with you. Can I come visit?"

"Of course, my house is your house. When can you come?"

"Would this afternoon be too soon? At your place after lunch?"

Vera hesitated at the suddenness of her request. "What is so important that you have to rush over like a fire engine to see me when you haven't called in four years?"

Andrea laughed and said, "It's important, but I really can't talk now."

"OK, you remember where I live?"

"Yes, I remember. By Clement Street," she said. "See you around one."

"Da. Dosvidania," Vera said and hung up.

Her next plan was to talk with Father Seraphim. Andrea called information for Mendocino Country and asked for the number of Transfiguration Monastery.

Remembering past times when she had visited monasteries,

Andrea thought the community would probably have finished the duties of the day and the Chapter of Faults. But perhaps Orthodox monks aren't so collectively neurotic as some Anglican ones and have dispensed with it altogether, she thought. She remembered, however, that Gareth once told her of an elderly monk who had confessed to eating a wild raspberry between meals.

A male voice with a mid-western twang answered, "Transfiguration Monastery."

"Hello, my name is Andrea West. I'm from the Episcopal seminary in Berkeley. I'm wondering if you have any space available for a brief retreat beginning on Saturday, November 3rd. I was hoping to speak with Father Seraphim. Father Mench suggested I call him. It's rather urgent."

"Father Seraphim is not normally available to see visitors. But please hold, I will see what I can do." The monk placed the receiver down and was gone for what seemed to Andrea a long time.

After five minutes, the young monk returned. "I'm sorry, Father Seraphim can't see you. It's his health. But you're still welcome to come visit."

Andrea did not show her disappointment, but thanked him and asked when she should plan to drive up there.

"We happen to have some space open on Saturday, since people don't visit as much this late in the fall. You can spend the night in one of our scetes if you wish."

Andrea thought about the old scetes in Russia, where the local hermits, called *Staretz*, lived. She had visions of staying in a primitive shack and hoped it had a few modern amenities. "Thank you," she said, "that would be terrific. I'll be there Saturday afternoon."

"Good. Dinner is at six. I will give you directions when you arrive. I'm Brother Isaiah. I'm the guest master."

"Thank you, brother," Andrea said gratefully. She knew how crowded monasteries could be on weekends and was grateful they had an opening on such short notice.

"Make sure you come before dark, because the road is bad. God bless you." And then he hung up.

3

Keith parked off Bryant Street and walked past three sleazy bail bonds joints, crossed Bryant and entered that great gray monolith, the Hall of Justice. Keith took the elevator up to homicide and spoke directly to the officer on duty.

The officer recognized Keith. "Welcome back. I hear you got roughed up."

"Thanks, Bart, I decided to use my shoulder as landing gear."

Bart called back behind the glass partitions, "Hey, Tony. There's someone here to see you." Then to Keith, "He just got in from a meeting with the Chief. Give him a minute."

The two of them debated baseball stats until Tony appeared, looking tired and sweaty. He nodded to Keith, "So, they let you out after all." He barely cracked a smile but Keith sensed he was glad to see him. "How's the shoulder?"

"Collar bone," he corrected. "Much better, but I can only move my arm a little."

Tony grunted. "Could have been worse. You're lucky you're not dead."

"When he hit me, for a second I wished I was! Listen, I came up to talk about the Beech case. I have to get some copy in to the paper or they're going to think I went to Hawaii."

"Come in my office. We've got things to talk about." Tony led him down the wide corridor to a glass Dutch door. "Coffee?" Tony raised a Styrofoam cup.

"Sure," Keith said, "Do you dispense it with IVs?"

Tony didn't crack a smile "You know where it is."

Keith poured some coffee and pulled up a chair. "Any news?"

Tony leaned back and spoke frankly. "We don't have much. We contacted this guy named Hart in New Jersey who runs this right-wing Catholic group called the Holy Virgin Society. They own the Icon of Kazan. We wanted to make sure the whole thing wasn't set up as some weird kind of insurance fraud or something."

"Well?"

"They're clean as God."

"What about their connection with Michael Beech?"

"Oh, Hart knew him all right. Said he had hired him to investigate this icon because over the years they had gotten so much screwy data about its authenticity."

"Did they know Beech was on to something?"

"I don't know. Hart didn't say."

"What do you think?" Keith honed in on him.

"They suspected something was wrong or they wouldn't have wanted a re-appraisal."

"Suppose Hart did know, and suppose Beech found out that the icon wasn't as old as they thought when they bought it. Do you think Hart would have tried to cover it up?"

"Possibly, but not by murder." Tony stretched back in his chair. "It wouldn't have been worth it. The Holy Virgin Society could have taken the high ground and gotten more just by suing the old lady."

Keith sat up in his chair. "Who is she?"

"We don't know. Apparently, Hart worked through this guy named Cecil Durant."

"We know about him," Keith said.

Tony raised his eyebrows. "We? Know what?"

Keith carefully explained what little he knew from Andrea— that the icon was appraised by Cecil Durant for a private owner and was exhibited at the New York World's Fair.

Tony took notes and asked for article references to have the assistants research them later. "No mention of the owner?"

"Diddily squat."

Tony sighed, "Hart didn't know either. We asked him. Hart tried to discover the name of the owner but Durant would never tell him. He said they wanted to remain anonymous."

"So it was a couple?"

"Could be."

"Where is Durant now?"

"Who knows? But we do know they still own property down in Santa Barbara and their taxes are up to date."

"What did you find down there?"

"An empty house but no sign of them. Their neighbors haven't seen them for weeks, months. No garbage collected, no mail, the usual."

"What about hotels or motels?"

"We're still looking. RVs and trailers, the works. His credentials are pretty cheesy, too—full of holes. Says he's an archeologist from Victoria but there were no University degrees, just mail order ones. He later claimed to be an art appraiser though we found no official license or credentials. It also seems he was some honcho in a New Age Church down in Southern California which drew in lots of followers: psychics, mediums, wizards, people into channeling, crystals; you know, outer space stuff."

Keith rolled his eyes, "Great! Phony psychics. Sounds redundant to me. Business is probably booming in L.A."

Tony grinned and said, "Twenty years ago they disappeared and popped up in the Bay Area and we think somehow latched onto this rich woman and the icon. There was no evidence of fraud or embezzlement, but it all sounds a little shady to me."

"Like a rotten banana."

"For all we know, they could be around here."

"They're not in the phone directories. I tried," Keith added.

"We did too. Both listed and unlisted."

"Maybe they don't need a phone—maybe they just read minds." Keith grinned, took out another Sherman and tapped it on the cardboard case before lighting it.

"If they ever tapped yours, they'd find nobody home." Tony handed him an ashtray.

Keith ignored the friendly jab. "What about the DMV, property records, tax records, false IDs?"

Tony gave him a what-do-you-think-I-am look. "We're working on it," he said. "We think someone's covering for them."

"You're a veritable fount of information this morning," Keith said, finishing his cup of coffee in one gulp. He stood up, "Why don't you teach Jergeson back there to make decent coffee?"

"We did. This is his good stuff."

"How can you stand it?"

"I can't. I drink tea."

"Italians and tea, that's obvious. Let me know if you turn up anything." Keith moved to the door.

"If I were you, I'd be careful about your Miss Seminary," Tony said, nonchalantly examining his pile of papers on the desk.

A wave of hot fury surged inside Keith. "What do you mean by that?"

"Just be careful. Something doesn't feel right. And I don't want you two doing any more amateur sleuthing. You could cause the whole case to be thrown out—which might be just what she wants. Maybe you're in too deep to see it."

"You're crazy." Tony's words stung Keith to the quick. "She's no more a murderer than my mother."

"We'll see. Now scram, I've got work to do. Stay out of trouble."

"Remember, Tony, I got work to do, too. Your department's going to look pretty stupid when you pin this on the wrong person." Keith crumpled his coffee cup and threw it into the trashcan as he pushed through the office door.

Keith walked briskly towards the *Examiner* Offices on 5th Street. He had a story to write but he also wanted to phone Andrea to warn her about Tony's suspicions. He longed to hear her voice again. He couldn't get Andrea out of his mind nor Tony's words, "You're in too deep." And he knew Tony was right. Whenever he was around her, he had the irrefutable evidence of his watery knees. He knew he was falling in love with Andrea West.

4

Vera Markevitch lived in the Avenues, off Clement Street, where she had her small antique shop. She leased the place so she could walk to work, as she had never learned to drive. Andrea pulled up in front of her house and stepped out of the car.

It was a small green single-story dwelling, almost a cottage, detached from its neighbors, which was unusual for that part of town. A small white picket fence stood overwhelmed by sweet red old-fashioned roses—tea roses in perfect health. Andrea admired them and wondered what she fed them with.

Vera greeted her at the front door with a traditional double kiss. "Darling, come in." Andrea noticed that she looked older, more haggard. Her hair was all gray; her body more stooped now that she was nearly seventy-five.

"Sit down. I make some tea," Vera ordered as she bustled into her 1950s kitchen.

Her house looked the same and still smelt the same—that odd fusty mixture of talcum powder and old ladies. She remained standing to inspect some of Vera's collections. In one corner, stood a glass cabinet filled with medals, silver thimbles, pins, jeweled snuffboxes, black lacquer boxes. She eyed the pictures and the perfume bottles on the mantelpiece. "You haven't changed a thing," she called to Vera who was busy in the kitchen. "It's just as I remember it as a child."

"What's to change?"

On the walls hung old tinted photographs of Vera with her husband and her son taken in Moscow in 1947. All three looked somber and grim, and somewhat malnourished. She remembered hearing from her mother how lucky Vera and her husband had been to escape from the Soviet Union in 1948. They had to leave their son behind. It broke her heart, and Vera never forgot. Her husband died soon after, leaving her with little money and painful memories.

There was a modest pink sofa, from the fifties, with a cheap-looking coffee table in front of it. Here, Andrea sat and waited, studying the smudged, rather homely icon of Our Lady of the Burning Bush, which hung in the upper right hand eastern corner of the room, traditionally called "the beautiful corner."

Vera came out bearing a hot pot of tea in one hand and a plate of crackers, hard cheese, sausage and some garnish of homemade eggplant rattatui.

"Can I help with the cups and saucers?" Andrea offered.

"Nyet. Sit, sit." Vera waved her hands, then came back with the cups and placed them with satisfaction down on the coffee table. "There," she said, falling back into the sofa with a martyred sigh.

"You didn't have to do all this." Andrea gave her a mock look of severity.

Vera patted Andrea's knee. "So, what else am I doing when my goddaughter calls up and says there's something important to talk about?" She took a sip of tea. "This tea is good. But they charge too much fancy-dancey prices for it. What is it I know you don't know?"

"Tatia Vera, I won't lie to you." Andrea cut straight to the point. "I am trying to find who took the Icon of Kazan. Do you know any icon appraisers by the name of Durant? Cecil Durant?"

Vera went silent and put her cup down slowly. Andrea thought a flicker of nervousness had flashed across her face. "A man called me the other day about icon dealers. I say nothing to him. Why should I talk with a stranger?"

"That must have been my friend Keith. He's helping me."

"You know him? He is not with the authorities?"

"No, he's quite safe."

"Oh, well, then. Police I don't mess in." Vera waved a hand with relief. She thought a minute. "No, I don't remember this Mr. Durant. But I do remember when Archbishop John wanted to buy the icon. It was in 1963, he wanted to build a big beautiful church."

"Yes, I know about that. Is there anyone you think who might know Durant, anyone at all? Someone who knows icons very well?"

Vera sat very still, as if struggling with something in her mind.

"Please, Tatia," Andrea pleaded, "lives depend upon it."

Vera sighed and said softly, "Ahhh, well, it must come out some day...." She looked at Andrea squarely. "Da, there is someone. Alexander Menshikov. He has fancy place here in the city. He buys and sells icons. He knows all about them. He might know. But if he asks how you know him, do not say me," she said firmly.

"Vera, thank you!" Andrea gave her an impulsive hug.

"Promise you won't say me." Vera looked at her sternly. "I write down address before you go."

"I promise."

Vera passed her the plate of sausage, cheese and crackers, "Now tell me all about your studies. And how is Nicky doing in his big penthouse in New York?"

5

It was almost 4 o'clock when Andrea left Vera's. She was driving down Geary Street when the beeper Keith had loaned her buzzed inside her purse. "Damn!" It kept beeping until she turned off onto a side street not far from the old Lone Mountain College campus. She jotted down the number, and then hunted for a phone.

She saw one by a 7-11 store and parked. Her heart pounded as she heard Keith's voice answer. She could hear Frank Sinatra crooning in the background. "Keith, I've been trying to reach you. Where are you, Jersey City?"

"At a '50s burger joint South of Market. How about meeting me after work at the M&M Tavern?"

"I don't know. It's been a long day." She was feeling drained, but still longed to see him.

"My treat," Keith coaxed her. "By the way, I stopped in for a chat with Tony Catelano. I think we need to talk." This was said more gravely.

Andrea's stomach felt as if it dropped fifty feet.

"He told me some new stuff about Durant. He has some property down in Santa Barbara but they haven't lived there for months." Keith told her the details of his conversation with Tony, all except the parts about Andrea. "Want to join me?"

"How about later, after seven?" she said. "I have to follow up on a couple of leads. Aunt Vera says I should visit this icon dealer near Alamo Square. I'd like to get right over there. The Haight's not far, I could meet you afterwards."

"Who is he?"

"A guy named Alexander Menshikov. I don't have time to talk. I'll let you know if it pans out." As she hung up the phone, Andrea noticed a surge of excitement inside her. For lots of reasons, she felt like a hawk circling its prey.

6

The setting sun lined the purple clouds with blazing shafts of light as Andrea pulled up beyond the three-story gingerbread Victorian facing Alamo Square. Lights shone through the lace curtains in the front bay windows. Finding no place to park in front of the house, she turned right onto Scott Street and found a space down the block.

The air grew colder as the light faded. Andrea buttoned her coat and walked up hill to the address Vera had given her. She turned left and stood in front of this Victorian Queen, marveling at the high turret on top. A blue historical landmark plaque was attached prominently on the side of the house.

Andrea took a deep breath and mounted the dozen steps, past the two white stone lions guarding the entrance, to the front door. She rang the doorbell beside the glass double doors. Electronic chimes sounded inside. Soon footsteps echoed down the long corridor. The door opened, and there stood a petite woman in her seventies with short white hair, luminous eyes, dressed in a simple blue skirt and white blouse. She smiled at Andrea and asked, "May I help you?"

"Please, I would like to speak with Mr. Menshikov. I'm interested in seeing his icons," Andrea's stomach knotted.

"Is he expecting you?" the woman asked pleasantly.

"No," Andrea said apologetically. "But I must see him. My name is Andrea West."

"Please step inside and wait here."

She led her into the hallway. Andrea waited dutifully as the woman opened the door and went off into a side parlor. Evidently other people were inside as well. She barely glimpsed the back of a tall, skinny brunette woman before the door shut. There was the low rumble of voices. Both men and women.

Andrea looked around the vestibule. She was stunned by the elegant Victorian decor: oak wainscoting, high ceilings, William Morris wall paper, huge Boston ferns potted in exquisite Chinese vases, a red velvet Victorian hard loveseat under the mirror.

After a few minutes, her guide returned and ushered Andrea into an oak paneled study off to the right of the hall. She opened the door and said, "Miss West is here to see you."

A large man stood in front of a large mahogany desk staring out the window, then turned and looked at Andrea. She wasn't sure if she saw a flicker of surprise—or was it distress—in his eyes, and wondered why. Whatever it was, he recovered well. He smiled graciously at her. "Hello. Alex Menshikov." He offered his hand. "What can I do for you?" He looked sternly at the woman, who softly closed the door behind her as she left the room.

Despite his bulk, Andrea thought he looked distinguished for a man in his late sixties. She held out her hand and stammered, "Sorry to barge in on you like this. I'm Andrea West. I'm doing some icon research and I was wondering if you could help me?"

He shook her hand cordially. "Please, sit down. How did you hear about me?" he asked innocently as they sat opposite one another in two red leather chairs.

"I saw your name in the yellow pages," she lied.

"Good," he smiled. "I'm glad they work. The phone company charges too much for them. What do you want to know?"

"I was wondering if you had icons of the Virgin and Child for sale?"

"Sure, plenty of them, but they're expensive," he said, looking her over. "I don't think they'd be in your range."

"I'm asking for a rich friend of mine," she lied again.

"Ahhh," he smiled. Andrea instinctively sensed he knew she was lying and wondered why he was letting her get away with it.

"Could I see what you have in stock?"

"Sure, let me go get a couple of samples. While you're waiting, why don't you look this over?" He handed her a large silver and white glossy catalogue with the index of his art goods for sale with the prices underneath. "I'll be back in a minute."

Andrea thumbed quickly through the catalogue. His stock included icons, jewelry, a full silver tea set, and elaborately jeweled Fabergé eggs.

She set the catalogue down and eyed the set of bookcases, filled with leather bound books, placed on either side of the door leading into another room. More books and pictures, together with a priceless cloisonné piece, sat on the shelves behind the desk, which dominated the room. Degrees, trade certificates and awards hung on the wall.

She noticed a small glass curio cabinet, not unlike Vera's, in the back corner to the left of the desk. This one, however, had a lock on it. It was jammed with crystal saltshakers, antique brooches, gold cigarette cases and amber necklaces, and a shelf full of black lacquer boxes.

Ever since she had been a child, Andrea loved looking at the stories painted in delicate gold and bright colors on these boxes. This was, in fact, one of the finest collections she had ever seen in one place. *I wonder if this is where Michael bought his box? He told me it was very rare.*

But the more she gazed at them, the more uncomfortable she felt about the place, as if there was a strange presence in the room. The space in the room dripped with it, as if the air was pea-green. Suddenly she knew what she had to do.

She listened for voices speaking in the next room to make sure she was safe. Acting on impulse, she hurried to the desk and began pulling open all the drawers. Then she froze.

There it was in the center drawer of the big mahogany desk. Andrea gasped. She lifted a paper away, revealing her missing photograph underneath. The one stolen from her home. "Bastard!" She grabbed her picture and quickly stuffed it into her purse.

A door slammed out in the hall. Footsteps grew louder. Hastily closing the drawers, Andrea rushed around in front of the desk and picked up the catalogue, just as the door opened. She felt her heart pounding in her throat. She took deep breaths to calm her panic. *Oh God, how do I get out of this?*

Alex walked in carrying three small icons. Andrea felt as if he was scrutinizing her closely. "Well, did you see anything you liked?" He laid them out on his desk.

She pointed to one of St. John on the left and one of Our Lady of the Sign.

"Yes, that one of St. John is very special. It comes from the late Novgorod school of icons. It was painted in the late 17th century. Very expensive. What do you think of this one?" He placed the icon under the lamplight. "Magnificent, isn't it?"

"Yes," Andrea managed to say.

He calmly showed off his collection. "These are the works of the chief student of the famed iconographer Andre Rublev...." He droned on about the intricacies of iconography. To her surprise, he didn't seem phased by her visit, but played along with her charade, even though she knew he knew who she was.

"They're the best I have," he said proudly. "I thought you'd like to see them. They're worth over $50,000 a piece. If you're interested, I could sell them to you on an installment plan."

"Thank you, but you were right. They are out of my price range. So sorry to bother you," Andrea said lamely. She was trapped and she knew he knew it. She felt weak, almost petrified with anxiety.

Just then the front doorbell chimed. "Sorry," Alex said and put down one of the icons. "I better get that." He left the study and opened the front door.

She saw a figure of a man dressed in a brown uniform with a clipboard under his arm, "UPS," he said. "Mr. Menshikov?" He took out a pen from behind his ear and offered it. "Can you help me with a couple of big boxes out there?"

Andrea grabbed her chance. She bolted through the opposite door at the other end of the study and found herself in a back hallway leading to a cramped kitchen.

There has to be a way out. She looked around desperately. Finding the back door by the pantry closet, she opened it and ran down a flight of wooden stairs into a yard. A light shone over the garbage cans on the right side. She ran quickly past them, opened the gate and ran down a short alley to her parked car.

She roared off as fast as she could down Scott Street. She looked into her rear view mirror and saw the figure of Alex Menshikov behind her, standing under the streetlight with his hands on his hips, as he watched her speed away.

CHAPTER 12

❧

"To risk nothing is to gain nothing. In our own lives cowardice does not apply solely to the material goods we sit on, like a hen on her eggs, and unlike her, without ever hatching anything out! It applies to everything in our lives, indeed to our life itself."

Metropolitan Anthony Bloom
Meditations: A Spiritual Journey

Andrea switched on her headlights and sped through the Western Addition as darkness descended over the rough streets and broken-down Victorians. Her hands shook as she squeezed the steering wheel and accelerated. "God, what have I done?" Glancing up into her rear view mirror, she saw that a green Mercedes, which had trailed her for many blocks, was gaining on her. What if it's him? She repressed the urge to panic.

She had to think quickly. The only safe place she could go was to her mother's house on California Street near the Palace of the Legion of Honor. The quickest way there was through the Park—especially since all the streets in the Avenues would be clogged with rush hour traffic. She made a sharp left onto McAllister Street and headed west until she reached Masonic Avenue, then made another left towards Golden Gate Park. Luckily, the green lights were with her, but she couldn't shake the Mercedes. "Damn!"

Andrea white-knuckled the steering wheel. Her car flew past the big cypress tree by McLaren Lodge, past the white dome of the Conservatory of Flowers, then the DeYoung Museum on her left and into the more isolated dark stretches of JFK Drive towards the center of the park.

Again, she checked her rear view mirror as she sped past the 8th Avenue exit. She saw that the Mercedes was about to flank her Honda. Andrea floored the gas pedal and whizzed past a car driving more slowly in front of her. Then a line of four cars drove past her from the opposite direction, giving the Mercedes a chance to gain on her.

As soon as there was a break in oncoming traffic, the Mercedes lurched to the left and began to pull alongside Andrea. She spun her head around to catch a glimpse of the driver, but on-coming head-lights blinded her.

A shot rang out. Andrea felt a bullet rip into her back fender.

"Oh, God!" Beads of sweat rolled down Andrea's back. Then another gunshot and the glass of her back seat window exploded with a pop as a bullet imbedded inside the interior roof of her car. Andrea shrieked and dodged the bullet, jerking the steering wheel as she tried to avoid being hit, narrowly missing a crash into a tree. With trembling hands, she regained control of the car and urged it forward as fast as it would go.

An oncoming car forced the attacker to fall back, but not for long. Undaunted, the Mercedes tailgated her until their bumpers were inches apart. "Oh God!" Andrea's heart thudded violently in her chest and her head pounded.

Just ahead, through the dark, Andrea saw the marked intersec-tion of JFK and Spreckels Lake Drive in the glare of her headlights. Having driven this road many times before on her way to her moth-er's house, she let her gut instinct take over. She released her foot from the gas and made the sharpest right hand turn she had ever made in her life. The squeal of tires shrieked in her ears.

Coming out of the turn, she didn't realize the parked car she almost sideswiped was a squad car sitting idle with its lights dimmed. Regaining control of the car, she again floored the gas pedal and kept moving. She checked her mirror again and sighed with relief. It looked as if she had shaken off the green Mercedes. "Yahoo!" Andrea cheered, raising a fist in the air.

She drove along, feeling quite pleased with herself, until she was startled to hear the loud whine of a siren behind her. Checking her mirror again, she saw flashing lights looming ominously.

A voice over the loud speaker shocked her eardrums, "Pull over to the right and stop."

Andrea slowed and pulled over onto the soft shoulder. She sat back in her seat, shaking uncontrollably; adrenaline raced through her body as if she was wired with the drug.

An Asian cop poked a flashlight in her direction and tapped on her car window. Andrea rolled it down.

"OK, lady, where's the fire?"

"Am I glad to see you!" Andrea looked up into the face of the officer who was immediately suspicious of her remark. "Somebody just shot at me."

The policeman looked behind him, "Where? When did this happen?"

"Right around the corner, just seconds ago, for God's sake. Look, I'll show you." As she unhooked her seat belt and moved her hand to open the car door, she realized it was shaking.

The officer was studied her suspiciously, as if he was hearing just another ploy. "Please stay in the car, Ma'am."

She sat back in her seat. "It's true! There are bullet holes in the back of my car. Look at the back window. You can see for yourself," she exclaimed. Andrea pulled bits of blue plastic glass out of her hair.

"All right, lady. Just calm down. Are you OK?"

"Yeah, I think. Just a nervous wreck." Feeling suddenly chilled, she hugged her arms and looked warily around her, afraid her pursuer might attempt to shoot her on the spot.

The policeman inspected the back fender with his flashlight and shown the light through the back window. "They look like a gun shot holes all right, but how do I know you didn't have them before?"

"There's glass all over the back of the car," Andrea protested.

"What kind of car was it?" he asked, taking notes.

"A green Mercedes. I don't know what year. I couldn't see the license plate."

"Get a look at the driver?"

"No, it was too dark. I don't think he was a very good marksman, or I'd be dead by now."

"Probably. You sure it was a man?"

"Well, no, not exactly. I think it was, but I don't know."

"Whether someone was chasing you or not, Ma'am, you were

still speeding. Can I see your driver's license and current registration, please?" She fumbled to get her license out of its plastic window in her wallet and showed it to him. He took them back to his flashing car, sat down and called his dispatcher.

He was gone so long, Andrea began to feel a little paranoid. She thought, "Maybe Menshikov reported a burglary?"

After several minutes the policeman sauntered back and handed her a clipboard with a ticket attached to it. He held out his flashlight, "Sign here," he ordered and handed her a pen. She signed the ticket, he tore off her copy and handed back her license and registration cards. "I'm going to report the shooting, but I think you better go down to the station to make a full report yourself."

"Thank you," she tucked her license back into her wallet. "Is it OK if I follow you out of the park?" she asked.

"You can go where you like, lady, as long as you don't go over the speed limit. I could have nailed you for reckless driving as well."

"Thanks a lot." She sighed with relief and prayed the Mercedes was gone for good. She turned on the ignition and followed the police car as it drove out towards Fulton Avenue. She checked her rear view mirror. No sign of the Mercedes, thank God. She zig-zagged her way through the Richmond District until she pulled up in front of her mother's house on Lake Street.

2

Marina opened the front door for her daughter. "Mama!" Andrea rushed in, pale and trembling. Andrea turned and double locked the door behind her. Her well-kept black hair was wild and askew; she breathed heavily.

Marina looked at Andrea and wrung her hands, "What's wrong? You look like you've been chased by a ghost."

"I almost just became a ghost," Andrea walked into the living room and pulled the drapes shut. "Somebody just tried to shoot me as I was driving here," she said.

"Oh, my poor darling!" Marina came over and clutched Andrea's shoulders to give her a big hug. Andrea felt like crying but didn't. She was in such a swirl of emotion she didn't know which one to feel first. She pulled away from her mother.

"Give me a minute. Let me pull myself together." She exhaled deeply and sank into the sofa. "God, I wish I hadn't given up smoking. It's times like these..."

Marina waited a few minutes. "Tell me what happened," she asked quietly. "You sure it wasn't one of those freak accidents? One of those freeway shootings?"

"In Golden Gate Park? No, somebody was trying to kill me! They shot at me but missed and hit my car." Andrea sprang up from the sofa and paced around the living room too anxious to sit. "I need a drink."

"What do you want?"

"Vodka. Straight up."

Marina came back momentarily with two medium vodkas on a hand-painted wooden tray and placed it on the coffee table. "Here, this will help you relax," Marina handed her daughter the drink. Andrea clutched her glass, took one large gulp, grimaced and sat back down. They sat close together on the overstuffed sofa, their knees almost touching.

"Mama, I lied to you," Andrea studied the pattern of her oriental rug. "Remember when I said I didn't have anything to do with Michael's case? Well, I lied. I've been trying to find out who killed him."

"I warned you, Andrea; I knew it would come to this." Marina had tears in her eyes. "I'm just glad you're OK." She rubbed her daughter's hand affectionately.

Andrea looked at her mother warmly. "I never could fool you, could I?" She set her finished glass down and picked up her purse. "Remember when somebody broke into my house, I told you the only thing I could find missing was our photograph?"

"Yes," Marina frowned. "But I don't understand."

Andrea continued, "You don't? Before Michael died, he wrote me a note saying that he had some documents, which pointed to a possible fraud relating to the Icon of Kazan. They were kept in a safe deposit box in a bank downtown. He told me the key to it was in a black lacquer box on his mantel. So this reporter, Keith Carlton, and I went to Michael's place to get the key, but somebody was there. He mugged Keith and stole the box."

"What happened to your common sense?" Marina scolded. "Have all those books rotted your brain? How could you get involved with something like this?"

"I know, I know. I couldn't help myself. Anyway, Vera told me about Alexander Menshikov, so I went to see him hoping he'd tell me something about Cecil Durant. That's when I found our photograph." Andrea pulled out the framed picture from her purse and set it on the table before Marina.

Her mother blanched. "You took this from Alexander Menshikov's house? He chased you just now?"

"Who else could it have been? This all happened just after I left his home."

"Did you actually see the one who chased you?"

"No, I didn't. I didn't exactly have time to take a good look."

"So, it could have been someone else," Marina argued.

"I don't think so," Andrea fumed. "Why are you so angry?"

"You could have been killed!" Marina fiercely dabbed her eyes with some Kleenex.

"Yes, I know, Mama, but I wasn't."

"What else did Vera tell you?" Marina asked grimly.

"Nothing. Why don't you tell me what she didn't?" Andrea's eyes blazed. "Why did this man have our picture? Who is he? What haven't you told me?"

Marina stood up, walked towards the living room window and turned her face away towards the outside view of the bay. "Yes, it's true," she said softly." I haven't told you the whole story. I have known Alex Menshikov a long time—since before you were born. Excuse me for a minute." Her mother disappeared into the kitchen and came back carrying the bottle of vodka.

Andrea sat still on the sofa as she watched her mother refill her glass. Her hand, dotted with age spots, trembled from emotion. Andrea could tell this was not easy for her.

"You know how you used to hear stories from Nicky about

Russians coming to stay at our house in Scarsdale? Well, Alex Menshikov was one of them. Nicky adored him. So did you, but you were too young to remember. Alex was a handsome man then, charming, with a glossy brown beard. Lots of fun, the life of the party. We became lovers. Sam hated him, of course. He didn't know about our affair at first, but I think he must have been suspicious. Then you were born.

"One night, both of them had too much to drink and he and Sam got into a bad fight. Sam called him a Commie and things got very ugly. It was during the McCarthy hearings when Sam thought everyone who wasn't in upper management was a Communist. It was horrible. So petty minded. That's why I ultimately left Sam." Marina wiped a tear from her eye.

Andrea sat there in a daze. "What else?"

"Remember when we moved to Burlingame and how we lived on Sam's alimony? That's when you and Nicky went to school and I started working in the Interior Decorating business. Alex followed us out here for a while. We usually met away from home. Those were the nights Vera would baby-sit for you, so Alex and I could have time together. But it couldn't last. He refused to stay put. He had no steady income. He didn't want a family, he wanted adventure. I was just a convenient port in the storm. We fought a lot. God knows how I finally screwed up the courage to end it with him. You were five when he left for good." Marina gulped her second glass of vodka.

Andrea gallantly tried to grasp what she was hearing. "So you and Alex had an affair. Why didn't you tell me before?" She fought back the tears.

"It was just too painful. To tell you about him would have been like cutting open an old wound. There were times when I thought I wanted to kill myself. Gradually, it seemed easier to let sleeping cats lie."

"Dogs, Mama," Andrea corrected her, always slightly amused by the way she mangled American idioms. "Did you ever see him again?"

Marina paused. "No, I never saw him again, not until the other night. He came over unexpectedly to ask me to warn you about this icon business. That's why I called you."

"To warn me?" Andrea stared at her.

"Yes, he's very concerned about you."

This didn't make sense to Andrea. "How could he be so concerned about me one minute and take pot shots at me the next? How did he know I was involved in this in the first place? And how did he find you?"

"I don't know," Marina sniffed. "You know how Russians gossip..." Marina sat down again on the sofa next to Andrea.

"Hmmmm," Andrea nodded. "But why didn't you tell me about the affair after he came to see you?"

"Things happened so fast. I didn't know he was mixed up with this thing! Although I should have known..." She placed her glass on the coffee table. "He and the black market used to be tighter than a pack of wolves. Who knows what he knows? Besides, I've kept the secret about him for so long, I couldn't find the courage to tell you and Nicky. I was afraid you'd hate me. I'm sorry Andrea. And to think I almost got you killed! Please forgive me." Marina burst into tears and covered her face with her hands.

Andrea gathered her mother in her arms. She hugged her, kissing her salt and pepper gray hair and rocked her back and forth, "That's OK, Mama. That's OK. I forgive you, Mama." The question she asked herself was, could she forgive herself?

3

Saturday, November 3, 1990

Next morning, Marina made breakfast for her and Andrea. Fresh ground coffee, scrambled eggs, juice and homemade honey nut filo pastry. Marina served herself after Andrea and sat down at the kitchen table.

"What are you going to do?" Marina poured Andrea another cup of coffee.

"What do you mean, what am I going to do?" Andrea stopped eating with her fork poised midair over her plate.

"Are you going to the police or what?"

"I don't know. You think I should turn myself in?" Andrea finished her forkful of eggs.

"I think you should tell them what happened. It's a lot better than if they found out on their own and threw you in jail!"

"True."

"Andreochka, do yourself a favor, do your Mama a favor. Go to the police," she pleaded. "Tell them what happened. It couldn't hurt!"

"I guess you're right. I'll stop by there when I leave."

"Good! Now, tell me about this reporter. Keith? What is he like? Are you seeing him? What kind of lover is he?"

"Mama!" Andrea blushed. "It's nothing, really." She sipped her coffee.

Marina sat back and studied her daughter. "No, there's more. I can tell. You're glowing." She put her elbow on the table with her chin in her hand. "Tell me. You never kept anything from me before."

Andrea smiled bashfully, "There's nothing to tell. Really." She shifted uneasily in her chair, "At least not yet," she said. "He's very different from the rest. Not like the Russian boys I used to date who were always so grabby, or critical like Michael, or even Gareth, who was sweet but so milk-toasty. Keith is intense but somehow more easy-going. He's funny too, and smart. I feel like I don't have to pretend around him. He's well-read, writes, and is a photographer. He speaks two languages, including a little Russian and seems as if he has traveled everywhere."

"Russian? He makes you laugh? That's good." Marina nodded with approval. "Sam had no sense of humor at all. Very bad. But he sounds as footloose as Alex was. Be careful, dear, you can never depend on those kind of men. What is that saying about a falling pebble?"

"A rolling stone, Mama," Andrea corrected. "The thing is, Keith is such a slob!"

"So, he's a bachelor! What do you expect, another Michael Beech?"

They both laughed. "Now, Mama! You have no respect. For all his selfishness, there were many wonderful things about Michael."

Andrea felt a lump gathering in her throat.

Marina raised her hands. "OK, OK, I won't say anything bad about the dead. I just want you to be careful this time."

Andrea kissed her mother's cheek and said, "I will, Mama. I'm over thirty now."

Marina snorted, "Age has nothing to do with brains. If anything, it gets worse."

Andrea grinned. "Thanks for breakfast. It was delicious." She collected her purse and coat.

Marina hugged her daughter and shook her shoulders gently. "Call me soon." She looked sternly into Andrea's eyes, "Be careful, promise?"

"I promise, Mama," Andrea kissed her and stepped outside. She stopped on the doorstep momentarily to take in the majestic panoramic view of the Pacific Ocean and the Marin Headlands painted a dusky sage green. She raised a silent prayer of thanks then walked to her car.

A piece of paper fluttered under her wiper blade. She pulled at it, "Damn, another ticket!" But it wasn't a ticket. One telling sentence, typed with capitals letters just like the first note, screamed from the white page. BANG, BANG YOU'RE DEAD.

4

The words "bang, bang you're dead", echoed in her brain as Andrea drove all the way to the Hall of Justice. She didn't look forward to seeing Detective Catelano again, especially after the grilling he had given her at their last meeting. She wanted to go home as soon as she passed through the big glass doors and saw the metal detector, but her mother's voice and the second death threat pushed her forward.

Andrea took the elevator up to Homicide Division and stepped up to the policeman at the front desk. She asked, "Hello, could I see Detective Catelano?"

An older Irish cop with a thick paunch, stared at her with bland eyes. "Do you have an appointment?"

"No," she admitted. "But I have some information about a case he's working on. It's important. My name is Andrea West."

He raised his eyebrows, "OK, let me see if he is in. He's been pretty busy. There's been a rash of killings in the Army Street projects again. Sign your name and the time of day here." He pointed to the sign-in sheet attached to the clipboard on the counter. He pressed the intercom buzzer and said to the back office, "Is Tony back there? Andrea West here wants to see him. She says it's important."

A flat female voice sounded over the intercom, "He'll be right out. Tell her to have a seat."

Tony Catelano shouldered his way through the door as if he was in a hurry and stopped cold. He looked surprised to see her. Andrea rose from her seat, "Detective, I need to see you."

"Come on into my office." He restrained his growl. She followed him into the inner sanctum. He offered her a chair. She sat down nervously.

"Mind if I call in my assistant?" He paused at the door. Andrea shook her head no. He shouted down the hall, "Hey, Jergeson, come in here for a minute." Officer Jergeson came in quietly, bearing a report form attached to a clipboard. He nodded hello to Andrea and sat on the edge of the side table. Tony sat down and leaned back in his chair. "So?"

Andrea hesitated. "I'm not sure how to begin," she stammered.

"How about at the beginning?" Tony smiled at her reassuringly. He sat down heavily in the chair next to hers, his body exuding exhaustion.

"Well, I think I know who burgled my house."

"Does this have anything to do with the icon and Beech's murder?"

"I don't know," Andrea stammered. "I went to this icon dealer's place in San Francisco. His name is Alexander Menshikov."

"How do you spell that?" Officer Jergeson interrupted. She spelled it for him and gave him the address.

"Alexander Menshikov lives on Alamo Square. I heard that he had a fabulous collection of icons, so I went to see them. When I got there, I was shown into his study. While I was there, I found the picture that was stolen from my house. He showed me some icons and when he stepped out of the room, I took back my picture," she spoke hurriedly.

"Then I left. As I was driving to my mother's house, somebody started chasing me, I think it was a green Mercedes. They took a shot at me and hit the back of my car. That's when a cop stopped me for speeding. You can find the police report on your computer."

"So why would he steal your photograph in the first place? And how do we know he actually stole this photograph. We only have your word for it."

"How else would it get from my house to his?" Andrea answered irately.

Tony looked up at the ceiling. His voice was more modulated. "And how did you find out about this Alexander Menshikov?"

"Through a friend of my family's. She was an old colleague of his once, used to be in the arts and antiques business. She's retired now."

"And she told you to go see her old friend Alex, is that it?"

"That's right," Andrea said more brightly. "He has an export/import business and among other things, he sells icons."

"We already know about your interest in the Kazan Icon." Tony leaned forward in his chair.

Andre felt cornered, "Yes, and not just that one. I have done a lot of research on Byzantine art."

"So you would have every reason to know about this man without your friend's help?"

"No!" Andrea said. "I never heard of him before."

"Are you sure?" Tony leaned towards her and riveted his eyes upon her. "Why don't you tell us the truth this time, Ms. West. Why did you really go to this man's place?"

"I told you!" Andrea protested.

"No, I don't think you did. We have all day. Why don't we start over again?"

Andrea's thoughts raced. She was trapped and she had walked right into it. She was close to tears. "OK," she sighed. Her face was red. "I've been looking for the Icon of Kazan," Andrea admitted, "even after our last talk."

"Was Carlton in on this with you?"

"No!" she blurted too strongly. Tony leaned back in his chair and studied her while Jergeson continued to take notes quietly on the side. "Keith had nothing to do with it." Andrea tried to recover her composure and changed direction. "I had heard about Menshikov's art business and then I remembered that Michael knew him. That's when I got suspicious and decided to pay him a visit."

"On the basis of this you stole the photo?" Tony glanced at Jergeson, "You searched Mr. Menshikov's place without permission, I presume."

Andrea flashed furiously at him, "Of course! It's mine after all."

Tony stood up and paced the room. "Let me refresh your memory a little. Back to the night Keith was hurt. Both of you went to Michael Beech's house that night, didn't you? After the team and I already searched the house."

Andrea nodded her head, falling for his bluff. She stammered, "How did you know?"

"They have a great neighborhood watch system in Pacific Heights. A neighbor heard a scuffle and later reported seeing two people matching your descriptions get into a car down the street. When I later visited Carlton in the hospital I knew he'd been up to something, so I just added things up."

"Well, somebody is still after me. Someone wrote me a death threat and left it at the seminary," Andrea admitted. "I stayed at my mother's house last night, but I found this on my windshield this morning." Andrea handed Tony the typed note.

He read it without comment and handed it to Officer Jergeson. "We'll keep this, if you don't mind."

"Be my guest! So, what do you think?"

"Ms. West, have you any idea how much trouble you're in? I could put you in jail for this, not to mention with charges of obstructing justice. The only reason I'm not going to is because your record is spotless and because I want you off this case!" He pointed at her. "You keep your nose out of this! I don't want to see you around any more. Do you understand?"

"Yes, sir." Andrea looked meekly down at the floor.

"And if you see your boyfriend before I do, ask him to drop by my office."

"Yes, sir," Andrea repeated. "Is that all?"

"Get outta here. I don't want to see you anymore," he dismissed her. "In fact, why don't you get out of town for a while and let me do my job. I think it will be safer for you. If you do, let me know where you're going."

Andrea got up quickly from her chair and backed out towards the door, "Thank you, Detective." She was glad she had already phoned Transfiguration Monastery. She closed the door behind her, signed out and went downstairs slowly, thinking pensively.

Tony grinned at his partner Jergeson and leaned back in his chair. "Well, how'd I do?"

"Hey, that one was a definite winner. A real Oscar perform-ance," he grinned back. "You weren't serious about arresting her, were you?"

"Just about. But we don't have enough evidence. I just hope I scared the shit out of her so she doesn't do something screwy again."

"Do you think she will?" Jergeson asked.

"I don't know," Tony tapped the tips of his fingers together. "It depends on how desperate she is. And why." He turned back towards his phone, "Let's run an FBI check on this Menshikov guy and see what we get. He sounds like a real scuzzball to me. We may have something here. Then maybe we'll go pay him a visit."

5

Andrea's session with the police frightened her in more ways than she had imagined. Everyone's right, she thought to herself. This is nuts. But she realized she was already in too deep, hooked into the drama like a drug, and she saw no way out.

As she drove away from the police station, pictures of what Keith had told her about Michael's death flashed through her mind. Imagines of Michael's body lying dead and the bloody knife stuck into the altar haunted her. Instinctively, something told her powers were at work here that went beyond the normal confines of evil.

"Oh, Michael, poor Michael," she said aloud and shot a short prayer upwards.

She stopped for a red light and as she waited, she suddenly felt a weird sensation, as if time had slowed into slow motion. She felt the temperature inside the car drop twenty degrees. All the hairs rose on the nape of her neck.

She distinctly felt as if Michael was sitting invisibly in the car seat next to her. She felt his transparent gaze bore into her soul. "Find her!" he said, quite audibly.

Great, that's all I need, Andrea laughed to herself, a haunted Honda! She wasn't sure she should speak towards the clouds or to the space in the car seat next to her. Now I'm really going crazy, she thought. "OK, Michael," she said aloud, "but only if you stop bugging me!" And as soon as she had made her decision, she felt the chill lift.

6

It was after lunch when Andrea finally reached home. She sank into her soft overstuffed sofa, exhausted and still shaken from the car chase, finding out about Alex, and the scorching diatribe she had just received from Tony Catelano.

She knew she was treading on dangerous ground, but her fascination and curiosity, as well as her wounded pride, wouldn't quite let her give up. She debated what to do and decided to give Keith a call.

She dialed his number and then sank back onto the sofa again. "Hi, Keith?"

"I was wondering what happened to you," he answered softly.

"I had a hell of a night last night," she said.

"Me too. I'll never have another vodka again! I missed you."

"Somebody tried to kill me last night." She told him her story from going to Alex's house, to the car chase and the police station, leaving out the part about Michael's ghost.

"Jesus, you sure all that happened in twenty-four hours? Are you OK?" he asked anxiously. "You weren't hurt?"

"Just shaken up a bit," Andrea confessed. "More by Catelano than anything...Though getting chased in the park was a nightmare."

"So you think this bastard killed Michael and stole the icon?"

"I don't know. He could have. I wonder if he could be the guy who jumped you at Michael's."

"How big was he?"

"Pretty tall," she said.

"I thought the guy who jumped me was short, but maybe I'm wrong. It happened so fast."

"That's not all," Andrea said, after debating whether she should tell Keith this or not. "Mama knows him. She said he was her lover when I was little back in the '50s. He used to smuggle icons from the Soviet Union to the U.S. and who knows what else. He has a pretty slippery past."

"He doesn't sound like the sort of guy a mother of yours would get involved with," Keith answered.

"I never knew about it. It's a real shock. She said he was very charming and fun back then. She flipped for him, I guess. I never knew she had a fast streak in her."

"Does she still see him?"

"No. She said he came to see her after Michael was killed to warn me to keep my nose out of the investigation. He must be involved with it somehow, but if he is, he never told her."

"How did he know you were involved?"

"I don't know. That's my question," Andrea said. "Did you discover anything at the police station?"

"I saw Tony too, right after you did. He tried to give me the same treatment. He said that if I had got involved in the case again he'd throw me in the slammer so fast it would make my head spin."

"What does your friend know about Durant?" Andrea asked.

"He knows Durant has a place down in Santa Barbara and that he was some kind of Canadian archeologist and art appraiser with questionable qualifications. He and his wife once started some New Age church and had a number of disciples. But he didn't have anything more on him."

"Keith, maybe we should hold off before things get more out of hand?"

"Not on your life! Not when I could get one of the best leads of my life."

"But we might get killed! Besides, I don't want to go to jail just so you can get a Pulitzer."

"Is that why you think I'm doing this?" he asked. Andrea could hear the hurt in his voice. "Just say I have a thing against seeing innocent people going to jail."

Andrea could feel her respect for him swell inside her. "I hate burdening you with my problems and I certainly don't want to get killed."

"Who does? It's no burden. What are friends for? You won't get killed, I'll be with you. Still, if you think we should hold off, I will."

Andrea debated within herself. Her reason fought with her heart. The real problem was that she was hooked on Keith and his unselfishness was digging him deeper in her heart. How could she refuse? And then there was her promise to Michael in the Honda. "Thanks," she sighed. "Catelano told me to get out of town for a while and I think it's a good idea."

"He's right," Keith said. "Menshikov might try to come back to your house, especially since he knows you have something on him."

"I think he's known that all along," she said ruefully.

"What are we going to do now?"

"Not we, me. Remember, I'm going to a Russian monastery up north. It sounds perfect, right now. I really need to get out of the City and to find some space. What about you?"

"I wish I could go with you. I could use some fresh air but I've got some work to do at the newspaper," Keith said. "Back to the old grindstone. I'll call you every day."

"I don't think the monastery wants many phone calls. Maybe I better call you. You'll be more accessible."

"I'll wait with bated breath."

Andrea laughed. "Please, spare me. Don't worry, I'll call." Then she placed the receiver down slowly, savoring the energy connection that had mysteriously leaped between them across miles of telephone wires.

CHAPTER 13

❧

"Judgment is not something which descends upon us from outside. The day will come when we shall stand before God and be judged, but as long as our pilgrimage continues, as long as we live in the process of becoming, as long as there is ahead of us this road which leads to the full measure of the stature of Christ which is our vocation, judgment must be pronounced by ourselves."

Metropolitan Anthony Bloom
Meditations: A Spiritual Journey

Transfiguration Monastery was an easy three hours north of San Francisco, past Ukiah, outside the small lumber town of Willits, home to lumberjacks, environmentalists, a few former and not so ex-hippies, besides the regular town folk.

The monastery nestled snugly at the bottom ridge of Sanhedrin Mountain, built obscurely in the forest off a rarely used fire road. "Sanhedrin Mountain" was an ironic name to have so close to a Christian monastery, Andrea thought, as she pictured Jesus' interrogation by Caiaphas in the Jewish Sanhedrin on Good Friday.

After she left Route 101, she drove on back country roads, along narrow lanes lined with huge gnarled California oak trees and green firs. The autumn leaves glowed in the late afternoon; a riotous profusion of orange and yellow dazzled in the fading sunlight. She hadn't seen such rich fall colors since she left Westchester County.

Andrea sped past flat green pastures and gnarled vineyards, their vines harvested and stripped of ripe red grapes, past farmhouses and whitewashed summer cottages. Then the county paved road ended abruptly and turned into a winding dirt fire road. Her car bounced and jostled for several miles over the pockmarked terrain until she came to the hillcrest and found the monastery perched in a sheltered, heavily wooded forest.

The "monastery" was not very church-like at all: more like a Northern Californian redwood summer house, a large ranch-style home with a wide deck that wrapped all the way around it, over-looking the variegated valley. Smell that piney air! She inhaled deeply.

Deciding to poke around before she went inside, Andrea climbed up the hill through a stand of pine trees towards a lovely wooden pioneer-style Orthodox chapel. Just like the one at Ft. Ross, she thought. It had a small gold cupola on top, double wooden doors in front and a bell off to the side. Beyond the chapel, she noticed a few cabins set apart from each other. She assumed these were used for guests.

A piercing screech sounded directly behind her, making her jump and spin around with surprise. A large plump blue-green crested peacock strutted before her eyes, bobbing its head back and forth, its tail spread out ostentatiously in full fan. "Oh! How lovely!" She spoke aloud, as her heart rate returned to normal. It squawked again so loud that Andrea covered her ears. Too bad they look like heaven but sound like hell, she smiled to herself.

Twenty yards off to the right, another squawk echoed from the woods. Then more calls from other parts of the woods and the drive-way; a nerve-wracking cacophony of territorial peacock calls. Others answered. Andrea counted six peacocks altogether. Then the noise stopped as suddenly as it began, while the one closest to her pecked the ground, shook its crown and stared shiftily at her with its beady eyes.

Remembering with amusement how Southern short story writer Flannery O'Connor often used peacocks in her writing, she surveyed the birds once more. They were ancient symbols of eternal life. Yes, Flannery would have enjoyed this. She felt, for the first time in days, the muscles in her neck beginning to relax.

As Andrea approached the main house, she saw a large cage containing six snow-white doves with red albino eyes. Their cooing sounded as mellow and supple as a babbling brook. In the waning warmth of the late afternoon light, she listened to them for a long while, soaking it all in, her eyes half closed.

She never even heard the tread of feet on the crunching gravel. "You must be Andrea West," a young man's voice said, startling her out of her reverie. "Did the peacocks scare you?"

"Only a little," she admitted. "They're beautiful birds!" She paused to examine the young monk with the shaggy red beard standing before her. Quite tall, he looked pale and gaunt from fasting, but with a face as fresh as any twenty-year-old farm boy. "You must be Brother Isaiah." she offered her hand.

He kept his hands under his scapular. "I'd shake hands with you but I've been in the garden," he apologized. Andrea noticed muddy timber boots below his frayed black cassock. He nodded to the peacocks. "We hope to breed and sell them some day."

"Aren't they too noisy?"

"Yes, they can be a real nuisance—and messy. Not the best crop to have around a monastery." His eyes turned shyly towards the ground. He changed the subject. "Have you seen the place yet?"

"No." She shook her head. "I presume that's the chapel. Are those guest cabins up there?" She pointed in their direction.

"We call them scetes."

"How long have you been here?" she pried.

"The monastery's been here fifteen years. I've only been here for five." He didn't seem to mind the question. He looks younger than his age, she thought. "Father Seraphim spent some time with the Camaldolese monks down at Big Sur, you know, the Benedictine monks, before coming here to start this monastery," he continued. "He was a missionary in Africa before that, with the White Fathers. He was nearly killed during the Congo uprising. Nearly had his legs cut off. Despite this, he has become a great scholar and speaks at least seven languages fluently. Now he lives here as a hermit."

"Does that mean he never speaks to anyone?"

"Not to outsiders, usually. He has taken a vow of silence, except, of course, for special circumstances or when he occasionally agrees to see someone for spiritual direction."

"I guess I've come all this way for nothing," Andrea sighed, hoping she could still contrive a visit. "Father Mench told me I had to see him, that his information about the Icon of Kazan was invaluable."

Brother Isaiah shook his head, "He hasn't spoken in a year. But Father Mench carries a lot of weight around here. It also depends on how Father Seraphim is feeling."

"Is there anything you can do?"

"No. He's very strict about his rule."

Andrea sighed. "Well, at least I can still enjoy the serenity of the place."

"Shall I get your bag?" Brother Isaiah offered politely.

Glad for a bit of old fashioned male gallantry, Andrea acquiesced. "Thank you."

Together Brother Isaiah and Andrea hiked up a steep path into the forest to her tiny cabin, fifty yards above the wooden chapel. "This is your scete," he said proudly.

"That means 'little hermitage' doesn't it?" she asked as she inspected the interior. A dose of solitude might just be what the doctor ordered.

He nodded, seeming pleased, and said, "Vespers is in an hour, then dinner, and Compline is at 7:15 p.m. Night vigil is from 1 to 2 a.m. but you don't have to get up. Then we go back to bed until matins and mass at 5:30. Breakfast is at 8 o'clock sharp. Enjoy your stay."

When they reached her cabin, he deposited her suitcase on the doorstep. Then, making a slight courteous bow with his hands tucked in his scapular, he turned and walked briskly down the hill towards the main house.

Nothing but twittering wrens and the random caw of a crow disturbed the absolute hush of the place. Andrea looked around and sighed contentedly. "What a peaceful life they live up here."

The wooden cabin was rustic and simple inside: a single bed, a small sink, an old throw rug, curtains on the windows, an oak bureau, an Orthodox cross over a small desk, a straight chair, a lamp and a used olive-green easy chair. The toilets and showers were communal. Andrea put her bag down and, feeling tired, lay down on the soft bed under a blanket, and quickly fell asleep.

At first, she thought she was dreaming when she heard a noise at her cabin window—the brittle metallic sound of tapping on glass. It was probably just a blue jay on the roof. But the tapping sound continued.

She pushed the curtain aside and found herself face to face with a short, swarthy, rather gnome-like white haired man. He had a military crew cut and was dressed in green khakis. He stared at her with fierce eyes.

2

Andrea let out a slight scream and jumped. The "gnome" pressed a finger to his lips, "Shhhh," he hissed, and urged her with the wave of a hand to follow him outside. Not quite sure at first if he was a guest, a local militiaman, or her would-be murderer, Andrea stood her ground.

"Who are you? What do you want?" Andrea placed her hands on her hips, silently praying she had locked her door.

The old man motioned to her to open the window, which she did. He whispered through the screen, "I know you knew Michael Beech and you're trying to find the Icon of Kazan." He looked around. "We can't talk here. I can help, but you will have to follow me."

Something about his pleading eyes made Andrea innately sense he was telling the truth. She decided to chance it. Her curiosity, as always, got the better of her. "OK, but only a little way."

She followed him up the steep narrow path behind her cabin into the woods. Andrea could tell that though the old man was short, his muscles bulged and he was in excellent condition for his age. He scurried up the hill like a deer, while Andrea, more out of shape than she would have liked, followed behind.

After a hundred yards, she could take no more. "Hold on," she said, and stopped. Her chest heaved. "I'm not going a step further unless you tell me who you are and where you're taking me."

The old man stopped and pointed at a log, "Sit here, Ms. West." His broad American accent contained the barest hint of having come from someplace else.

Andrea sat down. "How do you know about Michael and the icon? How do you know about me? Who are you?" she asked indignantly. She suddenly felt as if she had no more secrets left in this world. "I want to get those killers as much as you do." The man sat on a stone and peeled the bark off a twig with his fingernail.

"How do I know you're not one of them?" Andrea asked caustically.

"I was once, until they went off the deep end and let things go too far."

"You mean the murder?"

"Yes, and before that." He scanned her shrewdly. "Michael told me about you. He said you could be trusted. Right now, you're the only one I can turn to."

Andrea was stunned to hear Michael's name mentioned under such strange circumstances, but then again, nothing would surprise her any more. She did some fast thinking. "If you knew Michael, you must be in contact with the Holy Virgin Society. Were you the one who tipped them off about the Kazan Icon?"

He looked at her poker faced. "I can't answer that. All you need to know is that I can help. I can get the abbot to speak to you, but you have to promise me something first."

"It depends." She studied his face and wondered if he was Slavic and why he had turned against them, whoever "they" were.

"On what?" He picked his teeth with the twig.

"How safe it is."

"Safer than driving on the freeway."

Andrea shook her head. "Oh, that's reassuring. I don't understand any of this. OK, what is it you want?"

"I want you to meet me at the Russian Cultural Museum in San Francisco and pick up some papers for me. They're related to the icon. You know where it is, on Sutter Street. Go there this Wednesday morning, at 11 o'clock sharp."

"If you know so much about all this, what makes you think I won't call the police and tell them about the papers or you?"

"Because you need to see the abbot and I'm your only passport to him. If you call the police, the deal is off. Besides, I have nothing to fear from the police..."

"But from the killers you do," Andrea guessed.

He never batted an eyelash. "Will you do it?"

Andrea hesitated. "Not my idea of a nice cultural outing. Why should I go?"

"Because you won't get anywhere if you don't. Besides, if you don't, you won't get any reward money."

"I'm not in it for the reward money."

"Suit yourself," he shrugged. "$500,000 is a lot of money. Somebody's got to get it."

Suddenly the image of $37,000 dollars worth of student loans suddenly vanishing had great appeal to Andrea, but she would never have admitted that out loud. "All I care about is finding out who killed Michael."

"I've got evidence that will make some heads spin."

"Why don't you send it anonymously to the police?"

"I'd rather give it to you. It's safer. Meet me at the Russian Museum on Wednesday."

Andrea considered for a moment, and then said recklessly, "OK, you've got a deal."

"Good." The little man jumped up. "I'll arrange everything." With that, he dashed down the path again without even saying good-bye. Or thank you, for that matter.

3

Andrea sauntered back to her cabin and lay on her bed replaying the perplexing encounter over in her mind. This case is getting weirder all the time, she thought. She napped for twenty minutes until the bell rang from below for vespers and woke her.

After washing her face, she eagerly walked down the hill towards the pine trees surrounding the church. Grandmamma would have loved this scene. She remembered Babushka Anna fondly and wished she had a little finger's worth of her faith.

The little wooden church looked like something out of the Russian fairy tale books illustrated by Bilibin, which her mother read to her when she was a little girl. The green pine trees camouflaged it so well that the church seemed, from a distance, almost invisible at first.

The vespers service was lengthy. An older monk led the service in English. Nine monks dressed in black cassocks, all assorted ages and sizes, including Brother Isaiah, joined in. They chanted, prayed and sang for over an hour, standing most of the time. It seemed eternally long. Andrea joined in and enjoyed the service but also inspected the church's interior for the sake of her doctoral work.

Inside, the all-wooden church was divided into three sections: first, the nave, where a black potbellied stove glowed hotly; second, the choir area, where blonde wooden chairs lined either wall; and finally, the sanctuary itself, with the altar behind the iconostasis. Twenty large and small icons, some of them modern paintings, lined the iconostasis, while red votive candles flickered in front underneath them.

The chapel was filled with the woody smell of honey, burning cedar logs and spicy frankincense. She happily inhaled the pungent air with a satisfied breath. She felt as if she had come home at last. Slowly, all her spiritual angst began to melt away.

After vespers, a young sandy-haired monk carrying a tray kept warm by an aluminum cover, approached Andrea as she headed back to her scete. "Dinner," he said simply. "Leave everything on your front step when you're done. Have a nice. evening." He bowed and left her holding the tray.

After taking off her shoes and settling comfortably in her cabin's single chair, Andrea placed her dinner tray on her knees and removed the dish cover. The meal looked cheap and unappetizing: two boiled hot dogs, a pile of steaming grits, boiled zucchini picked fresh from their garden and a mixed green salad with a large slab of Russian brown bread and butter. When she picked up her napkin, she found a note scribbled in pencil on a piece of paper underneath.

It read: "Father Seraphim will meet you after breakfast tomorrow morning at 9:30. Brother Isaiah will get you." It was signed with an Orthodox cross.

4

Every night, since All Hallow's Eve, the ritual was always executed the same way. Just before midnight, after the servants had all gone to bed and Mrs. Saxon-Briggs lay fast asleep submerged in her mountain of pillows, they silently tiptoed downstairs in the dark. They went to the cabinet, retrieved the Crystal Skull and placed it reverently on the round table in the living room. A beeswax candle was brought from the front parlor and placed by the base of the Skull, then ceremoniously lit.

The room was pitch black, except for the light emanating from the Skull on the central table. Two hands picked up a black priestly stole which had been lying by the candle and put it on. They stood for some time in a circle staring at the Crystal Skull flickering in the dark, arms raised above their heads as they quietly mouthed ancient incantations.

Then it was time to stop. Time to wait and to watch.

5

Sunday, November 4, 1990

At 5 a.m., Andrea's alarm jolted her awake abruptly. The night before, Andrea had gone to bed early so she could rise before dawn to attend matins and the Divine Liturgy. To her grateful surprise, the monks here were surprisingly liberal about letting her receive Holy Communion.

As she dressed, her nose tingled with the smell of coming winter. Outside her warm cabin, the night chill clung heavily like an invisible icy slab in mid-air. Night frost had frozen the grass and leaves under her feet so that they crunched noisily in the darkness as she walked down the path to the chapel. Andrea loved this time of night. The black stillness of these early morning hours filled her with a strange sense of fullness, almost of expectancy.

The white luminous moon dangled low on the horizon; the stars looked especially clear and dazzling in the deep silence. Even the raucous chorus of frogs, which had croaked her to sleep after dusk last night, was still. She stepped softly, not wishing to wake any part of nature, especially the peacocks.

In the distant gloom, the golden cupola of the wooden church shimmered under the diamond stars and the velvet light of the full moon shone through the tall redwoods. The chapel stood as a kind of beacon in the darkness, and in its shadow everything was hushed and soft.

Andrea hurried inside to get warm, and took her place in one of the choir seats. Inside, the church was toasty, smelling of wood smoke, rose water and incense. All the monks were there, huddled in their chairs, wrapped in long woolen black cloaks, as they quietly prayed or arranged the ribbons in their breviaries before singing the morning office.

The black potbellied stove belched heat from the middle of the room. From time to time during the service, Brother Isaiah rose from his seat to poke the fire and set another log in its cast-iron tummy. The crackling fire, the shifting logs, the soft whine of air escaping then imploding in the green wood, combined with the long rhythmic chanting of the psalms, enfolded Andrea like a warm blanket.

The presence of God was palpable, the touch of holiness— almost physical. Her task was simply to accept it and let it in, grate- fully. Like air or sunlight. As she stood there, she imperceptibly felt as if Mary herself had come and wrapped her motherly arms around her. She had no idea how long this state of grace lasted. Though the service was long, it ended before she knew it.

Breakfast delivered on a tray, was simple: weak coffee, which Andrea hated, and hot steaming oatmeal, which she loved. Then, back in her cabin, she read and meditated until after nine.

When Brother Isaiah knocked on her door, she followed him without speaking, to a jeep parked by the main house. He opened the door for her, "We've got a ways to go."

"I thought he was just up the hill."

"He is—on the other side of the mountain. If we walked, it would take us nearly an hour to get there, but I've got work to do." He said this without any malice or impatience.

Their jeep turned onto a secret fire road conveniently hidden by the peacocks' coop and they drove silently for twenty minutes up a rutted dirt road to the top of the mountain. Stopping just below the crest of the ridge, Brother Isaiah said, "We walk from here. It's not far." He brought a bag of groceries and a large bundle of mail with him.

"I see being a hermit doesn't keep Father Seraphim from writ- ing lots of letters," Andrea commented.

"The abbot does important scholarship. He keeps up with peo- ple from all over the world. You should have seen his correspondence before he cut back." Isaiah's eyes danced. Andrea smiled.

They walked down a gently sloping path, overgrown with weeds and Scotch broom, until they reached the hermitage, a homey two-room cabin. A small vegetable garden with leeks, potatoes and beets, had been planted on the sunny side of the house.

Father Seraphim greeted them at the front door, his feet scuffling across the floor as he maneuvered ahead with two canes. Already a very short man, his disability made him even smaller. He smiled warmly and held out his stumpy hands to greet her.

My God, Andrea thought, seeing his pure white hair and a long flowing white beard, he looks just like St. Nicholas!

Brother Isaiah said goodbye. "I'll pick you up at 11."

"Thank you, if it's no trouble," she said and waved to Brother Isaiah as he climbed back into the jeep. Andrea surveyed the view. "It's so beautiful up here and I rarely get out of the city."

Andrea's remark seemed to please the abbot, who held out a hand. "Welcome!" said Fr. Seraphim in a thick French accent, pumping Andrea's hand warmly. "Father Mench wrote me about you. He called you the Kazan Icon lady." His light blue eyes sparkled. He showed her inside and caned his way back into the study, where he had been poring over some old manuscripts.

Inside, the room was sparse but self-sufficient, with a serviceable bathroom in back. There was a desk piled with books; lamps and two chairs; a makeshift kitchenette and a black pot-bellied stove, which radiated heat, keeping the room comfortably warm. He saw Andrea gazing at it. "The brothers made me get it," he confessed. "They said it would make my rheumatism better. I don't think it does, but it makes them feel better, so I have it. The only medicine I take is herbal tea."

He eased himself down into one of the chairs with obvious pain and set his canes on the floor; wincing slightly, he propped his short legs on a stool. "May I trouble you to bring the teapot over? I'm sorry I don't have anything else to offer."

Andrea fetched it. After serving themselves, Father Seraphim asked, "So, you are interested in the Icon of Kazan, yes?"

Andrea blew on her steaming tea to cool it. "The icon was on tour and a friend of mine, who was investigating it, was murdered when it was stolen."

Father Seraphim shook his head sadly. "I knew the tour was coming. *Très sacriligeuse!*"

"Father, tell me what you know about this icon. Is it really so special?" She took the picture of the Kazan Icon, which Luba had given her and showed it to him. "Have you ever seen this?"

"*Oui*, I have seen this one before," he nodded. "It is a holy icon, but of course, it's not the original." he looked at her knowingly.

"What do you mean?"

"Of course, you must know that after the original Kazan Icon was found, two other copies were made. The church used to keep one copy enshrined in the cathedral, and when they had to take the icon outside for other services, a duplicate would be used. The third copy was three feet tall and was kept at the St. Petersburg Cathedral. Later hundreds of copies were made in Russia during the 17th and 18th centuries."

Andrea blinked with amazement. "Hundreds?"

"Surely," he nodded.

"Why did this happen?" Andrea felt confused. "It sounds like a shell game to me."

Father Seraphim shrugged. "Maybe the original would not be stolen so fast, *n'est-ce pas*?"

"That makes sense," Andrea reflected.

"The Icon of Kazan appeared when Tsar Ivan the Terrible wanted to convert the Tartar Moslems in eastern Russia to the Tsar and to the Church. You know the story, no? In 1579, a fire burned Kazan and the Muslim leaders took advantage of this, claiming it was because God was angry with the Russians. The Church had to do something, so the icon appeared."

Andrea arched her eyebrows. "How convenient."

Father Seraphim continued, "You know how the Holy Virgin appeared to nine-year-old Matrona in a dream and told her to dig?" Andrea nodded. He continued, "And how on July 8, 1594, a new convent and cathedral was built in Kazan? The Russians believed it was the Virgin's answer to the Muslims. After this, in 1606, Metropolitan Germogen became Patriarch of all Russia. He probably took the original icon with him from Kazan to Moscow."

"It all seemed to fit into the Tsar's game plan conveniently, didn't it?" Andrea speculated.

"Or God's." Fr. Seraphim countered. "Later, Patriarch

Germogen was captured by Polish troops storming Russia; he was imprisoned and died in 1612, a martyr. Two copies of the original icon had been painted: one for the soldiers' use and one for the people. On October 22, 1612, Prince Pojarsky took the icon from the Kazan Cathedral in Moscow and gathered his troops to pray in front of the icon before they went to battle the Poles, who had invaded the Kremlin. The battle ended in victory and Our Lady of Kazan was greeted as the Liberatrix of Russia."

"Then in 1636, the Tsar built the Basilica of Our Lady of Kazan to commemorate the liberation of Moscow from the Poles. The Icon of Kazan was enshrined there until after the Revolution, when the church was destroyed. The basilica stood on Nikolsky Street near the entrance to Red Square diagonally across from Lenin's tomb. Sadly, in 1936, the Bolsheviks organized a vast crowd of 'militant atheists' and in one day, Poof!" The abbot's hands flew up like doves. "They dynamited it into oblivion."

"That was rather drastic, wasn't it?"

Father Seraphim nodded. "The other icon stayed in Kazan for two hundred years. Gifts of gold, jewels, money, and silk vestments poured into the shrine. Pilgrims traveled for miles to venerate it. Empress Catherine the Great lavished jewels on the icon and donated 25,000 rubles to build a new Kazan Cathedral, which was consecrated in 1808." He rearranged his leg painfully.

"But when Tsar Peter the Great moved the nation's capital from Moscow to St. Petersburg in 1708, the original Kazan Icon was moved with it. In 1737, a Cathedral dedicated to the Nativity of the Blessed Virgin was built on the Nevsky Prospect to enshrine the Kazan Icon, where it stayed until 1811. In 1812, this was the icon Kutusov took and paraded before his troops in order to defeat Napoleon. Tolstoy writes about this in *War and Peace*," he ended.

"I'm confused." Andrea's eyebrows knit together. "Where did the original Icon of Kazan go?"

"That is the big puzzle," he gave her a pixie grin. "In 1736, there were four Icons of Kazan. As of 1917, there were eleven Icons of Kazan officially recognized by the Church as miraculous.

"In 1963, Bishop Leonty, who worshipped the icon at the Kazan Shrine Cathedral in Moscow before the Revolution, positively identified this icon as the Moscow Kazan Icon," he said, pointing to Andrea's picture. "Before the October Revolution, a famous restorer of icons, Stephan Ryabushinsky, examined this icon you saw and gave the opinion that it had been painted over a number of times."

"So even if one of the three was the original icon, it was most likely painted over later?" Andrea asked, very puzzled.

"Perhaps," he smiled enigmatically.

"What about the original Icon of Kazan stolen from the Kazan Cathedral in 1904?"

"That was never found."

"So after the Russian Revolution, two 'miraculous' Icons of Kazan were missing: the Kazan version stolen in 1904 and the one that disappeared out of the Moscow Kazan Cathedral, right?" Andrea summarized, forming a clearer picture of the icon's history.

He waved his hand in the air, "You see, the search for the real Icon of Kazan is like searching for, how shall we say, one truffle in a forest of oaks. The Church, then and now, sees the question of 'which Icon is the real Icon?' as *très dangereuse*—because it pitted one city against another and leads people to idolatry. That is perhaps why they painted over it so many times. The point of an icon is not the icon itself, but God who stands behind it. Christ is the only real Icon that exists."

"I hope you're right, but I don't believe the Church was so high-minded. It looks like it got a lot of mileage out of that icon for four hundred years," Andrea said skeptically. "No wonder the Soviets blew up the Cathedral in Moscow!"

Father Seraphim made a Parisian shrug. "Lots of people do bad things for good reasons, and lots of people do good things for bad reasons."

"What happened to the Kazan Icon after the Revolution, and who has it now?"

"It went underground after the Revolution but reappeared in England in 1935. A rich businessman bought it and when he died, the Icon went to Christie's who sold it to an English explorer. After his death, his adopted daughter inherited it. She sold it to the Holy Virgin Society. They had it until it was stolen."

Andrea, who knew all this, sat on the edge of her seat, "What's the woman's name? Do you know where she lives?"

"Yes, I know her name and where she lives, but I don't approve of her." Father Seraphim stopped and looked at Andrea as if he was gazing through glass. A minute went by. "No. You are not yet ready to see her. You cannot go unless you first make your confession to me. Then, I might tell you where she is."

"Ready? Confession?" Andrea was stunned at his bluntness, but deep down, without knowing why, she felt it was important. "Why don't you approve of her?"

"I think we should not speak of such things in this holy place. Rather, you should think about making your confession."

"What time would you like?" she asked. She would never get anywhere by arguing.

"Today. After prayers and lunch. About 2 o'clock."

A sudden knock at the door startled Andrea. The Abbot beamed at her, "Brother Isaiah is right on time. Thank you, my dear, for an enlightening visit."

Andrea stood and shook his hand, "No, I should be thanking you. Later, then. By the way, have you seen a short man with the crew cut dressed in military clothes? Who is he?"

"But of course, that's the Major." He gave her a wink before he casually dismissed her and returned to his books.

6

Keith's collarbone was healing rapidly. Over the weekend, with time on his hands, he decided to do some sleuthing on his own. Resisting the temptation to phone Andrea, a friend drove him to his office and with the help of Susan, a veteran *Examiner* research assistant, he began to hunt for some noted icon experts.

They weren't too hard to find. Happily, Keith found one in his own back yard, more or less, at Stanford University. Getting him to meet with him and Andrea would be the real trick. As bait, he scanned a photograph of the Icon of Kazan, which Andrea had given him, along with a clipping reporting Michael Beech's murder, and sent them to him on the Internet.

Susan sat back in her chair and smiled with satisfaction as she clicked the computer mouse and sent Keith's message and material to Palo Alto. She looked up at Keith from under a fringe of blonde bangs. "No researcher worth his salt can resist this stuff. Ten bucks he calls you within a week."

"Twenty bucks. Two days," Keith smiled, as he sat with a leg dangling on the corner of her desk.

"Deal," she said, and they shook hands on it.

7

After lunch, Andrea was again driven up to the hermitage. She found the abbot seated by the pot-bellied stove with both legs propped up on a chair upon a pillow. He greeted her warmly and gestured her to sit down in a wooden chair opposite.

"So have you solved the mystery of the Icon of Kazan yet?" he teased.

Andrea felt only the faintest sting in his comment. "No," she admitted, "but I do have some questions." She had heard about hermits who had the gift of discernment and their ability to read hearts. In saints, such as Father Seraphim, this gift operated like a keen psychic sight: the insides of a person's soul would become obvious while the details of the body and persona disappeared. Here she knew she was in the presence of a Master, and she couldn't hide anything even if she wanted to. It was important to ask the right questions.

"But of course," he beamed kindly at her.

"Who is the Major?" Andrea asked abruptly, with intense curiosity. "How does he know about me and the Icon of Kazan?"

"I cannot answer your second question, but the first, I can. He is Major George Vashkovsky, now retired from the army. He is the son of Metropolitan Theodosius, and an old friend of our community."

Andrea nodded her head, as things gradually began to fall into place. "And he's an old friend of this lady, as well?"

"You will pardon me, but I can not answer that either," he looked calmly at her. "Ask me some other questions."

Andrea knew it was fruitless to pursue a direct tack, so she

changed the subject. "Brother Isaiah told me you paint icons yourself.
I know how icons are made in general—that the iconographer paints
them with much prayer and fasting, but I have never heard an iconographer talk about their inner experience. So, I have two questions.
What happens when you paint icons? What are icons really for?"

The abbot looked up at the ceiling and said, "Ahhh. Those are
beautiful questions. Not easily answered."

Andrea sat silently and waited with her hands folded softly in
her lap.

"I will answer the most important one first: what are icons really for? For God, of course, first, and then us. Have you ever drunk
six beers and then had a horrible accident? I have. The experience
sobers you up immediately. Icons are like that. They sober you up,"
he said.

"They are meant to wake you up?" Andrea said.

"That's right. Icons are like windows to God. They are like
doors, which open and take us into God's Holy City. Icons are
reminders that God is always with us. That is why in Russia they
used to be hung, not only in the eastern, beautiful corner of the
room, but also on wells and near springs, in shops, restaurants and
stables, even in train stations!" He almost giggled with joy at this.

"When you look at an icon," he continued, "you are not looking at it. Rather it is looking at you. It follows the movement of
your heart, cleans it, spreads it open and aims it towards God. Icons
are not meant to stir the emotions or reason, like secular art or
music, but rather to guide our hearts, our minds and bodies to their
true purpose: transfiguration.

"In the end, icons teach us that we are only pilgrims in this
world and that we have another home. They are the starting-point of
the inner path, as well as its end. Icons are the way and the means to
God: they are prayer itself."

As he spoke, Andrea noticed that his face shone with an invisible light, which reflected from his eyes and ruddy cheeks. He more
than glowed—he appeared almost to be ringed with fire. He was
quite oblivious to this, unaware that he embodied precisely what he
was talking about. Yet in this mystic state, he seemed utterly down to
earth, not rapt in some vague orgasmic trance. His piercing blue eyes

were exquisitely lucid and clear. He was both tender and passionately fierce at the same time.

A deep pang of longing swept over her as she gazed at him. She realized that she wanted nothing else: to reflect the same kind of fierce tender joy that he had. She ached for it like she had never ached for anything else on earth.

He continued, "When I used to paint icons, I did not paint them; the icon painted itself. Of course, I used wood and gesso, brushes and paint, but it came on its own. The work began with a commission and a special blessing by my spiritual director. I would read the life of the saint and pray to him or her every night. Then I brought the equipment to the church, blessed it with a special mole-ban to the saint, and prayed for help. I fasted while painting the icon, and when I was done, I had it blessed."

"Did every icon you paint change you?" Andrea asked.

"*Mon Dieu*! Of course! With some it was like Jacob wrestling with the angel." He chuckled and pointed to his legs. "That is why I limp so much..."

He stopped unexpectedly and looked kindly at Andrea. "You are too much in a hurry to become a saint, but you don't want to sacrifice anything to become one."

Unaccustomed to being understood so thoroughly, she wanted to hide under her chair. She stammered, "Yes, that's true. That is a problem I have..."

He nodded. "And what about the young man you are seeing?"

Andrea blanched. How could he have known about Keith? "Maybe I should make my confession now," she said with resignation.

"It is time," he said simply.

Her confession did not take long. Fifteen minutes perhaps. They sat there speaking face to face until he gave her absolution. The abbot concluded, "You are in grave danger. Your skepticism sometimes leads you into trouble, *n'est-ce pas*? I warn you, your spiritual pride may bring you to the point of death." He looked sternly at her.

"What should I do? What about the woman's name and address? What about the Major?" Andrea gulped, still stubbornly determined to find her.

"I cannot tell you what to do. You will do what you must. But I cannot tell you her name or where she lives, I do not want to be responsible for your life or for your soul. I can only pray." His eyes were an odd mixture of severity and compassion. He looked at his watch and said, "Now, you must leave. It is almost time for vespers."

Andrea managed to hide her disappointment and stood up courteously. "Thank you, Father, for seeing me. I will always remember you." Father Seraphim eased his legs off the pillow and slowly set each one on the ground, then he hoisted himself up on his canes. He paused and looked gravely and lovingly into her eyes, fathoming much more in her depths than she knew in herself. "And I you." He took her hands tenderly in his stubby ones and kissed them. "I will pray to the Holy Virgin for your protection," he said. Then he turned sadly away from her.

8

Unnerved by his last words, Andrea decided not to join the community for prayers. In fact, she was so worried that she decided to go home early. What was it he knew? Or feared?

After packing, she said good-bye to the monks, glad not to face leftover hot dogs and grits again, and drove down to the city: back to the noisy civilization and craziness she was mixed up in and could find no way out of.

She knew she could not stop her search now, but the idea left her with a lump in her throat. She felt sad, a little ashamed and very vulnerable; guilty as a child stealing cookies from a cookie jar, knowing the act itself kills the pleasure of their taste.

I feel like I've just left the Garden of Eden and can never go back, she mourned.

CHAPTER 14

❧

"Having blotted out of existence the Giver, we become possessors in our own right and exclude ourselves from the mystery of love, because we can no longer receive and we are incapable of giving. This is the very essence of sin—to rule out love, claiming from God, who loves and gives, that He should get out of our life, accept annihilation and die; this metaphysical murder of love is the act of sin, the sin of Satan, of Adam and of Cain."

Metropolitan Anthony Bloom
Meditations: A Spiritual Journey

Monday, November 5, 1990

Priscilla opened the door to Hannah's bedroom, balancing a silver breakfast tray, laden with a small thermos of warm milk, a teacup and a bowl of steaming Cream of Wheat in one hand and a paper in the other. Hannah, dressed in a powder blue night jacket, sat propped up against the gilded art deco headboard, looking like an aged and wrinkled Miss Muffet surrounded, as she was, by a mountain of white cotton pillows. She was pale as the lace frills that edged them.

Her two fluffy, pug-nosed Pekinese dogs lay panting at the foot of her bed; their little pink tongues hung out of their mouths, which were set in perpetual smiles.

"Breakfast," Priscilla said cheerfully.

"Oh, take it away," Hannah grimaced. "It probably tastes awful."

"Be that way," Priscilla said flatly, placing the tray daintily on the dressing table. She poured the warm milk and gave it to Hannah. "This will help settle your stomach."

She drank it quickly, with disgust and handed the cup back to Priscilla, then turned to her morning paper. Hannah weakly held the newspaper close to her face and tried to read the small print with a magnifying glass. She lay down the paper with frustration. "Damn, my eyes are really going."

Priscilla seemed concerned, "It can't be your cataracts again. You just had surgery. The doctor said they would be fine for years."

"I don't know what's the matter. I feel wretched. Absolutely good for nothing. Like an old dishrag. And I've had this horrible headache for the past two weeks," she held her forehead.

Priscilla came up and looked closely into Hannah eyes. They were red and puffy rimmed with pink eye. "They do look pinkish," she frowned. "I'll call the doctor and have him prescribe something for you."

"Please!" Hannah pleaded.

"And I'll get you some aspirin for your headaches." Priscilla handed her the hot cereal. "Here, it's cooler now."

"Do I have to?" she whined.

"Yes," Priscilla ordered. "It will do you good. I will be back shortly." Priscilla left, closing the door behind her silently.

One of the dogs nuzzled up to Hannah's side and begged for food. "Mopsy, what a spoiled child you are." She petted its golden coat weakly, and then fed it a dollop of hot cereal with her spoon. Mopsy licked it up greedily. "You'll get fat like Flopsy."

The other dog lay dejectedly at the foot of her bed. "What? Is Flopsy-wopsy not hungry?" She spoke endearingly to them but would never have dared to do so in front of another human being. "Poor Flopsy. Mopsy, be a good boy and lie down over there." She nudged the dog away. Compliantly, he uncurled himself and waddled to the other dog, then placed his paws over Flopsy's paws and lay his head down to sleep. "That's a good boy," she said. "I don't know what I'd do without my two babies."

She gazed at the Icon of Kazan displayed on the altar, which Cecil had designed for her. The eyes of the Virgin Mary gazed quizzically at her. "Is it because I have done wrong?" she asked again out loud. All was silent except for the soft wheezy snores of Flopsy and Mopsy at the foot of her bed. "Oh, I don't know. What does it matter, anyway?" She closed her eyes and was soon fast asleep.

2

During his mid-morning coffee break, Detective Tony Catelano was reading the pundits' predictions about tomorrow's election in the paper, when Officer Jergeson came into his office and tossed the pile of papers on his desk. "Take a look at these."

Tony hated interruptions. "What is it?" he sighed and gave the files a wary look.

"Menshikov. Seems he was in U.S. intelligence on the Russian front during World War II. The CIA tried to hire him after the war, but he refused. Said he wasn't interested in politics. In the '50s, he traveled between the U.S.S.R. and the U.S. more times than a fox can raid a henhouse. For a long time, the CIA thought his business selling icons and Russian antiquities was his phony cover as a spy."

"Was it?" Catelano raised his eyebrows.

"They could never pin anything on him. He never touched all the CIA material he had access to. Even double agents in the U.S.S.R. said he had dropped out of the spook business years ago."

"What about smuggling?" Tony asked.

"Nothing proven. He's either very good or very clean."

"Keep checking up on him. Anything else?"

"You'll like this. In the '50s he used to hang around New York society types in the Hamptons and Westchester County. His mailing address was in care of Sam and Marina West."

Tony shrugged, "So?"

"They happen to be the parents of our Ms. West."

Tony's eyes opened wider. "Oh?"

"Her parents separated in 1960 and divorced in 1963. Sam West is a lawyer who works for the State Department. He remarried and still lives in Westchester County. Her mother brought Andrea and her brother out to Burlingame in 1960 and got into the interior decorating business. She used her maiden name: Marina Roevich. The two kids were sent to school down the Peninsula."

"Any indication that Menshikov kept up with them?"

"No, he dropped out of sight after 1963."

"Why?"

"Nothing we can find so far."

"Where's the mother?"

"Out by the Legion of Honor, on California Street."

"Maybe we should pay her a visit. Good job, Jergeson." Tony swiveled in his chair and turned back to his overdue reports with renewed energy.

He had just started one report when his phone rang. "Catelano," he answered languidly but sat up immediately as the voice on the other end barked out orders. Tony jotted down names and numbers and ended by saying, "We'll be right there." He slammed the phone down and tore into his jacket. "Let's get a move on," he said, already halfway out the door.

Jergeson, who had never seen him move so fast, trotted beside him, "What's up?"

"That was the Chief. Says someone has left bomb threats against the Mayor and the two candidates. Wants every cop in the city on guard duty until after the election."

"Jesus!" Jergeson shook his head.

The two men walked briskly out the door on their way to City Hall. Their interview with Marina Roevich would have to wait.

3

Andrea had just finished teaching her morning class when Father Peter poked his head inside the classroom door, "How was the retreat?"

She turned from erasing the blackboard. "Oh, hi! It was fabulous. You would have loved it up there." She debated about telling him about the Major or the abbot's warnings about the icon.

"I want to hear all about it. How about lunch?"

A few minutes later, they were sitting together eating their sandwiches at a round table outside in the faculty courtyard. Andrea pulled a ham sandwich out of her bag. "You'd have liked Father Seraphim. He's very holy and looks just like a short, trim Santa Claus."

"He sounds right out of Tolstoy."

"Almost another Father Zosima. We had an incredible discussion about icons, about the rituals he used painting them. He also said there were lots of miraculous Kazan Icons."

Father Peter chuckled. "The Middle Ages in Russia must have been a fantastic time, if you believe all the legends they tell about it. By their accounts, icons were always falling out of the sky somewhere. It must have been positively dangerous to go out of your house."

Andrea smiled. "People were pretty credulous then."

"They still are," Father Peter observed. "There are always stories popping up around Calistoga about some self-cleansing icon." He bit into his crisp Granny Smith apple.

"Really?"

"Some art experts were sent to the Calistoga church and they determined that an unusual bacteria had formed on the icon's face which gobbled up all the dirt, grease and soot. Science is great, but it doesn't explain how these bacteria got there. That's a miracle in itself, I think. An Orthodox priest once said to me, 'Those self-cleansing icons are very well and good, but we must not confuse chemical reactions of paint with revelations from God.' Pretty astute, I say."

Andrea smiled at this paradox. "We also talked about the history of the Kazan Icon," she said. "The Russian army used to pray to it to destroy their enemies. What a horrible way to use a religious object."

Father Peter leaned back in his chair. "That's not new," he said. "I heard a story once in London from a Russian priest about a miraculous icon during World War II. A group of forty people, including Orthodox priests and nuns, tried to escape the Soviet Union through the Eastern Front. The only thing valuable they had with them was the icon of St. Seraphim of Sarov. At one point, they became trapped in the crossfire between the Americans and the Germans. They couldn't go back to the German Army, but in order to get to the American side, they had to go through the middle of the firefight. So their leader, Archbishop Andrew, held the Icon of St. Seraphim high over his head and processed them across the line. No one was shot—in fact, the battle stopped. They all attributed this miracle to the icon."

"And St. Seraphim of Sarov," Andrea added. "Now, that seems to me to be a much better way to view icons, I think."

"Quite," Father Peter said. "The old legends are wonderful, but the trouble with them is that they always lead to a misuse of power. Haven't you noticed that all the ancient stories end up being a tournament of icons? One medieval city with an icon pitted against another city with an icon. Jesus never used power that way."

Andrea asked, "How could something so sacred be used for bad ends? Wouldn't that in some way 'de-activate' the grace that had infused it?"

"That all depends on what you call holy. At first, in religion, people and things considered holy were set apart for special service to God. Over time, this 'set apartness' acquired power. In the Old Testament, God repeatedly warned the people not to come too close or touch Mt. Sinai 'lest I break out.' Remember how when Uzzah reached up and touched the Ark of the Covenant to stop it from toppling, he was struck dead? I suppose God's power was like a high tension wire breaking out in a gigantic power surge."

"Shades of *Raiders of the Lost Ark*!"

"Exactly," Father Peter, having finished his lunch, paused to light his pipe. He settled back in his chair and sucked on his pipe stem. "Now, icons do participate in the holy because of Christ, through whom all things were made. You know the verse in the beginning of John's Gospel, 'In the beginning was the Word...and through Him all things were made.' Because of this, icons somehow participate in the life of Christ. They mediate His presence in some mysterious way."

"You mean they're like sacraments."

"Yes, the outward signs of an inward and spiritual grace—well, sort of. They're not exactly one of the seven sacraments. People sometimes call icons and other holy objects 'sacramentals,' though I have never been able to understand the difference."

"I suppose it goes back to the issue of power, doesn't it? Quantity and quality," Andrea thought aloud.

"But there is something more to it than that because Christianity is supposed to be, at least theoretically, involved with morality more than most other religions. If Christ was supremely moral, then some mediation of His presence ought to exemplify his moral stance. Which then raises the question, how could His presence kill or enable armies to kill?"

"Perhaps it doesn't. After all, we are the ones made with free will. We're the ones who tend to pervert the good, not God."

"Well put," Father Peter said, withdrawing his pipe from his mouth. "Things which are intrinsically good can be used for evil purposes. Even the Eucharist can be used for evil things. That's where the power of the Black Mass comes from, because it is goodness perverted."

"But how can God allow that?" Andrea protested.

"That I wouldn't know. That God obviously can and does is another matter, which comes under the flamboyant theological title of *Theodicy*: 'why God does allow evil?' Fundamentalists—and the Gnostics before them—like to think of the Devil as some alternative power competing with God, as if everything was a battle between good and evil. Of course you know that, according to St. Augustine, evil is not a separate power in and of itself, but rather, is simply the absence of good."

Andrea was delighted by the intellectual rigor of this debate. "Yes, but is evil simply the absence of good? After all, absence is not evil in itself. Doesn't there have to be some intent related to it?"

"Yes, as the Dean of St. Paul's Cathedral once said, '"Evil arises from a disorderly and inharmonious motion.'"

"Hmmm. Gardeners often say that weeds are nothing but a plant in the wrong place, so I guess you could say that evil is a distorted good in the wrong place. Like cancer cells."

"When people intentionally pervert the good to achieve evil ends, it's not simply morally bad—it is wicked, despite the intention or conviction of the users."

"Like when televangelists use God's Word to bilk little old ladies out of their measly pension checks," Andrea said as she sliced into her plum.

"Or when politicians use their self-righteous rectitude to exclude, discriminate or even kill a particular segment of the population."

"That's what Father Seraphim said, 'Sometimes people do very bad things for good reasons, and others do very good things for bad reasons.'"

"Quite," Father Peter said with satisfaction. "And some people do very bad things for bad reasons." He knocked his pipe into his ashtray with three hard taps. "I should like to meet this abbot. He seems like a wise man."

"Perhaps one day you will." She smiled at the thought of this tall, black-haired spiritual giant meeting the short, white-haired one. It would be like St. Mutt meeting St. Jeff, she chuckled to herself.

4

Keith sat in his tiny pre-fab cubicle in the *Examiner* office; his five o'clock shadow had long since sprouted and he stared bleary-eyed at his green computer screen. He had just spent the last twelve hours with Manning, covering the breaking news about the bomb threats against the three candidates running for mayor. They had made little headway.

It was 8:30 p.m. He was so tired he felt as if someone had found a secret plug and drained all the red blood cells from his body. His feet hurt, his shoulder ached and his stomach rumbled with hunger. He had a copy deadline in half an hour and his brain was doing a great imitation of a pile of spaghetti. Throughout most of the day, he had functioned fine on his natural adrenaline, running around City Hall and following up on police leads; but whenever he stopped, like now, he couldn't get Andrea out of his mind.

He found himself thinking about her first thing in the morning, when he was in the shower and when he was standing in line at the deli. He could see her face in graphic detail: her shoulder-length wavy, black hair, her high forehead and sculpted cheek bones, her remarkable nose, her ivory skin, her large, brown, almond-shaped eyes framed under gracefully arched black eyebrows, her full, passionate lips, centered over a firm chin.

He loved how one half of her face sometimes seemed about to break out in mirth while the other half looked so solemn and grave. Under her academic exterior, he sensed there was something wild and exotic inside her, like a muted Firebird, longing to be set free. And increasingly, he yearned to be the igniting spark that would do so.

He knew she had received two death threats and that their actions to solve the crime had not lessened Tony's suspicions about her. He felt a little guilty about this and, in short, he worried about her. Then she went away up north and he hadn't heard from her in three days. He was distracted with worry.

He was vacillating between hurt, because she hadn't called him, and indecision, as to whether he should call her, when the phone rang. A male voice with a broad Bostonian accent asked for Keith Carlton. Keith sat up in his chair. "This is Keith Carlton." The voice on the other end suggested a time and place to meet over dinner.

"I'd like to bring a friend. Is that possible?" Keith asked. By all means, the voice on the other line answered, then the phone clicked dead.

Keith sat back in his swivel chair and smiled with satisfaction.

5

Back home, dressed in her bathrobe, Andrea sat curled up on her sofa in front of a roaring fire. She was grading papers after dinner and was so absorbed in her work that the abrupt ring of her phone startled her.

Keith's smooth voice sounded on the line. "Did you take a vow of silence at the monastery or what?" He tried to keep it light. "I've missed hearing from you."

"Sorry, I've been really busy." She spoke excitedly, oblivious to the hurt in his voice. "Lots of incredible things have happened. For one, I've met the Major."

"Who the hell is the Major?"

"Major George Vashkovsky." She described his odd appearance. "I think he's the one who tipped off the Holy Virgin Society about the Kazan Icon."

"Can you prove this?"

"Not yet, but he admitted he knew Michael and I suspect he's hiding from the murderers. He told me to meet him Wednesday morning at 11 o'clock at the Russian Cultural Museum on Sutter Street. He says he has some important papers for me. Want to come?"

"Are you sure it's safe? I don't want you going alone and I can't guarantee I'll be there. All hell's breaking loose at City Hall. Bomb threats to the mayoral candidates. Anything could happen between now and then."

Andrea couldn't hide her disappointment. "Of course, what you have to do is much more important."

"Sorry. It's not that I don't care, but I have other stories to work on. I'll call Tony Catelano and have someone go with you. I don't think you should go alone."

"The Major said if I called the police, there's no deal."

"It sounds crazy to me. I don't like it."

"Don't worry, I'll be fine. I have a feeling he's safe. He's on our side."

"I wouldn't be so quick to trust a double-crosser if I were you. But it's your call. How about meeting me later tonight—at eleven—and taking up where the Major made us leave off, groping in the dark?"

"Tempting but impossible. I have a mountain of papers to correct and I turn into a pumpkin at nine-thirty."

Keith persisted. "Then why don't you meet me tomorrow night for dinner instead? Before the polls close and they start tossing all the confetti. Six o'clock? At *Maxfield's* at the Sheraton Palace Hotel. I have a surprise for you. There's someone I think you ought to meet."

"Who is it?"

"I told you it's a secret. But I think he can help us find the Kazan Icon."

"And he's joining us for dinner? When you put it that way, who can resist?"

6

Alex sat in his study, listening through his headphones, as curious and perplexed as Andrea. He jotted down the time of her meeting with the Major on a piece of paper, tore it off the pad, and stuffed it in his shirt pocket. Without removing his earphones, he drew long and hard on his cigarette, squinting at the ceiling.

7

Tuesday, November 6, 1990

The next day, tired from teaching all afternoon, Andrea found it impossible to concentrate. She pushed the papers aside and threw her fountain pen down with disgust. Staring out her office window, she watched as students briskly climbed the hill to the seminary library with their collars turned up, hunched against the foggy wind. Soon it would be dark.

She debated what to do as the clock ticked conspicuously in her office. Reason told her to mind her own business, but she had to find out who murdered Michael and where the icon was, not simply for Michael's sake, but for her own. All the authorities in her life, her mother, Father Peter, the abbot and the police, were telling her to keep out of this, but something inside her rebelled against them.

She felt compelled to get to the bottom of this mystery, no matter what the cost, no matter what her fear. She knew this puzzle kept nagging at her because, deep down, she sensed that solving the mystery wasn't simply about finding the icon or Michael's murderer—it was about finding some long lost part of herself.

Andrea flicked on her desk lamp and watched as her hand opened a book, which she had borrowed on inter-library loan, *The History of Orthodoxy in America*. She turned to the index to corroborate Luba's information.

She ran her finger down the index columns, looking for the name of Metropolitan Theodosius, the Major's father, and soon found it. She read: "Metropolitan Theodosius: Theodore Nicholiavich Vashkovsky, born in Odessa and arrived in San Francisco in 1880 as an Orthodox missionary. He had married and raised two children before he was ordained a priest in 1907. He served as Dean of the Russian Church on Powell Street in San Francisco."

"He returned to Moscow with Archbishop Tikhon to serve as Chaplain to the Russian Imperial Army during the First World War, leaving his pregnant wife behind, where she barely survived the birth of her twins, only to die in 1920 during an influenza epidemic.

During these years, Andrea guessed, life in Russia for him must have been cruel and chaotic. She wondered, how a man so high in the Russian Church survived, especially after the Patriarch's arrest. In 1922, he returned to America, was tonsured a monk and consecrated Bishop by order of the Holy Synod that year. He stayed in Chicago until he was transferred as Bishop, to replace Metropolitan Platon in San Francisco in 1931. In 1934, he was created Orthodox Metropolitan of All America and Canada.

Still, the twins, sent into the care of relatives, must have been an inconvenience for him. She knew that in the Orthodox tradition, unlike Roman Catholics, priests could marry—if someone wanted to become a Bishop, he had to be celibate and unmarried. It wouldn't do to have children hanging around the future Orthodox leader of all America and Canada. She wondered how this had affected the Major. Andrea had become so engrossed in her reading that she jolted when Sally poked her head into Andrea's office. "Looks like you're the last one here. Can you make sure the lights are out before you leave?"

"What time is it?" She glanced at her watch. "Oh, Lord! It's 5:30 and I have to get ready for dinner." Andrea rushed out of her chair.

"Is it this hot date you've been telling me about?" Sally arched her eyebrow knowingly.

"Not quite. Keith's bringing company. He say's it's a surprise." Andrea quickly stuffed her papers and books into her tote bag and raced into her overcoat. "I'll walk out with you." She flicked off her office light and they left together.

8

Keith adjusted his tie in the hall mirror before entering *Maxfield's* swank bar at the Sheraton Palace in downtown San Francisco. His brown hair was neatly trimmed. His brief stint in the hospital caused him to lose weight; he looked fit and handsome. For once, he had arrived early. No sign of his secret host. At least he has good taste, Keith thought.

He scanned the room with admiration and sat down on a barstool to bask in the golden glow of the large oil painting that stretched behind the bar. It was Maxfield Parrish's famous "The Pied Piper of Hamlin". He liked what Parrish did with amber light in his art.

He watched the slick, red-haired bartender make his martini. Clearly he knew what he was doing. He set the chilled glass in front of Keith, pouring his concoction out of an ice-cold steel shaker. Keith tasted his drink. "Excellent!" He hoisted his glass in the air. "You've been doing this a long time?"

"Fifteen years," the bartender smiled, displaying a silver incisor in his upper bridge.

The man sitting next to Keith leaned over and said discreetly, "If you really like good martinis, you should try Boris', up at the Assyrian Zam Zam Room on Haight Street. The best in the business."

"Thanks for the tip," said Keith, swallowing his olive. "I'll try it sometime."

Andrea rushed in a little breathless, searched the room and saw Keith sitting at the bar. She was dressed in black stockings and heels, a short, tight, forest-green dress with a silk paisley scarf around her neck, and a black suede coat. Her wavy black hair was fashionably wild and loose. She tapped him on the shoulder.

Keith turned and broke into a smile when he saw her. "Wow!" He spontaneously kissed her, brushing his lips over her ear. "Mmmm. You look terrific and smell even better. I see you have your legs on."

"I don't wear heels very often," she smiled shyly, feeling her blood pulse. "Since you suggested this place, I thought I'd try to look decent. You look pretty good yourself. A tie, no less..."

Keith twirled it for her playfully and posed. "I always send my valet to Nordstrom's. I'm famished; let's sit down." He looked at his watch. "Our mystery host should be here any minute."

"Don't keep me in suspense," Andrea demanded. "Who is it?"

Keith said, "An art historian who specializes in icons. I sent him a photograph of the Icon. His name is James Templeton. I got his name through the Byzantine Arts Research Institute at Dumbarton Oaks in Washington, D.C. He came highly recommended by a Dr. Wassermann of Princeton, who is an expert on iconography. Templeton works at Stanford and has published in a lot of scholarly journals."

"How and when did you dig all that up?"

"Hey, I'm an investigative reporter," he grinned.

Keith took his martini from the bar and they followed the waiter to a pine green booth in the corner under several old black and white photographs of Mayor Christopher with Eisenhower and Kennedy, taken in this same room. As they moved to their table, Andrea felt her body flow with electricity when Keith gently placed his hand in the small of her back.

They had just sat down when a very tall, distinguished-looking man with a short gray mustache, dressed in a crisp navy suit and a burgundy bow tie, stepped into the lounge. He discreetly gave his name to the waiter, who ushered him towards Keith and Andrea's table.

Keith moved his chair to stand up, but James Templeton waved his hand, "No, no. Please don't."

Andrea studied him and thought he reminded her of a State Department bureaucrat from the 1960s. Part of the Kennedy Think-tank. A Boston Brahmin, no doubt. This will be interesting.

Keith extended his hand warmly. "Thanks for coming. I know you're a busy man. Andrea, this is Dr. James Templeton, whom you've heard of, I'm sure. And this is my friend, Andrea West, soon-to-be-professor of Anglican Studies and Theology at the Graduate Theological Union."

James Templeton clasped her hand and studied her with a sharp eye as he said to Keith, "You didn't tell me she was such a ravishing beauty." Andrea blushed. He sat down and neatly placed his white napkin on his lap, revealing a set of gracefully tapered hands. "Actually, before Keith phoned, I had heard of you, Dr. West." He smiled knowingly.

"Oh?" she arched her eyebrow, intrigued.

"Yes, Michael Beech sent me your paper on Byzantine mysticism. Admirable work. Well done."

Andrea blushed again with pleasure. "Thank you. Call me Andrea, please. I didn't know you knew him, but I'm not surprised. Michael always was ubiquitous, especially in the higher circles of the art world."

James glanced sadly down at the white tablecloth. "A tragic loss. If there's anything I can do to help. Of course, I knew the icon was coming to town. I was hoping to confer with Michael about it and I would have, if I hadn't been sent on a wild goose chase to Greece."

Andrea and Keith caught each other's eye across the table. "So you know about the Icon of Kazan?" Andrea asked amazed.

"Of course, though not as well as some people. I've never actually studied it up close, but I've had my doubts about it for a long time. I was hoping Michael's research would confirm my suspicions."

"You wouldn't happen to know Cecil Durant, would you?" Keith stabbed his toothpick into the green olive at the bottom of his martini glass and popped it into his mouth.

"That charlatan! I wouldn't be caught dead with him at Le Père Lachaise cemetery! He once tried to convince me that the Icon of Kazan was the original, but his research methods were half-baked. His excuse was he didn't carbon date the icon because he didn't want to chip any of the paint off. Rather, he said he used a binocular microscope with infra-red and ultra-violet photography to determine that it was painted in Constantinople between 1250 and 1300 CE."

"That would make it over seven hundred years old." Andrea was skeptical already.

James put his head back and laughed, "That's what he wanted everyone to think. He even suggested it was painted by a man who had studied art in Rome because it exhibited the techniques of Greek iconography but with Roman influences. Unlike Russian icons of a later period, he said it didn't have any canvas underneath it, whereas the Russians always put a canvas dipped in gesso over the wood. Durant told me this one had none, but it had three layers of gesso of varied coarseness sanded onto it instead so paint could be applied to the top layer along with the gold and silver leaf. He said it could have come up from Constantinople along the Don River on some trader's boat to Kazan. The last was pure poppycock, of course."

"Father Mench said that Cecil told him it was painted in fact in the 15th century," Andrea said.

James looked sympathetically at her. "I'm not surprised. Good art appraisers can date some of their pieces pretty closely. Their livelihood depends upon it. No real appraiser throws around separate dates without losing their credibility. Especially three hundred years apart."

"Maybe he was just trying to be cautious," Andrea suggested, playing devil's advocate.

"Maybe he's pulling a scam," Keith countered.

"Has anyone come up with any contrary dates?" Andrea asked.

"Well, I think Michael was about to," James said "Art history studies show quite clearly that the decline in the quality of Russian icon painting began around the middle of the 16th century. It was gradual at first but increased at a faster pace through the 18th and 19th centuries. In this period only pastiches of sacred art were produced."

James Templeton paused to butter a piece of French bread and continued, "My own studies lead me to think that the decline in the art of icon painting mirrored the inner decline of the authentic spiritual life of the church. That it did not disappear altogether is testified by the literary revival of spiritual writing in the 19th century. I'm referring here mainly to Theophan the Recluse, the editor and translator of the *Philokalia*." He glanced at his two companions to see if they were following him. Andrea nodded appreciatively, while Keith shrugged his shoulders in ignorance.

The waiter, who came to show Keith the wine, interrupted James' lecture. He swiftly uncorked it and poured Keith's glass, which he drank with approval, making it clear to Andrea that he didn't enjoy all this fussiness but had enough good manners to know what to do. They took a moment to decide their choices from the menu, and the waiter left with their orders.

James resumed his monologue. "Everything related to this Kazan Icon comes from the later decadent period, which most historians of Russian art consider to have begun by the middle of the 16th century—in other words, before the so-called discovery of the original Kazan Icon in 1579. The icon you are interested in is an obvious example of 'religious kitsch' of the late 17th or early 18th century, the period when baroque sentimentality had taken over from Byzantine austerity."

"Religious kitsch!" Andrea laughed. "You don't mince words, do you?"

"I was being charitable." James smiled wanly, clearly enjoying the chance to pontificate. "The icon photo you sent me, Keith, compared to a Kazan-type icon painted, say, in the late 1500s, is inelegant and banal. The features of your Kazan image are more naturalistic: someone attempted to introduce a Western European technique of plastic modeling so that the nose is bulbous and fleshy and the mouth full and voluptuous. The 17th century painter, Simon Ushakoff, first introduced these mannerisms, after which they were widely adopted.

"They are in marked contrast to the pure and sacred artistic style of the Middle Ages. The style then was to make the Kazan image with a small mouth and a long, thin nose, like those of the iconographer Rublev. In his work, the long narrow neck and the generally schematized, mathematical treatment give his figures an air of remoteness and timelessness enhanced by the inward, contemplative gaze of the Mother of God. In contrast, the more sentimental approach, coupled with the jewel-studded riza, causes your icon to seem crude and vulgar. You can reasonably expect that this icon was painted sometime around 1740. More likely much later."

"So let's get down to the bottom line here," Keith was feeling a little overwhelmed by all the details. "How much is it really worth?"

James paused to do some calculations in his head, while he swirled his wine glass in the candlelight inspecting the clarity of the red wine. "I would not value your icon, without the riza, at more than $5,000. The jewels and gold, of course, would be worth considerably more and could be sold at their face value."

Andrea raised her glass of wine to her lips. "So much for the great treasure of the Russian people."

Keith whistled. "I heard it was worth five million. No wonder Michael was so secretive. He was possibly about to uncover one of the biggest art scams of the 20th century."

9

She went to the cabinet, retrieved the Crystal Skull and placed it reverently on the round table, as she usually did every week at this time of night. From the front parlor, she took a beeswax candle and set it by the base of the Skull, then lit the wick. The air smelled of sulfur, smoke and honey.

The light again danced and glimmered from the sockets of the Skull in an almost life-like, demonic gaze. The room was dark except for the glowing Skull on the table.

She placed a black priestly stole around her neck for her usual private ritual. The house was as silent as a stone. She stood with her arms raised above her head before the Skull, silently mouthing ancient incantations, and then waited.

Many religions seek to exile the Dark, but her vocation was to embrace it—not simply to balance the light within herself in a kind of yin-yang dualism, but to push the light out all together. She wanted to contain within herself the power of the Black Hole, which is even more powerful than any light, which could get sucked into it.

She gave herself completely, with keen intention and purity of thought, to the Source—the power of the Black Hole. She felt the deeper dark slithering up inside her thighs like a black flame, licking all her longing into a fiery passion, until her very heart was smoldering in a conflagration of malice.

After perhaps twenty minutes, she stilled her mind to the same frequency of sound and light as the Skull's. Her inner eye saw two images. The first was of Andrea West sitting engrossed in conversation at Maxfield's with two men. She recognized the reporter Carlton, but studied the second man closely and made a note to herself to find out who he was. Almost overlaid on this image was a second image—the Major busily writing letters at a wooden desk in a remote cabin.

Instinctively, she knew that they were linked. She reflected aloud, "So that's what she's up to...She's going to see the Major. How convenient!"

Solemnly, she raised her hands high over her head in thanksgiving, and held them there for some minutes, chanting a deep guttural chant.

Then quite suddenly and unexpectedly, the flame from the burning candle snuffed out, as if all oxygen had been lost to it. The white smoke drifted upward like a loose string dangling in the air. Then she made a profound bow to the Source and the Skull and left the room.

CHAPTER 15

❧

"To be sure to go through life unscathed we hide in an ivory tower, close our minds, stifle our imagination, harden our hearts, make ourselves as insensitive as we can, because above all we are afraid of being hurt, wounded—and we become at best like those little marine organisms that, frail and vulnerable, secrete a hard shell which will keep them safe but also imprisons them in an unyielding coral armor which slowly kills them."

Metropolitan Anthony Bloom
Meditations: A Spiritual Journey

As the dinner lingered on, the wine, the filet mignon and the sparkling conversation went to Andrea's head. In fact, it went to everyone's head. James Templeton grew quite tipsy; he slurred his consonants and waxed sentimental about his twenty-year-old three-legged cat, Tripod, which he and his wife Muriel had recently decided to have the vet put down.

Keith didn't drink as much as the other two, but he had enough to lubricate his tongue. His conversation was dazzling. Brisk, serious and entertaining all at once, he was a natural-born storyteller. He told story after story about characters he had met while on the job reporting: funny stories, improbable stories and sad stories. He even did expert impersonations of both the mayor and his opponent, O'Shaughnessy, with running commentary. James and Andrea laughed so hard that Frank, the bartender, gave the trio some sideways glances.

Andrea, for her part, was feeling no pain. In fact, she was quite relaxed. She hadn't been happier in years. All during their conversation, however, she sensed tugs of kinetic energy exuding from Keith's body, as if he was magnetically pulling her to himself. Sometimes, their glances met and she could feel the charge of Keith's smoldering gaze. Her own desire within herself almost left her breathless.

As the evening wore on, Keith, an adept interviewer, persuaded everyone to talk about some of their deepest longings, including his own.

James grinned foolishly. "Of course, I just want to be rich, write books at my leisure, get a five-year tenure in Athens and own a house on Lake Como rent free for the rest of my life. What about you, Andrea?"

She toyed with her silverware. "I don't know. Get a teaching post at some seminary or University, preferably here in the Bay Area. Do some important research and publish. Travel to Russia, find my roots. Maybe find someone special. I wonder if it's not too late to have a baby..." Her voice trailed off at the last. She avoided Keith's eyes, which she could feel caressing her profile.

"And you, Keith?" James smiled genially and rested his elbow on the table with his chin slung in his hand. He had definitely exceeded his limit, but he still had eyes in his head.

"Me? I've done enough traveling for two lifetimes. I want to do some good journalism and political commentary someday. Maybe write some of those stories I've picked up along the way. And I want to settle down." His eyes searched Andrea's.

Suddenly feeling flustered and exposed, she realized she'd crack open and all her need would come pouring out if she stayed there another minute. She glanced at her watch, "Oh, my! Look what time it is. Keith, I thought you had to cover the election. I'll drive." She stood up from the table, but suddenly found herself wobbling.

Keith smiled kindly at her and stood up to steady her elbow. "Sorry, sweetheart, you aren't driving anywhere tonight. Let me drive you home. Manning will have to cover the first part of the returns for me."

James Templeton also stood up politely. He had to hold onto the wall to balance himself, "Nonsense! It's much too late to drive Andrea to the East Bay. And you have an election to cover, young man. Let me get her a room upstairs and I'll just call a cab for myself. I can stay with my sister here in the city."

Andrea protested, "James, really, you're very kind but that won't be necessary." But as she did so, the room began to suddenly weave and she plopped unceremoniously down in her seat again like a well-dressed rag doll.

James wagged a finger at her and teased, "I told you so. It would be my pleasure." He pulled a credit card out of his coat pocket and handed it to the waiter with as much dignity as possible for a man as fuddled as he was. "Dinner's on me too. I wish Muriel could have been here, I haven't had so much fun in years. Now, if you don't mind, I'll leave you two love birds while I go and order your room."

2

Upstairs on the forth floor of the Palace Hotel, Andrea and Keith stepped into her opulent bedroom suite. Andrea closed the door behind her and surveyed the spacious room. Her eyes glowed as she said to Keith, "You didn't arrange this did you?"

Keith shrugged and gazed modestly down into Andrea's face. "No, so help me God! I'm not that organized." He leaned towards her lips and stroked her chin with his finger tenderly. "But I'm glad somebody is." They paused self-consciously for a minute before Keith backed away.

"I better get going," he said awkwardly. "The election." If he'd had a fedora hat, he would have fumbled with it, Jimmy Stewart style, in his hands.

Andrea took a deep breath, "Right. The big election. May the best man win." She summoned a brave smile. Keith turned to leave. Impulsively, she stepped forward, "Sure you can't stay? At least for a ritual cup of coffee?"

"No, I better not. I have a long night ahead of me. This is a really important story," he smiled apologetically. "I'll call you in the morning before you go see the Major." With that, he stepped out of the room quickly.

Andrea sank down on the arm of the overstuffed sofa with disappointment and frustration. Trying to keep a level head, she decided the best thing to do would simply be to undress, take a hot bath then crawl into bed. She switched on the radio to the local classical station, which was playing a meditative Schumann string quartet.

Stepping out of her clothes and lace underwear, she filled the tub with hot water and stepped in the bath. The bath sobered her up considerably, but she felt so lonely, her insides ached.

Presently, there was a knock at her front door. "Who is it?" she called out from the bathroom.

"It's Keith." His muffled voice sounded from behind the door. "You left your purse in the dining room."

"I'll be right there." She grabbed a towel, hastily dried herself and ran a brush through her thick black hair. Having no bathrobe, she wrapped an enormous dry white bath towel around her naked body. Padding barefoot to the door, she opened it.

Keith held out her black purse, "You'll need this." His piercing sherry-colored eyes, so full of tenderness and longing, penetrated her very core. "How about that coffee?" he asked shyly.

Without a word, Andrea took his hand and pulled him inside the room as Keith simultaneously closed the door. They fell into each other's arms, backing up hard against the door with a marked thud. She pressed her mouth passionately onto his. They both softly whimpered with need. As they kissed, she undid his shirt and belt buckle, letting her bath towel drop noiselessly onto the floor.

3

Wednesday, November 7, 1990

Andrea, who was a morning person, woke first. She propped herself up on her elbow, cradling her head in her hand, and gazed at Keith affectionately for a moment as he lay sleeping beside her. Then quietly and slowly, she rolled out of bed, found his white shirt, put it on over her naked body and headed straight for the kitchenette.

Five minutes later, she climbed back into bed with some steaming coffee. Keith drowsily rolled over and stretched, "That smells good."

"Hmmm. Want some?"

"Where's my IV?" He sat up and yawned. He scratched his head. "What time is it?"

"7:30. How's your collarbone feeling?" She rubbed his back gently.

He moved his shoulder cautiously in its socket. "Much better.

Your Jacuzzi tub last night did wonders."

"Oh, I thought it was me."

"And you too!"

"Gee, thanks. I get to play second fiddle to the hotel plumbing..."

He gently grabbed her, pushed back the shirt and kissed her bare breast. "We're going to have to start working on your inferiority complex. Just what did your ex-husband do to you anyway?" He sucked her nipple.

"Nothing, that was the problem. Hey, watch it!" she giggled. "This stuff's hot!"

"So are you. Forget the coffee."

"You win." She put the coffee cup down and returned his kisses with equal passion.

After they had made slow, passionate love, Keith pulled the blankets up to his shoulders. "That was great. Good night, dear."

"No, you don't!" She ripped the covers off him. "We've got too much to do. What about the election? You've got a story to write and I have to find the Major."

Keith flopped back onto his pillow. "Spoil sport! Just when it was getting fun."

Andrea snuggled up to him and whispered in his ear, "There will be plenty of time for that later."

"Promise?"

"Promise." Andrea kissed him, slid out of bed, and went into the bathroom with her bundle of clothes.

"Where do you plan to meet this Major?" Keith asked.

"I told you," she shouted above the running hot water, "at the Russian Cultural Museum on Sutter Street. At 11. I'm going over to Mama's to change my clothes first."

"I'd feel better if I could go with you to see him."

"So would I! Where will you be this morning?" Stripped naked, she poked her head out of the bathroom and asked, "Could you meet me there during your lunch break?"

"Lunch's out." Andrea went back to her bath. Keith called, "I have to stop by City Hall to get the final results, then go to the Hall of Justice to see Catelano."

He rolled out of bed, stumbled into his dress pants and loped around the hotel suite in circles, half-asleep, holding a cup of hot coffee, while he hunted for a newspaper. Finally he found one outside by the suite room door. He read it over his second cup of coffee, while he waited for Andrea to free up the bathroom. He suddenly realized how contented he was.

He was shaking his head at the point spread on the Cal–Oregon State game when she came out, dressed in her slip and beaming. "What was that you said?"

"I said I have to see Catelano at noon." He looked up admiringly at her from his newspaper, "Do you really have to go alone?"

"I like it when you're protective." She kissed the top of his head and went to fetch another cup of coffee. "Do you think Catelano will tell you anything more?"

"Don't know. It can't hurt to ask."

"You guys sure have a weird relationship."

"No shit!"

Andrea went back into the kitchenette and peered into the cabinets. They were empty except for four small boxes of cereal, a bowl of fruit and some cheese and crackers wrapped in plastic containers. "Don't they have anything to eat for breakfast around here?" she complained, feeling her stomach growl. "A parakeet eats more for breakfast than this."

"That's because they want you to spend millions on their breakfast buffet downstairs in the Garden Court Restaurant," he mumbled, absorbed in his attempt at handicapping the college football scores. "Why don't you call room service?"

"I don't want to take advantage of James's generosity. I'll catch something at home before I come back into the city," she said, as she pulled her stockings up her thighs and slipped into her tight green dress. "I hope you can still get out to the Russian Museum."

Keith put the paper down, stood up and wrapped his arms around her. "You're not going so soon?"

"What do you mean? It's almost 8:30."

"You sure we couldn't have another little quickie?" He nibbled her ear. They kissed long and leisurely, until Andrea reluctantly pulled herself away.

"Sorry, got to go."

"You really know how to make a guy feel wanted."

"What do you want, me or the story?" Andrea shot back.

"Who said I have to choose?"

"That's what I thought," she smiled. "I'll see you at the Russian Museum, I hope."

"Be careful."

"I'll be fine. What could happen in a museum?"

4

By 10:30, that same Wednesday morning, the Major was already in the musty attic of the Russian Cultural Museum, busy sorting through the ancient piles of paper and archival material which mostly belonged to his father. Downstairs in the curator's office, the noise from the radio blasted strains of Russian folk music up the stairs. Fifty years of dust and no ventilation made the room stiflingly hot and close.

The floorboards creaked as the Major sorted papers in a circle around his desk. Some he would discard and others he was preserving for the Museum library. He also laid aside two small piles—one to add to those in the bank vault, and one for Andrea.

Thinking he heard something, he stopped and listened for another sound, but there was nothing so he returned to his work. He heard it again and turned around to see Alex Menshikov pointing a gun at him.

"You're losing your touch, George," Alex smirked. "You left too many clues."

The Major stood motionless, remaining outwardly calm and clutching some papers in his hand. "Look, Alex, let's make a deal. You're being framed for first-degree murder and armed robbery. Not much of a position to call the shots."

"It looks the other way to me," Alex said, glancing at his revolver. "You're the one in no position to deal, since you double-crossed us. Give me the papers and the keys. On the table," he waved the nozzle of his gun.

"Look, I can explain everything," the Major pleaded.

"I'm sure you can, but I don't want to hear it. Do it!"

The Major shoved the whole pile of papers and the deposit box keys towards him.

Alex took them and stuffed them into his jacket. "Now sit down and put your hands behind your head."

The Major put his hands behind his famous crew cut. He was furious but helpless. "You'll never get away with this," he spit at Alex hatefully.

"Maybe I will, maybe I won't," Alex said as he raised his arm.

Moments later, Alex walked briskly out of the building. A green Mercedes sat idling kitty-corner across the street. The person inside watched Alex get into his car and drive off, then switched off the ignition, locked the Mercedes and strode briskly towards the Russian Cultural Museum.

5

Andrea arrived at the Russian Museum a few minutes later. She glanced at her watch: 11 o'clock exactly. The large three-story brick Victorian building with its yellow and white stucco front loomed in the middle of the residential neighborhood like a large schooner surrounded by a crowd of dilapidated tugboats.

She took a deep breath and walked inside, passing through the iron gates that guarded the building when it was locked. Inside the dingy foyer, doors led off to what appeared to be offices. In one of them, Russian folk music blared from a tiny radio. Otherwise, the place seemed deserted.

"Anybody here?" she called aloud. Her voice echoed up the stairwell.

She walked up a wooden flight of stairs and came to a set of large double doors that opened into a large assembly hall. It had a worn parquet floor and an old-fashioned stage, with footlights and a tattered red velvet curtain hanging heavily from behind the art-deco proscenium arch. Half a dozen long tables and wooden chairs were set up in the middle of the room.

As she entered, her heels echoed conspicuously through the hall. She felt self-conscious.

Two Russian senior citizens were there busily, but silently setting the tables for the regular Senior Meal Program. One was a stooped babushka, dressed in a 1950's dress and scarf with an apron tied around her neck. The other was a frail elderly man with slick brown hair and deep furrows etched into his forehead. What was most alarming was the large Dracula-like widow's peak that plunged from the top of his hairline into his brow.

They hadn't noticed her until Andrea said hello in Russian. They looked up, mumbled a response and returned to their work. She spoke louder in Russian. "Do you know where Major Vashkovsky is?" The man looked up at her and pointed upstairs. "Spasibo," she thanked him and headed up the next flight of stairs.

Passing through another set of double doors on her left, she found herself standing in a large, dark Victorian room; the only light came from the large opaque windows on the street side. The room was empty except for rows of glass museum cases placed along the walls.

Seeing no one there, she stood at the foot of the narrow stairs to the third floor attic where she had heard the archives were kept. The door to the third floor was open and a dim light shone in the garret above. She went up the narrow, rickety stairs to the third floor slowly. Each step creaked noisily. "Hello?" she called out tentatively. No answer.

At the top of the stairs on her left, she was immediately accosted by numerous large oil portraits of Tsar Alexander II, a pale, bearded Tsar Nicholas II and an oval photograph of Nicholas' young son and heir, the hemophiliac Tsarevitch Alexei. Near the portraits were glass cases filled with memorabilia from the Tsar's Winter Palace in St. Petersburg.

Ahead of her, she saw a light coming from behind a flowered curtain. She pushed it aside and poked her head into a small chamber. Along one wall, the attic space was filled with metal filing cabinets, glass plate photographs and stacks of yellowing émigré newspapers.

She turned to look on her right and gasped, "Oh, my God!" She felt too frightened to scream. In the darkened corner of the room lay the body of a white haired man, sitting sprawled over a wooden desk. He lay face down on a pile of papers in a pool of blood. His throat was slit.

"Oh, no!" She approached the body. It was the Major. She touched his hand; it was still warm. She suspected he hadn't been dead half-an-hour.

A black lacquer box lay open on the desk. Both the top and bottom were smeared with blood. She turned the lid over and saw Michael's familiar Firebird design. It was all beginning to make sense. But who wanted him dead? And what did Alex Menshikov have to do with it?

She began to utter a prayer over him, when she heard a noise from the other side of the wall. Feet clattered down the squeaky stairs.

"Who's there?" Andrea called. No answer. Oh, Lord! The murderer is still here! Andrea bolted out of the attic undercroft after the intruder. But the door slammed shut before she could get to the bottom of the stairs. She ran down the stairs and tried the door handle. The door was locked.

She shook the handle and pounded the door with both fists, "Let me out!" she screamed. She pounded two or three times more, praying the two seniors in the auditorium could hear her over the music. There was no response.

"Think fast, Andrea," she said aloud to herself. She took her pick and nail file from her purse. Frantically, she began jimmying the old lock. Finally, it clicked open.

She burst out of the door, and ran down the corridor into the big hall. Vaguely smelling a familiar scent, she realized someone was standing close behind her. She had started to turn just as something hard crashed into her head. A split second of biting pain, then everything went black. She slumped down indecorously, like a bag of sand.

6

When she came to, she felt like a sledgehammer was imbedded in her skull. Her scalp felt wet and sticky with blood. She groaned and raised her hand. "Better not touch it," the paramedic ordered. She was lying on the floor with her head propped up. A young paramedic had just bandaged her head and was getting the equipment ready to take her to the hospital.

Andrea spoke to the medic and struggled, feeling still goofy, to rise from the floor, "They killed the Major! He's upstairs."

He held her back, "Hold on, you're not going anywhere." Feeling dizzy and faint, Andrea felt in no mood to argue and lay back.

Keith squatted down and placed a blanket around her shoulders. "They know all about that. They found him after I found you. I heard about it over the dispatch in Tony's office."

"What happened?" Andrea turned to him with a flood of gratitude and relief.

"That's what you're going to have to tell us." Tony Catelano, who had just arrived, looked down at her with concern and annoyance.

Andrea said weakly, "Did anyone see the murderer leave?"

"Jergeson is upstairs questioning the older couple in the senior dining room. I just came by to make sure you weren't dead. I'd prefer to strangle you myself. When you're up to it, I want to see you in my office."

Andrea nodded obediently.

Two hulking paramedics bent over her, lifted her gently up and slid the stretcher under her. She gritted her teeth but remained silent. Keith winced as he watched her in pain.

Andrea moved to watch where they were going. "If you can, please keep your head steady," one medic instructed. She could hear the radio dispatch of the police walkie-talkie click on and off and the sound of men's voices and feet upstairs in the attic. "Where are you taking me?" Andrea asked.

"To Kaiser Hospital," the paramedic grunted as they lifted her up. "I'm no doctor, ma'am, but you got an awful crack on you head. You might need stitches. Just don't move too much, OK?"

Andrea smiled bravely. "What time is it?" she asked Keith.

"Almost noon. Is there anything I can do for you?"

"What about your story?"

"Don't worry about that," he said. "I'm coming with you."

"Then, can you call my mother? Marina Roevich. Her number is in my purse. Tell her what happened and where I'm going."

Keith said he would as soon as they reached the hospital.

The paramedics covered her with a sheet up to her shoulders and strapped her into the metal stretcher with the expandable wheels, then carried her down the stairs to the waiting ambulance. Keith anxiously held her hand the whole way.

7

Alex Menshikov strolled into the Bank of America dressed in his best coat and tie, and walked briskly over to the service counter. He asked the Asian teller, "I want a safe deposit box. Your small size." After receiving his money and checking his IDs, she gave him a form and two keys to box #78. "Sign here," she pointed. Alex scribbled one of his usual aliases. The teller showed him his new box inside the vault and left him alone.

Alex spotted the camera hanging from the ceiling and stepped just out of view to slip on his clear surgical gloves. He unlocked his new box and then deftly opened box #36 with the keys he had just stolen from the Major. Inside was a large manila envelope containing the Major's papers. He opened it and found many letters, photographs of the Inner Circle and their names, including a separate picture of himself, and papers documenting the sale of the Kazan Icon. He suspected the Major, who was always a stickler for details, had kept a full dossier on them.

Alex thoroughly searched the papers for any mention of himself and cut them out with a pair of scissors. Then he divided the papers into two piles, one containing "useful" papers for himself for "future use" and one for the Major's box. Then he did two significant things: he stored the stolen papers in his new box #78 and replaced the Major's censured papers back into safe deposit box #36.

He placed the safe deposit keys to box #36, with a typed note stating the name of the account, the bank, and the street address, into a pre-addressed envelope and left the vault. Outside, he dropped it in the corner mailbox and walked towards a BART station.

CHAPTER 16

∾

"God sends us moments when we are brought up short by illness or accident, but instead of understanding that the hour of recollection, of withdrawal and of renewal has come, we fight desperately to return as fast as possible to our former state, rejecting the gift concealed in that act of God which frightens us."

Metropolitan Anthony Bloom
Meditations: A Spiritual Journey

Thursday, November 8, 1990

Andrea raised her head and groggily watched as the nurse jotted down some notes into the chart at the foot of her hospital bed. Her head still pounded.

"She's awake." The plump, freckled nurse smiled brightly. "Hello, Andrea, I'm Gina. How are you feeling this morning?"

"Not terrific," Andrea blinked, touching the bandages on top of her head. She was painfully aware that a patch of hair had been cut from her scalp. "How many stitches did they put in?"

"Not too many," Gina answered, "about four or five. The doctor said you had a slight concussion, but you'll be fine. He thinks you'll be able to go home later today. Just don't go jogging around the block."

"Don't worry!" Andrea lay back in her pillow. "What about my cat? Did anybody call my mother?"

"Mr. Carlton called her. She came in to see you last night but you were asleep. She said she'd be back after lunch. She left a message saying she had to go feed your cat this morning and bring back a change of clothes."

Andrea sighed in relief and turned her head away to control her urge to weep. So much had happened during the past twenty-four hours that she felt her usual mask of calm and reserve had been shattered to pieces.

The redheaded nurse noticed this. "Is there anything I can get for you?" Gina asked kindly. "Feelings like this are normal after the kind of shock you've just had."

Andrea pulled some Kleenex from the box on her bedside table and wiped her eyes. "No, I'll be fine. Thanks."

By noontime, Andrea was sitting up in bed washed and dressed in her hospital bathrobe. She heard a faint knock at her door. "Come in. Mama, is that you?"

"'Tis I," Keith shouldered open the door carrying a tray with lunch, three red roses in a bud vase and the perpetual newspaper under his arm. "And God said, 'Let there be life!'" he declaimed. "How are you feeling?" He put the tray and the roses on her bedside table, and then kissed her softly on the mouth. Dropping the *Examiner* at the foot of her bed, he flung himself into a chair.

"More like a half-life," Andrea beamed at him through wet eyelashes. "I thought you were my mother."

"Disappointed or relieved?" Keith quipped.

"What do you think?" Andrea reached over and picked up the vase to smell the roses. "They are lovely. Red, my favorite. They even smell like rosy-cinnamon. Thanks." She leaned toward Keith and kissed him again. He put the vase down on the bedside table for her.

Keith studied her face closely. "Are you OK?

"Just a little reaction to the shock. I'll get over it. The trouble with pain pills," she added, "is that they don't take the pain away, they only take you away from the pain. I feel like my headache's still here, but I've gone to Chicago."

"Not a bad place this time of year, but a bit cold. Bring me a juicy combo with peppers and a slab of Russell's ribs when you come back," he grinned.

He pulled his chair closer to her bed. "Well, you were certainly up to your ass in alligators! You must have come in just after he was offed. No idea who it was?"

"None."

"Not even a guess?"

"There was a certain smell." She said. "Perfume. I can't quite pin it down. You know, Keith, the Major had the Firebird lacquer box."

"I know. I saw it. I bet he was the one who jumped me at Michael's house."

"A seventy-year-old man?"

"The paramedics said his body was as solid as a rock. All muscle. He may have been old but he had the body of a healthy forty-five-year old."

"He was lying on some papers. Did anyone think to get them? You know, his father, who had been Chancellor for the Russian Patriarch, had access to all the Church papers and valuables after the Russian Revolution. I bet the Major had enough evidence from him to tip off the Holy Virgin Society."

"Blackmail is a great motive for murder."

"Yeah," she said ruefully, "and so is being at the wrong place at the wrong time."

"Luckily you're OK." Keith stroked her arm. "By the way, Tony called to see how you were. He said he wants to see you."

Andrea groaned, "I remember... He's going to kill me."

"He can't do that until you get well again," Keith smiled. "Besides, he can't pin anything on you." He handed her the after-noon paper proudly. "But take a look at this."

Andrea glanced at him. "So this is why you seem so excited." She opened it and read the three column headline: EX-WAR SPY KILLED: Murder at Russian Cultural Museum. She saw Keith's byline. She scanned the columns briefly until her eyes fell upon her name... "A local seminary professor linked to the murder victim and now a victim herself."

"It's a little sensationalist and premature, don't you think?" Her voice was icy.

"Premature for what? News is news and you have to get it while it's hot."

"I thought we both agreed not to print anything until the time was right. I thought you cared more about me than this?"

"Andrea, I do! But I'm a reporter, remember? This is how I earn my living. This is one of the best breaks I've had in years!"

"I see. So you're getting ahead at my expense?"

"Would you rather I kill the story and not tell the truth?" Keith's face flushed with anger.

"What about me?" she cried. "This will really go over big with the Dean, not to mention the Bishop! Do you know what this could do to my career?"

"Perhaps you should have thought about that before you got mixed up in all this."

"No thanks to you! Who was the one pushing me all the way? All you care about is your stupid Pulitzer, never mind what happens to anybody else!"

"Well, you weren't exactly digging in your heels, you know."

"What about Tuesday night?" Her eyes narrowed. "Or was that just part of your plan to get a good story? Or a good lay?"

"Andrea, look." Keith modulated his voice, seeing things were escalating too fast. "You've had a bad knock on the head. I don't want to say anything I'll regret." He stood up. "You're tired and being irrational. I'm going home. I'll check in with you tomorrow at home when you're feeling better."

"Irrational?! Do me a favor and save your gas. I don't want to see you again!"

"Andrea!"

"Get out!" She flung the newspaper at him. Picking it up off the floor, Keith hesitated, and then left her room, indignant and confused. He strode down the corridor and slammed the elevator button. "Women!"

2

Andrea hugged her pillow to her chest and wept. Not loud tears—but prolonged, unrelenting tears. She smothered her face in her pillow. Pain, exhaustion, anger and confusion washed over her like multiple waves of an inner ocean she was unable to ignore any longer. She hadn't cried like that in years—not since Gareth left her to re-join the order. And now, she had kicked Keith out of her life. Even more, she felt her headstrong pride and interfering ways had somehow thrown up an impenetrable wall between herself and God. If there was ever a lost sheep that needed rescuing, it was she.

Alone in her room, she wept silently until there were no more tears to weep. She tried to watch television but there was nothing on but soap operas, so she switched it off and tried to sleep but couldn't.

There came a firm knock at her door. She put on her bathrobe, both fearing and hoping it was Keith again and opened the door. To her surprise, she saw Father Peter standing before her. He was wearing his full black clericals. He smiled warmly at her, "Keith called the seminary. I heard what happened. I thought you might want some company."

"Peter!" Andrea didn't know whether to laugh or cry.

After a measured hug, Father Peter gently walked her across the room. "Don't you think you should be in bed? You've had a nasty shock." He eyed her calmly.

She climbed back into bed. "I thought it was someone else."

He pulled up a chair alongside the bed, sat down, and asked with concern, "How are you feeling?"

"Fine," she said with false brightness. "Much better. My headache is almost gone and I can walk around without getting dizzy. They're going to let me leave later today."

"Good," he said. "Now, tell me what happened." He leaned forward, resting his elbows on his knees, and looked intently at her. "You've been crying. What's this all about?"

"I forget how much you know." She wasn't sure how much to tell him.

"You told me a little about your meeting with the abbot, then Keith told me last night how you found Major Vashkovsky's body, and now this. I met him again on the way up. He also said you blew up at him, which I found hard to believe. But I want to hear your version." He sat back. "I have plenty of time."

Andrea suddenly felt as if her waterworks button had been pushed. Her chin trembled. When she got like this, it didn't take much when a trusted ear was ready to listen. And Peter was that trusted ear. Nevertheless, she wasn't sure if she wanted to burst into tears again or run and hide. "I guess I was hard on him. This is all very embarrassing. Stupid, really. I should never have gotten mixed up in it at all." She looked around for the Kleenex box, clinging to one last shred of self-control.

He nodded attentively. "Go on."

She babbled on, "I knew it was wrong but I had to find out who killed Michael."

"Isn't that the police's job?"

"Yes, but I felt a duty to Michael and the icon."

"A duty? Is that all?"

Andrea hesitated, "Well, I have to admit, I was being selfish too—I wanted to save my own skin. And there was a little revenge sprinkled in there too, I guess. I wanted to get whoever did such a blasphemous thing. Then things just spiraled out of control, that's all." She looked away from him.

"There's no need to be ashamed," he said gently. "You can let it all go now. God understands. I understand."

That was it. She burst into tears, "No, I don't think God understands! How could He after what I did?"

"What did you do?"

"It's hard to explain," she blew her nose again.

"Try," he insisted softly.

"Well, when I went to visit Father Seraphim, I was sure I was on some sort of divine mission because of my dream about Michael. Father Seraphim warned me that this obsession was nothing but spiritual pride but I ignored him. And then, of course, when I agreed to meet the Major at the Russian Museum, he made me feel as if I was the only one who could save the situation, which I know now was pure spiritual arrogance."

She glanced at him to see if any shadow of disapproval crossed his face. There was none. He guessed accurately, "So now you feel as if your disobedience has separated you from God."

"And not only Him. It's getting in the way of my relationships with other people. I slept with Keith the other night and it was wonderful. But now I've just kicked him out of my life," Andrea blotted her tears with her Kleenex.

"You fear you've made a few bad mistakes and now you're feeling at the end of your rope, is that it?"

"I guess I am," Andrea admitted. "But the thing is, after yesterday, I feel totally cut off from God."

The empathy in Father Peter's eyes and voice were clear, "Are you really? It seems as if your Guardian Angel has been working over-time the last twenty-four hours. You could have been killed yesterday."

"Then why do I feel so hopeless?"

"I think there's a psychological term for something as traumatic as you just have experienced—post-traumatic stress. Feeling depressed is normal. The problem with this kind of despair is that it feels so overwhelming. You say you think God saved you once, but because of your self-will, he won't save you again? No second chances?"

"Once burned it's a mistake, twice burned it's stupidity. Right?"

"And you think that only a stupid God would keep loving you after what you've done?"

"Would you?"

"Yes, but that's not the point. It sounds like your God has a pretty short fuse. Not exactly the God of unconditional Love we've all been led to believe in."

"But don't you see? God didn't abandon me, I abandoned Him."

"I see," he mused aloud. "C.S. Lewis once wrote: 'If God seems distant, who moved?'"

"Exactly," she said. "You're like the sheep who left the flock, can't find her way back and is stuck in a thorn bush bleating in the wilderness. The more you try to save yourself, the more it hurts."

"Bleeding is more like it," she smiled ruefully.

"You know, in the spiritual life there are always five possible reasons for the kind of feelings you're having: physical, psychological, emotional, spiritual or a combination of them all. Which do you think it is?"

"I don't know. I thought it was purely spiritual. At least that's what it feels like. Are you saying it could simply be psychological?"

"Or more realistically, all of the above. People can't simply be reduced to neat little scientific or theological boxes, as if they were freeze-dried pre-packaged entities."

"So you think it is depression?"

His eyes brightened. "Maybe. With a healthy dose of physical and spiritual fatigue thrown in as well. You've had a bad shock. You could have been killed. It's been like Christ wrestling with the demons in the desert, hasn't it?"

"It hasn't been fun."

"I think it's a tribute to your courage and faith, not to mention God's grace, that your soul hasn't shattered. It sounds very exhausting."

"It has been!"

"But you are a lot stronger than you think. And as for the depression... After all, when have you had time to grieve for Michael, or for that matter, your divorce from Gareth? Or if you really want to do some emotional archeology, consider your own parents' divorce?"

3

Andrea momentarily pictured her mother and father, Sam and Marina West, as she had known them when she was five. A panorama of memories sailed through her head: Sam in one of his bright moods, playing with her, Nicky and the dog; Sam sitting morosely behind the newspaper; Sam being away a lot; Sam arguing heatedly with her mother in French over the dinner table; Sam throwing his shot glass through the living room window; her being wrenched from Sam.

"I thought I had gotten over their divorce years ago."

Father Peter was about to respond, but was interrupted by a knock at the door.

Marina hurried into the room. "At last you're awake! Andreochka, how are you?" Marina enveloped Andrea with a big Russian hug. Then, seeing Father Peter, she stepped back. "Sorry, I'm interrupting."

"Nothing that can't be revisited later," he said amiably. "You look splendid today, Marina." Marina showed off her new purple winter coat and paisley scarf. "I'll leave you two together. Call me, Andrea, when you get out of the hospital." She nodded to him. He bent down and kissed her goodbye on the cheek, then stepped out of the room.

"The nurse tells me you'll be fine. But how do you feel?" Marina surveyed her daughter anxiously. "I'm glad to see your color has returned."

"Much better. I probably should start getting dressed. The doctors tell me I can go home later."

"Maybe you should come and stay with me where it will be safer?" Marina suggested.

Andrea thought for a minute and put on her best face, "No, I need to get back to my own bed. Besides, there's Gwyneth and the garden to take care of. Thank you for helping. I'll be all right. You don't need to worry about me."

"Why shouldn't I worry about you when you go playing detective and running after murderers!"

"I know what I did was crazy, but I wonder—do you know what you're doing?" Andrea paused, debating whether to broach this subject, but realized it was too late now.

Marina sat down on Andrea's bed. "What do you mean?"

"Mama, do you have any idea who Alex Menshikov is? How could you even talk to that man?"

"He's not what you think."

"Mama, he's a smuggler who might have stolen the Icon of Kazan. And maybe he killed Michael and the Major! Maybe he almost killed me? I thought I knew you, but I just don't understand how you could have anything to do with him, much less have been his lover!"

Marina, who had a volatile temper herself, suddenly became defensive. "You think you are so high and mighty, Miss Smarty Pants, just because you work for a seminary! What are you accusing me of? Sleeping with a murderer? I hadn't seen him in years until last week."

"Yes, but when you were lovers you knew he smuggled icons,

didn't you?"

"Not at first. I suspected it for a long time, until finally I ended it with him." Marina turned her face away.

"But why did you let it drag on so long?"

Marina snapped, "Because I was in love with him, that's why. Obviously, you don't know what being in love is like, or you'd understand."

"How could you say that?" Her mother's words stung because there was a grain of truth in them. "You know that's not true," Andrea said soberly. "Not now at least..." Not after the other night with Keith.

"You have no idea what it was like for me then. You think I wanted to go around with a person like that?"

"So why did you?"

Marina burst into tears and covered her face with her hands. "Because he is your father."

Andrea felt the firm ground of her normal inner reality crack into painful fissures. "What?"

"He's your father," Marina repeated simply, wiping her eyes.

Andrea shook her head and felt the room begin to spin a little, "Alex Menshikov is my father? What are you saying?"

Marina sat down beside her, "Remember I told you we were lovers? Well, I got pregnant when Sam was away on one of his long trips to Washington. There was nobody else. And when Sam came back, I made sure I slept with him immediately. Fortunately, he never knew because both he and Alex were dark haired and you have their coloring."

"But how did you know?" Andrea asked with tears in her eyes.

"Oh, I knew immediately. His face is written all over you. Sam always said you took after me, but I knew better."

"So Nicky is my half-brother? And Sam isn't my father at all?" Andrea felt bereft. "So that's why Alex stole my picture."

Marina nodded her head.

Andrea let her tears fall freely. "Why didn't you tell me this before? How could you have lied to me all these years? I don't even know you anymore. My whole life has been a lie!"

"I'm sorry, Andrea," Marina pleaded. "Please forgive me."

"I don't know if I can right now," she said stiffly. "Does Nicky know?"

Marina said, "Of course not! Though he may remember Alex more than you. He came to visit as often as he could after you were born. He kept pressuring me to divorce Sam. You have no idea how much he loved you. He called you his little jewel. Finally Sam began to get jealous and suspicious. That's what was behind all the fights we had. Finally, I gave in to Alex; I left Sam, took you and Nicky and came out here."

"Why didn't you marry Alex then?"

"Because I wanted him to settle down and find decent work and not go traveling around the world like he did. He tried at first. He even went to work in a bank, but he could never hold a desk job for long. He hated it. Then he got caught up with a fancy antiquities dealer who was married to some Russian Count. Finally, I couldn't take it any longer and I put my foot down. We fought and he left. Part of me died when he left. I never saw him again, not until this mess with Michael, though I heard about him from time to time."

Andrea was confused, angry and sympathetic all at once. She managed to say, "I can't imagine how hard that must have been for you."

Marina continued, "I had to find work on my own. And Sam was stingy about his alimony payments. You don't know how much I scrimped and saved. The hardest part was doing it without Alex."

"You really loved him, didn't you?"

"Your father, Alex, is a good man. He has his faults but he has a big heart. He was fine until he met this Countess," she said bitterly.

"Who is she?"

"Her name is Irena Glazanova. I only met her once, not long after we moved here. She was a little bit older than Alex, maybe four years. Very sophisticated. I remember her pearls with a white crystal at the end and her blonde hair always floating like a cloud around her head. She married into an old aristocratic Russian family. But even on her own, she had connections with high society and the Church. Alex said that her aunt had been lady-in-waiting to the

Tsarina. She told Alex that Rasputin came to dine with her family at her grandfather's house in Kazan long before Irena was born."

Fascinated, Andrea asked, "What was he like?"

"She said he was scruffy, had dirty hair and sharp, pushy black eyes. When he entered the house, something powerful, almost inescapable, entered the house with him. Rasputin went up to Irma's mother, dropped his hand heavily on her head and plunged his gaze into hers with absolute force. 'Someday, you will have twins,' he predicted, 'and your twin daughter will be mine.' More strange, within three weeks, he was assassinated."

"I wonder what he meant by that? Who was her husband?"

"He was a priest in the Church. He served as chaplain in the Tsar's army during the First World War and later assisted the Patriarch."

Andrea stared dumbfounded at her mother. "Metropolitan Theodosius."

"Why, yes, now that you mention it. He had served in San Francisco before going back to Russia," Marina looked quizzically at her daughter.

"Do you know what this means? She's the twin sister of the Major who was murdered yesterday. She's our link to the icon!" Andrea was breathless with excitement.

Marina's face clouded. "Andrea, be careful. I don't trust this woman. She's up to no good."

"Mama, you know everyone in the Russian community. Where is she?"

Marina shook her head. "I don't know. Call Vera. She used to have business dealings with her. She might know."

"So Vera knew about Alex and you."

"Yes," Marina admitted. "I had to tell somebody back then. It was hard to keep that inside for so long. You do understand, darling?" She stroked Andrea's hair. "I wanted to tell you a hundred times, but the time was never right. You were either too young, or off to Italy or something. Then you ended up at seminary and I was afraid you would hate me."

Andrea kissed her mother's hand. "I don't hate you, Mama, but I wish you had told me sooner. I guess there is a reason for everything," she sighed. "Though we don't always know why..." She still felt uneasy about Alex. "Mama, you know Alex. Do you think he could kill someone?"

Marina looked at Andrea squarely. "Believe me, the Alex I know would never have done a thing like that. But he could have changed. The Countess could have spoiled him. I can't answer that for you. If you do discover something against him, promise me you won't turn him in."

"Mama!" Andrea frowned, "How can you ask me that?"

"Promise me! He's your flesh and blood. If not for him, do it for me."

"I don't know if I can do that."

"Think about it."

"I will, Mama." Andrea kissed her forehead. "I promise I will think about it." Then Andrea reached for the phone.

"What are you doing?"

"Calling Vera, of course," Andrea said. "I have to find the Countess."

"And what will you do once you find her?"

"Go see her tomorrow, when I'm feeling better."

"Remember, you can't break through a wall with your forehead," Marina sighed. "I think the Countess is dangerous. Promise me you'll be careful."

"I will, Mama."

CHAPTER 17

❧

"St. Seraphim of Sarov, when asked what it was that made some people remain sinners and never make any progress while others were becoming saints and living in God, answered: 'Only determination.'"

Metropolitan Anthony Bloom
Living Prayer

Friday, November 9, 1990

Detective Catelano opened the door to the interrogation room and ushered Andrea across the threshold. He was followed by Officer Jergeson, who carried a tape recorder. Tony gestured to a wooden chair at the end of a long table. "Please sit," he said firmly.

She sat down gingerly, careful not to make sudden moves. With the help of some strong Tylenol she was feeling practically normal again, except for the bruise on her head and her stitches, which ached. Despite this, she could feel Tony's anger simmering under the surface. The air in the room was tense.

The two men sat across from her. Jergeson set up the tape recorder and took out a note pad. Tony nodded to him to start taping.

"I'm glad you're feeling better, Ms. West," he said coolly. "Do you have any idea what you've been doing? You could have gotten killed."

"I know." She looked ashamed, still rattled from the experience. "I'm sorry."

"Sorry? Is that all you can say?" He glared at her. His voice became dangerously quiet. "Look what's happened. Major Vashkovsky is dead. Now the whole Russian community is up in arms and the Mayor has the Police Chief crawling all over my back."

"Would it help if I said I was *really* sorry?"

"I'm not finished," he snapped at her. "Carlton told me everything." Tony sat down opposite Andrea and thrust his face close to hers. "What did I say to you last Saturday? 'If I see you involved again with this case, you're under arrest.' Did you think I was kidding?"

"No, sir."

"You're a smart woman. What's gotten into you? Was this your idea of some kind of adventure? Cheap thrills? Well, it's over."

"I went out of town, like you said," Andrea explained as calmly as she could, "but when I reached the monastery, the Major was there. He asked me to meet him at the Russian Cultural Museum. He said he had something for me but wouldn't give it to me if the police were involved. It was my only chance!"

"So that's where he went," Catelano looked at Jergeson. Andrea could see this brought him up short. He paused. "What a strange coincidence. When Vashkovsky's sister came in and identified the body, she was very upset. Hysterical. She said he disappeared three weeks ago. He was a retired World War II Army intelligence officer and she was afraid that his past might have caught up with him. Said she filed a missing person's report but we can't find any. Apparently, he followed a regular routine and then couldn't be contacted."

"What was her name?" Andrea asked suspiciously.

Catelano hesitated and then said her name, "Irena Glazanova."

"I thought so," Andrea nodded. "She's his twin, but I don't get the impression they were terribly close. She married into a Russian royal family, which is why she goes by the name of 'Countess Glazanova.' I do know she has some connection with Alex Menshikov, which points back to the icon." Andrea was careful not to mention her mother.

"What are you suggesting? That she's hooked up to this murder and that she was lying about her brother?"

"Could be," Andrea said with satisfaction, glad to be of use and on the right side of the law this time.

"Carlton told us Wednesday that the Major was the one who tipped off the Holy Virgin Society about the icon," Tony waited for her reaction. She nodded again. "He said the Major showed some papers to John Hart and Michael Beech which contained enough damning evidence for them to start their own investigation."

"You think he might have been blackmailing someone?"

"Quite possibly."

"Maybe the Major deliberately disappeared after Michael's murder but showed up long enough to steal the extra safe deposit key from Michael's house."

"Why would he bother?"

"He had put those papers in a safe deposit box and gave Michael the extra key. But when he learned Michael was dead, he had to recover it. That's when Keith and I bumped into him. He had the black lacquer box from Michael's house with him when he died. I saw it by his body."

"You can positively identify it?"

"I know it well. It was Michael's favorite."

"What's really strange is that the Major went down without a struggle, yet the coroner said he was built like a tank. It doesn't make sense. Not an old army man like him. With a gun yes, but not a knife. He had a huge contusion on his head and his throat was slit, like Michael Beech's."

Andrea winced as he said this, remembering Keith's description of Michael and picturing the sight of the Major's snow-white hair lying on the desk in a pool of blood. She turned her face away.

"Sorry," Tony said. "The coroner says someone knocked him out first and then came in for the kill."

"Why didn't the murderer kill him outright instead of knocking him out first? Maybe it was a conspiracy?" Andrea reasoned. "What about the Countess? Maybe she lied about filing a missing person's report?"

"Maybe."

"I wouldn't believe everything the Countess says."

"I don't think you can consider yourself a paragon of honesty either, Ms. West." Tony gave her a piercing glance and leaned towards her. "What time did you get to the Russian Museum?"

"Just after 11. When I touched the Major's body it was still warm. He wasn't dead for very long. Then I heard somebody run down the stairs; he or she, I don't know which, closed the door and locked me in. I banged on the door and yelled for someone to let me out, but no one came. Then I used a nail file to undo the lock. I was attacked just outside the door. You know the rest."

"Did you see who did it?"

"No," she said. "I was hit from behind."

"You were very lucky. Somebody obviously wants you out of the way. You know too much. I'm surprised you didn't get your throat cut too. The next time I find you involved with this thing, not only am I going to arrest you, I'm going to break your neck!"

Andrea looked him squarely in the eye, "Is there anything else you have to tell me?"

Tony returned her steady gaze and sighed. "No, just use your head while you still have one."

"I will," Andrea rose from her chair.

"Now, get out of here!" he growled. "I don't want to see you in here again."

She turned at the door. "Thank you for keeping up on this case. I know the election threats have kept you all very busy."

"Goodbye, Ms. West!"

Andrea left the room, shaking but much relieved.

Officer Jergeson turned off the tape recorder. "Do you think she's telling the truth?"

Tony tapped his pencil on the table. "Everything she told me was true. What I want to know is what she didn't tell me," he mused. "Russians can be pretty tight-lipped. Even the best of them." He stood up and made for the door, then stopped abruptly. "She's onto something. Follow her. She might have a better chance of staying alive."

"Who should I send?"

"Rosko. And see if Chipetti is back. I don't want her to empty her garbage cans without them knowing about it. Maybe she'll end up being more help than she knows."

2

When Andrea came out of Catelano's office, she was surprised to see Keith waiting by the elevator with his hands in his pockets, looking sheepish. His face softened when he saw her.

"What are you doing here?" Andrea asked, though she was pleased to see him.

"Waiting for you. I thought you'd like to see a friendly face after the grilling you just got." He flashed her a lovable smile.

"Thanks. How did you know I'd be here?"

"You're not the only one with intuition, you know." He asked with real concern, "How are you feeling?"

"Better. Not so dizzy anymore." She paused, trying to find the right words to say. They both spoke at once: "I wanted to," she said. "Don't worry," he said. They stopped in embarrassed silence.

"You go first," Keith offered.

"Sorry I blew my stack at you yesterday," she blushed. "I'm not seeing things too clearly. You were just doing your job."

"You had a right to be angry. I should have talked with you about it first." Andrea appreciated his humility. He added, "Besides, it's not everyday you find a dead body and get bludgeoned."

"No kidding."

"So how about a relaxing cup of espresso?" Keith grinned. They drove separately to one of the hip new cafes south of Market. The place was decorated with huge spray painted canvases and odd faux sculptures of twisted aluminum foil. Inside, the cafe was filled with local artists in black leather jackets, with spiked blue hair. Paper clips with razor blades dangled from their ears. One tee shirt read: "Theater is Life—Film is Art—TV is furniture." Andrea glanced warily around the room and was glad she was with Keith. They ordered two lattés.

"So what do we know so far? Let's play it out." Keith took out a piece of paper to jot down notes.

"Well, we know that Michael was first contacted by the Holy Virgin Society to reappraise the icon by carbon dating it," Andrea said, holding her latté in her hands to warm them.

"The Major, of course, was behind it all. He wanted to blow the whistle on the whole icon scam," Keith declared. "But why?"

"He told me he had been part of the group, whoever 'they' are, but that they went too far. Maybe Durant planned to murder Michael all along?"

"That's possible. And if the Major was blackmailing someone, then he got added to the hit list. People don't get killed for being particularly nice, you know."

"Luba said the Russian Church never trusted Cecil Durant. She said Archbishop John was always suspicious of him, and he's not the suspicious type. I wonder what Durant did to make him distrust him so. And why didn't the Holy Virgin Society examine his credentials more closely?"

"Gullibility, perhaps," Keith speculated. "Complacency has many faces. Maybe they didn't want to find out so they wouldn't have to admit they had been suckered."

"I think the Holy Virgin Society so desperately wanted it to be the real thing that they were willing to overlook major discrepancies, like credentials. A classic case of 'my mind is made up, don't confuse me with the facts.'"

"But after a tip-off by the Major, the Holy Virgin Society couldn't ignore things anymore, so they contacted Michael," Keith countered. "He takes you to see the icon the very night he begins the crucial carbon dating, then somebody kills him. But how did they know what he was up to and when?"

"I vaguely remember Michael spoke about the icon to a Russian colleague. Do you think that was Alex?"

"Could be. Maybe he double-crossed him?"

"Maybe, but what was the motive?" Andrea glanced as a woman with neon orange hair rose from the next table.

"Money, of course. Five million is nothing to sneeze at. Or if Cecil did it, maybe he was some sort of professional rival."

"Could be. Michael was not the most diplomatic person."

"I think Menshikov sounds like the perfect hit man," Keith said. "Didn't you say he and the Major used to be a spies during the war? Blackmail can be dangerous, especially if the Major knew about

Alex's smuggling in the Eastern Block. Maybe he murdered the Major because of some old grudge."

"We don't know if Alex murdered him," Andrea answered defensively, feeling both shame and fascination about him. She wanted to tell Keith everything, but decided to wait. "Mama told me that Countess Glazanova used to work with Alex. What's bizarre is that she happens to be the Major's twin sister. She told the police the Major had been missing for three weeks and claimed to have filed a missing persons report, but Tony said they couldn't find it."

"So it's a conspiracy?" Keith sipped his coffee.

"It sounds like it." Andrea counted off with her fingers, "OK, let's go down the list. We know that Durant is in the middle of this thing. So are Menshikov and the Countess. I suspect they are all somehow connected with this anonymous lady who was the original owner of the icon."

"You said you saw other people at Alex's house. Would you recognize any of them?" Keith asked.

"I only saw them fleetingly. I'm not sure."

"If this is a conspiracy, how do you know Alex was the one who chased you through the park?"

"I don't know. I just assumed it. I thought the others had gone by the time I left."

"Maybe they did, maybe they didn't," Keith said, writing a note to himself. "Maybe this is some kind of cult thing. Remember, both Michael and the Major had their throats slashed. I bet the coroner discovers even more similarities."

"Like one of those satanic cults?" Andrea shivered. "I hate those. A father of a friend of mine was an organist in an Episcopal Church in Ohio. He came in late one night to practice and found hundreds of wax candles burning all around the church. They were placed on the altar and in the windowsills. The altar linens were messed up and there were blood stains on the carpet."

"I thought things like that went out with the Middle Ages."

"Not if you heard the recent horrendous stories of people who've been ritually abused," she countered. "This has all the markings of it."

"The whole thing sounds fishy to me."

"No kidding. What I do know is that the Major was staying up at the monastery last week. He must have been hiding from somebody. Could it have been his sister? What does she know? Why is she lying?"

"So we have to find the Countess."

"That's why I'm going to see Vera."

"I thought Catelano warned you off this case."

"He did."

"So why are you going?"

"Can't I go see my own godmother?"

"I'm coming with you."

"Please don't. If you don't mind, I'd like to go alone. Personal stuff."

"I hope you're doing the right thing," Keith looked warily at her, but he didn't want another painful argument. He was just glad she was talking to him again.

"Quite sure. I'll call you later." She smiled seductively and gave Keith a big kiss, then left.

Not totally pleased with the way things had turned out, Keith sat back in his chair and tossed his cloth napkin onto his plate.

3

Andrea knocked loudly at Vera's front door. She could hear the patter of Vera's slippers limping on the hard wood floors as she came down the hall. "Andrea! You give me a surprise! Are you well? Your Mama tells me you were in hospital."

Andrea again kissed Vera twice on the cheek in the traditional Russian greeting. "I'm fine. Almost one hundred percent. I need to talk with you."

"Of course, of course." Vera stepped aside and showed her into the living room. "Sorry, I have nothing to give you," she gestured weakly. "So little money. Would you like some tea, toast and jam?"

"Tea would be nice." Vera shuffled out to the kitchen to turn on the kettle.

Andrea surveyed the many pictures on Vera's wall with a purpose. They had always hung there but they held no meaning for her, until now. She stopped at a photograph of three people. A tall, thin, dashing man dressed in a baggy zoot suit of the 1940s with wide lapels was flanked on one side by Vera who was then a dark-haired, moderately attractive woman with soulful eyes, and a beautiful blonde bombshell, tanned and dressed in white shorts, on the other. Somewhere she had seen that face before, or one like it—but where? She made a mental note to ask Vera about it.

Vera returned shortly bearing the tea tray, which swayed as she tottered into the living room. They sat down on the couch across from the fireplace. Andrea thankfully accepted the hot black Russian tea, and then Vera poured for herself. "Aunt Vera, I have some important questions to ask you. I want to talk with you about Alex Menshikov. I know everything, Vera. Mama told me."

"Ahhh," the old woman sighed heavily and nodded. "So this has finally come. I could not tell you before because your Mama swore me to secret. I knew Alex well, many years ago, when you were child."

"When was this?"

"Maybe 1959, 1960. Your mother brought Nicky and you from New York and you came to stay with me, remember?"

Andrea nodded, "I remember. I think I was almost five. I remember especially the old rose bushes in your garden with the honeysuckle that climbed up the back wall."

"Your mother had no money except for what Sam gave her. I started antique store but needed help with the big art because of my bad leg. Marina said she knew this man who was good art dealer. He sold wonderful icons, Fabergé eggs and gold cigarette cases. When I saw his things, I thought he must have good family connections or he is a swindler. He told me everything was OK but I never really believed him. But I couldn't go to police. I had to be careful because of my visa papers. The government didn't trust us Russians then."

"What was he like?" Andrea asked.

"He was tall and very handsome. Big brown beard. Always excited about everything. He was fun at parties. He used to sing old Russian songs as your Mama played piano. Such a fine deep voice!

He was very charming when he wanted to be. He was good buyer but he was tricky. He disappeared for long time and did not say where he was. Once he told me he was going to London to buy antiques. Later, when he did not return for many weeks, people said he slipped into East Germany."

"When was this?"

"Maybe 1960. Before those monsters put up the wall in Berlin. When he came home, I told him I could not use him as a buyer. My residency papers I did not want to lose. He just laughed. He said he was doing me favor because of Marina and you. But by then she had work. They fought, then he disappeared."

"Have you ever heard of Countess Glazanova?" Andrea sipped her tea.

"That impostor!" Vera said bitterly. "She's no Countess, but she calls herself one just because she married into money. Besides, those titles mean nothing anymore. She made Alex go bad, I think. All that glamour went to his head."

"What do you mean?" Andrea asked.

"She made dresses. She was very talented. Big beautiful blonde. When she was twenty-five she went to Hollywood because some big shot film producer saw her photograph at a modeling studio and offered her a role in films. But they discovered she was better at making fancy clothes than acting, so she sewed for movies, and later for big movie stars. Some say she whored her way up the ladder. Then she met this so-called Russian count and danced into high society. This was big thing for Alex, I think. I often wondered if he was her lover. She was like spider, that woman. She ate all the men up."

"Like the man in the photograph with you and the Countess?"

Vera blanched and slowly set her teacup down in her lap. "Da," she nodded. Tears wet her eyelashes. "After my Victor died, he was my boyfriend, but she stole him from me."

Andrea clasped Vera's bony hand, "Life has not been easy for you, has it?" After a pause, she asked, "Vera, why did you send me to Alex's house when you distrusted him so?"

Vera pressed her face with her handkerchief. "I hoped that if he saw you, he might change. You look so like Marina when she was young. Deep down, I think his heart is good. Besides," Vera patted Andrea's hand, "I don't want my goddaughter to be illegitimate any more."

Andrea flushed with emotion, but continued. "If the Countess' father was Metropolitan of the Orthodox Church, how could she have gone so bad?"

"To him, his children did not exist. She and the Major, God rest his soul," Vera crossed herself hurriedly, "were raised secretly by two aunts. That is why Irena Vashkovsky turned her face against her father and against Mother Church."

"She turned against the Church?"

"Most certainly. She met a man with a church where everyone talks to dead spirits. She became his disciple. Very bad."

"Do you know this man's name?" Andrea asked.

"I forget. He used to be archeologist who went bad because of some special rocks. But spirits, I do nothing with. Very dangerous."

"With rocks?"

"Yes, magic rocks which can cure you."

"Oh, you mean crystals!" Andrea laughed. "An archeologist? Would that be Cecil Durant?"

"Da! That's him."

"Do you know where the Countess lives now?"

"But of course, in the house her husband bought her before he died in 1978. It is on 8th Avenue by Lake Street."

"How do you know all this?"

"I used to play cribbage with Olga, one of her aunts, who disapproved of her and told me everything."

"What about her brother, Major Vashkovsky?"

"The Major never met his father. He went into the army and I heard he spied in Germany and Russia after the Second War. I think he saw his father after the War, but close, they never were."

"What kind of man was he?"

"Smart. Very smart, very tough. He spoke many languages: Russian, English, French, German, and Flemish. He knew science too. And he was very strong. Olga said he was always crazy about exercise and vitamins even after he retired from the Army. Every year he cut a cord of wood, just for fun."

"Was he married?"

"Sad to say, his wife died of cancer last year. He became angry and bitter. So, now you know everything." Vera folded her hands in her lap.

"I don't know about that," Andrea said modestly and placed hr teacup on the coffee table.

"Now I will get address for you." Vera rose stiffly from the couch and limped to her desk. She took out a small well-worn address book from one of the drawers and slowly turned the pages filled with neat, flowery cursive handwriting penned in blue ink. She pointed to the address in the book, "You must read, my eyes no good." Andrea wrote down the address.

"Can't you stay longer?"

"Sorry, Vera, I must go. Another day," Andrea kissed her good-bye. "I promise."

"You are always hopping off like a grasshopper! Where will you go now?"

"To see the Countess. I'll say I was a friend of her Aunt Olga's."

Vera chuckled, "Then she may not let you in."

"Well, then a relative of Alex's. That would certainly be the truth," she said ruefully.

"Ahhh, then you might get lucky."

Andrea held up the photograph of Vera, the Countess and her lover. "By the way, may I borrow this for a few days?"

A puzzled looked momentarily flashed across Vera's face, but waved her hand. "Of course, it makes me too sad to look at it."

"Thank you for everything." Andrea kissed Vera twice again at the door, then she hurried out to her car and drove home.

4

Jergeson came into Catelano's office and handed him the computer print out. "You'll want to look at this."

Tony swiveled around in his chair and took the paper from his hand. He read it quickly. "So, Menshikov had a ticket for a flight to

London on the 22nd, but he never took it."

"No, and he didn't buy it himself. The Visa card is held by a Priscilla Thorpe."

"Who's she?"

"A secretary in Piedmont for someone named Hannah Saxon-Briggs. Apparently, she's been with the family for thirty years."

"Saxon-Briggs? Where have I heard that name before?" Tony pulled out the Beech file and poured through the reports. Finally he stopped. "Got it!" He held up a piece of paper from the IRS. Tony looked at Jergeson with a sly grin, "I think we've got them where the hair is short."

"How's that?"

"Hannah Saxon-Briggs was the person who sold the Kazan Icon to the Holy Virgin Society."

"Are you telling me some blue-haired matron from Piedmont did all this?"

"I don't know, but I think it's time we went to see how the upper crust lives."

"Don't forget, the Chief wants us to question that bombing suspect they just picked up in the Richmond district."

"Terrific, a chat with some wacko just makes my day." Tony flung a paperclip into the wastebasket. "We'll have to visit the blue-bloods later." They collected their coats. "OK, Jergeson, you're driving this time."

5

Andrea sat on her sofa, staring at Vera's photograph, which she'd placed in front of her on the coffee table. Ordinarily, she never considered herself much of a psychic, but this picture filled her with foreboding.

She said a short prayer, closed her eyes and, relaxing slowly, fell into a trance. Memories and faces from the past two weeks flooded her consciousness: images of Michael's cufflinks at Greens, of the Cathedral, the Kazan Icon, and the monastery. It was an odd kaleidoscope of faces: the priest at the Cathedral who stared at her oddly was, she now realized, Alex; the face of her mother weeping; Keith's sardonic smile; Father Peter's compassionate face, and finally, the malicious face of a dark-haired woman she had never seen before. The image of the woman's face was transparent as if the woman's skull was made of quartz, not of human bone. She began to shiver violently which snapped her out of her trance. She crossed herself, said the Jesus Prayer a few times and then went to retrieve a sweater.

6

Andrea sat by the phone for a long time, debating whether she should phone the Countess. Detective Catelano's voice echoed in her mind: "Not only am I going to arrest you, I'm going to break your neck."

Common sense told her she should drop the whole thing and to stay clear of it. But the shock of discovering that Alex was her father had turned her whole world upside down. She didn't know who she was anymore. It was bad enough that Sam West, whom she doted on and thought was her father, had divorced her mother. She had gotten so used to his loss, like a splinter dug too far into the skin to feel anymore. But now this revelation brought her grief flooding back to her.

What's more, this recent knowledge had raised some buried memories that had never surfaced before. Most persistent was her sudden memory of her third birthday party. She remembered the pink and white birthday cake, the party hats and noisemakers. She could see her mother, looking radiant in her nice dress and apron, and the big burly man who pretended to be a bear and gave Andrea and her friends rides on his back. She squealed with laughter as he growled at her and rubbed her face with his thick brown whiskers.

It was the same man, now thirty-three years older, much heavier and clean-shaven, who so graciously showed her his favorite collection of icons. Now she understood the look in his eyes.

She couldn't bear to think that her own father murdered Michael and the Major. It was impossible. She had to know the answer, no matter what. If not for his sake, then for her own.

7

She rehearsed her conversation with the Countess over in her head. She couldn't be too direct, that was too dangerous. What was the Countess' weak point? She gave her intuition breathing room and went to water her plants on the deck.

It came to her while she was watering the white cymbidium. "Vanity!" she said aloud. I'll say I'm doing an article on Russian American celebrities and their contribution to culture for the Russian Heritage Monthly. She can't refuse that.

Andrea dialed her phone. An older woman answered, "Hello?" "Hello, Countess Glazanova? My name is Alexia Chernoff, I hope I am not disturbing you."

"No. What do you want?" She sounded cautious.

"I'm with the *Russian Heritage Monthly*. I was wondering if I could interview you regarding your many contributions to American culture?" Andrea put on her best professional voice.

"My goodness," she gasped. "To what do I owe this honor?"

"I was researching Russian-Americans in Hollywood and dis-covered that you were part of a vibrant sub-culture that sprang up around the movie industry after the War. All roads lead to you. After all, Countess, between your modeling and your designing career, you were the heart of the fashion industry back then."

"You've been doing your homework," the Countess twittered.

Andrea stroked her ego, "I thought the article might also include other San Francisco talents such as Michael Smuin and oth-ers from the art world as well."

"When would you like to come over?"

"Is tomorrow too soon? How about in the afternoon, about two? I'll have a photographer of course."

"I'm just an old woman with nothing to do," she feigned. "That's fine with me."

"You're sure this wouldn't be an inconvenience?" Andrea was glad Keith would be with her.

"Not at all. It would be splendid! See you about 2 o'clock tomorrow. You know my address? How to get here?"

"No," Andrea lied. "You better tell me."

"It's 475 8th Avenue, at Lake Street. Mine is the gray Queen Anne house. Magnificent of course. The second from the corner."

"Great! I look forward to seeing you then."

"And I you," the Countess gushed.

Andrea hung up the phone thinking, now I'm getting somewhere! Then she went to water the rest of her plants.

8

The Countess replaced the white and gold receiver of her antique phone and jotted down the number that had flashed across her caller ID display machine. She checked it with the number Edith had scribbled from the Cathedral guest book and it matched. She dialed immediately. "Edith darling, it's Irena. Is Cecil there? Yes, put him on, won't you?" There was silence while Edith went to fetch Cecil.

"Irena, I hope this is urgent," Cecil growled.

"This will appeal to your sense of urgency, my dear," she purred. "I just received a call from Andrea West, who's claiming to be a reporter. She wants to interview me tomorrow."

"Well, what did you say?"

"I told her to come, naturally."

"Is that wise?"

"Putting her off would only make her more suspicious. I know how to handle this. Don't worry, my dear. She also said she'd be bringing a photographer."

"Reinforcements, no doubt," he grunted.

"I'll try to put them off somehow."

"However you do it, just get her over here. It's the only way we can shut her up."

"I thought you'd say something sensible like that. We should be in Piedmont before three."

"We'll be here waiting for you."

"I think I will enjoy our little cat and mouse game," she cooed wickedly.

CHAPTER 18

There is a remarkable passage in the writing of Fr. John of Kronstadt, a Russian priest, in which he says that God does not reveal to us the ugliness of our souls unless he can espy in us sufficient faith and sufficient hope for us not to be broken by the vision of our own sins."

Metropolitan Anthony Bloom
Meditations: A Spiritual Journey

Saturday, November 10, 1990

"OK, OK!" Keith stood with a towel wrapped around his waist, dripping water from his shower onto the carpet, and grabbed the phone. "Hello," he bellowed.

"Grumpy, are we?" Andrea teased from the other end of the line.

"Andrea! I just got out of the shower. Let me dry off a sec, would ya?"

"What a great way to start a conversation," she laughed when he returned on the phone. "I kind of like the idea of you wet and naked."

Keith chuckled, "Me, too. What's up?"

"I think we're getting closer to solving this case," Andrea said, trying to contain her excitement. "The Countess has agreed to see me, tomorrow at 2. I told her I wanted to interview her for an article and you're going to be my photographer. Can you come? That should give us enough time to meet her and then see each other later. Can you get the afternoon off?"

"Not till about three. Why don't I meet you there?"

Disappointed, Andrea asked, "Sure you can't come any sooner?"

"No, the police have a live suspect from the City Hall bombing fiasco and I have to cover the story tomorrow with the Chief of

Police. But I'll be there around three."

"Great. Afterwards, we could go out for a drink."

"Hey, I heard about this place in the Haight called the Assyrian Zam Zam Club where they make the best martinis in town. Want to go there?"

"Your selection of original spots never ceases to amaze me. I'll try almost anything, as long as it's with you."

"Terrific. By the way, you're lucky I know how to use a camera."

"We'll need it," Andrea said. "I have a suspicion she's as vain as a fifty-year-old ingénue."

2

Dark, flat-bottomed clouds marched ominously across the morning sky like china statues of gray soldiers. A cold damp wind whipped in from the ocean. The air smelled dank and pregnant with rain. Catelano was busy raking the pile of leaves on his front lawn when his wife, just back from jogging, called him from the house. "Honey, telephone."

Tony shouted back. "Tell them I'm not home."

"It's Doug from the station. He said it's urgent. You better take it."

Tony threw his rake down and stormed into the house. "A guy can't even get one damn day off around here!" He took the phone from his wife and barked, "What is it?"

"Tony, we got the mail."

"Beautiful! You call me on my first day off in a month to tell me you got the mail. Why don't you sort it all now and then you can go potty?"

"Somebody sent us a pair of safe deposit keys."

"Convince me this is important."

"They're from the Bank of America on Market Street. We think it's connected to the icon case."

"The banks close at one, I'll meet you there in an hour."

"Got it, boss." They hung up.

Tony's wife, Marisa, still sweaty from her run, sipped her bottled water, "What is it?"

"I've got to go into the City for a couple of hours."

"What about Jenny's soccer game?" She didn't look happy.

"I'll try to be back in time. Don't wait for me." Tony slipped into his coat and kissed her good-bye. "I'll get to the game as soon as I can. I think we just got a break in a case."

"Be careful," she gave him that imploring look she got every time he had to leave like this.

"Ain't I always?" He kissed her goodbye.

3

Andrea drove to the end of the street and parked by a stand of tall, gangly eucalyptus trees that looked to Andrea like live drawings by El Greco. The thick smell of menthol that filled the air reminded her of the horrible Vicks and wool sock remedies her mother used to inflict upon her as a small child. It was not quite 2 o'clock.

The Countess' Queen Ann Victorian stood at the far end of the short street. At the ornate front door, Andrea figured the antique brass doorknocker alone must have cost a fortune.

The Countess opened the door with a flourish. "Ms. Chernoff, I presume?" Her accent was very polished. She tossed a finishing school smile at her.

"Not too late, I hope."

"Right on time. Come in, come in," she swung the door open for her with great drama. "Where's your photographer?" she asked.

"Unfortunately, he can't come until three. I hope this doesn't upset your schedule. Maybe we should arrange another time?" she asked suddenly, having second thoughts.

"Not at all," the Countess said, looking surprisingly pleased.

Andrea noticed that the Countess was astonishingly well preserved for a woman her age. She was small, but her snow-white hair, pulled back tightly into a bun, made her look quite stately. She wore a fitted lavender knit dress made of angora wool, several gold bracelets, a long string of pearls and a piece of white crystal surrounded by diamonds that hung at her right collar bone. Always aware of perfume, Andrea could detect the distinct scent of Channel No.5.

She ushered Andrea into her cozy living room. "I call this my salon." She seemed to Andrea a strange combination of self-consciousness, drama, arrogance and graciousness rolled all into one. "Would you care for a drink?" she asked, as Andrea settled down on the gold and pink silk settee opposite the fireplace.

"I never drink alcohol while working," Andrea said, admiring the early 19th century Russian watercolors hanging in gilded frames.

"Tea, perhaps?"

Andrea, who normally could never pass up a hot pot of tea, said cautiously, "No, thank you."

"I made myself a little something in the kitchen. I'll be right back."

While she was gone, Andrea immediately sprang up and snooped around. She studied a huge oil painting of Tsar Nicholas II over the fireplace then the glass bookcase filled with old leather-bound books printed in Russian and a few Nabokov novels in English. There were also assorted silver spoons, painted Russian Easter eggs, colorful lace, and a few large chunks of rose quartz crystal.

She saw many family photographs, most of them fashion portraits taken of the Countess over the years, looking dewy eyed and surrounded by a halo of blonde hair. The photographer had used an unfocused lens, a popular camera technique in the 1930s and '40s. A kind of Russian Greta Garbo, Andrea thought, with less of the come-hither look, but probably every bit as vain.

There was a series of photographs taken in the '60s all of the Countess, Major Vashkovsky, a younger Alex Menshikov with a brown beard, and a short sandy-haired man with the same woman who had met her at Alex's house, but looking younger. She guessed these might be Cecil and Edith Durant. There was also an elegant couple, whom she didn't know, but whom Andrea guessed were the original icon owners.

The pictures stunned her. My God, these people have known

each other for thirty years! Where were they? What were they doing together? In each, the group always remained the same, except in the last photograph. Here, the portly gentleman looked as if he was laughing and pointing. But at whom? And who took the picture? In each one there was that missing person, the invisible photographer.

Andrea hastily moved away from the picture towards one of the glass cabinets. The Countess came in bearing with her scotch and some hors d'oeuvres. She noticed the Countesses' hands, mottled with brown age spots, especially her bony fingers, which dripped with clusters of gold and diamond rings.

"Admiring my Fabergé eggs?" asked the Countess as she deposited the tray on the cherry wood coffee table. "Of course, they are some of his finest."

Andrea doubted this immediately, but nevertheless said, "They're lovely."

The Countess drifted down on the sofa while Andrea sat next to her. The Countess began the conversation. "Is this just for a magazine or are you also writing a book?" She eyed Andrea shrewdly.

Andrea did not expect this curve ball right off but she caught it deftly, "I wasn't planning to write a book, though there may be one or two spin-off articles. What I have in mind instead is a history of Russians in Hollywood and the entertainment world." Andrea knew that if she was going to get anywhere with this conversation, she would have to go on the offensive. "You were once a leading figure in the fashion world. What do you think of it now?"

The Countess grimaced. "Fashion certainly isn't what it used to be. Those were the days when people knew what style was!" the Countess lamented.

Andrea was right in assuming that the Countess' favorite topic was herself. The woman unraveled her memories with relish, while Andrea dutifully took notes. The details of it all were long-winded and almost too egotistical for Andrea to bear. "Of course, John Ford was a beast of a man," the Countess gushed. "Very disorganized. He had a vile temper. It was I who positively saved his productions..." This charade went on for half an hour.

Andrea kept asking her questions, always trying to lead her on to the subject of the 1960s, and her interest in the art world. "I see collecting is a hobby of yours. You have a number of marvelous Russian pieces."

"Yes, my dear," she said wistfully. "I know it's a trifle decadent, but I've always had to have the finest things—simply to live, you know. I cannot breathe with anything ugly around me. It helps me keep in touch with my art."

"How did you find all these wonderful antiques?" Andrea asked innocently.

"Through my various trips abroad and friends in the trade. For a while, I tried establishing a business of Russian collectibles but stopped after a time." She looked away momentarily. "I decided my true vocation was in fashion, art and film so I stopped. Now, of course, the films have become so degraded. Cheap. Nothing but sex and violence. I refuse to participate in an industry which does not cater to anything but the highest standards."

"Well, then you won't find much work in Hollywood."

The Countess sighed. "Life will never be the same again."

Andrea thought to herself, Thank God for small favors. "It must have been a difficult decision for you. Getting back to your brief experience in business, did you ever happen to run into an art dealer named Alex Menshikov?"

The Countess shifted slightly on the settee. "Yes, I knew him. He used to sell Russian imports. He specialized in icons. Are you very interested in icons, Ms. Chernoff?"

"Some what."

"Do you know much about this field?"

"A little," Andrea said modestly, realizing the conversation was slipping from her hands but was, nevertheless, going where she wanted.

"I know someone who specializes in appraising icons, perhaps you've heard of him. His name is Cecil Durant," the Countess said slyly.

Poker faced, Andrea responded, "Sorry, I haven't heard of him."

"No? Perhaps you have heard of the Icon of Kazan?"

"What Russian hasn't?"

"Cecil sold it to the Holy Virgin Society for Mrs. Saxon-Briggs. Do you know her?"

"No, but I've wanted to meet her for a long time," Andrea said candidly. "I've heard she is quite a collector."

"Have you?" the Countess said archly. She rose and fetched one of the group photographs for Andrea, "That's her, with her husband Edward," she pointed. "He's dead, of course. If you want to see her, you better do it fast. She's been battling a fatal illness. Would you like to meet her?"

"Yes, if it's not too much of a strain for her," Andrea said with real concern.

"Unfortunately, I can't drive much anymore. How would you like to be my chauffeur? I haven't seen her in years myself. I'm much too old to go gallivanting across the Bay to Piedmont. I would love to see her before I die. You would be doing me the greatest service."

Andrea couldn't pass up this opportunity. "I'd be happy to. But what about my photographer?" She looked at her watch with annoyance. It was after three. "He should be here by now."

"Can't you call him and reschedule?"

The Countess gave Andrea permission to use her phone. She let Keith's phone ring while trying to come up with another game plan. No answer. Damn! Andrea put the receiver down, "He's probably on his way."

Andrea tried to stall her but at last the Countess shrugged, "These things can't be helped. Let's go before I get out of the mood. At my age, impulses like this don't last very long."

Against her better judgment, Andrea decided to go. This was her last chance. Before they walked downstairs, Andrea said, "I've been admiring you necklace all afternoon. Where did you get such a beautiful piece of crystal?"

"From Cecil. Didn't I tell you? Cecil Durant is an expert on crystals."

"Really?" Andrea lied. So he has the Crystal Skull too, she thought. Her heart raced at the idea she might at last see the object of so much of her research. "I've always wanted to see a good collection of crystals," she said.

The Countess patted Andrea's hand. "My dear, now you shall have your chance." She smiled secretly as Andrea put her car into gear and headed for the Bay Bridge.

4

In the end, the interview with the Chief of Police made Keith arrive twenty minutes late. The eucalyptus trees creaked in the wet and blustery fog; their leaves shuddered like paper wind chimes. Keith zipped up his jacket as he approached the Countess' house. There was no sign of anyone. "Damn!"

He rang the doorbell at the Countess' gingerbread Victorian. No answer. He waited a few minutes and rang again. Still no answer. Damn again! Maybe there's a message on my machine?

Keith climbed quickly into his car and headed for the nearest pay phone. As he dialed home, he hit his head with his hand, realizing that, in his hurry, he hadn't reset his answering machine. Idiot! He felt guilty and furious with himself, both for being late and for letting Andrea go off on her own.

Maybe she ended her interview early, he thought. Hoping Andrea had gone ahead to the Assyrian Zam Zam Club, Keith jumped into his car and headed straight for Haight Street.

5

As Keith walked into the crowded Zam Zam Club, he passed a big, burly, white-haired man in a suede coat perched on a stool halfway down the bar. He was loudly telling a story to some buddies. Keith sat down a few stools away from them.

The bartender stood behind the bar wiping a glass with a clean white towel. Keith remembered his conversation with Frank at Maxfield's. "You Boris?" Keith asked.

Boris shot Keith a quizzical look, "Who wants to know?" he growled.

"I'm Keith Carlton. Folks down at *Maxfield's* say you make the best martinis in town."

"Is that what you want?" Boris asked gruffly.

"Chilled, with two olives." Keith deposited four bills on the counter. Boris turned and began filling the aluminum canister with cracked ice. When he was done, he dropped two green olives into the martini and handed it to Keith.

"Thanks," he said and took a sip, nodding his approval. "By the way, you haven't seen a beautiful dark haired woman come in here the last half hour, have you?"

Boris smiled, broadly surveyed his club and shook his head, "Nope. If she were beautiful, I'd notice. There was no woman." The group of men down the bar laughed as the older man finished his story with a flourish.

Keith shook his head, "That's strange. My girlfriend was supposed to meet me here after interviewing, can you believe it, this Countess. You sure you haven't seen her?"

"Positive." Boris continued drying glasses and arranging them on the shelf.

"Thanks." Keith sighed and decided to wait half an hour in case Andrea was late. He caught a few football scores on the tube then gulped down the rest of his drink and left the bar.

Soon after, Alex, who had eavesdropped on Keith's conversation, deposited his tip on the counter, then stood up and waved good-bye to his friends, "See you guys later." Alex stepped out the door after Keith and followed him for two blocks.

6

Unaware that he was being followed, Keith turned a sharp left on Ashbury towards the panhandle of Golden Gate Park towards his car and suddenly found himself face to face with Alex. Alex, who was six inches taller than Keith and almost twice as heavy, twirled him around, held him in a half nelson, then pressed him hard against the alley wall, and dug a hand-gun into his back. He hissed, "You reporters talk too much. So your girlfriend saw the Countess?"

Keith tried to struggle free but could not, "Where is she, you bastard?"

"How the hell should I know?" Alex puffed. "All I want is for you to fucking stay out of my face."

Keith winced from the pain in his shoulder, "She was supposed to be at the Countess's at three. You'll never get away with this."

"I wouldn't be so sure about that," Cecil said as he approached them.

Alex and Cecil flanked Keith and strong-armed him forward into a waiting sedan. "I think you've said enough already. We are going for a little ride. Walk natural, I don't want to have to use this."

"Where are we going?"

"Just shut up!"

7

Andrea and the Countess drove up the circular drive to the front of the huge mansion on Wildwood Court. "Go around to the back," the Countess demanded. "There's more room to park."

She drove down the gravel drive past a facade that was lit up like a European palace at Christmas, to the private lot near the servants' entrance. Four cars were parked there including a green Mercedes-Benz, which the chauffeur was hosing down.

"Beautiful car. Who owns that Mercedes?" Andrea asked as innocently as she could.

"It belongs to Mrs. Saxon-Briggs but she doesn't drive anymore. Her secretary drives it."

"I see..." Andrea began to feel very uneasy.

The Countess brought Andrea inside the front hall where presently, a tall, thin brunette stepped stiffly across the threshold. "Priscilla, darling, I brought some company," the Countess chirped. "I hope you don't mind. Meet Alexia Chernoff. She's the one I told you was doing the interview of me."

Priscilla Thorpe held out a hand in welcome and forced a smile. "Hello, I'm Priscilla Thorpe." Andrea took her hand but felt suddenly chilled. Somewhere from the back of her sub-conscious a sense memory was trying to push through, but she couldn't catch it.

As they walked past the massive descending staircase, Priscilla asked, "I do hope you can stay for dinner?"

Andrea hesitated, "Oh, I don't think so. I couldn't do that. This is so unexpected."

"Nonsense! She's staying," the Countess patted Andrea's hand, "Alexia says she wants to meet Hannah and see her collection of crystals."

Priscilla shook her head, "Mrs. Saxon-Briggs isn't feeling well, I'm afraid. But you're welcome to see her crystals. They're in here."

The Countess took Andrea by the elbow and led her into the inner drawing room where assorted pink, sapphire and white crystals were displayed in a well-lit glass cabinet. But it was the Crystal Skull sitting in the middle of a brown mahogany table, which made her stop dead in her tracks.

Andrea looked at the skull; her preconceived skepticism was immediately replaced with amazement. It was stunning. Immediately compelling and mysterious. The skull was about fourteen inches high and five inches wide, and it seemed to be made from glass. An unlit candle was placed next to it. Trying not to give away how much she knew, it took her a few seconds before she could speak, "What a crystal!"

"There is nothing like it," Priscilla boasted.

Andrea caught the fanatical glint in her eye, which made her nervous. She tried to appear calm, "Where did you get it?"

"Mrs. Saxon-Briggs said it was found in the jungle as her father was exploring the Temple City, Lubaantun, in British Honduras in 1927," the Countess added. "Who knows, it might even come from the lost city of Atlantis."

"Is that so?"

Priscilla took the Skull and held it up close to Andrea. "It is made from a block of pure quartz crystal. See, there's not one chisel mark on the skull," she said proudly. "No one knows how it was made."

Andrea was acutely aware of Priscilla's cold, astringent presence before her and the distinct smell of Shalimar perfume. Andrea's inner Geiger-counters suddenly went off with alarm as two scenes flashed through her mind. First, she realized whom she bumped into as she was leaving the Cathedral the night of Michael's murder. Second, she remembered the scent of the person who attacked her at the Russian Cultural Museum. Both times someone had been were wearing this unmistakable fragrance, and both times this person radiated a piercing chill, characteristic of someone trapped in spiritual winter.

Andrea then knew, without a doubt, she had to leave that house immediately.

"The collection is really amazing. Thank you for letting me see it but I really must be going," she said to the Countess and Priscilla. "I'm sorry I wasn't able to visit Mrs. Saxon-Briggs, perhaps another time." She approached the front door when Cecil Durant suddenly stepped into the hallway in front of her, holding a gun.

"Not so fast, Ms. West," he frowned.

She stopped, stunned with amazement. O God! She thought, what a fool I am! What a damn fool!

CHAPTER 19

"There is always a moment in the experience of discipleship when fear comes upon the disciple, for he sees at a certain moment that death is looming, the death that his self must face. Later on it will no longer be death, it will be life greater than his own, but every disciple will have to die first before he comes back to life."

Metropolitan Anthony Bloom
Meditations: A Spiritual Journey

Cecil opened the door to reveal Alex Menshikov standing in the doorway holding a gun to Keith, who was tied and gagged. "Timing is everything," Alex remarked.

"Keith!" Andrea exclaimed and instinctively moved towards him but Alex drew his gun closer to Keith's body. "I wouldn't do anything rash if I were you. Not if you care about your boyfriend here."

Andrea stood there helplessly, torn between terror and rage.

Priscilla ordered Cecil, "Take them downstairs and tie them up. We'll deal with them later."

Cecil shoved the muzzle of his gun into her back, "Scream and you're dead." Then he and Alex pushed both Keith and Andrea past the large walk-in pantry, down to an old-fashioned laundry room in the basement.

2

Andrea sat back to back with Keith and found it hard to breathe with the gag stuffed in her mouth. Everything was silent, except for the occasional metallic churning of the furnace innards across the room. The air smelt damp and fetid, reeking of rusty metal and years of mounting dust.

Andrea twisted the rope tied around her wrists and was surprised that it had a tiny amount of slack. After only a minute, she wriggled her hands free. She pulled the gag off, gasping for air, and shook her hair loose. Keith grunted through his gag.

Andrea bent down and untied her feet and slid out of the ropes that bound them together. She untied Keith's gag and hands. Both free, the couple spontaneously hugged each other.

"Jesus," he said in a hushed voice, rubbing his face, "I thought he was going to cut my jaw off." Keith looked admiringly at Andrea, "You must be related to Houdini!"

"I think there's a double-cross going on here," she whispered. "This was too easy."

"It's what those old spy thrillers called 'defecting in place,'" Keith whispered back.

Then Keith flicked on the lighter from his pocket and held it up, scanning the room. There was nothing but gray concrete walls and a huge antique furnace in one corner.

"I feel like we've been transported to a gulag on our way to the killing fields," Keith moaned softly.

"Your optimism will get us far," She quipped. "Do you always crack jokes when you're under pressure?"

"You should see me when I'm stuck in an stalled elevator! It helps to relieve the stress."

"Let's see if we can find a way out of here."

The rusty handle to the door of the furnace room turned easily, but squeaked loudly. With a pounding heart, she opened the door as slowly and as quietly as possible. The old wooden door groaned on its hinges. She cracked it open just wide enough to slip out.

They stood in the long, dark basement. At the far end was a door with a frosted glass window leading outside. Andrea silently pointed at it.

Keith hurried over and tried the window, but it was sealed tight. "It's stuck," he whispered. "You look at that end, I'll check the other side of the stairs."

Andrea went further into the bowels of the basement past the laundry room. Outside, a light bulb shone by the back door, illuminating only a small radius. Her eyes had grown quite accustomed to the dark. She felt like a sparrow trapped in a dark narrow room, flapping its wings against the windowpanes in a futile effort to find freedom.

Near the center of the room, cut into the wall a few feet off the ground, was a small three-foot square door. She opened it and, to her surprise, saw a large old-fashioned dumbwaiter.

"Keith! Come here," Andrea called out in a whisper. He stood by her side in a second. "Look at this! I haven't seen one of those since my grandmother's house. It probably goes all the way up to the third floor, where I bet they keep the linens. This is our way out."

Keith examined it and pushed on the floor of the dumbwaiter. "It looks too small for two people. I doubt even one of us could squat in it."

"No, silly! Not in it. We're going on top of it. We can stand on it and hoist our way up. Pull the box down till it hits the bottom."

Keith pushed slowly and carefully. The ropes above screeched on their pulleys. He stopped. They listened for signs of steps upstairs. Their hearts thumped wildly. None came. Keith exhaled audibly.

"OK," she whispered, "Try it again."

He pushed down again, this time more slowly and more evenly. The ropes slid smoothly in place. He pushed it down until the dumbwaiter hit bottom of the shaft below the doorsill. This allowed Andrea a space of about two feet to look up the dark shaft. She stuck her head in, twisted her body and craned her neck up. She could see streams of yellow light coming through the cracks in the dumbwaiter doors on the first, second and third floors. "Great!" Andrea whispered in triumph.

"Help me up will you?" She sat on the sill as Keith awkwardly helped her hoist herself into the dumbwaiter shaft. She sat on the top of the dumbwaiter cabinet to catch her breath for a minute. "Thank God I'm not claustrophobic," she whispered down to Keith.

"Too bad I am! You're not getting me in that worm hole."

"Keith, what are you taking about? Not at a time like this! Get over it and get on up here!"

"So much for the pastoral touch."

Andrea's face peered out through the gap, "I hope this isn't one of your stress-relieving moments. Because if it is, it isn't working!"

"Hey, would I lie about a thing like this? Ever since Chucky Marchesi stuffed me down a manhole when I was ten," he whispered, "I've always had this horrible fear of tight places. Sorry, I can't help it."

"You'll be in a deeper manhole if you don't get your tail up here."

"I'm moving as fast as I can," Keith stalled.

"I'm going without you," Andrea fumed. She stood up on the roof of the dumbwaiter and began to pull at one of the ropes. The box moved an inch upward.

"OK, OK," Keith held the dumbwaiter. "Just hang on a minute."

"Believe me, I'm not going anywhere. Hurry up!"

Keith clumsily climbed through the gap and clambered on top of the dumbwaiter, sitting at Andrea's feet. "My worst nightmare," he groaned.

"But I thought you said you were in the war in El Salvador?"

"I was! At least we were outside. No problem. This is the pits."

"Stand up and help me pull this rope," she ordered. As Keith cautiously rose to his feet, they could feel the roof of the dumbwaiter creak and sag.

"What if it doesn't hold?" Keith looked down nervously.

"We'll never get out of here if we don't try," she said with determination. They shifted their weight to the corner of the box, which had the most support and grabbed the thick ropes. "Try not to hurt your bad shoulder if you can."

"Don't worry," he whispered, "It's already telling me loud and clear what to do."

She brushed away a few cobwebs with disgust, took a deep breath of the fusty air and hissed, "Now together, pull." Both of them gripped the coarse ropes that dangled down from the top of the house and grunted, pulling as hard as they could. Nothing happened. The dumbwaiter didn't move.

"Maybe we're pulling the wrong one." They balanced their feet and tried again, pulling the other rope. It squealed in its pulley up near the attic. They stopped and waited to hear if anyone upstairs had heard it. There wasn't a sound.

They drew the rope more evenly this time, which was harder, as it required continuous tension, but the ropes ran smoothly on the pulley. Very slowly the bottom of the dumbwaiter creaked off the basement floor.

Please God, let it hold! Andrea prayed. They hauled themselves up steadily and slowly, inching noiselessly up the dark shaft. The dumbwaiter held.

Andrea tried to guess how the dumbwaiter would fit into the scheme of the house. It landed in the basement near the center of the house right near the laundry, that means it wouldn't be too far from the scullery, between the kitchen and the dining room so that when the table cloths and napkins were removed, it would be easy to throw them down the shaft to be laundered. With any luck, the living room was at the far end, away from the kitchen and noise of the servants. The living room is where they would be.

They rose slowly. "Remind me to start lifting weights when I get home," Keith whispered as sweat poured down his face. No sooner had he said this, than they heard the sound of splintering wood above them in the shaft. They stopped pulling on the ropes. "What the hell was that?!" Keith froze.

"I don't know." Andrea, puzzled, tugged at her rope to test it. The rope held fine.

"Let's get out of here," Keith whispered nervously. "I don't feel like getting shafted today."

"Very funny," Andrea hissed. "Keep pulling."

By now, they had hoisted themselves nearly up to the first floor. They heard the muffled sound of the dishwasher in the kitchen and Andrea guessed they were in the scullery.

They stopped by the dumbwaiter door on the first floor and hung on the ropes, breathing heavily. "This would be a lot easier if there was only one of us," Andrea panted.

"And you're the one," Keith parried in hushed tones. Keith cracked open the dumbwaiter door and peeked through to make sure the cook had left the kitchen. "This is our stop," he squatted down to get out.

"Where are you going?" Andrea protested.

"What do you mean? I'm getting out. Where are *you* going?"

"I'm going to get the icon. I know it's in one of these bedrooms up there," she pointed.

"Are you crazy? You can't do that. Forget the icon. We gotta get out of here!"

"I have to get it. For Michael's sake and the Major's. You go on without me," Andrea ordered in a hoarse whisper.

"I don't like this. I don't like this at all. You're obsessed, that's what you are! You're as bad as these maniacs."

"How can you say that? If you're not with me, just forget the whole thing."

Keith tried his last card, "Andrea, either it's me or the icon—which do you want?"

"Who said I have to choose?" Andrea said defiantly. "Why don't you make yourself useful and get some help!"

Keith glowered at her but realized this was no time to argue. "I'll try. I'll meet you at the back door in twenty minutes. If you're not there by then, I'm going to the police."

"Good luck! I'll be there." Andrea said.

Keith shook his head and despite his misgivings, climbed out of the dumbwaiter and stepped out onto the kitchen floor, closing the door silently behind him before he looked for a place to hide.

Andrea stood up in the dark shaft and surveyed her possibilities. The Countess had said Mrs. Saxon-Briggs wasn't well, so she'd probably be lying in bed in the master bedroom on the second floor. Like most stately homes of the past, she knew the third floor was usually set apart as the servant's quarters. She hoped these would be near the far end of the house by the back stairs, as far away from the master bedroom as possible. That would be her way out.

3

"But dear, you can't just take them out and shoot them as if they were pesky rodents that had invaded your cellar," Edith paused and peered up from her knitting. She sat on the sofa by the fireplace with knitting needles and a sweater on her lap, a string of blue yarn stretched down to the big bag at her feet on the floor. She turned back to her knitting.

"Nobody said anything about murder," Cecil scowled at her.

Edith drifted from the thread of the conversation and gazed at the Crystal Skull, propped upon a stand on the table. "Look how the Skull glows," she murmured. "She's so lovely!"

Cecil looked at it and grunted his approval. "Edith, don't change the subject." He leaned on the mantelpiece and kicked the bottom log burning in the grate into place. "No one wants to kill them, but let's be practical. They know too much."

"I don't like this one bit," Edith answered nervously.

"Well, it's too late now," he snapped.

"Stop bickering." Priscilla paced back and forth. "I need to think." She turned and glared at the Countess and Alex. "You were both stupid to bring them here. Really stupid. Who knows if they weren't followed?"

"Don't get nasty with me, you witch," the Countess hissed at her. "I've had enough of your high and mighty airs. Of course we weren't followed. Who's going to chase after a young woman taking an old lady out for a spin in her own car? The police have better things to do."

"And I made sure I wasn't followed," Alex said as he sprawled opposite Edith in a high-back easy chair. "What else could I do? Kill Carlton on Haight Street and throw him in the Bay in broad daylight? All this would never have happened if you had followed my directions in the first place." He folded his arms stubbornly. The fire crackled and sputtered brightly.

"So it's all my fault?" Priscilla flared back at him.

"Who else? And what about that idiotic idea of those death threats? That was effective. Why didn't you wave a red flag in the air and say to the police, 'Here we are, over here!'"

"If you were in London right now, as we originally planned, we'd be a lot safer," Priscilla retorted.

Cecil slammed his hand on the mantel, "Shut up! I'm tired of this arguing. I say we get them out of town immediately. Then we decide. Maybe they can be bribed to keep their mouths shut?"

"Not likely." Alex said glumly, "Carlton earns his living by blabbing and she's too high-minded for that."

The Countess said, "We've already kidnapped them, soon it will be front page news. No, we have to decide here, tonight."

Edith tried to change the tone of the conversation. "I'm sorry Hannah couldn't be here with us. I'd like to know what she thinks."

Priscilla said, "Yes, poor dear, she isn't feeling well. She has been lingering for quite some time." She glanced at Edith, who seemed honestly concerned.

The Countess sighed, "We can't live forever...." and picked up a magazine and started to thumb through it.

"Well, at least we can be assured that there will be a brighter place for her in the spirit world," Edith chirped optimistically.

"Oh, God!" Alex rolled out of his chair and stood up. "I need a drink. Anyone else?"

The women declined, shaking their heads. Cecil said, "I'll have a scotch on the rocks. Make it a double."

Alex strode into the dining room and opened the liquor cabinet. The whiskey was gone. Thinking an extra bottle was stored in the kitchen, he went past the scullery and furtively searched the pantry shelves, hoping to find another bottle.

Keith froze in the pantry broom closet, the one place worse than his worst nightmare.

Alex was too busy hunting to notice that the closet door was slightly ajar, or that he was being watched through the crack. As Alex rummaged among the bottles, he noticed an unusual bell-jar stashed on a back corner shelf. He pulled it out and twisted off the lid. The jar was half full of a white powdered substance. Powdered sugar? Arrowroot? Cocaine? He wondered. He smelled it, then ran with fear to the sink and quickly washed his hands thoroughly with hot water.

"Cancer, my foot!" Alex muttered aloud. He replaced the bell-jar in the pantry, wiped off his fingerprints with a towel and finding, a fresh bottle of whiskey on the pantry floor, returned with it to the living room.

And Keith knew another murder was in progress.

4

Andrea had heard the cabinets opening and closing in the scullery below and stopped hoisting her way up. God, I hope they haven't found him, she prayed. Then she heard one pair of steps treading heavily out of the kitchen and she breathed a sigh of relief. She waited for several minutes after the footsteps retreated before beginning again.

Slowly, she continued to hoist herself and the dumbwaiter upwards. Well on her way, she dangled nearly two stories up the narrow, airless shaft. Sweat poured down her back as she held the ropes against her body. She held both ropes tightly, trembling with fear and exhaustion. She heard the pulleys occasionally scrape up at the top where they were joined to the roof. Then her worst fear happened.

Distantly overhead, she heard the sound of wood splintering. She looked up and felt the dumbwaiter jerk as one of the clamps tore away from the wooden beam.

Feverishly, she hoisted the dumbwaiter up until she was nearly level with the second floor. She grabbed the ledge with both hands just as the clamp pulled loose on one side and the dumbwaiter dropped six inches. The clamp fell past her in the shaft and clattered onto the roof below her feet. One of the ropes dangled limply in the air.

She pulled her torso onto the ledge, shouldering the dumbwaiter door open slowly until she poked her head out to survey the hallway. She panted for fresh air. No on was in sight.

She slipped off the dumbwaiter ledge and tiptoed cautiously to hide in a corner, where she debated which way to go next. To her right the dark corridor went along, then turned sharply to the left, presumably towards the back stairs. She looked towards her left and saw a long runner that led past bedroom doors to an end room. A light shone through the crack at the bottom of the door. The master bedroom, she deduced.

She felt torn. Her survival instinct told her to go right. She had to save her own skin and get out of there. But something else kept pulling her towards this last room. She had to know what or who was behind those closed doors.

She heard someone coming up the front stairs. Andrea bolted into one of the side rooms and hid inside a dusty closet. She heard a door open, then close. She heard a tiny dog bark and the sound of muffled, inaudible voices.

After a few minutes, Andrea heard Priscilla's voice at the door. "I'll check on you before bedtime." The door closed. Andrea felt like sneezing, but stifled it. The steps continued on down the stairs.

After a long pause, Andrea slipped out and tiptoed down the hall towards the end bedroom. She turned the doorknob and heard a faint whining at the foot of the door. She opened it slowly and stepped inside. She knew immediately where she was and whom she was with.

5

"I thought you would never come," Hannah Saxon-Briggs croaked weakly from her bed. Andrea saw a shriveled old woman, gaunt with blackened palms and purple fingernails, lying in a valley of white lacy pillows piled up around her head. She noticed the old woman was nearly bald, with strands of white hair scattered on the pillow. Her face was bony and blotchy.

A thin Pekinese dog languished at Andrea's feet by the door. Barely alive, the poor dog looked as if it had been molting. Clumps of dog hair lay about the rugs. There was a sweet sickly smell of death in the room.

Fearful the old woman was dying, Andrea went to her bedside table to inspect the several plastic bottles of medication lying there. Demerol, morphine and heavy doses of Vicodin. She took Hannah's pulse. It was dangerously slow.

Hannah looked up at Andrea's face and rasped, "You're my Guardian Angel."

Andrea couldn't tell if the woman was delirious or senile. She patted her arm. "I'm not an angel, my name is Andrea West."

"You're my angel just the same," she smiled weakly at her.

Andrea asked firmly, "Mrs. Saxon-Briggs?" Hannah nodded her

head weakly. "Where is the Kazan Icon?"

With effort the old woman raised a long bony finger and pointed to the tall dresser opposite her. Andrea turned around and saw the Icon of Kazan, dazzling and radiant, with its emerald gemstones bursting through the gold filigree placed on Cecil's altar. "I've been praying for a miracle," Hannah said.

Once again, it was not the rubies and diamonds which caught Andrea's eye, but the kind face of the Madonna herself that peered lovingly out from her precious encrustment. Andrea stepped towards the Icon, when she noticed the body of another Pekinese dog lying dead in the corner by a water dish.

"Oh, no!" she bent over and inspected the animal. The odor was foul.

She stood up. "He's dead." Clumps of dog hair lay all around the floor. Andrea had been a gardener long enough to know the effects of a variety of toxins. "Arsenic poisoning," she concluded out loud.

"I know," Hannah wheezed. She rolled over, and began to cough violently from her difficulty swallowing. Then she began vomiting into a bedpan by her side. Andrea covered her nose and mouth with repulsion. "They killed Flopsy just as they're killing me," she lamented. She looked at her dogs mournfully, "All I want is for the three of us to die together."

"Who's killing you?"

"They are. Downstairs. All of them." She smiled ironically. "Even my faithful Priscilla."

"But why? How?"

"I don't know. But they are. I gave her everything. She had no reason to complain." Tears welled in Hannah's eyes. "She should have been grateful. My husband doted on her before he died. Since we had no children, I even put her in my will. She was all I had. She could have had it all. I don't understand. She should have been grateful."

"Some forms of pride would rather die than be grateful," Andrea mused and considered Hannah's situation. "It looks like you have been sick for weeks."

Hannah nodded yes. "I hoped getting the Kazan Icon back would heal me, but it has done no good. I have gotten worse."

"Did you also arrange the break-in and Michael Beech's murder?"

"I had nothing to do with him." Hannah gasped for air. "They did everything. Later, they told me Mr. Menshikov murdered him. He was such an awful man, I wasn't surprised."

"Who told you Alex murdered him?" Andrea persisted.

"Priscilla did. She does everything for me. Nurses me, feeds me," Hannah turned her face to the wall bitterly. "I thought she loved me, but it was a sham."

Andrea did some quick thinking. "Were you also planning to sell the Crystal Skull and the Kazan Icon again?"

Mrs. Saxon-Briggs nodded her head. "If the icon couldn't cure me, yes. We needed the money. My debts are horrendous. I expect she thought they were hers."

"Do you think Priscilla is behind all this?" No doubt she killed Michael and the Major too, Andrea thought to herself. Unfortunately, killing gets easier the more you do it.

"I don't know what to think," the old woman answered weakly. "I don't trust her any more."

"Mrs. Saxon-Briggs, you're very ill. You need a doctor immediately."

She said bluntly. "I'm afraid it's too late. I don't think I can walk anymore."

"All the more reason to get help. I'm sorry, but I'm going to have to take the icon. Then we're going to get you to a hospital."

Hannah shook her head. "No, don't."

"The doctors can save you, if you let them!" Andrea said, "God works as much through doctors as through icons."

"It's no use. You can take the icon. I'm afraid God and I are not on speaking terms anymore. I don't believe in God."

"You may not believe in God, but I suspect God still believes in you—no matter what you've done."

"Maybe," she answered apathetically. "You'll need to turn off the alarm system if you want the icon. There, on the wall." She pointed weakly to the switch by her bed.

Andrea took Hannah's cold hand in hers. She fixed a piercing gaze on Hannah and said fiercely, "I'm going to get out of here. I'll call an ambulance for you. Just hang on until they come." She squeezed her hand. "Just hang on!"

Hannah's eyes filled up with tears. "Why are you doing this for me?"

"Because I must," she said honestly. "I'll be back. Don't worry. Just pray for me. Hard."

"I don't know how anymore," she complained.

"Just pretend like you do and the rest will come naturally."

Andrea flipped the switch and turned off the alarm system, and then she unhooked the Icon from above the altar. It came off easily. It weighed almost ten pounds. Andrea momentarily thought the eyes of the Holy Virgin looked alive, gazing back at her with a look of reassurance. The gold, emeralds and the diamonds, which studded the riza, dazzled brightly in the light.

"You'll be all right," Andrea took Hannah's hand and said a brief silent prayer. "Don't give up." Then she slipped out with the icon under her arm and headed for the back stairs.

6

Andrea tiptoed slowly down the narrow, spiral staircase, trying not to make the boards creak, but the old wooden stairs groaned and screeched with protest at every step. She clutched the Icon tightly to her chest. Just as she rounded the last curve, she was greeted with the sound of a female voice, "Those stairs are the best burglar alarm we have."

Cecil and Priscilla stood at the bottom of the stairs and Priscilla was pointing a handgun straight at her. Andrea tried to dash up the stairs again, but Alex, who was holding another gun, was descending from above.

"I don't think that would be a very good idea," he said, spinning her around. He thrust the gun nozzle into her back, "Move!"

He stuck right behind her.

"Where's Carlton?" Priscilla snapped at Andrea as they walked to the living room.

"I don't know," Andrea answered honestly but with defiance. She had quickly sized up the situation when she realized how easily she had slipped out of the ropes. Clearly, there was more than one double-cross going on, but she couldn't tell which way.

"I'll go look for him," Cecil said, striding out.

Priscilla waved her gun briskly and barked, "Edith, close the drapes." Edith immediately pulled the tall flowing drapes across the bay windows. As she did so, rain began pelting the windows until it was a heavy downpour.

The Countess took the Kazan Icon from Andrea with a proprietary smirk. "You won't be needing this anymore," she said and placed it on the mantel over the fireplace.

"Over there," Priscilla said coldly, waving her gun. Andrea stood by the fireplace near the icon. The Countess sank into the sofa and coolly lit a cigarette.

Andrea saw the Skull, nearby on the table, glowering ominously at her. Cecil had returned and now stood at a safe distance. Alex stood not far from Priscilla, pointing the gun at Andrea, so that the three of them were positioned in a triangle. Andrea glared at Priscilla holding the gun. "Why don't you tell them the truth?"

Priscilla laughed at her, "What's there to tell?"

"Why don't you tell them how you betrayed them? You used them all to make sure the real value of the icon was never discovered. What were you planning to do to them after they had done their duty? Were you going to give them a cut of the take? Or kill them one by one, like you killed Michael and the Major?"

"You don't know what you're talking about," Priscilla said contemptuously and eyed Alex's gun. "Alex, she's just lying to get out of here."

"Shut up! I'm interested," Alex said. "Let her talk."

Andrea began with calculation, "First you framed Alex and Cecil to make it look like either one could have killed Michael."

"Prove it," Priscilla said.

"Because I saw you at the cathedral that night. Don't you remember? You wore a beige coat and a paisley scarf. And your perfume then is the same as you're wearing now. Shalimar, I believe."

"That's what Priscilla always wears!" Edith said naively.

"So you were there after all?" Cecil questioned angrily.

Priscilla stood motionless, "Quiet! It could have been anybody. I wasn't there."

"Well, you certainly weren't here." The Countess narrowed her eyes at Priscilla.

Operating on a hunch, Andrea added, "Then you chased me through the park in the green Mercedes. Aren't you the only one who drives it?"

Alex, Cecil and the Countess glared at Priscilla, while Edith stared wide-eyed.

Andrea continued, "I had thought it was Alex but I was wrong. All of you met at his house when I interrupted you that day." Andrea tried a bluff. "You pretended to leave suddenly with the rest, but instead you stayed behind waiting to get me."

"That's crazy," Priscilla said more wildly. "She's making all this up."

"Is she?" Alex eyed Priscilla. "I didn't chase her."

"You also betrayed yourself with those death threats you left me." Andrea riveted her gaze on Priscilla. "Your secretarial skills betrayed you. Like all good professional secretaries, you typed two spaces between the period and your next sentence. I doubt Alex, Cecil, Edith or the Countess would have thought to do that. But you had to tie up all the loose ends. You had to kill the Major because he betrayed you. Was it remorse, or didn't the idea of murder appeal to him? He had papers and hid them in a safe deposit box downtown, and then he gave Michael the extra key. Was the Major blackmailing the whole group or just you?"

Andrea turned to Alex, "You tapped Michael's phones. That's how you knew I was going to the cathedral, but you didn't plan on Michael being killed. Your job was simply to steal the icon, but Priscilla set you up both times. She's tall, but was too weak to take down either Michael or the Major alone, she needed someone big and strong to knock them out for her. You were the perfect patsy. Your mistake was to take my photograph." Andrea looked at him knowingly.

"Go on," Alex said. He held his gun steady, never taking his eyes off Priscilla.

Andrea turned back to Priscilla, "Your third mistake had to do with the black lacquer box. If Alex had murdered the Major, I don't think he would have left that rare lacquer box by his body. Chances are, Alex would have taken it for his fine collection. But you knew nothing about lacquer boxes or Alex's collection, so you left it lying there on the desk. You followed Alex to the Russian Cultural Museum and let him knock out the Major to get the safe deposit keys. Were you planning to kill Alex for the papers, too? Or were you," Andrea turned to Alex, "also planning to blackmail Priscilla for them?"

"At first I was, but then I had a better idea," Alex confirmed.

"Unfortunately, Priscilla, I caught you in the act at the Russian Cultural Museum once again. You wanted to kill me ever since I bumped into you at the cathedral, and now you had your second chance. But you weren't strong or quick enough. If you had been, would you have pinned that on Alex as well?"

"This is ludicrous!" Priscilla turned pale.

"Now you're poisoning Mrs. Saxon-Briggs with drugs and arsenic." Andrea accused. "She's lying nearly dead upstairs right now. Who's the fall guy now, Priscilla? Is it Edith, the Countess or the cook? Go see for yourselves."

"Is this true?" Cecil scowled at Priscilla.

"You should see the jar of arsenic she has hidden in the pantry," Alex said.

"You bitch!" The Countess spat out.

"She's just making wild guesses. She doesn't know what she's talking about." Priscilla's eyes shifted around the group.

"Edith," Cecil ordered, "Go check on Mrs. Saxon-Briggs in her bedroom." Edith picked up her knitting bag on the mahogany table where the Crystal Skull stood and briskly walked out.

"She's been lying to you all along," Andrea accused.

"Shut up!" Priscilla snapped desperately.

"Why did you do it?" Andrea lashed back. "Were you against the sale of the icon to begin with? Did you know it was a fraud? Or was it because you couldn't wait to get Hannah's money, the icon and the Crystal Skull for yourself? Who's good name were you trying to protect, hers or yours?"

Suddenly, a noise erupted in the hallway, men's voices shouting. The groundskeeper came in, hauling Keith by the collar, and shoved him over to the fireplace next to Andrea. "I found him prowling in the garden." Obviously, the scene in the living room did not disturb him.

"Good job, Xavier," Priscilla nodded to him. "You can go now. Keep an eye on things outside." He nodded and left obediently.

Priscilla surveyed Keith, who stood there dripping wet from the rain. "Now this is a convenient turn of events," she gloated. "Two for the price of one."

"It will never work," he panted. "We know everything. The arsenic, everything," He glanced over to Andrea reassuringly, their eyes met fleetingly as Andrea gave him a quizzical look. How did he find out?

"So it seems," Priscilla crooned maliciously. "All the more reason to get rid of you both." She smiled a sweet, crazy smile.

"You can't mean here?" Cecil said with dismay.

"Why not? All the less trouble for us," she pointed her gun at Andrea and moved closer towards her. "You have no idea how much debt I will be inheriting. The Kazan Icon, as an original, would have paid off all of it. And it cost too much to keep the Major quiet. He would have ruined everything, just as you're doing now," She glowered menacingly at Andrea and Keith and raised her gun arm.

Andrea instinctively backed towards Keith. Keith suddenly grabbed the Icon of Kazan, and jumped in front of her, using the icon as a breastplate to shield Andrea and himself. "Shoot and you shoot the icon," he shouted.

Priscilla laughed bizarrely. "Who cares? You said it was a fraud anyway." She raised her arm, taking aim.

Suddenly glass shattered behind them, and everyone jumped as two shots exploded in the room.

"Hannah!" Priscilla exclaimed and cried out with pain as her gun shot wildly. Her bullet glanced off the icon and dug into the ceiling. But as she fired her gun, Alex fired too and shot Priscilla in the shoulder.

Blood trickled through Priscilla's fingers, clasping the gaping wound as she stood there, watching Hannah Saxon-Briggs leaning weakly on her stick in the doorway. The old woman stood barefoot in her nightgown before the shattered remains of a Ming vase, which she had just smashed with her cane. Then Hannah collapsed unconscious onto the floor.

Everyone froze, except Priscilla, who with determined eyes as beady as a marmot's, lifted her gun towards Andrea.

Another shot exploded. Priscilla doubled over and twisted with surprise, to see Alex pointing his gun at her. "You bastard!" she swore as she slumped to the ground. Alex stood still, holding his gun steady, to make sure she couldn't get in a final parting shot.

Terrified, Cecil ran out of the room. The Countess sat nervously pinned to the sofa. She contemplated Priscilla's bleeding corpse with disdain. "Do you think she's dead? Oh dear, that gorgeous Persian rug will be ruined!"

CHAPTER 20

"It is not enough to be granted forgiveness, we must be prepared to receive it, to accept it."

Metropolitan Anthony Bloom
Meditations: A Spiritual Journey

Andrea and Keith huddled together, clutching the icon and each other. Andrea stared in horror at Priscilla's body lying stretched on the floor dead, as the carpet soaked up her red blood. They watched anxiously, as Alex bent one knee to the ground to briefly inspect Priscilla's body. Her gun lay on the floor by her hand. He didn't touch it.

The Countess made a move towards the door. Alex cocked his gun and yelled, "No you don't. You're not going anywhere. Sit down on that couch and don't move!" He pointed the gun at her. The Countess glared at him but silently obeyed.

Looking soberly at Priscilla, Alex said, "She was too smart for her own good." He pulled a set of keys from Priscilla's pocket and jangled them in the air; "Getaway keys," he grinned. "I always liked that green Mercedes." Slowly, he stood erect and faced the couple. Keith gulped. Alex saw this and said, "Don't worry, I'm not going to hurt you guys."

Andrea and Keith visibly breathed easier with relief. Keith examined the icon. "Hey! The bullet chipped the corner here." A top part of the gold riza had a chunk blown off.

Alex inspected it also and laughed, "So it did! The most expensive bulletproof vest I ever saw. Who said miracles don't happen?" He took it from Keith and replaced it on the mantel.

Alex pulled some rope from his pocket and tied the Countess' hands and feet. "Make sure you stay with the Countess until the police come." He said to Keith, glaring at Irena on the sofa.

"My lawyer will skin you alive," the Countess hissed at Alex contemptuously.

"Not if they can't catch me," Alex retorted.

Hannah still lay on the floor, motionless. Andrea was already at her side, checking her pulse and gently slapping her face to rouse her. "Hannah, Hannah, can you hear me?" She said loudly into her ear. There was no response.

Alex nodded to Keith. "You better call the ambulance," he said, stuffing his gun into his belt. Keith went to find a phone.

Hannah groaned and attempted to sit up. Andrea collected a wool throw by the desk, went quickly to her side and wrapped it over Hannah's shoulders. "Don't move. The ambulance will be here in a few minutes." She placed a sofa pillow under the woman's head. "Better?" Hannah nodded vaguely. "Hang on, they'll be here soon."

"Did you really think I would shoot you?" Alex looked down at Andrea as she knelt by Hannah. "My own sweet daughter?" There was only the slightest hint of mockery in his eyes.

"I didn't know." She looked at Alex squarely. "Thanks," she said, feeling suddenly awkward. "I guess I owe you an apology. I underestimated you."

He smiled back at her, "I don't blame you. How could you know? You and Marina had only the past to go on. I have suspected Priscilla for quite a while. I was just waiting for the perfect time and place to get her. Now I can call it self-defense."

Rising from her knees, Andrea asked, "What now?"

"I'm going to get the hell out of here. With my history, another burglary and this will put me definitely out of the ball game." Alex moved as if to go, leaving the Icon of Kazan behind.

Keith returned. "The Durants have definitely gone," he announ-ced. "You're not taking the icon?"

"Are you kidding? That thing is so hot I couldn't sell it to a tribe of Pygmies."

"Where are you going?" Andrea's face reflected genuine concern.

"I don't know. Besides, it wouldn't be safe for you to know." Andrea nodded sadly. "Don't worry, you'll hear from me." Alex grinned at her. "I like giving surprises."

"No kidding," Keith chuckled.

Alex waved a finger at him, "You treat her right, young man," he said with mock severity. "Not like her father."

"Yes, sir," Keith saluted, but looked puzzled.

Alex turned and scowled at the Countess, "I hope they give you life!"

"I hope you rot in hell!" she spat out maliciously.

"Ohhh," Hannah Saxon-Briggs groaned as she lay on the floor. "Gotta run," Alex said brightly, ignoring her. "By the way, Andrea, your phones aren't tapped anymore."

Andrea felt too choked up to speak. She merely whispered, "Thanks." Alex winked at her as he left towards the back door.

"The police and an ambulance will be here pretty soon." Keith said, as he wrapped his arm around Andrea's shivering shoulder.

"I better phone Mama." Andrea said. She moved toward the phone but stopped as the doorbell rang.

Keith opened the door and exclaimed, "Don't you guys know enough to come in out of the rain?"

2

Detective Catelano stepped over the threshold, wearing a rain-spattered trench coat, and surveyed the two women on the floor. "Jesus! What happened here?"

"You missed the fireworks," Keith remarked.

"Not by much, obviously," Tony stooped and touched Priscilla's wrist, then let it flop to the floor.

"Mrs. Saxon-Briggs is alive but needs to get to a hospital immediately," Andrea said.

Minutes later, the Piedmont Police and Fire Department arrived. The paramedics wheeled in their stretchers and carried Hannah out, then roared off to the hospital with wailing sirens. Officer Jergeson escorted the Countess, now much subdued, towards a squad car for questioning.

A rookie cop inspected Priscilla, "She's dead, sir."

"I can see that, you idiot. Get forensics over here fast," Tony growled. Tony went to inspect the icon. "Nice jewels. Looks like it needs a little repair." He placed his hands in his pockets and scrutinized Keith and Andrea, "OK, who's first? I got all evening."

They looked at each other, and then Andrea explained everything. "Priscilla Thorpe killed Michael Beech at the Cathedral. She also killed Major Vashkovsky, and she was poisoning Mrs. Saxon-Briggs."

"And she was about to kill us," Keith added.

"Keep talking."

Andrea told the sequence of events in detail, "...and as she was about to shoot, Alex shot her. Keith saved my life. You can see where her bullet glanced off the icon."

"Lovely lady. You wouldn't happen to know where Mr. Menshikov went, do you?"

"No," Andrea answered truthfully.

Tony looked sharply at her, "If you did, would you tell me?"

Andrea didn't say a word, unsure how to respond.

"I thought as much."

"Oh," Andrea said, "he stole the icon all right, but he didn't kill Michael or the Major." Andrea suddenly felt defensive for her father. "Priscilla Thorpe tried to pin both murders on Alex."

"Ahhh," Tony said. "So that's why Alex killed her?"

"He saved our lives," Keith said.

"He had a good reason to do so," Andrea volunteered and took Keith's hand. She stammered, "He's my father."

Keith's mouth gaped open, "So that explains it. Why didn't you tell me?"

"I'm sorry." Andrea looked sheepishly back at Keith. "I tried to but there wasn't time."

Tony raised his eyebrows, "That's special. How long have you known this?"

"Only a few days."

"A few days? What about Sam West? No, wait," Tony held up

his hands. "I'm tired and this is much too complicated. I'm taking you both in for questioning."

Two of the officers who had been out looking for Alex and the Durants came back panting, "Sir, there's no sign of anyone. The staff has left too. It looks like three cars are gone."

"Damn! Did either of you two see the cars?"

"One was a beige Buick, maybe 1985, the other was a new green Mercedes," Keith answered.

"Find them! Get them in here!" The young officers blinked and dashed out to the squad car.

Glancing at the mahogany table, Andrea gasped and grabbed Keith's arm, "Look! The Crystal Skull is gone!"

"Holy shit!"

They stared at the empty table, then their eyes met. They spoke simultaneously, "Edith..."

· "Will you people please tell me what the hell is going on? Tony demanded. "What Crystal Skull?"

"Come on." Keith patted him on the shoulder. "We'll tell you on the way to the station."

"Get ready," Andrea moaned. "This is going to be a long night."

3

The four of them sat around the table as Andrea told the whole story, speaking clearly into the tape recorder. Tony crossed his arms. "How did you know it was Priscilla Thorpe?"

Andrea sat opposite him, "I didn't know until I saw her face to face. Her perfume was the give-away. I smelled it the night I bumped into her at the cathedral and when she tried to kill me at the Russian Museum. The rest was easy, simply a matter of deduction and bluffing until she admitted it."

"What makes you think Menshikov didn't do it?" Tony asked. "He had the means to kill and the motive. Maybe Michael ran into him in the course of the break-in?"

"No, it seems clear he knew what Michael was doing and want-ed him out of commission, but Priscilla had a stronger motive for murder. Alex was hired to manufacture a duplicate icon and switch it for the original. He just wanted to get out of there as cleanly as possibly. Her plan was to have it all."

"The jewels looked original enough."

"Yeah. But the icon's a fraud," Keith said. "It's not nearly as old as everybody thinks it is."

"I suspect the real reason Priscilla wanted it back was because of its supernatural power," Andrea concluded. "I recognized the look of spiritual greed in her eyes. With the Crystal Skull and the Saxon-Briggs inheritance she'd have everything she wanted. That explains the ritual slaying of Michael: power was her ultimate motive."

"Maybe," Tony said, "but didn't you say that Mrs. Saxon-Briggs wanted to be cured? That could have been another reason. She was dying, after all."

"Thanks to Priscilla."

"So much for the miraculous icon," Keith quipped.

"Who's to say God didn't have something to do with it?" Andrea countered. "That's what theologians call 'Providence.'"

Keith shrugged. "You're outta my ball park. I thought Providence was the capitol of Rhode Island."

Andrea grunted. "Please, it's too late for puns."

"Let's get serious folks. I'm tired and I want to go to bed." Tony rubbed his forehead. "So you think Priscilla also killed Major Vashkovsky to cover her tracks?"

"She told us he was blackmailing her, for Christ's sake," Keith exclaimed. "She had plenty of motive."

"Seems he was blackmailing his sister, too. These are interesting deductions, but the case hangs on Alex, if we ever catch him. It would help if we had the Durants." Tony arched his aching back and yawned. He glanced at Jergeson. "Tomorrow we pump the Countess some more."

Tony looked at his watch. It was 1:30 a.m. Keith slouched in the chair by Andrea, looking heavy-lidded. Andrea yawned. Tony threw down his pen. "OK, let's call it a night. I think we got enough for one day."

Officer Jergeson started packing up the tape equipment.

Tony looked at them. "We'll call you if we need anything."

"What will happen to Alex if you catch him?" Andrea looked concerned.

"I sure hope he's got a good lawyer, because he's got a hell of a lot of explaining to do." They rose to leave.

"One thing more." Andrea turned to Tony, as she and Keith stopped at the threshold. "How did you find out where we were?"

"We had you followed and we got a lucky anonymous tip off. This morning, somebody sent us the safe deposit keys and when we saw the papers we came here as soon as we could. We had already tracked Alex's ticket to London and discovered Priscilla had ordered it. We also dug up some old CIA material on both Menshikov and the Major, so a trip to Piedmont was inevitable."

"Alex!" Andrea and Keith spoke simultaneously again.

Tony waved at them. "Now, go home."

Keith stretched. "I've got to get up early and pound out a story before I get canned. OK, Andrea?" She grinned, remembering their agreement and nodded. "Don't worry, Tony," Keith said, "I'll say what a great job you did in breaking this case."

"You better or else your ass is grass the next time you come in here."

"Hey, there won't be a next time. I'm moving up to the city desk. Just watch."

"Wait!" Tony rummaged through some files, "I almost forgot. The two of you will be getting some reward money."

Andrea and Keith gasped with surprise, "Really?"

"For finding the damn icon. Hart put up five hundred big ones. So Carlton," he ribbed, "lunch is on you until I retire."

4

Sunday, November 11, 1990

Sunday afternoon, Keith sat at his computer in his cubicle in the *Examiner* newsroom proofing his article about the Kazan Icon. He was in mid-sentence when his line buzzed. That's strange, Keith thought, nobody ever calls me here on Sunday.

He picked up the receiver, "Mr. Carlton?" A voice with a deep accent spoke.

"Yes? Who's this?"

"This is Alex," His voice sounded husky and very sober.

Keith sat up in his chair. "Where are you?"

"I need to see you. Meet me at Pier 39, by the carousel."

"Sure. What's this all about?"

"I tell you when I see you. At 3:30 p.m., at the carousel."

"OK." Keith hung up the phone and sat back in his chair to ponder this. He thought it was too weird that Alex should be Andrea's father. He wasn't sure he liked it. It could spell trouble down the road. He was glad he'd now have an opportunity to really check this guy out.

He shook his head and continued working on the last section of his story. An hour later he sent the copy to the city editor's computer. He tapped the desk twice with his pen as a sign of triumph. Then he collected his jacket and sauntered out the door, taking out his box of Shermans as he went.

By the elevator, he stopped, studied the cigarettes and realized he had suddenly lost his taste for them. Very slowly, he realized he had lost his taste for other things as well—like his need for total independence and his plan to stay unattached. Even some of his natural skepticism had taken a beating. Maybe there was something to all this religion after all, he thought. Uncle Isaac had always intrigued him. Maybe he'd explore some of his Jewish roots someday. It couldn't hurt.

In the meantime, he knew what he had to do. He started by tossing the full box of Sherman's cigarettes into the trashcan.

5

Monday, November 12, 1990

Father Mench slept with his mouth open as he lay in bed on the fifth floor of Pacific Presbyterian Hospital. The nurse bustled past them, adjusted the clamp on his IV, and then gently touched his shoulder. "Father Mench, you have some visitors."

He woke and saw Keith and Andrea, bearing a bouquet of golden mums, standing by his side. He extended a long bony hand to Andrea. His skin was transparent and thin as tissue paper. "Ahhh, the icon lady," he smiled weakly. "I have been praying for you."

"I don't doubt that," Andrea beamed back at him and took his hand. "I sure needed it."

The priest nodded his head knowingly. He pointed at Keith. "Who is this man, your husband?"

Keith smiled and enjoyed watching Andrea squirm. "No," Andrea stammered, "Just a friend. This is Keith Carlton, a reporter with the *Examiner*."

"I see. So, why have you come to see an old dying priest? This is not such big news."

"No, we've got good news for you," Keith announced. "We found the Icon of Kazan! And the person who killed Michael Beech and the Major."

"Yah?" he blinked. "Who?"

"Priscilla Thorpe," Andrea stated.

"The secretary to the rich English lady?" he asked.

"Yep."

He frowned. "I knew she was no good."

Andrea explained, "She wanted everything in Mrs. Saxon-Briggs' estate, including the Kazan Icon and the Crystal Skull. If it leaked out that the ic...." Keith touched her elbow. Andrea paused, "There were some underhanded dealings and she was afraid of a lawsuit."

"The love of money is the root of much evil," Father Mench sighed. "I knew the Holy Blessed Mother would fix it up OK."

Keith intervened, "You mean you suspected them all along?"

"Of course," he said, tapping his nose. "I can smell these things. I had faith it would be all right. But not without danger." He glanced at Andrea. "Or sacrifice." He looked at Keith. "Maybe that is why the Blessed Mother let it be stolen in the first place."

"So, you knew about the icon?" Andrea asked with surprise.

"That it's not the real one?"

"The real icon? There are many holy Kazan Icons! Many originals! It does not matter in the end, because God uses them all—if God wants. We westerners are always so worried about originals. Which one is the real one? Which one is the first one? It does not matter. They are only windows to heaven. The important thing is heaven itself. That is, God."

"What about life down here?" Keith asked. "Isn't that important too?"

"Same thing." He looked radiantly at him. "It's only how you see things. It is all one." He closed his eyes with exhaustion, but Andrea could feel the sweet river of peace flowing out of him like water.

Andrea squeezed the priest's hand. "You must be very tired. We only came by to see how you were doing and to pass on the good news. You'll also be glad to know that I'm sending some money to Russia to help fund the building of the new Kazan Church in Moscow."

"The Russian people suffer much now. It will help them. God will bless you." He patted her hand.

Andrea had tears in her eyes, "Goodbye Father Mench." She bent down and kissed him on the forehead. "Pray for me."

"I always do." He beamed and patted her cheek. "For you too," he winked at Keith. "Although you're a tougher case. But not hopeless."

"Thanks." Keith stuffed his hands in his pockets. "Andrea says I'm a St. Jude special."

"Perhaps..." Father Mench waved. "Goodbye. God bless you both."

Andrea and Keith stood somberly in the elevator as it descended to the lobby. Andrea broke the silence. "Did you see how frail he looked? I bet he won't last the week." She had tears in her eyes. "I know this sounds crazy, but I wish the icon was here to heal him. It just doesn't seem fair!"

Keith wrapped his arm around her. "It isn't fair. Life's a bitch! But maybe he has something better than the icon."

"What's that?"

"Heaven. And he knows it. Not many of us can say that—but I think he can."

"I hope you're right," Andrea said as the elevator door opened.

Keith glanced at his watch as they stepped out, "We gotta hurry or we'll be late."

"For what?"

"You'll see." Keith pulled her elbow and walked her briskly to his car.

6

"Here you are. The Emeryville Train Station," the Indian cabby announced in his clipped accent, above the noise of sitar music blaring from the radio. "That'll be twenty-two dollars and forty-five cents." He glanced over his shoulder at Keith and Andrea and pulled the meter handle, then jotted down the time and mileage on his route sheet.

Andrea fumed in the back seat with her arms folded as Keith dug for his wallet, "I don't see why we couldn't have driven ourselves!"

"Because it would have been too risky."

"Risky for what?"

Keith handed the cabby the bills as they climbed out of the taxi. The cabby's eyes bugged out at the extra fifty-dollar bill in his fist. He poked his head out of the window, "Many thank-yous! Did you vin the lottery?"

"Nope, something much better." He glanced warmly at Andrea, then he hooked his arm in hers and together they walked into the pseudo Art Deco train station.

"Really, Keith, you shouldn't be throwing money around like that. We haven't gotten our money yet."

"What do you mean? I got a promotion, we cracked a super case, two hundred and fifty grand is coming my way and I got you! Right now, I'm the richest guy I know. I can afford to spread it around a little. Isn't that what it's all about?" He beamed, then stopped and faced Andrea. "I do have you, don't I?"

"Keith..." She felt flustered and a little pushed.

"I'm serious, Andrea." His eyes probed hers. "You're the best thing that has ever happened to me. I love you. Marry me."

She stared back at him speechless. They stood in awkward silence as dry brown oak leaves scuttled across the cement sidewalk and the icy November wind bit into her cheeks.

"I'm sorry," Andrea said at last, "I'm so surprised." Keith held his breath, preparing for the worst. "Don't get me wrong, I really care for you. You're terrific, but marriage?"

"You don't have to soften the blow for me. Just tell me. Do you love me?"

"There hasn't been enough time. Not yet." She smiled coyly at him. "Let's keep working on it."

"What are you, the new St. Augustine? 'O God, please make me married, but not yet.'"

"I see you've been boning up on mystical theology in your spare time."

"I'm a man of many talents, Andrea. A storehouse of hidden treasures." He put his hand to his brow melodramatically: "Someday she will come to her senses and then they will live happily ever after."

"I see you're full of something," she laughed at him.

"How about some poetry? Will some Kenneth Patchen work?" He spread his arms expansively and proclaimed passionately, "'O my darling troubles heaven with her loveliness—she is made of such cloth that the angels cry to see her...'"

"I love his poetry!" Andrea laughed and clapped.

"You should see mine..." he said suggestively.

"And I thought you were an old cynic," she snuggled against his shoulder playfully.

"Not as much as I used to be... You've changed all that." He gathered her in his arms.

Andrea resisted a little. "Keith! This is a train station, for God's sake. Look at all these people." She blushed. "Why did you drag me down here anyway?"

Just then, Alex Menshikov emerged like a tall fullback from the milling crowd. "To see me," he smiled at her awkwardly. He was carrying a small suitcase.

Keith saluted him, "I'll leave you two alone. I'll just be at the coffee bar getting my fix."

7

Alex and Andrea sat down together in two black oval seats near the wall. "I'm not very good at these kinds of things," Andrea said shyly, "but I just wanted to say, I'm sorry you and Mama never married."

"If you really knew me," Alex grunted, "I'm not so sure you'd say that."

"Maybe. Well, I'm glad I was wrong about you."

"Why is that?"

"Because I couldn't stand it if I found out my father was a murderer." Her eyes were full of emotion.

"Oh, so running from the police is OK?" he bantered, trying to keep things light. "And stealing?"

"No," she stuttered. "Of course not."

"Don't worry, I'm used to it. It's how I've always made a living. I do this." He lit a cigarette and spit out a bit of tobacco.

"I'm just sad to see things end up this way, that's all."

"You mean you're sad to see I'm your father?" He leaned towards her, placing his elbows on his knees. He twiddled his cigarette nervously in his fingers.

"Well, no. Well, yes. It's hard having you on the run." She looked around the room. "I wouldn't wish that on anybody. What will you do if they catch you?"

"Go to prison."

"Have you been to prison before?"

"Once in Moscow. They thought I was a spy. American prisons are like Club Med by comparison," he said grimly.

"Did they treat you badly?"

Images of torture chambers had haunted his memory and he

didn't like conjuring them up now. He inhaled and winced, "I'm lucky I'm alive, which is better than most."

"Well, I'm glad you're alive, too," Andrea admitted. "If it weren't for you... Thank you for saving my life." She reached over and squeezed his hand.

Alex looked down at his feet. They sat silently. Andrea noticed his face had turned red.

He looked over at her proudly. "I can still see in your face the little girl I once knew. You were a jewel at four. Full of darkness and light, just like your mother. I wanted to keep you forever, but I knew that if I stayed everything would go bad. Just like things always do. I knew nothing about love then, only fooling around. Now I wonder where it's all got me." He sighed. "I've been doing time all my life but the bars caging me aren't made of steel." He finished his cigarette and smashed it with his foot on the floor.

Outside, the train to Los Angeles rumbled noisily up to the station and screeched to a stop right on schedule.

"We all make mistakes," she said. "Sometimes, things deserve a second chance."

"Yeah, but I've run out of all my lucky chances."

"I'm not so sure about that. You're not dead yet."

He looked away. "Give Marina my best. I just wanted to say goodbye." He choked up a little. "I have to go."

They strolled out onto the platform under the purple neon Emeryville sign. Keith walked up to Alex and the two men shook hands gruffly. Alex turned back to Andrea and, gazing at her with soulful eyes, he kissed her twice on the cheeks, "Thank you. *Proshchaite*."

She nodded and answered, "*Proshchaite*." She touched his arm, "Take care of yourself." She felt a lump gathering in her throat and her eyes grew misty as she watched her Papa Bear head for the waiting train. She felt she was ten once again, watching with a broken heart as her father walked out of their lives forever.

The silver Amtrak train steamed idly and impatiently on its tracks as passengers said their farewells and quickly climbed on board. Keith put his arm around Andrea as she blew her nose. Alex saluted to them as he climbed on board. They waved back.

"Do you think we'll ever see him again?" Keith asked.

"I don't know," Andrea said, sadly. "I just don't know."

"What did he say to you in Russian?"

"*Proshchaite*. It means goodbye. It also means forgive."

8

Alex found his seat and hoisted his bag into the overhead luggage rack. He peered sadly out the window at them as the train jerked into motion and pulled away with a mechanical grumble.

He sat down in his seat. Across the aisle, Cecil was reading his newspaper and Edith was busy knitting a baby blue sweater. She pulled her yarn from a skein which lay in her knitting bag next to the Crystal Skull. "Glad you made it." Cecil folded his paper. Edith smiled weakly at him as her needles darted and clicked together.

"I wasn't sure I would."

"I do hope someone gives Priscilla a nice funeral, don't you, dear?" Edith smiled benignly and Cecil rolled his eyes.

Alex smiled and stretched his long legs under the shabby train seat. He took his cap out of his pocket and dropped it over his face, "Wake me when we get to L.A."

ABOUT THE AUTHOR

PAMELA CRANSTON is a poet and a writer whose work has appeared in the:
*Adirondack Review, Anglican Theological Review, Tales for the Trail: Adventures
in Air, Land & Water* by Birch Brook Press, *The Blueline Anthology* published
by Syracuse Press, *Forward Movement Publications, Mystic River Review,
Penwood Review,* and many other publications. Formerly an Anglican
Franciscan nun, she majored in Russian History and Journalism in college
and ultimately received her BA in Interdisciplinary Social Science from
San Francisco State University in 1984. She received a Masters of Divinity
degree in 1988 from the Church Divinity School of the Pacific, (CDSP),
Berkeley, California. She was ordained as an Episcopal priest in 1990. For
the past fifteen years, she has served churches and hospices in the San
Francisco Bay area, where she lives with her husband.

This book is available from:
BIBLIO DISTRIBUTION (a division of NBN)
15200 NBN Way
Blue Ridge Summit, PA 17214
Phone 800-462-6420
Fax 800-338-4550
e-mail custserv@nbnbooks.com
http://www.bibliodistribution.com/home.shtml